D0179451

IN THE ARMS OF A MARQUESS

"Every woman who ever dreamed of having a titled lord at her feet will love this novel."
—Eloisa James, *New York Times* bestselling author

"Immersive and lush . . . Ashe is that rare author who chooses to risk unexpected elements within an established genre, and whose skill and magic with the pen lifts her tales above the rest."
Fresh Fiction

SWEPT AWAY BY A KISS

"A breathtaking romance filled with sensuality."
—Lisa Kleypas, #1 *New York Times* bestselling author

Churchill County Library
553 S. Maine Street
Fallon, Nevada 89406
(775) 423-7581

By Katharine Ashe

The Devil's Duke
THE PRINCE
THE DUKE
THE EARL
THE ROGUE

The Falcon Club
HOW A LADY WEDS A ROGUE
HOW TO BE A PROPER LADY
WHEN A SCOT LOVES A LADY

The Prince Catchers
I LOVED A ROGUE
I ADORED A LORD
I MARRIED THE DUKE

Rogues of the Sea
IN THE ARMS OF A MARQUESS
CAPTURED BY A ROGUE LORD
SWEPT AWAY BY A KISS

And from Avon Impulse
THE PIRATE & I
KISSES, SHE WROTE
HOW TO MARRY A HIGHLANDER
A LADY'S WISH

ATTENTION: ORGANIZATIONS AND CORPORATIONS
HarperCollins books may be purchased for educational, business,
or sales promotional use. For information, please e-mail the Special
Markets Department at SPsales@harpercollins.com.

Praise for the Novels of Katharine Ashe

THE DUKE

Amazon's Best Romances of 2017

"A romance that Kathleen Woodiwiss
herself would be proud to have written."
—*Booklist* (★Starred Review★)

THE EARL

"A tender and gripping romantic adventure."
—*BookPage* (TOP PICK!)

"A rollicking page-turner."
—*Publishers Weekly* (★Starred Review★)

THE ROGUE

"Powerful, suspenseful, and sensual."
—RT Book Reviews (TOP PICK!)

"The desperate yearning—and dangerous secrets—
between the star-crossed lovers had my stomach
in knots until the very end of this hypnotic book."
—Amazon's Omnivorous, Best Books of the Month

I LOVED A ROGUE

"Passionate, heart-wrenching,
and thoroughly satisfying."
—All About Romance, Desert Isle Keeper

"A blissful read."
—*USA Today*, Best Romances of the Year

Churchill County Library
553 S. Maine Street
Fallon, Nevada 89406
(775) 423-7581

KISSES, SHE WROTE

"Finished it with tears in my eyes.
Yes, it was that good."
—Elizabeth Boyle, *New York Times* bestselling author

HOW TO MARRY A HIGHLANDER
RITA® Award Finalist 2014
Romance Writers of America

HOW TO BE A PROPER LADY
Amazon's Best Romances of 2012

WHEN A SCOT LOVES A LADY

"Lushly intense romance . . . radiant prose."
—*Library Journal* (★Starred Review★)

"Sensationally intelligent writing,
and a true, weak-in-the-knees love story."
—Barnes & Noble "Heart to Heart" Recommended Read!

The
PRINCE

A Devil's Duke
Novel

Katharine
Ashe

AVONBOOKS

An Imprint of HarperCollinsPublishers

This is a work of fiction. Names, characters, places, and incidents are products of the author's imagination or are used fictitiously and are not to be construed as real. Any resemblance to actual events, locales, organizations, or persons, living or dead, is entirely coincidental.

THE PRINCE. Copyright © 2018 by Katharine Brophy Dubois. All rights reserved. Printed in the United States of America. No part of this book may be used or reproduced in any manner whatsoever without written permission except in the case of brief quotations embodied in critical articles and reviews. For information, address HarperCollins Publishers, 195 Broadway, New York, NY 10007.

First Avon Books mass market printing: June 2018

Print Edition ISBN: 978-0-06-264174-8
Digital Edition ISBN: 978-0-06-264175-5

Cover design by Patricia Barrow
Cover illustration by Anna Kmet

Avon, Avon & logo, and Avon Books & logo are registered trademarks of HarperCollins Publishers in the United States of America and other countries.

HarperCollins is a registered trademark of HarperCollins Publishers in the United States of America and other countries.

FIRST EDITION

18 19 20 21 22   QGM   10 9 8 7 6 5 4 3 2 1

If you purchased this book without a cover, you should be aware that this book is stolen property. It was reported as "unsold and destroyed" to the publisher, and neither the author nor the publisher has received any payment for this "stripped book."

For my son, slayer of (bad) dragons.

Inspired by true stories,
mingled together and set aright.

I fled in confusion, anxiety and pain.
I find them banished at your command,

—SAADI,
Gulistan (13th century, Persia)

Let us then first fully realize that this is not a new idea.

—ELIZABETH BLACKWELL,
Address on the Medical Education of Women (1856, England)

Chapter 1

A Disguise

September 1825
Surgeons' Hall
Edinburgh, Scotland

*N*eck cloths were a lot tighter than she had imagined. And trousers pinched a person right up the center of where she least wanted to be pinched.

But no one had noticed her. Even the students on the benches to either side, murmuring to their companions about the dissection in the center of the U-shaped operating theater, had not glanced twice at her.

Obviously the whiskers had been a stroke of brilliance.

Nevertheless, Libby Shaw kept her shoulders hunched and head bent, peeking at the demonstration from beneath the concealing rim of her cap. As the surgeon peeled away the muscle to expose bone, a shiver of pleasure fanned through her.

She had sat in this theater before to watch public dissections and surgeries. Disguised as a man now, it all felt different: the medical men with their wise brows and hands that worked miracles; the scratching of students' pencils in notebooks; the cringes of the curious public drawn to the lecture; and the stench of the flesh on the table, slowed in its natural decay by the cool cellar in which the surgical assistant stored it each afternoon to preserve it for the following day's lecture.

For a sennight already, Edinburgh's most celebrated surgeons had been performing a system-by-system dissection, but Libby had not bothered attending until today, the day reserved for her favorite part: the skeletal system. The human skeleton was sturdy, stable, such a pleasure to study.

"That is the fibula," the young man on her left whispered to his companion.

"It is?" the other whispered uncertainly.

No.

Libby bit her lips together. The whiskers disguised her face, not her voice.

"Of course, numbskull," the first one said. She recognized that haughty tone. She had met plenty of this sort when her father invited his students to dinner. They thought their arrogance impressed her.

"I've been to dozens of these dissections already," he added.

Yet he did not know a fibula from a tibia.

"What's that?" the other whispered, pointing.

The soleus.

"The tibialis anterior," the haughty one said. "Clearly you haven't read Charles Bell's *A System of Dissections*."

Clearly he hadn't either.

Their whispers had grown louder. Libby inched forward on the bench and turned her ear toward the floor below.

"Watch, Pulley," the haughty one said. "Now he will use the lithotomy forceps to pluck out the muscle."

Libby jerked her chin aside.

"He will not," she whispered in a low pitch. "He will use the curved knife to protect the muscle while exposing the bone. Now do be quiet so the rest of us can hear." She turned her face back toward the stage. She wasn't here to admonish ill-informed students. She was here to learn.

With each new revelation the lecturing surgeon offered, Libby scribed a detailed note, carefully lining up each sentence at the left margin, to be easily readable later. Finally the surgeon draped a linen cloth over the table, and the hall erupted in applause.

"This calls for a pint," the haughty student said, as though he'd done the dissection himself.

"Invite the new lad?" his friend said with a glance at her as she closed her notebook and stood.

The arrogant lip curled. "The riffraff can find their own pub."

They moved off.

"Dinna fret o'er Cheddar," a youth said cheerfully beside her. "He's a bushel o' mean stuffed into a barrel o' privilege. Family's got money an' he's clever as a fox. Doesna think he's got to be decent to anybody. Good on you to take him down a peg, lad."

She could not pretend the youth was not speaking to her. Reaching up, she touched the brim of her cap. For weeks she had studied men's gestures, as well as their gaits and facial movements, then practiced them before a mirror.

"I dinna know you," the youth said. "An' I know everybody." He thrust out his hand. The mop of ginger curls over his pale freckled face jiggled. "Archibald Armstrong. My mates call me Archie."

She turned away.

"Here now!" he said, scanning Libby's fine coat and trousers. "You're no' too smart to shake a fellow's hand, are you?"

There was no avoiding it. Libby grasped his hand and shook it hard.

"Smart," she mumbled. "Joseph."

"Fine grip you've got there, Joe! I always say you know the measure o' a man by his handshake. Matriculating this session?"

In her dreams.

She nodded.

"Excellent," Archie declared. "Always happy to meet a bloke cleverer than me, 'less it's Cheddar," he said with a wink, and clapped Libby on the shoulder, sending her lurching forward. "The lads are off to the Dug's Bone for a pint. Got to wash away the stink," he said jauntily. "Join us."

"Obliged," she said, and he moved off.

Euphoria bubbled up in her. All three students had believed she was a man!

The disguise did not, however, solve her greatest problem: finding a surgeon with whom to apprentice. For that she needed connections in Edinburgh's surgical community. Those connections would also pave the path to enrolling in courses on anatomy, surgery, and chemistry to augment her apprenticeship. Miss Elizabeth Shaw, daughter of renowned forensic physician John Shaw, had those sorts of connections in spades. The newly created and entirely friendless Joseph Smart *did not*.

But women were not allowed to apprentice as surgeons. Thus her disguise.

Below, only two students were asking questions of the lecturing surgeon. Questions crowded her own head, yet boys like Archie Armstrong didn't even bother staying to learn more.

As Elizabeth Shaw, she had never met this surgeon. She could chance asking her questions without being recognized. Tucking her notebook beneath her arm and starting toward the stair, she cut a swift glance across the thinning crowd.

Her steps faltered.

A man sat across the theater, alone as the tiers emptied.

It was not because he was the only person Libby recognized in the place that she abruptly could not move. For he was not. She had noticed several of her father's friends in the crowd.

And she did not halt because this man was attractive; for he was, with a strong tapering jaw, black hair swept back from his brow, and deep-set eyes. His arms clad in a fine coat and crossed loosely over his chest were muscular, and the crisp white of his cravat shone brilliantly against his skin. Libby had never particularly cared about external beauty; her interest was a body's health. And she had been stared at before. It was not due to his dark gaze trained upon her that she remained paralyzed.

Her feet would not move now because in that gaze was thorough recognition. He knew her.

They had met only once, two and a half years ago, exceedingly briefly. Yet the gleam in his hooded eyes now told her that he knew her at this moment to be Elizabeth Shaw.

With a regal nod he offered her a slow, confident smile of pure deviltry.

Panic seized her. It required only a single person to unmask her. If she did not move swiftly now, this man with the keen eyes and dangerous smile would.

EXCEPT FOR THE whiskers, she was perfect.

Watching her across the theater, Ziyaeddin wondered if she knew the whiskers were horrendous. But they helped serve her purpose: none of the men here realized that a female hid as one of them. None save he.

For two hours the attention of every person in the theater had been on the demonstration. Although Ziyaeddin preferred the earlier stages of a surgical dissection, when the body was whole and the muscles still plump with blood, he appreciated the entire series. A man could not properly depict the exterior without knowing what lay beneath.

Also, Edinburgh's medical community was large, sophisticated, and prosperous. He had friends as well as patrons among the men here. It was useful to occasionally be seen in public.

And then there was the girl.

With a sober face she had listened to the lecturing surgeon, scribbling in a notebook set atop her trouser-clad knees, making no move that might reveal her femininity. But he knew the girl beneath that disguise. He had once encountered her at Haiknayes Castle, the home of the Duke and Duchess of Loch Irvine. He remembered her perfectly.

Her fingers clutching pencil and notebook were long with very short nails, and darker than the visible bits of her fair chin and cheeks. The nose was neither large nor pert. The eyes, shaded by her hat, were almond-shaped, narrowing in the centers at equivalent arcs toward the dip at the bridge of her nose, the left a bit smaller than the right. The lashes and eye color he could not discern at this distance, but he knew them to be, respectively, golden brown and brilliant blue. The whiskers obscured her lips.

Those lips had given him trouble.

Considerable trouble.

Her father, John Shaw, was a respected physician. Ziyaeddin considered the likelihood that Dr. Shaw was aware his daughter now attended a surgical dissection dressed in men's clothing. From even the little Ziyaeddin knew of Miss Elizabeth Shaw: probably not.

She gazed with longing at the stragglers lingering about the lecturer. She mustn't realize how obviously her face showed that longing. He should probably tell her. That, and he needed to have another look at those lips.

Those lips.

Abruptly she turned her head and met his gaze, and the beautifully mobile features went stone still. Recognition sparked in the blue.

Aha. So she remembered him. No doubt she treasured the picture of her face that he had drawn at Haiknayes, probably keeping it in an intimate location: her bedside table or between the pages of her diary. Portraits by "the Turk" were coveted by ladies throughout Scotland and England. It was part of his mystique to rarely do likenesses of individual women, so that when he did they were especially valuable.

He inclined his head.

With a vexed glance at the lecturing floor below, she hurried from the hall.

Taking up his walking stick, he went out, greeting acquaintances along the way. The usual pain assailed him; he could never sit for long without it. He ignored it. He had far more interesting things to ponder now, two things: an upper lip and a lower lip.

By the time he came onto the street she had disappeared. Amidst the bustle of pedestrians, horses, and vehicles, he could not see her. Then, abruptly, through the window of a bookshop, he did.

A youth with a tight hat and too many whiskers stared at him above the edge of an open volume. The fire in the intelligent eyes dared him to reveal her.

Opening the door, he entered and looked into Elizabeth Shaw's scruffy face.

The hat was a clever contrivance, and like her cravat and coat, both of fine quality and understated. But the moustaches were all wrong, fashioned of goat's hair, and too coarse and ashy, and did not suit the golden strands of hair visible betwixt cap and collar. To conceal her smooth skin she had exaggerated the side whiskers till they were as thick and long as a sailor's.

He bowed. "Good day."

She ducked her head, moved around him, and darted out of the shop.

He followed.

As he half expected and half hoped, she was waiting for him in an alley not far away. Entering the secluded close he went toward her.

"You mustn't tell my father," she said without preamble. It did not surprise him. When they had spoken so briefly at Haiknayes she had been unconcerned with regular manners too.

"The color of the whiskers is unsuitable," he said.

Her nose crinkled. "It is?"

"It needs more yellow." Yellow ochre. And perhaps a touch of raw sienna.

She seemed to consider this. "I suppose you would know that, being a portrait artist."

"I would indeed," he said, bridling his amusement.

"Credible whiskers are remarkably difficult to come by." There was no anger in the eyes now, only earnest concern. "How did you recognize me?"

He stepped forward, closing the distance between them so that the precise shape and hues of her lips became clear to him—beautiful lips: nothing like the current fashion for red bows, instead wide and lushly pink.

"I have cause to know these lips well." Yet not well enough.

Before his encounter with Elizabeth Shaw at Haiknayes Castle, he had never seen a woman's lips and wanted immediately to touch them. Draw: yes. Paint: certainly. Touch: *never.*

"And these eyes," he added, because she was an unusual little woman and she did something to him—something alarming yet wholly pleasurable. She quickened his pulse.

And she made him want to stand in an alleyway chatting about false whiskers.

"At Haiknayes," she said, "you drew my face perfectly after seeing me only once."

Not perfectly. But close.

"You remember," he said.

"Of course I remember. I am not in my dotage, and you gave the picture *to me.* My father believed one of my friends drew it. He put a frame on it and hung it in the parlor. I pretended it fell off the wall while being dusted and the glass shattered. I told him I would take it to the shop to have the glass replaced but I threw it in the trash bin."

He laughed.

Her brows perked. "You are not offended?"

"Of course not."

"Truly?"

"If I wished, I could draw your face a hundred more times."

She blinked. "I must go." She glanced toward the alley's end. "I've elsewhere to be just now."

"A gentlemen's club?" He folded his arms. "Or a gaming hell? Perhaps the local public house?"

The lips twitched. "That is the simplest kind of humor."

"Well, you don't plan to attend a ladies' sewing circle in this ensemble." He allowed his gaze to travel down the heavy coat and trousers. She had most certainly bound her breasts, but there was no disguising the subtle flare of her hips. "Do you?"

"You are absurd. You won't tell anybody, will you?"

She had no reason to expect his discretion. And he was enjoying the dart that formed at the bridge of her nose, the shape of it like a pair of stalwart lovers forever separated by a mountain. Her beauty was conventional, a mingling of Scottish clarity and English delicacy. Yet the change-ability of her features fascinated him.

He found any sort of freedom of motion maddening—and inspiring.

"I should like to know the reason for your disguise," he said.

"I wanted to assess whether I could pass as a man," she said in a tone that suggested she thought him a simpleton. But he was accustomed to this. Even in this city of learning, and despite the popularity in fashionable society of all things Ottoman, he was occasionally treated to the scorn of people who believed the hue of his skin or his foreign features rendered him dull-witted, irrational, violent, cruel, or rapacious.

Yet this woman's eyes shone not with insult but sincerity.

"Congratulations for succeeding," he said. "Almost."

"I might as easily ask what *you* were doing there."

"Enjoying the vision of a pretty girl disguised as a youth."

Like sunlight sparking off the Mediterranean, her eyes flared. Abruptly she moved past him. He watched her lithe legs and straight back and stride that was far too confident for a woman.

"Miss Shaw, forgive my impertinence."

She paused. "I saw the portrait you did of the duke and duchess. It is very good."

That portrait of the Duke and Duchess of Loch Irvine

was not "very good." It was brilliant. Light and dark. Mystery and familiarity. Action and peace. Passion and reason. He had painted every facet of the pair in sublime balance.

Looking into the bright eyes now, he saw that Miss Shaw was well aware of this.

So this little woman of the earnest brow knew how to tease too. He should have anticipated that.

His body's reaction to this realization was, however, something of a surprise. Perhaps those slender legs were the trouble. Or thoughts of her breasts. Or the plump curve of her lower lip. Or the fact that she was standing before him dressed as a boy, duping everyone, yet apparently expecting him to keep her confidence.

"You will not tell anybody, will you?" she said. "The duke or Amarantha?"

"I believe they are in the countryside."

"That was a non-answer," she said. "Will you?"

"Your secret is safe with me."

"In truth?"

He nodded.

"Thank you." With a swift sweep of her gaze up and down his body, she hurried off around the corner.

Ziyaeddin walked the remainder of the route to his house slowly. Even when the way was long and his hip and back cramped, he disliked hiring a chair. Walking, he could study people.

Yet when he entered the foyer of his house, which was cool in the damp Caledonian fashion, he realized he had seen nothing of his surroundings for many minutes. He had been thinking of her.

Those lips.

Those damnable lips.

A letter sat on the silver dish on the foyer table, the

name *Ibrahim Kent* written across its well-worn exterior. It had traveled many miles, and he recognized the hand that had addressed it. He had received such letters before.

Greetings and blessings upon you, sir.

His sister's servant in the palace, Ali, never wrote anything in these letters that could identify any of them—no salutation, no name, no title—in the event that those unsympathetic to his mistress intercepted them.

She bids me beg you remain as you are, for he fears your return and does not cease his threats against those loyal to you. She insists that a time will come soon when your return will place none in peril. Until then, she bids you peace, as do I.

Ziyaeddin folded the letter and took it to the kitchen stove to burn. Then he went into his studio and penned a letter to London.

Again and again in seven years the foreign secretary had made Britain's position on the matter clear. *Bide your time, Your Highness. The situation is too volatile, the Russians too powerful, the Ottomans too uneasy, and Iran too little prepared for another war. If the tsar believes his ally now ruling Tabir to be weak, it would disrupt every other land in the region. Britain will come to the aid of Your Highness in time. We only await the ideal moment.*

In seven years nothing had changed: Westminster was still refusing aid; his sister was still a prisoner in the palace in which their father had once benevolently ruled; and he, heir to that realm, was still helpless, thousands of miles away where fate had thrown him. Yet his sister bid him to remain here.

After years of exile, captivity, and assassination attempts, the false identity he had adopted allowed him some peace. But he could not be content. What sort of man allowed his sister to be bound in a forced marriage with his enemy? What sort of son would not burn to avenge his father's assassination?

Disguise and fettered desire: these were the measure of his life now.

He would not keep Elizabeth Shaw's secret because she had asked it of him. He would keep it because he understood her.

Chapter 2

The Desire

*L*ibby slipped into the butler's pantry, hastily pulling off her cap and coat. The lecture had gone overlong and then that man had further delayed her.

That man.

Two and a half years ago when she had first encountered him he had discombobulated her too. He knocked her off balance, which was absurd given that *he* walked on a peg, not she.

He was too mysterious for her liking. Most people believed him to be Turkish, but he spoke many languages—Turkish, Persian, French, Russian, English, and some even said Arabic. He was a wildly popular portrait artist. Wealthy people commissioned his work for huge sums, and he appeared in the Edinburgh gossip columns as often as he went into society, which seemed to be infrequently by choice. Fashionable hostesses adored him. Gorgeously well-spoken and young, having fully adopted British dress and entirely eschewed whiskers, Mr. Ibrahim Kent was both exotically foreign and comfortably familiar. Apparently to high society that made him the ideal party guest.

Yet he remained largely a mystery. Why didn't anybody know from where exactly he had come? Why should it be secret?

Libby didn't like mysteries. They made her feel itchy and unsettled.

But she believed he would not expose her. The Duke of Loch Irvine had always been very kind to her, and Mr. Kent was his close friend. She trusted Mr. Kent's word.

She was peeling the side whiskers from her cheeks painfully when Iris Tate appeared in the doorway and burst into laughter.

"Whiskers and muslin! Mama needn't take me to London for a season after all, for I've seen everything there is to see now."

"Come button me up." Grabbing a pot of oil from the hiding spot, Libby shoved her trousers, shirt, and all the other bits of her disguise under the empty wine rack and started cleaning off the adhesive. "Have the movers finished?"

"They are loading your father's trunks onto the carriage now. They're to take yours to Miss Alice's house afterward. By the by, Alice's housekeeper has the fever and she is worried you might take it too."

"I never take fevers. I have a strong constitution." It made her the ideal candidate for the medical profession, if only the profession allowed women. "Thank you for helping me with this, Iris. You are a dear friend."

"I would invite you to come stay with me while your father is gone, but I would never inflict Mama on you. There! You look like a woman again, except for the red splotches around your lips."

Libby rubbed salve into her raw skin. "I must find a less abrasive adhesive. And more comfortable trousers."

"You cannot attend again anyway, not as a boy," Iris

said. "Now that you will be living two miles away in Leith at Alice's house, you will be too far away from the college. And where would you change into those clothes without detection? At Tabitha's shop?"

"I cannot. She was wonderful to make these clothes so I could move secretly about the docks." When Libby and her father had lived in Leith, Tabitha had applauded Libby's need to treat the wounds and minor illnesses of poor sailors off the merchant ships. "But after Thomas discovered it and told my father, I cannot ask Tabitha to keep this secret from him. An intimate relationship between a wife and husband must be built on trust."

"I suppose," Iris said with the blithe shrug of a fifteen-year-old.

"It really must, Iris." Yet here she was, keeping the secret from her father, whom she loved more than anyone in the world. "It is positively criminal that I cannot apprentice with a surgeon as myself."

"Elizabeth?" her father called from the front of the house. "Is that you?"

"Coming, Papa!"

The foyer was a familiar scene: her father surrounded by luggage. Through the open doorway she could see men hauling a traveling trunk toward the coach. She and her father frequently changed residences, following his aristocratic patients and projects for the police. Now they were moving again, this time, however, separating: he to London and she back to Leith to live with their friend Alice Campbell.

"I am here, Papa," she said.

At sixty, Dr. John Shaw had health and intelligence and kind, wise eyes, and now also a yearlong invitation from the Royal College of Physicians in London to lecture on his expertise: medical forensics.

"The driver wishes to depart. Where have you been?"

"At the bookshop." It wasn't *untrue*.

"Libby," Iris said, "I will call on you at Miss Alice's. Bon voyage, Dr. Shaw."

Libby cast Iris a grateful look as she went out.

"I am very excited for you for your grand adventure, Papa. You will be splendid at the Royal College."

"I hope I can be of use there," he said with the customary humility she admired.

"Allow me to go with you."

"You will be happier here, Elizabeth. Among friends."

In familiar places, he meant.

"I could be happy with you in London."

He withdrew a kerchief from a pocket, and from another pocket the lorgnette he used for examinations, and began to polish the glass. This was difficult for him too.

"You must remember what happened the last time we lived in London," he said.

What happened. An understatement. Plunged into unfamiliar places, with all of her daily habits upset, she had felt overwhelmed and had swiftly lost weight, could not leave the house, and eventually refused to allow him to leave it either.

"Papa, that was years ago." Before she learned to love medicine—before she had found such satisfaction in studying the bones, muscles and nerves that made the human body move and run and dance and swim in rivers and climb mountains. "I believe I could be happy in London if—"

"If you could apprentice with Charles Bell." He tucked the lorgnette and linen in the same pocket. "Elizabeth, what makes you believe that Mr. Bell will take you on as an apprentice when no surgeon in Edinburgh will?"

"I have read every one of his books and essays," she said, plucking out the kerchief, folding it, and replacing it in the correct pocket. "I know more about anatomy and practical surgery than many surgeons you know. You have said so your—"

"Women will never be admitted to the medical profession, Elizabeth. You are twenty, old enough to accept this finally."

Words died in her mouth. She shook her head.

His features softened.

"I have upset you," he said. "And only minutes before I must leave."

"You have not said anything I do not already know, of course. You are weary of me," slipped from between her lips before she could catch it.

"Elizabeth."

"Are you?" It was unfair of her to ask, but the need for reassurance pressed at her urgently, as needs often did— questions that required immediate answers, worries that sought immediate reassurance. The mother she never knew had suffered from the same small madness. Unchecked, the unrelenting need had eventually driven her to her death. "*Are* you, Papa?"

"Of course not." But his tone hinted at impatience. He had long believed she would grow out of this too. Rather, he had hoped it. Yet she had disappointed him in that hope.

He took her hands into his, the dry and warm and wonderful hands of a physician. Raised entirely by her father, cared for and given ample affection, she adored him.

"Daughter, you must accept reality."

"Papa, how will the profession begin to even consider admitting women if qualified women do not seek admittance?"

"I have no doubt there has never been a woman more qualified to apprentice to a surgeon than you, my brilliant child. I wish I could change the world for you. It pains me that I cannot."

She could bear his pain no more easily than her own.

"You are the best father imaginable." She squeezed his hands. "I will miss you."

"You know what you must do now, Elizabeth. Here in Edinburgh and in Leith are young women of conversation with whom you can make friends so that your days will not be so aimless."

"They are not aimless. I am studying, Papa. You know that. And Iris, Tabitha, and Alice are the best friends a person could wish."

"Iris Tate is a child, Tabitha Bellarmine has a husband and shop now to concern her, and Alice Campbell, while an excellent person, is forty years your senior. You need friends of your own situation." Taking up his light medical case, he paused at the open door. "The choices you make, Elizabeth, affect others."

She hated the worry etching his features. He needed reassurance now too.

"I will try to make new friends, if you wish. I promise." He started out.

"Papa," she said to his back, the need tightening her throat. "Please tell me that you are not weary of me."

"How could you ever imagine it?"

"Say it, please." She needed to hear the words.

"I am not weary of you," he said patiently. "God be with you, my dear child."

But God was never with her, only that fierce need telling her what to do and say.

When the carriage drew away from the house she watched until it disappeared from view, because the need told her to do that too.

ZIYAEDDIN AWOKE FROM the dream in much the same manner he always did: soaked in sweat and probably shouting.

He wasn't entirely certain about the shouting. He had not kept a manservant in years. Now in the middle of the night there was no one to rush into his bedchamber with a worried frown asking ridiculous questions and begging to aid him. The housekeeper came daily except Sundays, and the manservant came thrice weekly. He lived humbly and preferred it that way, especially when the dream came.

Yet the usual images did not linger before his eyes now open to the darkness: fire and wicked smoke against a sapphire sky. No scent of desperation filled his nostrils. No panic compressed his lungs. Instead his bedchamber was redolent of the coming winter, and before his eyes was a pair of lips.

Rubbing a hand over his face, he shrugged into his dressing gown.

The house was narrow, flanked on either side by similar houses. He had not purchased it for its fine wood paneling in the parlor or elegant façade or lofty foyer, but for this single-story hexagonal chamber with north-facing windows and two adjacent smaller chambers. He lived entirely here, where the light was clean.

Crossing the studio past his current piece, a trio of fair Scottish maidens, he went into the little chamber he used as a workroom. He reached for a portfolio tucked behind the worktable and drew forth the pages within.

In the lamp glow her features in pencil and pen were as familiar to him now as they had been in the daylight of Surgeons' Hall, the bookshop, and the alley. The whiskers notwithstanding, he would have been a fool not to recognize her.

On their first encounter at Haiknayes she had entered the library where he was reading, and he had seen her standing there beneath a grotesque of Saint George and told her she resembled nothing less than an angel at the feet of the triumphant Lucifer. She had departed as abruptly as she had appeared.

Then he had drawn these.

Mobility. Feeling. Thought. They were all so thoroughly on the surface of her features, as though, unlike all others in this land of curious constraint, she alone had never learned to mask her thoughts and emotions, or simply did not care to.

But he had never gotten the lips right.

He carried the drawings to the easel, set the lamp beside him, and found a pencil.

By the time he finished, dawn was arriving. It was too late to return to bed, and the pain was too great from sitting for so long. But satisfaction hummed through him now and he required no sleep.

He dressed, donned his hat and coat, and went in search of coffee. For in this city thousands of leagues from his home he was not Ziyaeddin Mirza, Prince of Tabir, surrounded by servants and sycophants to do his bidding. He had not been that in seventeen years.

Here he was simple Ibrahim Kent, portraitist. And honest labor made a man hungry.

Chapter 3

Inspiration

"*How do* you manage to contrive such clever golden curls, Miss Shaw?" The speaker was young and fashionably gowned. Her lips smiled, but her eyes did not.

The little group of society maidens had been discussing the clothing and hair of other people at the party for a quarter of an hour already. None of them had spoken to Libby since she had approached them, until now.

"I haven't anything to do with the qualities of my hair, actually," Libby said. "Children naturally possess the physical traits of their parents. For instance, you and your brother share the same straight brown hair and hazel eyes, due to your father and mother's similar traits."

"Is that so?" the girl drawled without any evidence of interest, then turned her body, blocking Libby from the circle entirely.

"Sister," a man said laughingly at Libby's shoulder, "you are snubbing Miss Shaw."

"Dear me, brother, how beastly of me." Her painted lips

shaped an insincere smile. "What would you like to converse about now, Miss Shaw? Teeth and chins, I daresay?"

Her friends tittered appreciatively.

"Come now, sister," her brother said with a grin. "Play nice."

"This isn't play," Libby said. "This is the most common form of social dominating. Your sister has brought attention to a trait of mine that others consider attractive, my blond curls, and wishes to be noticed instead of me. So she noted it first, aloud, while however insulting me to show others she has power over me. But I have no ambitions so she needn't worry. None of you have read *A Treatise on Exclusion* by Mr. Harper of the Plinian Society, have you?"

They all stared at her as though she had grown floppy ears and fangs.

"No. Of course not," she muttered, feeling the hated heat rise in her cheeks. "Good evening." Pivoting, she heard one of them whisper, "She is such a child."

Walking swiftly past the clusters of people, Libby left the drawing room.

She had come to this party solely so that she could write to her father that she had, and to please her half-sister, Lady Constance Sterling, who liked to bring her along to parties hosted by physicians, like this one, so Libby might become acquainted with young men who shared her interest in medicine.

Now Constance was chatting merrily with a cluster of lawyers and politicians who, though she was married, still enjoyed flirting with her. Constance was very beautiful, heiress to a duke, and delightful. She did not know that the last thing on earth Libby wanted was a beau, and that her father's wish for her to marry was so painful that she could barely think about it without her palms growing damp.

Most of Edinburgh physicians' houses had good libraries.

When her mind was busy acquiring information, it quieted. She would find the library here and regain her equilibrium.

Ahead, the glow of candlelight peeked through a door that stood partially ajar. She pushed it open and discovered her goal, well stocked and with comfortable furniture.

"Excellent," she said.

A feminine cry of distress came from across the room. A man's thick grunts followed.

Libby had heard such noises before. Living wherever her father's patients required, in the homes of wealthy families with randy sons and unwilling servants, hiding in stairwells and cabinets, she had *seen*.

She rushed forward around the sofa.

There was abruptly a lot of movement: the woman dragging a sumptuous gown up over her breasts, the man leaping up from between the woman's thighs and clutching the open fall of his breeches to cover his genitals, and both of them gaping at her as though they had caught *her* half naked and not the reverse.

"Oh, it's only her," the woman whispered. Her jewels tinkled as she giggled.

So. Apparently neither unwilling nor a servant.

Libby pinned her gaze to the floor as they made sounds of putting themselves in order. Then, with laughter and more giggles, they were gone.

She felt cold all over, and a little nauseated.

Moving to a bookcase, she plucked out a volume. But the words entrapped her, and she looped back again and again to memorize them. She could not remember them well enough, yet she *must*.

Shoving the book onto the shelf, she put her back to it and tried—*tried* to draw slow, even breaths. She needed her surgical instruments in her hands now, or her model bones, to touch and feel and know their familiar shapes again. They would calm her enough to be able to read. They always did.

Casting her gaze about for such an object, she caught the gleam of a painting illumined by the hearth's light.

Done upon some ancient mythological theme, it featured a woman draped in filmy white cloth that amply revealed the curves of her hips and breasts and even her aroused nipples. Beneath a pomegranate tree she danced, her arms and legs and neck gracefully lissome. Before her knelt a man clad in a suggestion of a cloth about his loins. With both hands he was offering her fruit.

Moving toward it, Libby stared at the god's glorious body. Endowed in the musculature, like a laboring man, but one who had plenty of nourishment to support thick muscles, he was likewise lush, and anatomically perfect. Even his position kneeling before the woman was balanced; Libby could practically feel his knees digging into the earth, his heels against his buttocks, the shifting muscles in his limbs. The woman was the same: ideal without exaggeration. They were both entirely human and gloriously divine.

Libby sighed. To be able to study the human body freely—as this artist obviously had—and to understand it so well was her dream.

The artist had made his signature in the lower corner, barely visible against the dark grass: *I. Kent*.

Now she understood how he had recognized her despite the disguise, and how two and a half years ago, after speaking with her for only minutes, he had drawn her face with perfect accuracy. To render the human form and features so honestly as he had done in this painting, a man must perceive them as few did.

Abruptly the sounds of conversation in the drawing room came into the library and the young gentleman from earlier entered.

"Miss Shaw," he said, closing the door. "My sister feared that you took offense at her teasing and bid me come after you to beg your pardon."

"Pardon granted," she said, crossing the room. "Good night."

"I cannot be happy unless I am certain you know she meant you no insult."

"Of course she meant insult. But I am nearly impervious to slights, so it hardly—"

He moved swiftly, blocking her exit.

"Miss Shaw, allow me to seize this rare opportunity of privacy to tell you how ardently I admire you."

"Admire me? You don't even know me."

"I have been watching you from afar, afraid to make myself known to you."

"That is certainly a lie, for I haven't any great beauty to admire from afar. Please, sir, I wish to leave this room now."

"You must believe me, Miss Shaw. I haven't approached you before because I was—well—intimidated." He offered a crooked smile. "You must know that you make a man feel weak and foolish."

"That is ridiculous. A woman cannot make a man anything he is not already." She reached around him for the door handle. "Now you must—"

He grabbed her shoulders and his mouth descended upon hers. Then his arms were around her and his tongue pushing at her lips.

Libby tore her mouth away and shoved against him. "Release me now or I will scream."

"That you haven't already shows me you want this."

That she had not already was because she loved Constance and her father and did not wish to shame them. She had come into this room alone. For years she had known better.

She hauled her knee into his groin.

He staggered back, gasping and clutching his crotch.

Hurrying back to the party, she found Constance and her husband, Saint.

On the carriage ride home, she barely attended to Constance and Saint's conversation.

"Libby," Constance said after a time. "Did you hate it so much?"

Yes. "No." She wanted to ask Constance why a man would thrust his tongue into a woman's mouth. And if it was uncomfortable doing sexual congress on a sofa. And what exactly happened when two people who were engaged in sexual congress were interrupted in the middle of it.

"You seem distressed," Constance said, and kindly.

The need to ask the questions was climbing up Libby's throat and tightening her chest. "I cannot speak of it now," she forced herself to say.

"I saw you escape to the library. What did you discover there?" Constance knew distraction helped. She was a wonderful sister.

"A painting. It was beautiful." Extraordinary.

"That reminds me of excellent news I heard this evening, Libby. It seems that just as your father is traveling to London, Mr. Charles Bell is journeying here to Edinburgh for a brief visit to deliver a trio of lectures at the Academy. Isn't this marvelous? You will finally have your dream of hearing him lecture."

Libby's dream was not to hear Mr. Charles Bell lecture, but to apprentice with him.

"How did Libby's mention of a painting in the library remind you of Charles Bell?" Saint said.

"Mr. Bell is an artist."

"I thought he was a surgeon."

"He is both," Libby said. "His artistic studies have allowed him to understand the body better than any other surgeon or physician in—" Her heartbeats were abruptly quick. "In Scotland."

An idea was forming, a brilliant idea that could enable her to formally study surgical medicine.

Only one man could make it possible: a reclusive portraitist whose mysteriousness would be the ticket to her dream.

Chapter 4

A Proposal

The knocker sounded precisely as the sun withdrew its blade from the scabbard of the horizon and set the girls beneath his brush aglow. For this reason he had positioned the canvas as close to the window as possible, to capture the light required to bring these insipid maidens to life.

The clack came again at the front door.

It was early for his housekeeper to arrive, and unusual for her to forget her key. But Ziyaeddin had been sitting too long. He needed to move. Snuffing the lamp, he went forward through the house still sunk in darkness as the knocker clacked thrice more.

He opened the door not on Mrs. Coutts but on a young woman.

"I need your help," she said. She wore a straw hat atop her riot of golden curls, which were cinched with a ribbon, a plain cloak of unbecoming brown wool over a likewise dull gown. Yet her cheeks were bright with morning's chill and her breaths puffed into quick little silvery clouds.

No insipid maiden, this one.

"We are clothed according to our sex this morning, it appears," he said.

"It appears we are," she said, giving him that up-and-down sweep of appraisal that she had in the alley. "Do invite me in."

Briefly, Ziyaeddin considered his options.

Those lips. Unconcealed this time by false whiskers.

He opened the door wide.

"Why did you answer the door?" she said. "That is, I am glad you did. It is much more convenient than waiting in a parlor for you to see me, which is what I assumed would happen. Actually, I thought I would probably be turned away, but I brought a calling card in that event. Do you not have servants?"

"They have not yet arrived. I don't suppose you noticed it is barely dawn."

"Of course I have. I couldn't wait." She seemed to balance on her toes. "Shall we go to the parlor now?"

He gestured toward the parlor door.

"Oh, I like this!" She circled the chamber, then halted at its precise center. "It is perfect."

Perfect for what, he could not imagine. She did not seem the sort of young woman to be happy sitting at a tea table for long.

"Don't you?" she said.

"Don't I?"

"Don't you have round-the-clock servants?"

"I don't. Miss Shaw, I am under the impression you are not aware that this is an unusual call."

"I know it is. But I don't care about social conventions and I assumed you don't either. You are obviously a recluse.

Amarantha says you rarely go anywhere even though you are invited everywhere and that you even declined an invitation from the Academy of Edinburgh to lecture on painting. And you said that you would not tell anyone I had gone to the dissection dressed as a man, so you are unconventional too."

"An impressive list of evidence, to be sure. Nevertheless, as a gentleman it behooves me to note that you should not in fact be in a bachelor's home, even at dawn."

"Then you are unmarried?"

That a frisson of warning slid through him now, accompanied by a rather focused awakening, made him pause a moment before he replied.

"I am."

"Excellent," she said. "That will make this much easier. A wife might need to know all of your business and that could ruin everything."

Ziyaeddin had allowed her into the house from curiosity and because the Duke of Loch Irvine, the man to whom he owed his life, and the duke's wife held great affection for her. He was reconsidering the wisdom of that decision.

"You have succeeded," he said. "I am thoroughly perplexed. What could my nonexistent wife ruin by knowing?"

"The subterfuge in which I am hoping you will engage with me. Soon. Beginning today, if possible. Time is of the essence. Charles Bell will arrive in Edinburgh momentarily and I haven't any time to waste if I am to convince him."

"Convince him of what?"

"To help me become a surgeon."

He stood entirely still, saying nothing, and the urge to say more pressed at Libby. Instead, she counted silently. Waiting for any response was extraordinarily difficult for her. But her father had taught her that men often had difficulty following her speech; her mind moved too quickly for them.

Nothing about Mr. Kent moved at all. He was *remarkably* still.

"A surgeon," he finally said.

"Yes."

"It has been my impression—correct me if I am mistaken—that in this country women do not practice medicine," he said as though they were conversing about any subject. *A good sign*. Perhaps this man's mind moved more rapidly than most men's.

"That is not precisely true. There are women all over Britain with medical knowledge who are wonderfully capable of caring for patients. It is in fact perhaps the strongest point in our case, as regards mere power, both physical and intellectual, that women have been able to do so much while debarred from the advantages of early education open to most men. Women are midwives and nurses. We are not permitted to be physicians and surgeons."

"You wish to be the first."

"I don't care if I am the *first*. I only wish to be a surgeon. Not one of those hack barbers that removes teeth and such." The sort that lopped off men's limbs in battlefield hospitals, that had no doubt done so to this man's lower leg. Mr. Kent was young, but old enough to have fought as a youth in war. "I don't wish to hang a red and white striped pole before my shop. I wish to be a true scientist, the sort of surgeon that understands the complexity of the human body and, through that understanding, heals people."

"Your ambition is admirable, Miss Shaw."

"Rather, it is rational. I am more intelligent than most men, and my father gave me an excellent education in mathematics, chemistry, and mechanical philosophy, not to mention Latin and some Greek and of course the modern languages. I am already remarkably learned in medicine from studying independently and from assisting my father for years."

"I see. I don't, however, see what your rational ambition has to do with me."

"To become a surgeon, I must first apprentice under the direction of an established master surgeon."

"Aha. Thus your interest in Mr. Bell."

Her heart skipped. "You know of Charles Bell?"

"I have made his acquaintance."

"You *have*? How? He has lived in London for decades."

"I came to know him at the Royal Academy there."

"Where the greatest artists in Britain gather?" This was too good to be true. "How extraordinary! But you are exceptionally talented, after all."

He lifted a single brow. "Am I, then?"

"Of course you are. I said that about the portrait of the duke and Amarantha to tease you as you were teasing me. This is marvelous! Even better than I imagined. Last night I saw one of your paintings hanging in a physician's house. The figures were beautiful. You must have spoken with Mr. Bell at the Academy about painting the human form."

"If you have come seeking painting lessons, Miss Shaw, you have come to the wrong man. But you needn't despair. There are plenty of artists in Edinburgh happy to teach painting to fashionable young ladies."

"I am not at all fashionable and I don't need those men. I need you."

His gaze sharpened for a moment. Then he gestured with his hand that she should continue. He had beautiful hands, long-fingered and graceful. He walked with such awkwardness: the pole that served him as a right foot and ankle made his stride uneven. That he could break his stillness now with such a satiny gesture startled her.

She could not lose courage. Her future depended on this.

"I would like to commission you to paint a few pictures," she said. "Of people. The figures must be at least as unclothed as those in the painting I saw last night. And it would be best if they were of sick or injured people, the sort that Charles Bell paints."

"You have come here to commission work on behalf of your father?"

"No. My father is in London now, for an entire year in fact. I want these paintings for myself."

He regarded her thoughtfully while the pressure rose in Libby to continue speaking. His eyes were full of perception, rich dark brown with long, ebony lashes. There was a quality to the set of his mouth that suggested natural arrogance yet an unwillingness to actually *be* arrogant. She could not imagine those full lips sneering, not even in mock pleasure as the rapacious young man had done at the party the night before.

"My work is not inexpensive," he said.

"That is inconsequential." If she must, she would borrow the money.

"Unfortunately, my schedule is full at present."

"Yes. I have heard your works are sought after. You are outrageously fashionable. Everybody wants a portrait by the Turk. You must know they call you that? Not by your name. Only the Turk. It is disrespectful. Although it's true that you are unique in Edinburgh. That is, there are plenty of foreign sailors in Leith, of course, and many other foreigners, in this city too. Why, there is a taxidermist from Jamaica right down the street from here. But I don't believe foreign *portrait artists* crowd Britain's salons, at least no more foreign than Americans or Irishmen."

"At least." He was smiling a bit now, barely, but it made him even handsomer. A suggestion of morning whiskers ran along his jaw and about his mouth, carving his lean cheeks into further shadow. She had rarely seen a gentleman unshaven. It rendered his good looks rather fierce.

"Certainly no other Turkish portrait artists," she added. "Are you actually Turkish? Some people who have traveled abroad with the East India Company or the military believe you may be Persian rather than Turkish. They wonder aloud why you wear no beard or robes or turban. You can tell me."

"Yet I will not."

"As you wish. Still, I think it's shabby that gossips do not refer to you by name, although of course the newspapers mostly do."

"I appreciate your concern. My schedule is still full."

"They could be small paintings."

He smiled again, but only a slight lift of one side of his lips.

"Very small paintings," she said.

"Aha, I see. Then perhaps I could do one or two very small pieces. Between other projects." A teasing gleam lit his eyes. She ignored it.

"The sooner the better," she said. "And the pictures must include a particular detail."

"What detail is that, Miss Shaw?"

"I require my name at the bottom. As the artist."

The amusement drained from his features.

"I do not mean you any insult," she said hastily. "I assure you."

"And yet," he said shortly.

"Truly. Anybody would be proud to hang one of your paintings on her wall. I don't know why that physician had his hidden away in his library, except perhaps some callers wouldn't like the scantily clad god and goddess. Most people are uncomfortable with nudity. As a student of medicine, of course, I am not. It is only that Mr. Bell must believe I painted the paintings."

"Must he?" The muscles in his jaw had contracted and

the sinews in his neck were tight, and abruptly Libby realized that he was not fully dressed. He wore a dark dressing gown over trousers and a shirt without stock or cravat. He had not even buttoned the shirt at the neck, leaving the hollow at the base of his throat and the contours of the clavicle wholly visible. And *beautiful.*

From skin to bones, every part of the human body always fascinated her. Never, however, had she studied another person and felt hot tingles erupt in her own body.

She dragged her attention up to his eyes.

"Yes," she pushed out between her lips. "No man will seriously consider me for an apprenticeship. Occasionally my father's colleagues and friends speak with me about medicine, and some have even admitted they're impressed with my knowledge. But Mr. Charles Bell is unique. His work is original and brilliant. I think this is because he has learned about the body through studying art, and he uses his own paintings and drawings to teach others. If he sees that beyond our mutual love of medical science I am also a talented painter of the human form, he might believe that I have enough natural ability to study medicine. He could aid me in finding a surgeon to take me on as an apprentice and also help me gain admittance to a school to study anatomy and chemistry. He has enormous influence, still, despite his falling out with the instructors of anatomy that precipitated his move to London." She gripped her hands together. "Don't you see? With the support of a man of Mr. Bell's eminence, I could become a real surgeon. An *excellent* surgeon."

"I begin to suspect you could."

"Do you?"

"Your mind clearly functions outside of the usual tracks. But I will put no one's name on my work save my own, least of all a woman's."

Panic was bleeding into her. "You say *woman* with such scorn."

"I do not paint watercolors of flowers, Miss Shaw."

"Exactly. You paint the human form, which is precisely the reason I have not asked this of anyone else. I beg of you. Won't you consider this commission?"

"My answer remains no. This interview is at an end." He walked into the foyer.

Nerves splintering, she followed him.

"I will pretend to be a young man again," she said. "You may sign the name Joseph Smart to the pictures and be not ashamed."

The parlor had been pale with dawn through the open curtains. But the foyer was nearly dark and she became fully aware of his size. Above average height for a man, he was neither bulky nor slender, rather lean with broad shoulders. So close to him now she felt his energy, like the energy of a mighty river that had been dammed: power impeded, hidden behind calm.

"Good day, Miss Shaw."

"Don't you see?" she said. "It is the only way."

"I see that your imagination far outstrips mine. Do you truly believe you can succeed in pretending to Mr. Bell that you are a man and then reveal to him the truth once he has allowed you to fool everybody in Edinburgh, including him?"

"It's true: he would be furious." She nodded. "It will be best to remain a man until I pass the entrance exams to the Royal College of Surgeons. Surgical apprenticeships are typically seven years, but I am already accomplished, and apprentices are allowed to sit for exams after four years if they wish. And of course I could take the diploma exams after three sessions. I have been my father's informal apprentice for all intents and purposes since I was a child. Without a full apprenticeship I will simply have to pay a higher fee to become a fellow in the college. But if I must I will."

"Your dreams are impressive, Miss Shaw, as is your confidence. But your thinking is ludicrous. Not only will people recognize that you are a woman—"

"They didn't at the lecture."

"Consider your servants. Will you take them into your confidence, hoping that they will not betray you?" A razor seemed to slice each of his words now. "I assure you, one rarely knows from which direction betrayal will come until it is too late."

"I will find a way to conceal it from them." She must.

"What of your neighbors? When they see a young man who could be the twin of Miss Shaw leave and return to your house each day, for how long will they remain oblivious to the truth? A fortnight? A month?"

Desperation was slithering through her. "You seem to have thought through this swiftly."

"I have some experience with concealment."

Libby knew little of him except that he had the friendship of the Duke and Duchess of Loch Irvine. And she knew of his extraordinary art. And now she knew that he lived alone. *Without servants.*

"I will live here," she said. "With you."

There was complete silence in which, in the foyer that was finally taking on the light of morning, she saw his features slacken.

"You will most certainly not," he said.

"Don't you see how ideal this is?" Excitement was scurrying up through her. "You rarely go out or entertain. Amarantha has said so. Now, finding yourself desirous of company, you will become the patron of a young surgical student. I will be a relative of a close friend of yours—the

duke or somebody else you trust not to ask questions and
who lives comfortably at a distance from Edinburgh. It
will be the easiest story to tell your servants, I think, one
they will certainly believe. Everybody else will too. You
will take in this young surgical student to make him acquainted with Mr. Bell and others of the medical community.
And he—I, that is—will accomplish the rest with my
brilliance and hard work."

"But I am not in fact desirous of company."

"It is a *pretense*."

"And now you are not only a youth but a distant relative
of a duke?"

"My mother was actually a duchess."

The black brows rose. "Your mother?"

"My father is not my real father. My mother was the
Duchess of Read, but the Duke of Read is not the man
who got me on her. I don't know exactly how it happened,
for she perished when I was an infant, and nobody speaks
of it. John Shaw raised me as his own. He and the Duke of
Read have been friends for decades, and we visited Read
Castle frequently throughout my childhood. Constance
and I share the same color hair, and I am the image of
the portrait of the duchess that hangs on the wall at Read
Castle. Even you would marvel at the likeness."

"Would I?" The cutting edge had gone from his tone.

"In this house and neighborhood nobody will know
that Joseph Smart is a woman. And I will have privacy to
study. It is ideal, really. And I won't bother you. I will hide
myself away in a corner of the house that you don't use.
Is there a corner you don't use? There must be. Without
servants living here, there are probably empty servants'
quarters above, and you are unlikely to even go up there
anyway."

"Aren't I?"

"Of course not. I can see quite clearly you walk with pain. And it wouldn't be forever. Once I have proven myself equal to the men in my program—indeed, their superior—I will reveal the truth and they will all have to accept me. Please. You must help me."

"I mustn't. Miss Shaw, this plan is preposterous, every detail of it."

"The greatest advances in science have come when people have attempted the preposterous. It is not the same in art?"

"Perhaps. But you are accepting a lot on faith."

"On faith? What do you mean? That I will prove—"

"You know nothing of me."

Alarm wound its way from the base of her spine up into her throat. The intensity of his eyes seemed suddenly as foreign as his bronzed skin and the soft accent that inflected his English.

"It is true," she said. "I know almost nothing about you. But I know that the Duke of Loch Irvine entrusted you with his home. And I know that Amarantha admires you."

"Would you tell them of your charade?"

He was not refusing her.

"No. I would not wish to oblige my friends to lie on my behalf."

"But you would have no qualms requiring me to lie. You assume I haven't the morality of an Englishman or a Scot."

"No! Not at all. That is, I don't know what sort of morality you have. But that hardly matters." She twisted her hands together. "Don't you see? I have *no* other potential allies."

He moved the step forward that brought him within inches of her, and he made no sound, not the tip of his cane or peg, his entire body in control. It must certainly cost him great effort to move with such silence, and that alarmed her.

"In pursuit of this scheme you would make yourself entirely vulnerable to a man you do not know." His voice was low. Intimate.

"It is not a scheme. It is my dream." She lifted her chin. "It has been my dream for my entire life. And I will succeed at it. I am determined to."

His gaze traveled over her features slowly.

"Have you no concern for the shame this would bring upon your father?"

"I must press forward now while he is away, while I have opportunity."

"For a woman of great intelligence you are remarkably ignorant."

She backed away a step. "What exactly do you mean by that?"

"Even were I to agree to this charade, an artist of Mr. Bell's discernment would notice the similarity between my style and this pretend Joseph Smart's."

"Then you can make the paintings unalike. Mine can be imperfect. Slightly imperfect. Enough so that Mr. Bell will be impressed but will not notice the similarity."

"Would you give a person imperfect medical care?"

"Of course not. But this is different."

"Not to me."

She understood. He had standards, just as she did. But that meant he must also have desires, just as she did.

"I will pay you twice the proper price of each work. Thrice. I will pay for board."

"I have no need of your money."

"Then what do you want?"

"Nothing you can give me that I do not already possess, *güzel kız*. I cannot help you." He went to the door and opened it to the outside. "Good day, Miss Shaw."

Standing on the stoop, she watched the door shut her out with quiet yet firm finality.

Chapter 5

A Gentlemanly Agreement

"'Tis no' your finest work, sir. No' by far."

Ziyaeddin's housekeeper bustled about his studio, taking up teacups and straightening the curtains.

He rubbed a palm over his eyes. "Thank you, Mrs. Coutts. I appreciate your candor."

"I always prefer the truth to empty flattery," she said with the no-nonsense honesty of Scots that he had come to appreciate. "The lasses you finished last Saturday were less than your best too, if you dinna mind me saying."

"I do not mind it." Even as he had delivered it to their parents he knew the portrait of the maidens, over which he had labored for months, lacked something. Fire. Emotion. Depth. Movement.

Now this piece, of a wealthy lawyer and his wife, was suffering the same. They were an amiable pair. But the picture meant nothing to him: this man in his sober coat and this woman in her layers of lace. They wanted a perfect likeness, and he was able to give that to them. A perfectly uninspired likeness.

All of his work had gone thus since that girl had called. *Woman.*

Those lips.

Those eyes.

Those squared shoulders and those supple arms and that tongue from which so swiftly tripped words that came at the speed of a maddened camel.

He set down the brush and took up his sketching pad. Scraping the chalk over the thick paper, he worked swiftly.

"Oo, now, sir," his housekeeper said, leaning over his shoulder. "'Tis a bonnie lass, that one."

"I have not yet drawn her face."

"There be more to a lass's beauty than nose and lips and eyes, sir."

He paused. "Mrs. Coutts, how is it that you are not offended?"

"I brought seven bairns into the world, an' another ten bairns to my daughters too. I'll no' get my petticoat in a bunch over a wee nekked bum." With a firm nod she went to the door. "I'll be off now. Dinner's on the stove. But you'd best have an outin' tonight, sir. P'raps to one o' those parties you're always invited to." She shook her head. "A young man shouldna be so alone." With a rustle of starched skirts she was gone.

She was, of course, correct. In a fortnight he had not left the house except to call on this lawyer and his wife for sittings. Other than Mrs. Coutts, his manservant, and them, he had not spoken with a human in a fortnight.

Except Elizabeth Shaw.

The drawings of her remained where he had left them

following the public dissection. After her absurd proposal he had not taken advantage of the time he had spent that morning studying her features, as she pleaded her case to him.

The lips on those drawings would remain imperfect. Just as the painting before him would, the couple entirely without life.

Without life.

A reply to his letter had come from Canning. The foreign secretary urged His Royal Highness to remain patient.

But Ziyaeddin had heard from another as well: the Iranian ambassador, who in poetic Persian phrases had suggested that the Shahanshah was no longer averse to persuasion, that the Russian theft of lands in the last treaty could no longer be tolerated, that a prince of Persian blood must again rule there, not the imposters of the northern tribes who called themselves khans but were no more than cowards. In this reconquest Tabir would prove a welcome ally. The usurping general in Russia's pocket must therefore be unseated.

That time had not yet come. Respecting his sister Aairah's wishes, and to ensure the safety of her children and the people of Tabir, Ziyaeddin remained here, fortunate that Edinburgh society was content with his fabricated history, that he had traveled from some unspecified place in Ottoman lands to learn to paint portraits in the European style.

Biding his time.

While he did this, a little slip of a woman who refused to wait for the world's approval did not fear dressing as a youth and living in the house of a man she did not know in order to achieve her dream.

Standing, he slid paper and pencil into a portfolio and left his house. It was a few short blocks to his destination.

"Guidday," the girl draped over the parlor couch drawled.

The place was shabbily decorated, with threadbare upholstery and faded wallpaper. "Where've you been, sweets?
We've no' seen you in an age." She wore a robe that was
the suggestion of a gown only, her bosom spilling from
the bodice and the skirts parting to reveal an entire stock-
inged leg.

"Good day, Miss Dallis," he said. "I trust you are well?"

"Aye. Only longin' for a visit from you, o' course," she
said, stroking her fingers along her thigh in practiced
seduction.

"Have you an hour?"

She undraped her slender limbs from the chair. With
eyes bleary from whatever palliative she had consumed—
gin, laudanum, opium if she'd had work lately and could
afford it—she sauntered toward him.

"For you, sweets," she said, stroking a painted fingertip
down his chest. "I've the whole day."

"I cannot pay you for the whole day." Each shilling he
spent for his own pleasure was a shilling less for Tabir. That,
and he did not relish remaining in the brothel long enough
to attract any of the vermin resident in the upholstery.

"I might give you the whole day anyway." She chuckled.
"I'm wagering everybody'll be paying gold to see my picture
someday. I'll be a regular Mona Lisa."

He could not help but smile. That this woman, born
into poverty and selling her body for shillings, knew of
the *Mona Lisa* did not surprise him. On the whole Scots
were an informed, learned, wonderful people. His captivity
chafed at him, but he could not have landed in a better
place of exile.

"The solarium, if you will," he said.

She went ahead of him, dropping her gown before he
even closed the door. Hers was still a young body but worn,
Scots pale yet marked with the scars of a pox suffered in

her childhood. She wore it with ease, settling herself comfortably in a shaft of light from between the draperies.

He found a chair—blessedly without upholstery—and set the sketchpad on his knee and then pencil to paper.

"Certain you'll only be looking today, sweets? I'd no' mind if you touched too."

"No touching today, Dallis." *No touching ever.* "Only drawing."

With so few strokes of the pencil, life was welling up like a spring beneath his ribs. There was such beauty in the simplest flesh, such poetry in the fragile vessel of the human soul: color, texture, tempests, sunrises and fire. That he had been born to rule was his destiny. That he had been created to do this was his gift.

"Will it muck up your picture if I sleep?" Dallis said, her eyelids already drooping.

"Not at all. Sleep on, madam."

"I've been meanin' to ask you, sweets," she said, her head lolling onto one shoulder. "You've no' had an accident in battle or some such, more than the leg?"

"I have not."

"Then all your parts work aright?"

"They do." As proven by those parts working fantastically well when Elizabeth Shaw had been standing a foot away from him in his foyer. Inconveniently.

Dallis sighed. "A perfect gentleman you be, sweets. Every lass in this house would trust you with her life."

Well, there was something. He suspected it wasn't every day a house full of prostitutes gave a man such faith.

His father had also inspired faith in others. And he had had such faith in his people, in turn, that he had not seen the danger from within until it arose and struck him down.

Elizabeth Shaw would blithely wave away the threat of betrayal from one close to her.

Ziyaeddin knew better.

The figure taking shape beneath his pencil danced.

He wished he could justify to himself these visits more often. But he could not be seen entering and exiting brothels regularly. No whiff of licentiousness must mar the image he had cultivated in this city.

Mrs. Coutts badgered him about his solitude, but he had crafted his presence in Scotland with intention. He was no dashing dandy from the East, no court jester to entertain the fashionable set enthralled by the exotic. Instead, Edinburgh society gossiped about the enigmatic "Turk," and the mystery surrounding him made them always hungry to know more. Patrons clamored to commission his work and they paid him well. The portraits he did of individual women went for thrice the price of every other piece simply because he agreed to paint them so rarely. It was a dishonest scheme, but it had swiftly gained him both fame and gold.

That gold went into coffers he would take with him when someday he departed this adopted land to claim his birthright. Every guinea was marked for a purpose: a strong guard to protect his family; arms to protect the people; a modern fleet to carry the goods of Tabir across the Caspian; gold to secure Aairah's marriage to a strong ally and ensure his own alliances through marriage too.

This was his destiny, delayed while the general held Aairah's life beneath the blade, and the lives of her children and the people of Tabir. He would not jeopardize that to satisfy his desires now.

Something tickled his ankle. He reached down and plucked a flea from his skin.

"Allah, have mercy," he mumbled.

Tucking a banknote beneath his model's slack hand, he went out into the blustery autumn afternoon. The sky was brilliant blue, a color he had only ever seen once, here in Scotland: in the eyes of a girl who had stood in his house a fortnight earlier and pleaded with him.

What do you want?

She was extraordinary, a young woman of infinite determination and mad purpose. Brushing aside all rules, she had come to him and begged the impossible.

Güzel kız.

And she was beautiful. Despite her disregard for proper manners, despite her plain dress and forthright conversation and intense vivacity—rather, because of those—because of her intellect, warmth, and clean confidence, she was appealing. Outrageously appealing. Compelling.

And those lips.

Most people are uncomfortable with nudity. As a student of medicine, of course, I am not.

In the middle of the street, he halted.

No. It was an insane idea. Ridiculous. Preposterous.

I am not.

Hailing a hackney, he instructed the driver to make haste.

The Home of Miss Alice Campbell
Port of Leith, Scotland

"MISS SHAW?" ALICE's housekeeper poked her head into the bedchamber. "Have you no' heard me knockin', child?"

"I dislike being called child, Marjorie," Libby said, lifting her attention from the model pelvic bone in her palms. "For I am not a child, which should be clear to you by my fully mature breasts and my linens that must be sent to the laundress monthly for bleaching, if not by my ability to converse like an adult, not to mention my reminder to you any number of times that I am in fact not a child. So I can only surmise that you imagine me a child because I am unwed. But since I know many childish married women, that doesn't make any sense."

"You've a caller, miss."

"Oh. Please send Iris up."

"'Tis no' Miss Tate. 'Tis a gentleman."

"A gentleman?" Other than that dreadful young man from the party, she hadn't spoken to a gentleman in a fortnight, none who would call on her at least.

Except . . .

"Does he walk with a limp?"

"Aye, child."

Libby flew down the steps.

He stood by the parlor window. As she entered he turned from the view of the street toward her with that marvelous stillness she had noticed on each of their previous three encounters.

"You have decided to tell my father about my attendance at the dissection, after all," she said. "Or you intend to tell the duke, perhaps have already told him. For you cannot be here to tell me that you have reconsidered my request."

"Rather, your demand," he said.

"I requested," she said.

"Employing the word *must* several times."

"Well? Will you tell them? Have you?"

His gaze dipped to her hands. "What is that?"

She still clutched the model.

"A pelvis. Rather, a plaster cast of a pelvis. A woman's, of course. See the wide distance between the acetabula and the wider and shallower true pelvis than in a man's, not to mention the greater width of the sub-pubic arch." She set down the model. "Tell me at once why you have come."

"If you are to reside in my home, you must practice

better manners. While I am not in fact attached to all social conventions, I do appreciate politeness."

She jerked forward involuntarily, then caught herself.

"Then . . ." She could hardly breathe. "We are agreed?"

"We are agreed."

Air whooshed from her lungs.

"Thank you! I shan't cause you any trouble. I promise that I will be as inconspicuous as a mouse. You will hardly know I'm there."

"I doubt that. Nevertheless, I will require it of you. I must have quiet to work. And no interruptions."

"Of course, of course. And you will introduce me to Charles Bell?"

"I will."

"This is perfect! *Perfect.* I will go pack my books and instruments immediately. Mr. Bell will only stay in Edinburgh briefly, so we must arrange for me to meet him immediately. And I should enroll in anatomy and chemistry courses, and acquire more clothing. There is much to do."

"Upon one condition."

Her singing nerves clumped into a ball.

"I cannot tell my father. He would forbid it—for the obvious reasons. And I cannot tell Amarantha and the duke either. Out of concern for me they would certainly tell my father, or Constance at the very least. None of them can know. I beg of you, do not ask that."

"Begging again. It does not become you."

"Is that the condition? That I no longer say *I beg of you*?"

"No." His dark gaze now left her face to trail down her neck. Libby felt the caress of the perusal like the tip of a firebrand running between her breasts and down her torso to her belly, then lower. His warning returned to her, that she was unwise to voluntarily make herself vulnerable to a man about whom she knew nothing.

With a flowering of heat between her thighs, disappointment curdled her excitement. She had not imagined this of any dear friend of the Duke and Duchess of Loch Irvine. But men were above all physical creatures, driven by animal urges more often than not, lust among the foremost. And she had already told him that she would tell no one else about their subterfuge. Under these circumstances, she did not blame him now for turning her need to his own advantage.

She could do it.

He was physically appealing—so much so that the idea of lying with him aroused her. And he seemed healthy, virile in fact. She probably needn't fear disease. Pregnancy was a concern. Contraceptive methods were not always effective.

Yet to follow her dream she must take risks.

She set her shoulders back.

"What is your condition?" she said.

"Once each sennight you must sit for me."

"*Sit* for you? As a *model*? So that you can draw me?"

"And paint."

Relief spilled through her. "That is all? That is your one condition? Nothing else?"

"Nothing else."

He was so still, his gaze so intent upon her, as though he imagined she would object. But elation was filling up the holes drilled by anxiety.

"I accept! For how many hours in each sitting? I cannot spare too much time from studying. I will be apprenticing at a hospital as well as attending lectures so I will be very busy."

"Shall we agree to a minimum of one hour each sennight?"

"Yes. That would suit me." She went to him and thrust

out her hand. "We must seal this agreement as gentlemen," she added with a grin because it was simply too marvelous.

He took the walking stick into his left hand and grasped hers.

Palm-to-palm his hand swallowed hers in heat. His grip was much stronger than she had anticipated. Absolute. *Powerful.*

"As gentlemen, Mr. Smart," he said smoothly.

Libby snatched her hand away and pressed it against her skirt. This was no doubt the reason that men and women did not often shake hands. She could not dwell on how Archie Armstrong's clasp had not caused any of the sensations that were happening in her body now.

Anyway, as a man she must become accustomed to shaking men's hands.

"I have one condition as well," she said.

"You are not in a position to make conditions."

"Be that as it may, I should like to know something about you. Amarantha and the duke do not gossip, and they have never even shared any tiny detail about you, not even the name of the country from where you come. I think if I am to live in your house I should know."

"Yet you will not. Can you accept that or is this agreement broken already?"

Alarm skittered through her. "It is not. And one other matter."

"Another?" he drawled.

"It would be best if there were no regular callers to the house. I will remain in disguise as often as possible, but my skin will not support the adhesive for the whiskers unless it is given relief from it each day."

"You have already noted that I am a hermit," he said.

"And you replied that you are not."

"I did not realize you heard me say that."

"You were standing right in front of me. There was no one else present."

"You were a bull running toward a red cloak."

"That's new, to be sure. I have been compared to any number of creatures—a hummingbird, a magpie, a squirrel, a rabbit, even a monkey—but never a bull. I remember everything people say." The words, phrases, sentences spooled through her brain on constant repeat. "It is what makes me such an excellent student of science, which requires quite a lot of technical memorization."

"Yes," he said.

"Yes?"

"The housekeeper visits daily except Sundays, and my manservant every other day. Otherwise, the house will remain free of callers. But you must devise whiskers that suit your skin and hair. The present offend me."

"Is that another condition?"

"It is a request."

A smile tugged at her lips. "I will attempt not to offend you."

"Fine. Does this agreement suit you?"

"Perfectly. I must go prepare." She went toward the door.

"Miss Shaw," he said.

She looked over her shoulder.

He withdrew his hand from his pocket. "Your key to the house."

Nerves danced about in her stomach. This was *real*. Not a scheme or fantastical plan. Not a dream. For reasons of his own, this man was making possible the only thing she had ever wanted.

"Have you no other model?" she said.

"I beg your pardon?"

"I know you have plenty of commissions. Haven't you a model to come to your house and sit for you too?"

"I do not," he said.

She recrossed the room and reached for the key atop his extended palm. His fingers closed around hers.

"Are you prepared for this?" he said.

The brass was hard and cool, his strong hand imprisoning hers as though through this contact he meant to warn her too.

"Prepared for—?"

"Elizabeth!" Alice called from the foyer. "I have had a letter from your father, and again he mentions that flamboyant Frenchwoman."

He released Libby.

"I am more convinced than ever that he has—Oh!" With gray curls encased in a plain cap and an emblem of the Edinburgh Women's Abolitionist Society pinned to her collar, Miss Alice Campbell seemed the unlikeliest sexagenarian in Britain to have once been a London courtesan. Yet she had.

"Well, I would say good day," she said. "But it has suddenly become an *excellent* day. How do you do, Mr. Kent?" She curtsied.

"Good day, Miss Campbell." He bowed.

"Elizabeth, why didn't you warn me that a handsome young man would be calling on you this morning? If I had known, I would never have interrupted. At the very least I would have donned a more taking gown." Her eyes twinkled.

"He is leaving now," Libby said. "Aren't you?"

"Regrettably, madam," he said to Alice with a gallant smile that made hot little tingles erupt between Libby's thighs anew. "Miss Shaw." He nodded to her, and Libby knew that this was his manner of acknowledging silently that she was now—to him—a man.

Excitement chased the tingles.

When the front door had closed, Alice's bright stare speared her.

"You will explain immediately."

"There is nothing to explain. He—"

"You were holding hands with him."

"I was not."

"You were standing brow to brow, with your hand in his. Dear girl, if there is nothing to explain, then I lose hope for you entirely! Is Mr. Kent courting you?"

"No. Definitely not." He barely tolerated her. "How do you know him?"

"I made his acquaintance when we were all at Haiknayes. His portraits are shockingly in vogue. If that delicious man is not courting you, Elizabeth Shaw, what was his purpose here and why was your face full of guilt when I entered this parlor?"

"My face was not full of guilt."

"Do not attempt to convince me that it was only a social call. Have you been meeting that man in secret?"

"Please, Alice. Have I ever given you reason to believe I would engage in secret trysts with any man?"

"Of course not! You have never shown interest in gentlemen. But let me assure you that if you were to find any gentleman interesting I would never stand in the way of it, no matter where he comes from. If he captured your heart I would accept *even* an Irishman, although naturally *that* would pain me."

"Alice—"

"When a woman has entertained men from diplomats to dukes, she learns that they are all alike in the only manner that matters." A pencil-thin brow rose.

"The male sexual drive, I think you must mean. But I am sorry to—"

"I will hear no apologies! If you have finally fallen over

the moon for a man I could not be happier. Have I made myself clear?"

"Yes. You have always been the best of friends to me. Now please allow me to tell you the truth. For I cannot do what I intend to do unless you agree to keep the secret too."

"Thank the blessed Lord!" Alice clapped her palms together. "I have been praying for this day since you sprouted breasts. You are eloping!"

"*No*. Absolutely not."

"You should. His manners are sublime and he is positively gorgeous."

"That may be, but my secret is something else entirely."

Alice lengthened her spine and pursed her lips. "Elizabeth, what are you planning?"

"It is already planned." Her heartbeats were strong. "I am to become a surgeon."

Chapter 6

Mr. Smart Moves In

*L*ibby's possessions were spread across her bedchamber. Iris packed books, models, and instruments into a traveling trunk, while Alice sorted through clothing. Almost all evidence of her femininity would be left at Alice's for fear of his servants discovering it.

"Alice, please pack one gown and undergarments." She didn't suppose he wanted her to pose in men's clothing, and she could hide them in the locked trunk and wash the undergarments on Sundays.

"I am not entirely resolved to leaving you alone in that house with him, Elizabeth," Alice said, placing in her traveling trunk a stack of newly purchased neck cloths.

"But you were overjoyed when you believed I was eloping."

"Marriage, yes. Cohabitation is another matter altogether."

"Cohabitation?" Iris was peering at them.

"In his house, I will be a man," Libby said to Alice.

Alice pursed her lips. "To everybody except him."

Her brain spun around his final question to her, as her brain always did. She had told neither Alice nor Iris about the terms of the bargain—about sitting for him. She wanted to confess it to them now. But he was keeping her secrets, and she must keep his.

"Alice, I will be fine. He has told me he doesn't wish to ever see or hear me, and I will be far too busy anyway."

"This is the most exciting adventure I have ever had," Iris said, "and it isn't even my adventure!"

"Adventure indeed," Alice said with a knowing eye.

Three hours later, as the hackney coach approached the house in which she was to live until her father's return to Scotland, Libby's stomach was in knots, her palms uncomfortably damp, and the whiskers were already itching. But she ignored it all. For this was not an adventure, not a game played for amusement. This was real. Her life. Her dream.

The coach halted and she jumped out, reveling in the freedom of movement trousers and no stays allowed.

"This is the house," she said to the driver, pitching her voice low. The more she practiced Joseph Smart's style of speaking, the more naturally it came.

She counted the five steps to the stoop. Not all houses in Edinburgh's Old Town had stairs to the entranceway. He was either a glutton for punishment, or he had had a reason for purchasing this house that made the steps a necessary inconvenience.

The door was polished oak set in an elegant sandstone façade. She lifted her hand to knock, then paused. She was not a guest. He had given her a key.

Nerves tumbled through her stomach.

Once the driver had deposited her traveling trunk in the foyer, she shut the door. Dragging the cap from her head, she allowed herself a thick exhale.

"You have cut your hair."

His voice was fluid and smooth, like the depths of a creek rolling over rocks, rounding them as it passed. He stood in silhouette from light at the opposite end of the corridor, garbed in black and cloaked in stillness.

"I cannot always be wearing a cap indoors," she said. "I don't mind it. Iris—that is, my friend Iris Tate—collected the hair and will fashion it into an attachment piece so that I can wear it when I am obliged to see Lady Constance on occasion, as myself. As my other self, that is." From this moment forward she was both Libby Shaw and Joseph Smart.

Coming toward her, he withdrew a gold watch and fob from his pocket.

"Have you an appointment?" she said. When he had required her to leave him be, she had imagined she would rarely see him. Perhaps never.

"I do," he said. "But I am not consulting the time now." He grasped her hand and placed the watch upon her palm.

She blinked, wondering if he would take her hand each time they saw each other, and both hoping he would not and wishing he would. It was an odd thing to be held by a man who was not her father, unnerving yet pleasant. *Stirring.*

"This was my father's," he said. "I have no use for it, but you may. More importantly, it will help distract the eye from the shape of your hips." His hand slipped away from hers.

She was not voluptuous like Constance or even as curvy as Iris already. But this man was an artist. He would see everything.

She met his gaze and she did feel as though he saw her—all of her—with the most intimate awareness. It was the same awareness in his touch: as though, through all the senses, he was always studying her closely.

"Thank you," she said. "You needn't have."

"It is one hundred years old." He took up his hat. "Made by an ancient family of clockmakers who once served caliphs and kings."

"It *is*?"

"Yes." Ziyaeddin could not resist smiling just a bit. "So don't sell it to pay your rent."

About Elizabeth Shaw always seemed to hang a buzzing, vibratory tension. As she smiled now, he felt the slight release of that tension in her as though it was happening beneath his own ribs.

She delighted him. It was an uncomfortable sensation. That, and he had not felt raw desire for a woman in so long that it disconcerted him.

Of a lifetime of catastrophically unfortunate decisions and happenstance disasters, this was among the worst. He should not have agreed to this.

But it was too late now. He must simply stay away from this. From *her*.

"I wish you well in this endeavor, Miss Shaw."

She stared at the watch on her palm. "This is all very peculiar, isn't it?"

"Yes. But I would expect nothing less of you."

Her gaze snapped up. "But you don't know me."

"I know enough." Too much already. And all of it captivated him. "I will be out for the remainder of the day, so you may settle in at your leisure. My housekeeper, Mrs. Coutts, has prepared the rooms above for you. Use whichever you wish. As you guessed, I never go up there. She and Gibbs could have a running dice game on the third story and I would be none the wiser. I don't believe they do, by the way. She was far too happy to learn that another person will be living here. But if you find any dice, feel free to discard them."

"You needn't jest to put me at my ease," she said.

"On the contrary, I am entirely serious about the dice." He went to the door, feeling her clinical gaze upon him as though he were some specimen of incomplete manhood, a body to be studied in its imperfection.

That was for the best. She must never know that even in boy's clothing she roused the actual man. It would be to neither of their advantages.

"And after I settle in?" she said.

"After?"

Her nostrils flared. "Will you leave me alone then too?"

Aha. She did seem to understand men after all.

"Yes. Except once a sennight. Once a sennight for an hour, you are mine."

"As agreed upon," she said after a pause. "Is that what you meant yesterday, when you asked if I was prepared? Did you mean prepared to sit for you? For I will fulfill my side of our bargain. I will do anything to succeed in this."

"I believe that." He returned to her and looked down into her earnest eyes, into the face full of determination. "But, no. That is not what I meant when I asked if you were prepared."

"Then prepared for what?"

"To live among men each day. To learn their ways and mimic them and pretend to be what you are not so that they will not know you for what you truly are. To be always alone. That is what I asked, Miss Shaw. Are you prepared for that?"

"Yes," she said, her chin firm beneath the horrid whiskers. "For I must be."

He allowed himself to smile.

"You know that," she said. "You just tested me. When you said, *You are mine*, you wanted to see if I would flinch. If I would show fear."

"Perhaps. Or perhaps you give me more credit for

dispassion than I deserve," he said honestly, his gaze slipping to her lips momentarily. Lips he had not yet gotten perfect.

But he would.

The knocker sounded on the front door.

On the stoop stood a lad in threadbare clothes, holding a heavy wooden chest in his arms.

"My medical chest!" she said in a wholly altered timbre, low and throaty. "Where did you find this?"

The boy jerked his head toward the street. "Behind the pub yonder, sir."

"How did it come to be *there*?" she said.

"I watched the driver carry it up with the rest o' the luggage, but then back to the coach," he said. "Then I saw him drive off with it, so I followed him. S'pect he didna find aught he liked, 'cause he left it in the alley, though I'd say the box's as good as gold empty too! When I saw 'tis a doc's box, though, I said to myself, 'If a thief'd stole the doc's bag as which tended Mum after the loom collapsed an' snapped her leg right in two, she'd ne'er walked again!'" He thrust the chest toward her. "I didna nab a thingie."

"Thank you for your honesty. How is your mother's leg now?"

"'S all healed up." He shook his ratty head. "But she's got the aches in the spot somethin' awful."

"That is not uncommon in a badly broken bone that has mended. How much meat, eggs, and soft cheese does your mother eat?"

He screwed up his brow. "We'd a chicken Sunday."

"Every Sunday?"

"Naww. Anly when Pa's home from the drivin'."

"And does she eat the skin and fat of it, or do you?"

"Gives it to the wee ones, she do, them bein' the twins, sir."

"Of course she does. Any good mother would." She set

the chest on the floor, unlatched it, and withdrew a large brown bottle. "This is walnut oil." She wrapped the lad's hands around it. "Your mother must swallow a teaspoonful of it every day. After a fortnight or two, I think she will find her discomfort less burdensome."

"By drinkin' *oil*?"

"This oil in particular—and a few others, but this is the one I have on hand at present. It is very valuable," she said, her hands still surrounding his. "I do not wish you to sell it."

"Mum'll sell it herself to pay the rent!"

"She mustn't. She must consume it each day or she will not recover fully, and then she will not be able to sit comfortably before the loom ever again. So here is what you must do: hide it somewhere she will not find it and add it to her food yourself. I don't usually approve of untruths"— she cast Ziyaeddin a swift glance—"but you must do this for her. And when the bottle is empty, return here and give me a report. If it is helping to ease her pain, I will supply you with more. If it isn't, we will find another solution."

"Aye, Doc!"

She released him. "Now tuck that away so it won't break."

The lad tugged on his cap and scampered off. She latched the medical chest.

"I don't know how I could have forgotten this. I must have been more anxious arriving than I thought." Her eyes were troubled, and she held the box to her chest as though it were an infant. "And now I have just given away the gift that I brought for you in thanks for taking me in."

"The bottle of oil?"

"In my research I learned that walnut oil is the preferred medium for paint due to its lightness and that it does not yellow with age, but that many painters find it too expensive to use regularly. That particular bottle was derived from English walnuts. They are delicious, but I suppose that hardly matters to you of course, nor the cost of oil for that matter, for the furnishings in your house and your clothing are obviously costly, and I understand that your paintings are quite expensive."

"You researched painting oils?"

"Of course. If I am to live with an artist I must know what he holds dear. I am sorry I had to give it away."

Had to give it away, as though she had no choice but to help the lad's mother, whom she had never even met.

"I am not sorry," he said, opening the door. "You need not give me gifts." He was beginning to think her presence in his house was gift enough. "Good day, Mr. Smart."

LIBBY EXPLORED. ADORNED with plain, elegant furniture, the two bedchambers on the second story revealed the influence of their master in the exquisite Eastern-style rugs and a few small paintings. In the bedchamber whose window faced the street was a mirror and dressing table, which she required for donning her whiskers each day.

A painting hung by the door. It obviously depicted a marketplace, although not like any marketplace she had visited. Tent awnings shaded people and painted amphorae full of goods, and rugs like those on the floors of this house, and sunshine blazed everywhere. Amidst the activity of bearded men and veiled women, two boys raced, stirring up dust. Though foreign, it was a tableau of the most ordinary sorts of interactions—buying and selling and playing—and alive with life.

Libby leaned forward. The faces of the boys and all the market-goers were blurred, as though she were peering through sunlight too brilliant or shadow too deep to discern them. Each figure was colorful and vital, but in their anonymity, distant.

A frisson of fear wriggled up her center, the same she

had felt when he said those unexpected words: *You are mine.*

Withdrawing the watch from her pocket, she ran her fingertip over the engravings on the lid. Ornate, with delicate curls and loops, they seemed more than a mere decorative pattern, rather like words.

Caliphs and kings.

When he had come close to her, he had again moved smoothly, as though it did not affect him to move like that on his ruined leg. But she knew how the skeleton and muscles functioned, and she knew that his display of strength and steadiness could not in fact come without cost.

Reaching up to the painting, she ran her fingertips along the bottom edge of the frame and then onto the picture. It was cool and uneven. The toe of the dark boy's shoe barely arose from the canvas, but enough so that the texture itself created dynamism.

"The master painted that one."

Libby pivoted to the doorway. The woman there was mature, with as much gray beneath her cap as red, and shrewd eyes set in a ruddy Scottish face.

Libby bowed. "How d'you do, ma'am?"

"Wasn't that as fine a bow as any lad's ever given Nan Coutts? Aye, you'll do," she said with a nod. "Those pretty eyes might be trouble, but we'll darken those brows an' that'll help. Dinna worry over the master's man, Gibbs," she said with a wave of her hand. "He's no' the full shillin', that one. But keep your wits about you, lass." She bustled onto the stair landing. "I set dinner at six, then I'm home to my Rufus to cook for him, the dearie."

Then she was gone, leaving Libby shaking a bit.

He had told his housekeeper.

Checking her whiskers in the mirror, she left the house and walked to the university clerk's office. After paying the fees for anatomy and chemistry courses, she set off with a wide, youthlike stride for the bookshop.

"Joe Smart!" Archibald Armstrong waved from across the street, then jogged over. "Saw you come from the clerk's. Got your apprenticeship yet?"

She shook her head.

"I'm to apprentice with Myers. Jealous? Dinna be! He's my uncle. Mum said if he wouldna take me on she'd have his guts for garters." His smile was broad. This time when he smacked Libby on the back she dug her heels into the cobbles and remained upright.

He peered at her face.

"Beastly hot, those whiskers, aye? An' I'll tell you what, the lasses dinna care for 'em. Best shave 'em off afore you get a tongue-lashin' for scrapin' up some bonnie female's cheeks." He grinned even wider. "I'd best be off. Mum's invited the cousins for dinner. Canna be late."

THE SCENTS OF savory roast and freshly baked bread met Libby as she entered her new residence. The Holland covers had been removed from the dining table, and upon the sleek cherrywood, adorned now with fine linen, Mrs. Coutts had laid a feast, yet only a single place setting. A note beside the platter indicated that a cold lunch for the morrow was in the larder.

She ran upstairs, peeled off her whiskers, removed her neck cloth, and returned to the dining room. Striding about the city as a man had given her a powerful appetite.

She was halfway through her second plate when her host appeared in the doorway.

"See the salutation," she said, brandishing Mrs. Coutts's note. The housekeeper had written *To the Young Miss*.

"It seems I neglected to share with her your name."

Libby stood up. "You promised secrecy."

"Yet I did not promise foolhardiness."

"What if someone had called and seen this note? What if your manservant, Mr. Gibbs, did? Or have you told him too?"

"I have not. And no one will call."

"I am vexed with you. We had an agreement."

"An agreement I chose to amend. Slightly."

"Will you amend it whenever it suits you? At whim?"

"Possibly. This is my house."

"You are autocratic."

"And you are a young woman pretending to be a boy. Which of us, do you suppose, is overstepping bounds more grievously?"

"I do not trust you."

"You should not trust me. Now, sit. Continue your repast. A lad's brain requires fuel to function at its best."

"Do you not eat?" She tried not to scan his body but failed, as she was failing at maintaining any sort of calm around him. "I understand that artists can often be eccentric, so perhaps you don't eat."

"Eccentric? This, from you?"

"I met an artist once at a party Constance insisted I attend. He was thin and pale, as though he never ate. Some fashionable ladies believe frailty to be interesting. He was not, rather unhealthy as a man stricken with a complaint of the kidneys or liver. I was worried for him. Your musculature seems fit and sound, however." *Gorgeous.* "Not at all undernourished."

"I am glad to spare you the concern for my health. I called upon Charles Bell. He is eager to make the acquaintance of young Mr. Smart."

"Mr. Bell! When? He knows about me? Already?"

"I have invited him to lunch tomorrow to make the

acquaintance of Joseph Smart, a distant cousin of a friend of mine, now a guest in my home. Is it not as you wished?"

"It is! I only—"

"As agreed upon, Miss Shaw, I am here to give you what you most desire." He spoke the words slowly and without removing his gaze from hers.

"You are here because this is your house. And to secure your own desire."

The side of his mouth turned up.

"For a model," she added. "Don't intentionally misconstrue my words. I am nearly immune to teasing."

"Nearly? Interesting."

"You mustn't flirt with me."

"I am not flirting with you."

"Then what are you doing?"

He bent his head a bit and said, after a moment's hesitation, "Learning you."

Sensation twirled up her body. It felt like anticipation. *Ridiculous.*

"Learning me?" she said.

"The more I know of an individual, the more accurately I can depict her. Or him."

"It isn't only the exterior you study?"

"It is not."

"That is the reason you attended the dissection."

He nodded.

"At what day and time would you like me to sit for you?" she said.

"Sunday at ten o'clock."

"What of church?"

"Neither Mrs. Coutts nor Mr. Gibbs comes on Sunday." His hand tightened around the head of his walking stick. "Sunday at ten o'clock."

He left, and she cleared the dishes, trying only to think

of Mr. Bell's imminent call. But she could not quiet her mind.

Had he called on Mr. Bell before making his offer to her at Alice's house? Had he chosen Sunday morning for the sittings for his convenience, or hers? Had she offended him by mentioning church? Perhaps he was not Christian. And what was he learning about her when he studied her with his beautiful dark eyes and smiled as though he liked what he discovered?

Chapter 7

Allies

 $\mathcal{C}$ harles Bell called two days after the little woman
moved into Ziyaeddin's house and disrupted his peace
entirely. Her face and voice and the manner in which she
moved were maddening. The trousers, coat, and whiskers
should repel him. They did not. That knowing a female
body hid within made him thirst for her was pure insanity.
That he could not seem to control his tongue with her was
a lack of discipline he had never before known.

As Bell entered his parlor, Ziyaeddin found himself
hoping that she would fail, that the surgeon would discover
her ruse and depart in a fury.

With a steady eye and outstretched hand she made the
acquaintance of the famed surgeon. She spoke knowledge-
ably and at a pace that seemed to both bemuse and impress
Bell. A Scot of about fifty years and a man of both profound
faith and scientific brilliance, Bell had a thoughtful air
and intelligent eyes. Ziyaeddin trusted him.

After half an hour, Ziyaeddin excused himself. Visiting

Mrs. Coutts in the kitchen, he ensured that she had set the dining table for two only, and then retreated to his quarters.

Two hours later the false boy appeared in the doorway of his studio.

"He has invited me to call with him at the Royal Infirmary tomorrow! He wishes to see how I apply my knowledge in examining patients. I was obliged to invent a deceased uncle who was a surgeon in America. He wondered where I had gotten all of my knowledge and I could not invent an English or Scottish uncle, of course, because he would be able to research that too easily, even if my uncle were in the colonial service."

"I offer my condolences on the passing of your American uncle."

Her eyes shone as though the sun lit them from behind. "I worry that the physicians or nurses at the infirmary might recognize me. But I encountered one yesterday and he did not know me. And Mr. Bell believes that I am a young man! Rather, a boy, because of my youthful appearance. I do feel some guilt over pretending to be fifteen. At twenty years old it isn't remarkable that I should have acquired a vast knowledge of medicine."

"Of course not," he murmured.

"But at fifteen it really does seem impressive. Yet everybody believes it. It is incredible. Wonderful! And you have made it possible. I am more grateful than you can imagine. Mr. Bell and I discussed the advantages of taking courses at the university. Naturally I can augment those studies with courses at a private surgical school. Is this where you paint?"

She seemed never to breathe when she spoke like this, with such animation and spirit and energy. In the manner of a coach and six racing along a highway or a schooner at full sail cutting the sea, she was alluring, despite the trousers, despite the flattened chest and the cropped hair and the false whiskers. Despite all.

How this would all end he could not fathom. *Not well*, probably.

He had made a terrible mistake.

"Yes," he said. "This is where I paint. Recall that I require not to be disturbed."

"This is an exceptional occasion, of course." She gestured to the canvas on his easel. "I met that couple you are painting once at a party with Constance. She is always dragging me to parties, hoping I will meet a young man I can endure long enough to allow him to court me. I cannot contain my happiness! I want to celebrate. Will you come for a pint with me now? I've never done such a thing but Archie Armstrong mentioned it the other day. I know young men are fond of drinking ale. I must become accustomed to it so that if I am ever obliged to drink ale with my fellow students, the spirits will not go to my head too swiftly."

She balanced on the balls of her feet in the doorway, framed in darkness, light resting on the high bones of her flushed cheeks and pale brow and golden curls, as though it feared to settle and be dislodged as swiftly.

He *must* get away from her.

"Archie Armstrong?" he said instead.

"I made his acquaintance the day you saw me at the dissection. I am grateful for that day, that you happened to be there and recognized me. I don't believe that our agreement is fair to you, for there is so much more advantage to me in it than to you."

The horrifying whiskers were insufficient to mask her vibrant beauty. Charles Bell and this Archie Armstrong and every other man she had encountered while wearing this disguise who could not see this girl were imbeciles.

But it had always been his curse to see what others did not.

"I have all that I need." He did not believe this. Not any longer.

"Nevertheless, I am aware of the disparity. And grateful. Thank you. I cannot thank you—"

"If you weep, this arrangement is at an end."

"I am *not* weeping. I never weep. I only wish to thank you."

"You have thanked me. We have an accord. Nothing further need be said about it." He turned away from her and took up his brush. He needed the wood between his fingers. "There are tears in your eyes."

"The adhesive causes them. I must visit the apothecary I like in Leith, as Elizabeth Shaw of course, to ask him to devise a less noxious compound."

"You do that. Good day, Miss Shaw."

"You should always call me Mr. Smart. So that you don't accidentally do otherwise in public."

"When you are dressed as Joseph Smart, you should always speak to me in his voice. Then you will not accidentally do otherwise in public."

"Touché. You, Mr. Ibrahim Kent, are not so dull-witted after all."

Now he could not resist glancing at her. "You have not thought me dull-witted."

"No." She bit her lips together, and the whiskers jutted out preposterously. "So will you come with me now to drink a pint to celebrate?"

"I will not. I will never. Go now."

She remained. He could sense her there, as though her curiosity and thick, expansive joy, were actually reaching out and touching him.

"Ibrahim Kent is not my name," he said, and was abruptly aware of considerably more space beneath his ribs.

"It *isn't?*"

He looked at her.

"What is your name, then?" she said.

"You, I think, will address me only as Master."

"I will do nothing of the sort," she said upon laughter. It was short and choppy and musical in the manner of a drum, and wonderful.

"Then speak to me not at all." He was absolutely unable to not smile. "Now, be off with you."

With a brilliant flare of her eyes she whirled about and was gone.

He was in hell. And heaven. At once.

The only consolation: it was temporary.

FOR FIVE DAYS Libby did not see the man in whose house she lived. While away from that house her life became frankly unbelievable, within the house all remained as equable as its master, with the exception of a small and reckless intrusion.

On tiny legs it sped into the parlor where Libby had shelved her medical books, hurled itself into the grate to roll with joyful abandon in the ash, and dove past her feet to circle the table legs and then scamper out the door, leaving in its wake a trail of dust.

She had been determined to memorize George Kellie's commentary on the benefits derived from compression by the tourniquet. But the dawn was swiftly becoming morning and she was to accompany Mr. Bell to the Royal Infirmary. There he would introduce her to a surgeon who would take her on as an apprentice. She had trimmed her hair anew, and before she left the house she must fashion the shorn bits into whiskers more suitable for a youth of fifteen. That would take time.

Snuffing her lamp, she followed the trail of ashes to the kitchen.

"Mrs. Coutts, I suppose you have noticed that a piglet is running about the house?"

"Aye, lass." She was pressing dough into a pan.

"Is it to be . . . dinner?"

"There be no pork in this house! Leek an' peas tonight, an' kidney pie."

"It seems that Mr. Kent does not dine at home often."

"He's been takin' dinner down at the Gilded Quill."

"The coffeehouse in which artists and writers gather? Does he prefer dining there?"

Mrs. Coutts cut her a quick glance. "Now more than afore."

Clearly he had changed his habits because of her requirement that he invite no one to the house.

"I am sorry that you must prepare dinner for only me," she said. "May I help?"

"None o' that, lass. I'm glad you've come to stay. The master's too alone in this big empty place. 'Tis a blessin' you're here." She dusted her hands on her apron and gave a little closed pail to Libby. "This'll keep you till you come home tonight."

Home. As though this truly were her home, and not simply a hiding place from which to launch her subterfuge.

"If the pig isn't to be eaten, why is it in the house?"

"The master's onto one of his projects, I s'pect. Now, I'm off to market. Mr. Gibbs'll arrive shortly, so you'd best hide." With a big basket slung over her elbow, Mrs. Coutts departed and Libby went up to her bedchamber. As she entered she touched her fingertips to the painting, exactly where she had touched it on her first day in this house and every day since. The paint's silky, bumpy texture gave her comfort. Worries batted about in her head—about her preparation to formally study medicine, her whiskers, the surgeon she would meet today. Yet skimming her fingertips over the feet of the running boys in the market-place spread calm beneath her ribs. How singular that a picture of strangers in an alien land should feel like the safest, most familiar thing in her world now.

Drawing out scissors from the dressing table, the locks of her hair, and the noxious adhesive, she set to work.

THE ROYAL INFIRMARY sat massively upon a whole block of Old Town. Mr. Bell had assured her that she would have the finest surgeon in town as her mentor, one of only a handful with a permanent rotation at the infirmary.

"Ah, there he is," Mr. Bell said as they approached two men. "Mr. Bridges, allow me to make known to you Joseph Smart."

"But this is no more than a child, Charles," Mr. Bridges said, peering down his long nose at Libby. A man of advanced years, he had a narrow chin and a shock of grayish-sandy hair.

"Yet his mind is acute, Lewis, and his knowledge extensive already. I am persuaded you will be pleasantly surprised."

"We shall see." Mr. Bridges had already begun walking away.

With a delightfully conspiratorial nod to her, Mr. Bell departed.

Libby looked at the other man. The arrogant student from the public dissection stared back at her, his stance bristling with affront.

She put her hand forward. "How do you do?"

His aristocratic lip curled. "Think you'll win over Bridges and push me aside?"

Her hand dropped to her side. "I don't think anything of you at all." She set off after the surgeon. She had not entered into this charade to be sidetracked by the petty competition of other students. She had work to do. Nothing must come in the way of that.

BY THE TIME Libby found a low stone wall not far from the infirmary to plop down atop and open her lunch pail, she was both exhausted and exhilarated. Mr. Bridges was as brilliant a teacher as Mr. Bell had said. That he was cool and demanding Libby could easily endure. She only wished she could endure it without the company of his other apprentice, Maxwell Chedham.

One of the nurses had answered Libby's questions about him. From an old Derbyshire family, Chedham had first entered into politics but disliked it. Although new to the study of medicine, because of his intellect and temperament he was widely considered the most promising first-year apprentice in town.

Obviously he didn't like the prospect of competition for that role. As they moved through the wards, his glares at her were tiresome.

Yet even his disagreeable company and the itchy adhesive on her face could not dull her happiness. As though celebrating her triumph too, the air was crisp and the sun bathed the cobblestones and brick in warmth. Opening the pail she dug out a savory tart.

How marvelous it was to sit alone in a public place! The trousers gave her freedom to perch on the wall as though it were the most commodious couch.

A door nearby opened and a woman came onto the stoop. A gown of gossamer fabric glided over her long legs that seemed free of petticoats. Leaning a hip against the railing in a position that revealed a great lot of bosom, she turned to Libby. Beneath the rouge and kohl that decorated her face, she seemed young and unhealthily gaunt.

Libby gestured with a pastry.

With an arched brow, the woman lifted a bottle.

"Joseph!" Iris Tate's voice came clearly down the alley. Dressed in a pink and white striped gown and matching bonnet, with her dark curls spilling out every which way, she was grinning.

Libby jumped off the wall and hurried toward her friend.

"Cousin Joseph!" Iris practically giggled. "How diverting it is to call your name! Alice said I should not tease you, but this is already the most fun I've had since you left. Goodness, what have you done with your hair? It's positively *dripping*."

Libby had coated her hair with oil to make it darker and loosen the curls, then combed it straight over her brow and onto her cheeks, and Mrs. Coutts had given her a cosmetic to thicken her eyebrows.

"Come along, cousin." She drew Iris's hand onto her arm as a gentleman would, and led her away. "Before someone hears you being silly."

"Who would hear me? Oh!" She gasped. "*Libby*, is that woman a—"

"Quiet now," she whispered. "How did you find me?"

"The note you sent to Alice yesterday said that you expected to be at the infirmary this morning. I have been strolling around here for at least an hour—"

"Alone? Without a footman?"

"*You* always have."

The choices you make, Elizabeth, affect others.

"Anyway, I hoped to come upon you," Iris said. "And now I have!"

"It is so good to see you, Iris. Thank you for coming." Libby squeezed her friend's hand.

"I haven't anything else to do but sit around all day listening to Mama's complaints. And, truth be told, Alice and I miss you dreadfully. Without you I haven't any idea what to read, and Alice only sits and embroiders silently. It's downright *dull* at her house now."

"I miss you both too, Iris. But the more contact I have with anybody that I knew in my past life, the more likely I am to be found out."

"Your past life? Libby, do you mean to *never* be yourself again?"

"Of course not." Yet she felt more like herself now than she ever had. "Why have you come here?"

"Constance has invited us all to a picnic tomorrow. Shall we tell her that you are under the weather?"

"Constance knows that I am never under the weather. I must go."

"Alice intends to quiz you about Mr. Kent. She has been imagining the most shocking scenarios of seduction. It's awfully funny, Lib—"

"Cousin," Libby whispered, tightening her hand over Iris's as they passed a pair of pedestrians. "You must remember to address me as Joseph."

"They are fantastic stories, really . . . *Joseph*. In one scenario he is a powerful warlock, and he locks you in a tower to serve as his cook, but you are so clever that you become his acolyte and then his partner instead. In another he is a pirate! He spirits you away onto his ship and we never see you again. Alice says he has a peg leg. Does he? I didn't notice it, but I only saw him that once when we were all at Haiknayes. And in another of her stories he reveals himself to be a—"

"Iris, please."

"All right. But in any case, in all of the scenarios you are brilliant."

Turning the corner they nearly collided with Archie Armstrong.

"Joe Smart! I wondered if I'd see you again soon." His

eyes alighted on Iris. His mouth popped wide and his clean-shaven cheeks got dusky. "Good day, miss." He bowed. He carried a stack of books under one arm.

Libby's stomach knotted up in pleasure. She would have books for courses too.

"Good day, Archie."

"Capital weather we're enjoying today, aye, miss?" he said to Iris.

"To be sure." Iris released Libby's arm. "I'll run home now, Joseph," she said with blessedly light emphasis on the name. Making a sound that was dangerously like a giggle, she practically skipped away. Regret and soft grief tugged at Libby. That she had to abandon her friends in order to follow her dreams could not be right.

"Well there, Joe," Archie said, staring after Iris. "How d'you come to be strolling with Aphrodite today?"

Aphrodite? Men were infinitely silly.

"She's my cousin," Libby fabricated. "Distant."

"Cousin! Much obliged to you then for not introducing me, friend."

Friend?

"I beg your pardon," she muttered.

"Dinna fret," Archie said cheerfully. "There'll be another occasion."

Not if she could prevent it.

"I'm headin' to the pub to meet the lads. Thought we'd page through a few anatomy texts while enjoying a pint. Join us?" Archie's face was open and sincere.

She shouldn't. The more alone she kept, the safer her secret would be. Yet she nodded.

"Not much of a talker, are you? You needna be, o' course. I talk enough for three lads." He laughed.

In fact, Alice and Iris and everyone regularly pointed out that she barely ever ceased speaking. But silence was yet another practice she had to master now.

"See you took my advice an' shaved off those thick whiskers," Archie said with a sideways glance at her.

"Mm hm." The light, silky down she had achieved this morning did look much better.

"Don't suppose you shaved to impress a certain lass, now? Did you?" Archie lifted a brow. "Perhaps a distant cousin?"

"It's not like that with Iris," she mumbled.

"Iris? A bonnie name! An' she's no' spoken for?"

Iris's mother probably had a dozen titled suitors already lined up for her debut.

She shook her head again.

"Joe, I've a notion we're to be capital good friends. Here's the place," he said, stopping before a tavern Libby had passed hundreds of times, but into which she had never entered. The marquee read THE DUG'S BONE. The door opened and a group of young men came out laughing and talking. She heard the words "Aristotle" and "Epicurus" as they passed.

"Now look here," Archie said, facing her. "I'll speak plain, Joe: my mates an' I willna tease you about your age, so you needna wear those false whiskers again. We're interested in one thing only: the brain in a lad's head. Or, two things: the brain in a lad's head an' his favorite ale. In your case, his distant relations too," he added with a wink. "Understood?"

She nodded.

"Fine then," Archie said. "Now, I've a mind to toast to this city's youngest new surgical student."

Hovering between worry and elation, Libby followed him inside. But worry was an old friend. The elation, new and sparkling, seemed instead to want to settle in her heart.

Chapter 8

Sunday at Ten O'clock

he swine entered first, barreling in on tiny hooves with snorts and grunts. She followed it momentarily, moving into his studio like a storm moves across a beach: with magnificent energy.

"Thanks to the watch you have lent me I have been precisely on time everywhere I have gone for days. What splendid light this room has at this hour, so clean and pure! I understand now the reason that you bought this house. Yet the rest of the house is quite nice too. I don't know why you do not use the dining room and the parlor. But Mrs. Coutts has made it all very comfortable for me, you know. Shall I sit there?"

She walked to the high stool even as she spoke, and perched on the edge of it. She wore a gown of an ochre color that rendered her skin sallow yet made her eyes even more brilliant than usual. It fit snugly to her breasts and shoulders and arms.

Ziyaeddin had expected her to wear the men's clothing. He wished she had. He needed no more enticements to her femininity: he had plenty already in the crisp curves of her lips as she tried to hold them still and the delicate flare of her nostrils that revealed her struggle to do so.

It seemed difficult for her not to speak every thought she had. Yet now she was trying to.

He took up his sketching pad and pencil.

"What will you draw?" she said, her brows arching as though she meant to look over the edge of the paper, which she could not from six feet distant.

"You," he said. "I should have thought that obvious."

"Ha ha. How clever you are, sir. I am nearly breathless with hilarity."

Yet she was in fact breathless, her chest moving rapidly in shallow inhalations and exhalations.

"You needn't fear," he said.

The golden lashes fanned wide. "Why would I fear?"

"I shan't draw you as a monster." The lips. *The lips.* The bow of the upper appeared simple enough. Yet the lower . . . Neither too plump nor narrow. Uncomplicated yet unique. And the left side of the lower lip was slightly squared. Asymmetrical lips. Lips that were never still.

"I knew I would rarely see you," she said. "You made that clear. But I have always lived with my father and I see him regularly most days. Saw him, that is. So I think I have been disconcerted not to actually see you. It is odd to share a house with a person and not meet him even in passing. What did you spend your days doing?"

"Awaiting this moment," he said, more or less honestly.

She laughed and shifted her weight from one buttock to the other.

"Oh. You wish to remain enigmatic," she said. "The Turk," she added more thoughtfully.

There. The light danced upon her lower lip, a pinkish gold raindrop that defined the shadow beneath it. The skin on her chin was reddened, above her upper lip as well, and running beneath the length of each cheekbone.

"Are you actually Turkish?" she said.

"No." *Not entirely.*

"Then why does everyone call you the Turk?"

"You must ask them that."

"Perhaps they are ignorant, and one man of foreign features, skin, and accent seems equal to the next."

"Perhaps." *Most certainly.* Yet he had allowed this misbelief. He had at times encouraged it.

"If you are not Turkish, then from where do you—"

"Be still."

She was. For a minute.

"Are you still painting Mr. and Mrs. McPherson's portrait?"

"It is finished." Unsatisfactorily. Unveiling it had been as an undertaker unveils a corpse. The tip of this woman's nose in lead now showed more life than those two subjects combined.

"Did they like it?"

"Yes." They had rhapsodized. They did not know to expect more.

Not this woman. She was seizing life with both hands.

"Turn your face toward the window."

"It is a great relief to have the hair off my brow," she said, lifting a hand and swiping it over the short curls she had confined with a cloth band. She had strong hands, unlike a lady's, rather more like a woman of the laboring class, because she used them.

He wondered if she had ever used them on a man—*not medically*—and then tried to strike that from his imagination. Unsuccessfully.

"Mrs. Coutts suggested that I comb it forward to cover more of my face," she said, "but it is so short that it springs back. I employed oil to keep it still."

Long fingers. Blunt tips. Short nails. Wrinkled knuckles. Capable hands. She moved them swiftly yet with purpose. If she were not shortly discovered, if she remained, he would paint her hands. Her lips. The tip of her nose. And then the remainder of her. He would torture himself doing it. But he would not resist the desire to do so.

Every other desire regarding this woman, however, he would resist.

His original intention in seeking her as a model he now knew could simply not be. It was challenge enough to his self-control depicting her fully clothed.

"Does the skin irritation on my face cause you trouble?" she said.

Her entire existence caused him trouble.

"No."

"You don't intend to sell these pictures of me, do you?"

"No."

"Then for what purpose do you wish to draw me?"

He looked up into her eyes. "For your beauty."

"You are teasing now. I know beautiful women. Constance is beautiful. Amarantha is beautiful. My features are unremarkable. Ordinary. I am not beautiful."

"You are to me."

She stared at him, her lips parted slightly, the harsh pinkness around them as on the face of a child who had enthusiastically consumed pomegranate. But her eyes were not a child's eyes; they were full of clean intelligence and honest wisdom.

"They are studies only," he said. "Not a portrait."

"May I see?"

He nodded.

She leaped off the stool and came to him without any grace, only movement, always movement.

"Oh," she said. "One feature at a time. Lips. Nose. Fingers. Why not my entire hand?"

"You have not remained still enough for me to capture either hand entirely."

She trapped her lips between her teeth and met his gaze.

"Capture?" she said.

"Study," he amended.

"I think you meant capture." Her eyes were gloriously bright, and spots of pink stained each cheek, mingling with the rash.

"Return to your perch, *güzel kız*. The eleventh hour has not yet arrived."

She did so, this time setting her feet on the lower rungs, which tightened the gown around her buttocks and thighs.

"What other features will you study?" she said. "My ears?"

"Undoubtedly."

"Chin? Neck? Feet?" She wiggled a foot shod in a plain slipper. "Eyes?"

"Yes." Never her eyes. Not again. Not since drawing her eyes at Haiknayes had changed his life. Too much of her soul shone in those eyes. To draw them would be to drink in that soul and make himself drunk on it.

"What language were those words—*goo-zell kuz*?"

"Turkish."

"But you said that you are not Turkish."

"You speak English?"

"Obviously."

"Yet the language of your homeland is Scots."

"Then am I to assume that you come from a place that is now within the Ottoman Empire?"

He should have guessed she would have knowledge of such a thing.

"No." Rather, a place that had existed for a millennium before the Ottomans ever came, and had broken from the ancient Persian Empire, and which still maintained its freedom from both.

"You won't tell me," she said.

"As I have already said."

"Will you tell me what *goo-zell kuz* means?"

"It means beautiful girl."

"Does it? How dull! I imagined it something like *nasty harpy* or *persistent irritant* or some such."

"I think I should be insulted."

"You must truly lack imagination, which is intriguing given the beauty of your paintings. But I have heard of artists whose work is extraordinary turning out to be deeply uninteresting people. Perhaps you are one of those."

Minx.

"Perhaps," he said.

She smiled, and her teeth showed white and even between the maddening lips.

"Don't," he heard himself say.

"Don't what? Tease you as you are so fond of teasing me? Oh. You thought me humorless. I don't blame you for it. Most people do."

"Don't smile."

That wonderful dart formed between her brows, the one that reminded him of lovers separated by land that could never be traversed.

"Why not?" she said. "Are you trying to draw my lips now?"

"Always."

"That is mysterious."

"Your smile affects me," he said. "Acutely."

Her mouth shut. Briefly.

"How so? I recently read a treatise in which the physician

claimed that regularly seeing a smile could actually thin the noxious humors in a melancholy person. The physician was an Italian, of course. Englishmen would never bother themselves with matters like smiles. They would not consider it sufficiently scientific. Or even interesting. And the theory of humors is passé now. You are not melancholy, though. At least there are no indicators of melancholy about you that I observe."

"Lay your hand upon your knee and do not move it."

She did so and her fingers arched, the tips resting on the fabric as though prepared for imminent flight.

"Why don't you wear a suitable prosthetic device—an actual foot?"

The perfect arc of her forefinger came onto the page as though a benevolent spirit guided his pencil.

"You would walk much more comfortably," she said. "What is your age?"

"Twenty-five."

"You could delay or even entirely deter the damage to your spine that is the result of an uneven gait. I have studied every treatise on the alignment of the spine that has been wri—"

"Miss Shaw—"

"*Mr. Smart.*"

"When you appear in this studio wearing men's clothing and speak only as a man, then I will call you Mr. Smart."

"You must now too."

"I really mustn't."

"You do not want to hear my advice. I am thoroughly versed in the muscular and skeletal and nervous systems beyond even surgeons of my father's acquaintance who have years of experience. I have been reading treatises for years, and watched surgeons perform complex surgeries as often as possible. I have cared for my father's patients often too and assisted him with surgeries. In the hopes of someday meeting Charles Bell, I read every one of his works on the nerves, brain, and spine, as well as his colleagues' works, works by Dutch, French, and American surgeons, and even the works of Arab surgeons that I could find translated into European languages. I am an expert."

"You are arrogant."

"I am not. I am in fact very knowledgeable. Yet you will not heed my advice. Is it because I am a woman?"

"No."

"I don't believe you."

"Believe what you wish," he said. "This hour is an at end." Signaled by the chime of a clock in the parlor. "Did you purchase that clock?"

"No. I simply wound it. I cannot wear a man's watch while I am sitting here for you, after all." She rose to her feet, but remained standing by the stool. "I am sorry."

"For winding the clock that I did not remember I owned?"

"For badgering you."

Grasping his walking stick, he stood and went to her.

"You did not badger," he said, looking down into her face, tracing the swell of her lower lip with his gaze and feeling it in him—against his lips, beneath his fingertips, in the pigmented fibers of his paintbrush. "You asked questions. I answered those which I wished to answer and did not answer the others. Now, your time here is finished. Leave me."

For a moment she said nothing, and her features were quiet. At rest.

"Until next Sunday," she said a bit unsteadily.

Then her gaze dipped to his mouth.

Desire passed through him like a trail of fire across a ship deck.

He must be dreaming. It could not be that she was staring at his lips as though she wanted him to kiss her. It was not possible that he did to her what she did to him, that he made her thirst and hunger and feel entirely at a loss.

Even if it were so, it would not matter. This reality—this city, this house, this world, *this woman*—was not his destiny.

Those lips. Unique. *Perfect*.

Two and a half years ago he had been in hiding, pretending that he did not exist. Then she had appeared.

These lips.

These eyes. Eyes like the blue of the sea, lit with thought and intelligence and unfettered passion. Eyes that were a little hazy now.

Slowly they turned upward to his.

"You have plenty of commissions," she said in a register that was neither Elizabeth Shaw's nor Joseph Smart's, husky and soft, that made him imagine reaching up and twining his fingers through the golden curls and tilting her face so that he could capture those lips beneath his. "Your paintings are sought after," she said. "The other day a piece in the newspaper said that your talent is as great as Lawrence's or Beechey's, and that you lack only the royal patron who will hurl you into stardom, but that such a patron will inevitably come."

He couldn't *think*.

"Isn't that so?" she said, her breasts rising upon a heavy inhalation.

"Did you ask a question?"

"I need to understand. Why did you agree to this? My friend Alice Campbell is suspicious of your motive for agreeing to this arrangement."

"You have what you wish," he said. "Why do you ask me this?"

"Is it only because you find me beautiful, however mistaken you are about that?"

It was simply not possible to resist touching her a moment longer. He lifted his hand and, smoothing a single fingertip over her brow, tugged a silky curl free from the band around her head. It sprang forth.

"That's better," he said.

Her eyes were wide pools of blue— blue from a childhood he had nearly forgotten, aglow now from the Scottish sun.

"Yes," he said. "It is simply because I wish to have the freedom to draw you. That is everything, Miss Shaw. There is nothing more. Does this answer satisfy you?"

"Nothing satisfies me," she said. "My father has said so often, since I was a little girl, that nothing ever satisfies me, I always ask for more because there are always more questions to ask. And he is correct. For my beauty only? My nonexistent beauty?"

"For your nonexistent beauty only," he said. "Now, good day."

"Good day," she almost whispered. "Tomorrow I begin attending anatomy lectures."

He laughed.

"Do not laugh! I am experiencing an excess of nerves at present. No woman has ever enrolled in an anatomy course at this university—not to anybody's knowledge at least. I am afraid my knees will shake, and as I will be wearing trousers Professor Jones will see it. That is the physician teaching the course. Rather, everybody would see it, my classmates as well. I apologize for mentioning knees, by the way. You cannot be accustomed to women speaking of their knees and such to you. But since you are an artist perhaps you don't mind it. Or perhaps from where you come women and men speak of such matters all the time."

"Not typically."

"From where *do* you come?"

"It was so long ago, I hardly remember."

"In some ways you seem more Scottish than Constance's husband and even Amarantha, after all."

He fought a smile.

"Amarantha is rather worldly," she said, "having lived in the West Indies. Still, she is English and speaks like an Englishwoman. And neither she nor Saint, who is English from the West Indies, have lived in Scotland for even half as long as you have. And your accent is inflected in places with Scots. Having grown up in Edinburgh and the port of Leith and so many other places in Scotland and England, I notice such things. I notice everything."

"I am coming to see that. My mother was Turkish, my father of Persian blood."

Her beautiful lips parted.

"That, *güzel kız*, is all that I will tell you."

She pinned those lips together.

"Your knees will not shake," he said.

"I hope they don't. All right. I am going now." She backed away and walked across the room. But she paused in the doorway and turned her shoulder so that she was looking at him. She was lithe, small but strong, and there was an economic control to her movements. She was not haphazardly in constant motion as he had thought, rather, in a continuous struggle to bridle that runaway motion.

"I used to tell my father everything," she said. "Every detail of my day. Now I am commencing the most extraordinary experience of my life and I have no one to tell about it all."

"Tell me," he said and wished he could have remained silent.

"You won't mind it?"

He shook his head.

A smile lit her face. She began to turn away, but swung back again.

"That is to say, I don't mean to suggest that you are like my *father.* You could not be less like him." Her gaze skittered along his body. "That is, you are young, and handsome of course, and—" Her neck constricted and the patches of irritated skin fused into a blush.

"You should learn to control that," he said.

"Of course I should," she muttered, covering a cheek with her palm. "There are bound to be any number of young and attractive men in my classes."

"Study them," he said. "Study them as you studied my leg earlier, and you will again forget that you are a maiden and instead be only a surgeon."

Her chest rose upon several great, jerky inhalations.

"Thank you," she said.

"There is no need to thank me again."

"But I must."

He bowed.

Whirling about, she left him, finally, in peace, and the piglet scampered after her. It was a while, however, before peace actually felt peaceful again.

Chapter 9

The Silence

*A*t first her knowledge proved vastly superior to that of her peers. But there was more to learn than she had dreamed possible. She filled the notebook within a sennight, then bought a dozen more, labeled each with the date of each Monday, and stacked them on the writing table in the parlor.

The first time Chedham answered a question more swiftly than she, his pompous grin was unendurable. That night she dragged out her father's thickest text on surgery and reread it. When she had taken so many notes that her fingers were too sore to hold the pen, finally she closed the tome and crawled to bed.

An hour later she was pasting on her whiskers and oiling her hair to throw herself into her studies anew. She could do this. She would.

When she entered her host's studio on Sunday morning he said, "Today you will be silent."

He lifted his gaze, and Libby's stomach tightened as it always did when he looked directly into her eyes.

He was handsome in a manner that made her feel hot inside. And after the previous sitting, she had had the impulse to kiss him.

She had never wanted to kiss a man before. The blush that had rushed across her skin at that moment still made her prickly with fury at herself. A woman of medicine could not behave like a bashful maiden.

This man affected her differently than other men did. She must simply learn to live with that—with *him*.

She nodded.

"Can you be silent?" he said.

She nodded again.

The piglet trotted beside her to the stool and settled itself by her feet.

She bent to trail her fingertips between its ears. "Have you named th—"

Slowly he lifted a single brow.

"I am sorry I talked so much last time. I can in fact be quiet." Turning to the windows through which only pale light now shone, Libby reviewed in her mind her notes on the week's lectures.

She glanced at the artist. Only his hand wielding pencil and his eyes moved, his gaze shifting between her hand and the page before him. He wore black trousers, a coat of burgundy, and a patterned waistcoat, and the white of his shirt was a striking contrast with his skin. In her sennight at the university she had, in fact, encountered no young man as handsome as he, nor one who made her stomach frolic like spring lambs in a field. She had not had the impulse to kiss any of them.

"Why do—"

The pencil halted.

She clamped her lips shut.

"Ask it," he said.

"Why do you draw people? And paint? Portraits. Why are you an artist?"

"To be able to afford to feed the pig." He returned to his work.

"Honestly," she said, biting back her smile.

After a moment he said, "I find the human form inspiring."

"You do? The shapes of skulls and spines and whatnot?"

"The lyricism and shadows and motion," he said.

"Lyricism?"

"Poetry."

"You see *poetry* when you see a human body?"

"I do."

"How extraordinary."

"What do you see, Miss Shaw?"

"Scoliosis of the spine. Splay foot. Cleft lips. Bowed legs. Scars. Goiters. On Friday I assisted Mr. Bridges in examining a woman with a fractured radius. She was in considerable pain, but her two young children were with her, so I drew diagrams of the bones of the arm on their own arms, which of course made them giggle since it tickled."

"That was kind of you," he said, his eyes on her knee now.

She shrugged. "It distracted her, which was my purpose. But even as I did it I could think of nothing except that bone and the manner in which Mr. Bridges was setting it so that she would have full use of that arm for the remainder of her life."

The muscles in his jaw were taut. It looked like he was trying *not* to smile.

"That is poetry of a sort," he said.

"No. It is entirely prosaic. I also see natural bone structure." She allowed her gaze to trace the firm, tapering line of his jaw and then his lips. Pleasure twittered about in her belly.

"You are studying my bone structure now," he said, "aren't you?"

"Not . . . quite." Any moment she would tell him that she was wondering how it might feel to touch his face, that jaw, his skin. The words ached to be spoken aloud. A distraction was necessary. "I am learning so much each day. Mr. Bridges is wise and careful. And he treats me and Chedham similarly, even though Chedham is wealthy and aristocratic and attractive, and I am not."

"This is not, by the way, silence."

"At the last sitting, you said that I might share with you news of my studies."

"I did."

"Are you now retracting that offer?"

There was gentleness in his eyes at times, yet shrouded by a sharp sort of darkness, as though the world had taught him to overcome that which was most natural to him. Perhaps he had learned that darkness in the accident that had taken part of his leg.

"Who is Chedham?" he said.

"Maxwell Chedham is the other student apprenticing with Mr. Bridges. He is intelligent and arrogant."

"And wealthy and aristocratic and attractive."

"Yes. Although not as attractive as you are."

He glanced up, then down again at his sketchpad.

"I have so many questions," she said. "More than I can ask Mr. Bridges or after anatomy lectures."

"I have no doubt of that."

"It frustrates me." As soon as she wrapped her mind around the answer to one question, three more popped up in its place. "I am grateful to you for—"

"Do not thank me again."

"I must."

"Then I will plug my ears and hear nothing. Ah, there is anger in that brow now. Interesting. Hold that, could you?" His pencil skipped across the paper.

"There is not *anger* in this brow. Rather, exasperation. I don't know why you would object to hearing that I am grateful for your help."

After a silence during which she tried to focus her attention on the branches of the tree in the garden behind the house, he finally spoke.

"Did your father never teach you not to repeatedly tell a man that you find him attractive?"

"No," she said. "He has rarely spoken to me as a regular father speaks to a regular daughter, I think. He has been infinitely kind and generous. Constance and Alice have tried to teach me proper behavior. It hasn't taken. If it had I would not be here, of course. Do you mind it?"

"Mind it?" He lifted his eyes to hers. "No."

How the touch of a man's gaze could send the blood rushing into her face and also her female organs at once was an extraordinary thing. It made her want to be touched by more than his gaze. Her lips even felt tingly. Her nipples too. A soft throbbing had commenced in her genitals. It was certainly sexual desire.

She made herself look away from him again. Across the bedchamber door stretched a bar perhaps eighteen inches below the lintel, attached to both posts. Each time he walked through that doorway he must duck.

"What is the purpose of that bar in your doorway?" she said.

"To slam my head into the next time I consider taking in a boarder. It jars rational thought back into the skull."

"Ha ha. Injury to the skull often does exactly the opposite."

"The next time you are attempting to study, I will sit nearby speaking constantly. That should prove amusing."

"I would not mind that. I enjoy having company." She shifted on the stool. "Are we finished yet?"

"For twenty more minutes, Miss Shaw, you—"

"I am yours. As you have decreed."

For the remainder of the hour he said nothing and she did not speak. Instead she spent the time cataloguing in her mind every detail she knew about sexual response. It amounted to very little. She had more questions than knowledge, a lacuna worse than in any other area of anatomy.

When the clock chimed in the parlor, she slid from the stool. "Until next week?"

"Until next week."

The piglet followed her to the door and out. She did not pause to ask the myriad other questions bubbling to her tongue: Had he named the creature? What purpose did it have in this house? Did he never eat pork? Was he a Muslim? Why had he come to Scotland? What was the real purpose of the bar across his bedchamber doorway? And did he not know that a man could not simply tell a woman he found her beautiful and expect her to forget it—as though men told her she was beautiful all the time—and as though he weren't a great hypocrite to forbid her from doing the same?

THE FOLLOWING DAY, after a heated debate with Chedham concerning round sutures, to which Mr. Bridges listened carefully, Libby welcomed the peace of the alley that had become her lunchtime refuge. Settling on the wall she opened her pail.

The door to the brothel flew wide and the same young woman from before came onto the stoop. A man exited behind her. He had long hair and a jagged nose. Slapping her on the behind, he strode away whistling.

The woman glanced at Libby. She seemed as thin as before. Whatever that man paid her, it wasn't enough.

Digging into her lunch pail, Libby withdrew a boiled egg and bread, jumped off the wall, and walked to her.

"You must eat or you will waste away to nothing." Grasping the woman's hand, she put the food in it. She had none of the outward signs of syphilis—swollen lymph nodes, rash on her palm, or ulcers about the mouth. "Are you in need of medication of any sort? I cannot give you laudanum. But if you require other medicaments I will see what I can do."

"Who's offerin'?" the woman said, not closing her fingers around the food.

"I am a surgical apprentice at the infirmary yonder." It still felt wonderful to say it aloud. "Do take the food. It is either you or those gulls, and they already seem far better fed than you."

The fingers curled over the egg and bread.

"Go off then," the woman said. "Or do you think you'll stand there watchin' me eat?"

"I will in fact stand here and watch you eat. For I do not fancy you sharing it with someone else."

The woman cocked a brow. "Now why would I be doin' that?"

"Obviously you do not feed yourself sufficiently. Yet you clearly have customers. At least one. And he seemed happy. That is sufficient evidence to suggest that you are giving your earnings to someone else."

"Clever lad."

"Now, do eat that so I can return to eating my own lunch."

"You've any left?"

"Plenty."

"But you've nothin' to drink. Here now, take a nip o' this." She offered the bottle.

"Thank you, no."

A laugh like broken glass came from the woman's throat.

"Afraid if you put your lips where I've put mine, lad, it'll get a rise out o' you?"

A rise. Could a man really become aroused after drinking from the same bottle as a woman? It seemed implausible.

She imagined sharing a cup with her housemate, and heat gathered so swiftly between her legs she gasped.

"No," she said quickly to cover the sound. "It is only that I've got to keep my head clear for working with one of the most famous surgeons in Britain."

"You're no' the usual sort, are you?"

"The usual sort of student? No, I am not."

Her companion laughed. "You're a sweet one, pretendin' you canna have a wee nip so you dinna have to share my bottle, instead o' tellin' me I'm a poxy wench. Name's Coira."

"I am pleased to make your acquaintance, Coira." Libby bowed. "I am Joseph Smart. Now I've got to be heading to lecture. Do promise you will eat that."

"Aye." Coira leaned close. "In return, here's a wee bit o' advice: try no' to smile too much. Men rarely do."

ACCORDING TO MRS. COUTTS, the student of surgical medicine now residing in his house left shortly after dawn each morning, returned at dusk each evening, ate dinner in the dining room, and then repaired to the parlor to study until the wee hours.

"Eats a healthy plate, she does, sir," his housekeeper said with a satisfied nod. "As fine as a real lad."

"But you are concerned," he said.

"'Taint healthy for a lass to spend so much time with

her nose in a pile o' books. Turnin' pale as a specter, she is. Next we know it, she'll fall ill an' be needin' to physic herself."

Ziyaeddin had seen no evidence of ill health when she had last sat for him, only the same eyes filled with curiosity and thought, the same skin reddened in patches by the adhesive, and the same damnably impossible lips.

He had expected more conversation—regarding what, he could not guess—for she had an expansive mind. But she had remained silent throughout the hour, saying nothing except in parting, and then only "Until next Sunday" again.

"Have you shared this concern with her?" he said to his housekeeper.

"Ach." Mrs. Coutts waved a dismissive hand. "She's got a way about her, sir, I'd no' care to cross."

He understood. Along with her forthright purpose, a flinty energy prickled. It was the same energy that came forth in burbling warmth when she thanked him repeatedly, the same intensity of spirit that always seemed to need release in speech or movement. That the thought of it made him want to take her into his hands and discover how that intensity responded to lovemaking only proved he was wise for remaining at a distance from her.

That evening, returning home through a drizzle, as he approached he saw the drapery in the parlor parted and the false lad and young pig watching him through the rain-spattered pane.

They met him at the door.

"Why don't you hire a chair?" she demanded as she seized his umbrella and bolted the door. "One needn't be an aristocrat to go about town in a chair. I know any number of entirely humble gentlemen who do so."

All of them aging and gouty, no doubt, like the man

whose portrait he was now painting. Mixing gray into the pallid whites of the gentleman's skin, Ziyaeddin had thought of this woman, and had added a dollop of Permanent Rose to the palette to please himself. His patrons, the man's children, would appreciate it too. They would not know the reason for their appreciation—that he had made their father appear more alive than in reality. But they would be pleased.

"Thank you for this unsolicited recommendation." He removed his cloak. "I will take it under advisement."

"You won't," she said. "You are displeased with me for saying it. I can hear it in your voice. But I am vexed, so frankly I don't care. This walking could seriously and permanently damage your spine. Irreversibly. Either you do not understand that, which would make you extraordinarily obtuse in your observational powers, and I know you aren't that, or you *choose* to walk despite the damage it is causing you, and the pain, which makes you a fool. An arrogant fool."

"By all means, don't mince words. What would be the fun in that? How did you come to be standing at the window then, just as I returned?"

"The pig knew it." She gestured to the runt snorting at their feet. "It sits by the window and watches people going by. Suddenly it got very excited, dancing about on the chair and making a lot of noise, so I went to see the reason for its excitement. It was your approach. Apparently it has a great deal of affection for you. Are you certain it's not a pet?"

"If you are finding yourself peering out the window over its shoulder, you should be asking yourself that question."

"Touché." She was again studying his lips.

Taking up the lighter walking stick he used inside the house, he moved away from her tempting lips and brilliant eyes that invited him to do what he must not—*what he ached to do.*

"What is the advantage," she said behind him, "of having an expert in the skeletal and muscular systems, not to mention a student of the most recent scientific theories concerning neural pathways, living in your house, if you do not heed her advice?"

"Give me time," he said, entering his quarters. "I will probably think of one."

She did not follow him inside, which he accounted a miracle of sorts. Closing the door and leaning his shoulders back against it, he ran a hand over his face and tried to steady himself. The habitual pains in his hip and back were old friends; he knew how to endure them. The lust that even the sound of her voice ignited in his body was another matter altogether.

She had no idea.

It must remain so.

With no possibility of relief, he went to bed. Despite the pain, sleep came easily.

Waking came violently, covered in sweat and gasping for air. But his throat was not raw; at least he had not awoken shouting.

Climbing out of bed, he bit back on the discomfort, dressed, and went into his workroom. On the table beside mortar, pestle, paints, and oils was a small jar. He palmed it now.

Light stole from the parlor door, which was cracked open several inches—wide enough for a piglet to squeeze through if it should wish. Inside, the creature slept cozily on the cushion his housekeeper had set for it by the hearth.

Not for the first time, he imagined his mother's horror were she to see his household now. But she was gone, and his faith as well. And he had use for the little creature.

And for the woman.

She had told him that she was accustomed to regular companionship at home. He gave her none. The piglet must suffice.

At the desk, a lamp burned low by her elbow beside an empty cup and saucer. Surrounded by books, she slumped over the table, cheek pressed to the page of an open volume, sleeping. As he went toward her she did not stir.

Parted, her lips were the hue of dusty rose, and her limbs were entirely slack. She was never thus. He suspected that in waking she did not know how to be immobile.

She had removed the whiskers and discarded the neck cloth and waistcoat, but wore trousers and shirt and a loose coat. The shirt collar had fallen open and he saw no binding about her breasts, only smooth, pale, rounded skin.

He imagined waking her, drawing her to him, and tasting that skin, feeling it beneath his lips. When she looked at him there was more than clinical assessment in her eyes. There was agitation. And desire. She was far too well informed for the usual naïveté of young Englishwomen. He had no hope that, maiden or not, she did not recognize lust for what it was.

If he touched her, she would not resist.

Setting down the jar softly, he went to the hearth, piled wood on the embers, then left.

Chapter 10

Awakening

*L*ibby awoke to the parlor steeped in the gray of almost-dawn and the sense that a sound had nudged her from sleep. A shout, perhaps? Not from within the house, certainly. Despite his cane, her host was uncannily quiet.

Straightening, and stiff muscles flinching, she rubbed the bleariness from her eyes, scowled at the crinkled page of Russell's *Singular Variety of Hernia* upon which she had fallen asleep, and groaned when her fingers strafed her cheeks.

The skin irritation was unendurable. But before her mirror she had studied her face *sans* whiskers too many times to have any illusion that she looked like anything but a woman dressed in men's clothing. The whiskers, her hair treatment, and the darkening of her brows together had a significant effect.

But she had no uncertainty as to the real reason the

other students and her teachers believed her disguise: they did not think a woman capable of medical science. Even if they thought her unusually effeminate, it would simply never occur to them that a woman could accomplish what she was now accomplishing.

On the table beside Russell's study was a small jar.

It was not yet light out, still too early for Mrs. Coutts or Mr. Gibbs to have arrived. Which meant that her host had left the jar here while she slept.

Libby's heartbeat did an uncomfortable little stumble.

Prying out the cork, she discovered a thin, oily substance. She sniffed. It was nearly odorless. Perhaps it was a balm or soap, to soothe her rash. He had not complained about the blemishes on her face, but he mustn't like to draw them. Skimming her fingertip over it, she touched her thumb to forefinger. The digits stuck together.

Adhesive!

Shutting off the lamp, she took the jar to her bedchamber. As she dressed she heard Mrs. Coutts arrive, and shortly the scents of cooking twined through the house.

In the dining room, Libby poured a cup of tea and let the steam dampen her face. She tweaked a few whiskers. They held.

Setting down the cup, she went to the back of the house.

Pale morning light illumined the windows of his studio, casting him in a pearly aura as he stood at the easel. Arms crossed and stance remarkably solid, he stared intently at the large canvas.

"I am sorry I fell asleep in the parlor," she said.

"You may sleep anywhere you wish in this house," he said, not turning his attention from the painting. "But you may not disturb me while I am working. Begone."

"There is no evidence of brush or palette anywhere. You are not working. You are pondering."

"Pondering is part of the work." His arms tightened across his chest, making the coat strain at his shoulders. *Good Lord*, he was thoroughly virile. She could study the shape of his clavicles and scapulae—his entire pectoral girdle—for hours.

"The adhesive is marvelous," she said. "Miraculous, in fact. Extraordinarily light yet strong. Even dry it is elastic. What will dissolve it?"

"Linseed oil."

"Oh, of course. Its base is linseed. Ingenious. Where did you purchase it?"

"I made it."

"You?"

Finally he turned his gaze upon her. But he said nothing.

"You are a chemist?" she said.

"Among other talents."

"You must concoct your own pigments and solutions."

He nodded, again that regal tilt of his head that seemed to compliment her as it suggested a great distance between them.

"But human skin is entirely different from canvas," she said. "How do you know this adhesive would not be an even fiercer irritant than the adhesive I have been using?"

"Your new best friend helped."

"My new best—*oh*. Truly ingenious! Pigs are susceptible to many of the same ailments as humans, of course. And the piglet's skin must be at least as sensitive as mine. That was clever of you. The experiment did not harm it, I hope."

"The compounds were mild." The shadow of a smile crossed his lips. "The creature rather enjoyed the attention, I think."

"Now that you are finished with it—that is, I have not seen it this morning. Have you returned it to the butcher?"

"If I had?"

"You *haven't*."

"For a person of science you are a remarkably soft-hearted girl."

"One is not counterindicative of the other. And I am not a girl."

"No," he said, his eyes hooding as his gaze dipped. But he was looking at neither a girl nor a woman, rather a young man. "You are not," he said as though beneath the coat and waistcoat and trousers he saw her woman's body—her breasts and hips and thighs and fluttering belly.

He looked again into her eyes. "It is in the kitchen with Mrs. Coutts. Not in the pot. Rather, begging for scraps for breakfast. Now haven't you a lecture to attend, or some such?"

"Thank you. You did this even when you needn't have."

"The clarity of your skin is of interest to me." He returned his attention to the canvas.

When she passed the kitchen doorway the piglet scampered out and ran circles around her feet. Scooping it up, she examined it in the light from the parlor windows. On its stomach, a small square of fur had been shaven away. The skin there was healthy.

He had kept a farm animal in his clean, elegant house in order to devise an adhesive that would not irritate her skin. Yet he had no interest in talking to her, in drinking a pint with her, or in seeing her other than for a single hour each Sunday morning.

LIBBY HAD TROUBLE keeping her attention on Dr. Jones's lecture. The whiskers felt too light, her cheeks too elastic, and she could not stop thinking that the adhesive had failed and had fallen off and she would be exposed before everybody.

"Fine news, what?" Archie whispered beside her.

Below, Dr. Jones was pointing his baton at a diagram of the vascular system.

"What news?"

"What news? Jones has announced we'll have cadavers come January! You know what that means."

"What does it mean?"

"Means we've a month to find a private surgery course an' have ourselves practice dissectin' afore Jones is watchin' our every cut. 'Tis the only way to have a jump on the others." His freckles bunched up in a frown. "Under the weather, lad? Been stayin' out late with Cheddar an' his mates, have you?"

"Of course not. I am only a bit distracted today."

"Now I've seen it all. Joseph Smart, distracted from studies. Lad, get your head outta the clouds."

But she could not manage to focus, and when lecture ended she did not go to the library with Archie, as they had taken to doing after lecture, to be followed by a visit to the pub. Instead she went to the closest place she could think to go: her friend Tabitha's modiste shop.

Through the small window she saw no one inside. The bell on the door jingled as she entered and went directly to the mirror.

The whiskers were intact. The adhesive he had contrived was light and essentially invisible. He was an extraordinary chemist.

And he was her ally.

"Good day." Tabitha said, coming around a wide screen from behind which women were speaking softly. They were probably doing measurements or a fitting on the dais, precisely where Tabitha had made Libby's first set of man's clothes. "I am Mrs. Bellarmine." Her soft West Indies accent, rounded shoulders, and gown of delicate muslin were a contrast to her wary eyes. "How may I help you, sir?"

Sir.

Men did not call at modiste shops. Having escaped enslavement in the West Indies, Tabitha had plenty of reason to mistrust men who behaved out of the ordinary. Married now to a Scotsman, still she was an outsider making her home in a new land, and vulnerable.

Just as Libby's housemate was.

"Mum needs a wrap," she muttered, gesturing at a display of shawls. "That'll do." Digging into her wallet, she slapped a banknote on the counter.

She kept her head down as her friend wrapped up the shawl and made change.

"I hope your mother enjoys it."

"M'thanks," she mumbled.

By the time she made it around the corner and out of sight of the shop she was dizzy. Dragging in a lungful of air, she stared at the paper package in her hands.

One of her closest friends did not even recognize her.

Are you prepared to be always alone?

He had warned her. But she had not truly understood. And she had not considered how it would affect him if she were discovered—how he, as a foreigner in this city, could be endangered by her ruse.

"What's in the package?" Archie said as Libby settled beside him at the table that was becoming their usual spot in the pub. Archie's friends Peter "Pincushion" Pincher and George Allan were already seated, with pints of ale.

"A shawl."

Archie pushed a teacup toward her. On her first visit here, she had made the mistake of drinking a whole pot of tea before discovering that students typically relieved themselves in the gutter in the alley behind the building. She sipped slowly.

"A shawl? If you've no' gone an' replaced yourself with

another Joe Smart, I'll be flabbergasted. Sure it's no' a bag o' bones?"

"Or a rat to dissect?" Pincushion said with a grin.

"Or surgical instruments?" George added.

They had taken her measure swiftly. Was she entirely transparent?

She frowned. The adhesive moved so easily with her skin she didn't even feel it. He was a *miracle* chemist. She wished she had half of his talent.

Tickling heat sped into her belly. To be here with her new companions yet thinking of him was strange and wonderful. Her life had become secrets upon secrets. Yet thoughts of him felt honest.

"It's only a shawl," she said.

"Perhaps for that pretty cousin?" Pincushion said, poking a knobby elbow into Archie's ribs.

"Fine news about the cadavers comin' at the New Year, aye?" Archie said in an obvious redirection. "Thought we'd have to wait till the next course."

"It isn't all it's made out to be," George mumbled. He had brown hair that spiked like a pitchfork and thick spectacles.

"Aw, Allan," Pincushion said, "you're only afraid you'll toss your breakfast again this year too."

"This year?" Libby said.

"George is repeatin' anatomy," Archie explained. "Failed the diploma exam."

George nodded in glum confirmation.

"Couldn't hold the knife steady enough to cut," Pincushion said, wiggling his brows. "Turned green every day."

"If you cannot endure dissecting, George, why are you studying surgery?" Libby said.

"He doesn't want to be a surgeon," Pincushion said. "Or a physician."

"Rather be a solicitor," Archie said. "But his father's a physician."

"And his father's father," Pincushion said.

"And my father's father's father," George said.

"The old man's a right bloody bastard," Pincushion said.

"An' he's got money. George finished last term—"

"In disgrace," George inserted.

"But his father's bought him back in again."

"That is a rotten deal, George," Libby said, imagining the women who would rejoice in having George Allan's money and liberty to study medicine in his place.

"Enough gloom, lads," Archie declared. "Despite havin' his head in the clouds, Joe recited the lymphatic system to everybody in lecture today. Jones was beamin'. A toast to our young mate!"

They toasted her and she drank lightly.

ON FRIDAY LIBBY gave the shawl to Coira.

Coira cooed. "What am I to do with a wrap bonnie as this?"

"Wear it to church," Libby suggested.

"Church! Laddie, you're a precious one, to be sure."

Libby suspected where the shawl would go: the same place Coira's wages went, a grandmother she had spoken of with affection.

With a jaunty bow, copied from the sorts of jaunty bows she'd seen Archie give women, Libby headed to lecture.

In the lecture hall, the physician stood at a dissection table upon which was a collection of jars.

"Gentlemen, today we will begin dissecting preserved organs," Dr. Jones said, gesturing to a man entering the theater. "Mr. Plath here will assist with dissections for the remainder of the session. He is an advanced surgical student."

Libby's mouth went entirely dry. Mr. Plath was the young man from the party she had attended with Constance and Saint, whose hands had made bruises on her arms.

Plath perused the tiers of students. Pausing on George, his eyes narrowed.

"Plath hates me," George whispered. "He told me I'm a mama's boy."

"Your saintly mum's the only reason you're no' a thorough bounder, lad."

"As soon as they open those jars I'll gag and he'll crucify me again."

Libby unscrewed the lid of a little tub of scented balm. "Rub this on your upper lip, George. It will mask the stench."

Archie and Pincushion swiped balm above their lips too. Libby couldn't; she had no idea how the adhesive and balm would mix.

"Mr. Smart and Mr. Chedham," Dr. Jones said. "Your marks are at present the highest. You will begin."

"Perfect," she heard Chedham mutter.

Palms damp, she approached the table.

"Mr. Chedham," Plath said. "You will dissect the heart." He looked directly into her face from a yard away. "Mr. Smart, you have the brain."

He had no idea.

"The rest of you," Dr. Jones said, "open your notebooks."

"Dr. Jones," Libby said. "I have already dissected the brain several times and committed all the parts to memory. May Mr. Armstrong perform the dissection of this brain while I describe it?" From a family of prosperous farmers,

Archie only lacked experience to be a fine man of medicine.

"This is an unusual request, Mr. Smart. But you may. Mr. Armstrong, approach."

Archie sprang up from his chair. As he grabbed an instrument and began working, she felt Dr. Jones's gaze on her, and prayed it was approving.

"I DINNA KNOW how you bear it, lad." Archie's fuzzy eyes stared at where Chedham stood with his usual sycophants clustered around him.

"Bear what?" she mumbled, light-headed and not quite certain how she had come to be clasping an empty ale glass. The pub was full of students, all boisterous. George and Pincushion were chuckling over something, both looking merry as ploughmen on a Sunday.

Right. They were celebrating George's triumph over nausea. And she privately was celebrating the success of her disguise. Plath had not recognized her. Even Tabitha had not recognized her. And these boys believed she was one of them. Her transformation into Joseph Smart was complete. When Archie had bought her a pint, celebrating seemed in order.

"Apprenticing alongside Cheddar," he said. "He's got a coldness I dinna trust, as though he's got no fellow feelin'. But enough o' him." Archie smacked the table. "Let's talk about females."

"Gotten up the courage to invite Joe's cousin for a stroll yet?" Pincushion said.

Archie's cheeks flushed pink through the freckles.

"It ain't the *courage* he's got up for the lass," George said, laughing. "Aye, Archibald?"

"Look at him!" Pincushion cried. "I'll bet our lad's gone stiff as a cadaver at only the mention of the girl."

"Sod off, Peter," Archie said cheerfully, but he cast Libby a worried glance. "Pincher was raised in a barn, Joe. I've nothin' but respect for your cousin. Dinna take it amiss, will you?"

"Why should I?"

Archie's gaze shifted over her shoulder, then abruptly widened in alarm. Libby followed it with hers.

Eyes rolled up in his head and mouth hanging open, Pincushion was slowly stroking his ale glass up and down, then gradually quicker. He started moaning. George chortled madly.

Archie's complexion got even redder. "Odd's blood," he said desperately. Casting his gaze about, he called out to a pair of students nearby. "How about a game tomorrow, lads? I'll bring the ball."

An hour later, Libby walked home in a haze, her vision bleary and thoughts thoroughly muddled. That action Pincushion had been doing with his glass . . .

It was certainly sexual. And George's reference to "up" seemed clear enough.

Obviously Archie had a tendre for Iris. After only one meeting, that seemed silly. But attraction for a female did often cause a male erection. The female body functioned similarly, although much less obviously. Anatomy texts glossed over both, describing the functions of the muscles and fascia and blood vessels, but little about how it all actually *occurred*. They needn't elaborate on male arousal; all those books were meant for only men to read.

Inside the house she went into the parlor.

"P'raps the French will have something to say." Her consonants slurred. Pulling a thick volume off the shelf, she opened it and blinked hard to bring the words into focus. But even the French text was vague.

If her father were home, he would tell her.

No. He wouldn't. He would say that the least appropriate place for her to be was in a pub with young men making lewd gestures. Then he would look at her with eyes full of affection and pity and her heart would implode.

He loved her. He wanted the best for her. But he knew her weaknesses.

She should not go to the pub with Archie and the lads. They had accepted her as a man. What other purpose had she for socializing with them?

Loneliness.

It was weakness. She had the company of Mrs. Coutts and the piglet. And she was accustomed to being alone— truly alone, even with her friends. Alice, Constance, and Tabitha cared for her, but they did not share her love of medicine. Iris just liked to laugh, and Libby provided plenty of fodder for that.

To none of them was she fully herself.

She went to her bedchamber, changed into her nightshirt, and sat at the dressing table. The kohl that extended and thickened her brows went first, wiped entirely away with cream. The whiskers followed.

She stared at her reflection, her eyes very wide and soft in the lamplight. With her cropped hair, bare features, and man's nightshirt open at the collar, she was neither youth nor young woman.

"I am me. I am only me," she repeated, louder.

She wondered what he saw in these lips that fascinated him. She touched her fingertips to her lower lip. Heat skittered about her belly. With a quick little breath, she skimmed her fingertips over the tender skin where the whiskers had been. The pink was fading already. He was a master draughtsman, an exceptional painter, and a genius chemist.

When she had come into the house earlier, she had

seen light beneath his studio door. She could not wait for Sunday to thank him. Pulling a dressing gown on over her nightshirt, she went from her room.

As soon as she opened the door to his quarters she understood the real reason she had not been able to wait for Sunday. Here she felt at home. Here in his studio she was both woman and student. Here lived the only person in the world who knew the entire truth about her.

Pushing the door open, she stepped inside.

A lamp by the easel illumined the chamber in an amber glow. The purpose of the bar across the doorway to his bedchamber was now entirely clear.

Stripped to only breeches, his arms and torso glistening with sweat, and eyes closed, he was pulling himself up and lowering himself down and repeating that action slowly and at an exact, even tempo: up, down, up, down, without a missed beat. The muscles were well developed, finely cut, elastic and lean, contracting and relaxing, each a miracle of function, and all together a thing of power and great beauty.

Now she comprehended the silence and fluidity with which he could move. No human body, however well-conditioned, could entirely overcome his lack. But the strapped muscles of his abdomen, chest, and arms would allow him temporary speed and stealth that many men with both feet could not achieve.

Why he wanted to be capable of speed and stealth, she could not guess.

In a scampering rush, the piglet flung itself past him and into the studio, its sleepy snorts elated as it cavorted about her feet.

Taking a silent step backward, Libby prayed he would ignore the noise.

He opened his eyes.

Chapter 11

An Interruption

She should move. She should leave. She should at least turn around until he donned a shirt.

Instead she stared and her pulse beat a battle drum against her ribs, her cheeks and entire body filled with heat, and a thousand questions clamored onto her tongue.

He lowered himself to his bare foot and grasped his cane that was propped against the doorpost. The loose fabric on the right leg of his breeches was pinned up. Obviously the peg had not been surgically attached. No wonder he had such pain; he was walking on a wholly deficient replacement.

He said nothing. Except for the deep inhalations and exhalations that shifted shadows across the contours of his chest and abdomen, he did not move.

The piglet scuttled across the room and into his bed-chamber again.

"Apparently," she said, "it is content in having revealed

me here and will now return to its bed and the sweet dreams of the innocent."

"Why are you here?" he said in an unremarkable tone, as though he weren't wearing only breeches and standing with damp hair and trickles of sweat caressing his superb musculature. "Are you unwell?"

"No. I have been out at the pub with friends, and I think I did not realize until just this moment quite how intoxicated I am. I came to—"

He walked toward her. Without the support beneath his right leg, the muscles in his arms and shoulders and chest quivered with the extraordinary effort. But he barely limped, effectively using the walking stick as a leg. A scar two inches long carved a slender track in his waist.

"I came to tell you how well the adhesive functions," she forged ahead. She had seen men's bodies before. She was a medical scientist, the daughter of a physician. The naked male torso was nothing but a collection of muscles and bones and—oh, *good Lord*, he was exquisitely beautiful. "It is light." *So beautiful*. "And flexible. Yet it holds the whiskers firmly. In only two days the irritation to my skin has vanished."

"I know how well it functions," he said, halting so close that she could feel the heat from his body in the chill air between them, and watch the muscles relax into sculpted beauty. "I tested it thoroughly before giving it to you."

Other small scars marked the perfect flesh here and there. She wanted to ask him about them. Then she wanted to explore each with her fingers.

"I realize that, of course," she said. "But—"

He lifted his hand and wrapped it around the side of her face. She did not resist the urging of his grasp that turned her face upward as his fingers sank into her hair.

In the darkness his gaze upon her features was like midnight.

"You should not be here." His voice was rough, but his fingers were twined in her hair and he was so close—*so close*—as though he had no idea what his body close did to hers.

"You are telling me I should not be here and holding me, at once." It came out as a reedy whisper. "That is irrational."

He was looking at her features, one at a time, studying as he always did, but differently now, as though he'd all the leisure in the world to do so.

"You should not be here," he repeated. Then his gaze dipped to her lips.

Explosions of pleasure made her body feel raw. *Vulnerable.* She wanted to lean her cheek more snugly into his hand, to *be held*, to turn her face and feel the sensation of his palm against her lips.

"I wanted to thank you," she said.

"You have thanked me already."

"Admittedly, the ale has robbed me of acute thought. But I think I would have come to share this news with you anyway, even without the drink. It is, you see . . ."

A droplet of moisture made a trail along his cheek to cling to his jaw, which was dark with whisker growth. She had the mad, wild urge to lick that trail and taste his saltiness.

She set her fingertips on his chest. His breathing hitched and his hand fell away from her face.

Splaying her fingers over his pectoral muscle, she brought her palm flat to his skin. His heartbeats were quick, his flesh hot and damp.

She was affecting him.

Her hand, pink from scrubbing, shone starkly against

his golden brown skin. Staring at his nipples she felt hers prickle to achy peaks. How would it feel to press them against his firm chest, to give her body what it obviously wanted?

It would feel *good*. So good.

Sliding her hand over his ribs, exploring the hard controlled beauty of him, she leaned forward.

Then her hand was hovering in emptiness.

She watched him walk across the studio and into his bedchamber. The door closed.

Breaking free of paralysis, she returned to her bedchamber in a muddle. Removing the dressing gown and nightshirt, she climbed beneath the covers and felt the soft linen slide over her skin, caressing her as she had tried to caress him.

He found her beautiful. His flesh had responded to her touch. Why wouldn't he allow it?

Her body was strung with tension, her head swimming. The tight peaks of her breasts practically wept with need.

Slipping her fingers over her breasts, she stroked the firm tips, and a moan began in her throat. Around the puckered nipples her breasts were soft. She had bound them into wrappings dozens of times already, flattening them as much as possible, but she had never done this—she had never allowed herself to truly feel her own flesh. What sort of person of medicine was she, to ignore a physical response that she could so easily study?

The sort of person who had never felt this physical response—this lust—before living in this house.

Sliding her palms over the curves of her belly and hips, she explored, noting the sensations the caresses aroused. But her lips were parted, her breaths quickening, and she was not thinking of medicine. She was thinking of him, of how it would feel were his hands now where hers explored, reveling in this voluptuous examination, this fantasy that came so easily.

Perhaps he found her only beautiful as a subject of study, just as she found her patients fascinating. Perhaps she did not rouse in him the desire that looking at him—hearing his voice, touching him, meeting his gaze—roused in her.

That would explain it.

She slid her fingers between her thighs. Sweet urgency grew as she let herself think of his male beauty, his scent of sweat and cologne, and his skin beneath the fingers that were now waking her body, stroking, probing, slick and wet and unrestrained. Picturing his hand on her, she arched into the caress. Whimpers of pleasure escaped between her lips. With the covers tangled about her, she tried to imagine herself like other women: at twenty years old a wife by now, who knew a man's touch.

But she was not like other women. She was a man.

Chapter 12

A Request

She found him at the Gilded Quill. In this modest place, decorated in dark wood and white linen, and smelling of beeswax, sage, and cakes, Ziyaeddin met friends for dinner or tea, and occasionally clients.

Most often, however, he was alone here, with a cup of coffee—which he had taught the cook to prepare with sugar—a newspaper, and his thoughts. His sketchbook was always open, his pencil ready should an interesting character present itself for study.

Today he was only sitting, neither drawing nor drinking, alone as he was rarely now in his own house—sitting at a table by the window and staring sightlessly at the street.

He was not especially surprised when she appeared. She was Joseph Smart whenever she left his house, and she was Joseph Smart now, feathery whiskers and all.

She came directly to him. "May I join you?"

He inclined his head.

With the ease of a youth who had been doing so a lifetime, she lifted the tails of her coat to avoid sitting on them. She was intelligent. Clever. Quick. Observant. Of course she would perform even the minor act of sitting as she did all else: with purpose and perfection.

Weeks earlier Charles Bell had sat across from him in the seat she now occupied, marveling at young Mr. Smart's knowledge and abilities and wondering aloud if this was merely the shine on a new penny. Ziyaeddin had replied to the surgeon that it was, rather, the honest glow of a guinea.

Now that guinea looked him squarely in the eye.

"Last night at the pub I drank to excess," she said. "I have never drunk so much, and I was too caught up in celebrating to study the effect it was having on my thoughts."

"Celebrating what?"

She waved a dismissive hand. "What I am saying is that I hadn't the foresight to halt myself from going to your quarters last night. Actually, it is a fascinating study in compromised reason. When I had the impulse to speak with you, I was imagining you exactly as you are whenever I am there. With the spirits confusing my thoughts I did not consider that when you are in your chambers you are not always standing or sitting before the easel, fully clothed. It was careless of me and I am ashamed for that."

"For that?"

"Yes. I have the most wretched headache and sour stomach as proof of my carelessness too."

"For only that?"

Her eyes widened, two pools of deepest sea that made him want to drink from her. *Allah, how he thirsted.*

"Yes," she repeated, then with another frown: "I should not have drank as I did. Drunkenness and disorderliness are prohibited by the terms of my indenture, of course. But I am not ashamed of seeing a partially naked man, if that is what you mean to suggest."

"Perhaps I did mean to suggest that." He folded his arms. "I am now reconsidering."

"I am a person of science," she said in exaggeratedly crisp syllables. "I have seen many men unclothed."

"I am also now reconsidering the respect I had been holding for your father."

"Of course my father never allowed me to see a fully unclothed man. Only parts."

"What a relief," he murmured.

"Yesterday in anatomy we began dissecting preserved organs. I was invited to demonstrate."

"Ah, thus the celebrating."

Her lips snapped together. Those lips were so different now than the night before when they had been parted with expectation, shimmering with moisture, and entirely ready to be kissed—without words *asking to be kissed*. Now they were uncertain.

"Have I mistaken it?" he said.

"No. I was indeed celebrating that. It is a great honor to be chosen to lead the first dissection of the session."

"I have no doubt you impressed Dr. Jones and your classmates."

She tucked in her chin a bit. "You remember my professor's name."

"Would you prefer I forget the details of what you tell me?"

Markedly deep, quick breaths were swelling her chest. Beneath the wool and linen it was flat as a boy's, and he wondered how she could move with such energy and comfort though she was bound into this costume.

"Thank you for remembering the details." She spoke

quietly. "I beg your pardon for interrupting you last night. And for touching you as I did. I hope you will forgive me."

"It was I who behaved rudely."

"It was my fault to be there. Not yours, of course. I am sorry. Will you forgive me and shake hands?"

He simply couldn't. Touching her the night before had been a grave mistake. This entire charade was a mistake. But at least this one aspect of it he could control.

If he touched her hand now he would want to touch all of her.

"Here is a lesson, young Joseph: do not offer your hand to a man who does not deserve your civility."

"But you do deserve my civility. I am not naïve. Nor ignorant. I am aware of what can happen to a woman who makes herself vulnerable to a man as I did with you last night."

"I know not whether to rejoice that you think me such an honorable man or despair that you are certain I am one."

"You needn't despair. I don't know you well enough to be certain. I barely know anything of you at all, except what I have seen of you in your paintings."

"Do not mistake the art for the artist," he said.

"Even so, I know you are generous, if selfishly so—"

"A contradiction."

"For you have done all of this for me for so little compensation. And you are . . . strong. In character. You live in a foreign land among those who probably understand you very little, and you have made a life for yourself here. That requires strength. And courage."

This required courage: pretending she did not affect him, that the night before he had not nearly grabbed her and done to her everything he had been dreaming of doing to her.

"You are also physically strong," she said. "I have noticed that before. But it was especially clear to me last night. Your body is in extraordinarily good form."

He could not resist smiling.

"Do I speak an untruth?" she said.

"I should have anticipated this."

"Anticipated what?"

"That you would say this. Aloud. To me. As though it were the most normal conversation between a man and a woman."

Her brow crinkled. "There is no woman here now."

Despite all, she had no idea that to him her whiskers and trousers might as well be ribbons and skirts.

"You speak every one of your thoughts," he said.

Her perfect lips parted, then closed on unspoken words.

"I see," he said, smiling. "You are demonstrating that I am wrong about that."

"No. I am thinking that women must be happy with you."

"Women?"

"With your physical strength. With your body. It is impressive, beautiful, as male bodies go. Your lovers . . . they must . . . enjoy it."

He said nothing in response, only stared at her, while Libby felt the heat climb into her neck and cheeks.

He stood up, grasped his cane, and left.

Flinging coins onto the table, she followed him. She caught up to him easily. On the peg he walked with only a minor limp, but by no means quickly.

"Wait," she said as she came side by side with him. "I—"

He halted, and in the middle of the footpath with people passing by on either side he said, "What in the blazes sort of comment was that?"

"What do you—"

He set off again. It had begun to rain and the cobbles were glistening. Questions like the rain battered her.

"I only wonder," she said when she ascended the stoop of the house behind him.

"Oh, do you?" he said between tight teeth, fitting the key in the lock and pushing the door open with such control she might think she only imagined his anger if not for the taut tendons and muscles in his jaw.

He was waiting on the stoop for her to precede him, apparently forgetting that she was not a woman.

"Yes," she said, passing him by to enter. "I wonder *everything*. I know nothing about you, and you will not tell me. But here I am living in your house and where there is no information to supply reality my mind always invents scenarios. So, yes, I was wondering."

"What else have you wondered?" He spoke coolly. "Whether I am accustomed to pleasuring half a dozen women at once, or perhaps in succession? Whether the harem I kept numbered in the dozens or the hundreds? Whether I pray to idols? Whether I spend each night polishing my collection of daggers so that I can steal out and sacrifice Christian infants to my heathen gods? Or perhaps your wonderings have been of the more plebeian sort. Perhaps you wonder whether I eat with a fork and spoon or on my hands and knees like a dog?"

Her stomach churned. "No."

"None of those? For I assure you, I have heard each of those questions while residing in this land. I won't be surprised to hear them again, and any other wonderings your fertile imagination can add to them."

"I think you must know by now that although I am insatiably curious, I am neither ignorant nor without thought."

His eyes were obsidian.

"For instance," she continued, "I know that Muslims believe in the same god as Christians, although they call that god by a different name. When the American Thomas Jefferson insisted on that, many people made a fuss about it, but I think it makes perfect sense. And I know that idols are prohibited you. Admittedly I don't know anything about harems . . . and such. But I don't understand how anybody schooled in Scripture could think a child would be a useful religious sacrifice, for of course Abraham, who was the father of Judaism, Christianity and Islam, made that mistake with his own son so that the rest of us needn't ever after. In general I am not taken to fanciful notions, for I read a lot—a lot more, that is, than the caricatures of Byron or Morier. And I don't depend on the ridiculous portraits of foreigners one sees at the opera to inform me. I regret that is not the case with every Englishman or Scot you have encountered. If I could slap them all, I would."

For a long moment he did not speak.

"You would slap them," he finally said.

"Yes. For I don't have a collection of daggers. Although I do have surgical instruments, it's true. So I suppose I could inflict some fairly grievous wounds if necessary. I haven't yet taken an oath as medical men do, so it would not be strictly unethical, although certainly immoral. But I would do it for your sake. Please let me know if you ever wish me to."

His beautiful eyes changed, and Libby felt seen—truly seen—as though he not only believed her words but understood her. All of the sensations of pleasure lingering in her body from the night before surged anew.

She tried very hard not to look at his lips. "Could we now call it a draw?"

"We could," he said in an oddly low voice.

"But there *is* something I should like to know about you. Something in particular."

"Aha. Here we are again."

"How did it happen?" She gestured downward.

He only stared at her, but now without anger.

"Was it an accident? A wound turned septic? An incurable fistula from a bullet wound, perhaps, or shrapnel—"

"Miss Shaw—"

"Shh! Gibbs is probably upstairs," she whispered. "You must call me Mr. Smart."

"Saved by the valet." He began to move away.

"Please," she said to his back. "It is a professional curiosity, of course." The partial lie tasted flat on her tongue.

She was opening her mouth to tell him the truth— that she simply wanted to know—that she wanted to know *him*—when he said, "It was the price I paid for my freedom."

His *freedom*?

"Thank you for telling me."

He continued on to his studio and shut the door behind him. Libby was trembling from her stomach outward. It was the most horrible sensation, and entirely unwelcome.

Gathering up her books from the parlor, she stuffed them into her satchel and went out. Last night she had had enough ale for a lifetime. But she wanted companionship, and a plateful of pie to calm her stomach.

Her friends were not at the pub. Maxwell Chedham sauntered toward her, glass of ale in hand.

"Studying on a Saturday?" he said with a superior nod toward her books spread on the table.

"Your patients would benefit if you did too," she said.

"You won't win, Smart. I'll prove you are a fraud."

Acidic heat crept through her.

"I know you want to be Professor Russell's surgical assistant next year," he said.

"The chair of clinical surgery? No. I simply want to prac—"

"You are a boy playing at a man's game, Smart. It's only

time before you make a mistake. And I will be there to take you down."

He strolled away.

You are a fraud.

She wanted to make him explain his words. The need pressed at her to pursue it. She fought it, redirecting her thoughts to her books, but she was damp all over with perspiration.

As she ate and her stomach settled, she paged through her notes. At the next table, a pair of students had their heads bent over a philosophical text.

This was a miracle: sitting alone in a pub, medical books before her, young men all around with their minds turned toward learning. She had dreamed of this. She had planned and worked and striven for this. Her father had taught her by example to never settle for defeat, even when adversaries seemed to be winning.

Women will never be admitted to the medical profession.

This time he was wrong. She would not accept defeat. Her father might have raised her to speak like a Brit and converse like a man, but she was a Scotswoman. No arrogant English blueblood would undo her.

BY THE LIGHT of a single candle Libby was trying to read the tiny text in a volume of chemical science that had clearly been printed for ants, when the parlor door opened. Lifting her head, she squinted across the shadows.

"Oh," she said. "What are you doing out of your cave?"

He smiled, only slightly, but it ignited a tickle of pleasure in her stomach. It was difficult to look at him without remembering how she had felt such pleasure in touching herself while imagining his hands on her.

She wanted to confess it to him. Sometimes the need to

confess her thoughts and actions grew so hot and desperate, she could think of nothing else. Confession always brought her such relief. But she had only ever felt that need to confess all with her father, and sometimes Constance and Alice, who were like family. Never a stranger.

Something had changed between them.

"I have come to apologize," he said, remaining by the door.

She swiveled to face him, and her skirts tangled in the chair legs.

"Barely a month, and already I've lost the knack of wearing a gown." She yanked at the hem. "How fortunate gentlemen are to enjoy freedom of movement at all times, day and night."

"The night I entered this room to give you the adhesive you were wearing trousers. Why not tonight?"

She didn't know.

"For what have you come to apologize? For assuming the worst of me? You needn't," she said, turning again to her books and taking up her pen. "I am accustomed to making wretched mistakes and everybody thinking me awful. I am forever apologizing to my friends for saying or doing something grievously amiss."

"I am sorry for speaking to you as I did."

She wrote a word. She'd no idea what word it was.

"About pleasuring women and harems and such?" The nerves were dancing about in her stomach again.

"Yes."

"Again, I say, you needn't," she said, writing another nonsense word. "I began it, after all, mentioning lovers."

He said nothing.

She looked up at him.

"It was ungentlemanly of me." His jaw was again rather tight.

"We could go on all year insulting each other and then apologizing for it, I suspect."

"You would rather we did not?"

"Shockingly, I do." She stood up. "In fact I have a favor to ask of you now. I have been considering asking you about it since yesterday, before the unfortunate interruption, and I would prefer to ask you now rather than to wait until tomorrow's sitting. I would rather not ask it in your studio, you see."

"I find it difficult to believe there is any question you would not ask in any location," he said with that almost-smile that made him even handsomer.

"Usually there isn't. But I am endeavoring to be respectful of your work space."

"Are you?"

"Yes. Belatedly. You know, you should acknowledge my good intentions in at least some matters. I am not all awful."

He walked to her, the cane making a quiet thump on the rug.

"I do not think you are even partially awful," he said, his gaze shifting over her features. She supposed he always looked at people like this, as though he were studying the curves and shapes and tones of their faces, much as she studied people's postures and humps and knobby knees.

Lyricism.

When he looked at her, did he see poetry?

"But you are," she said, feeling all the heat from the night before reaching up inside her with hungry hands.

"I am what?" he said.

"Awful."

"For giving you the run of my house and enduring interruptions at all hours?"

"This afternoon you left me with the bill after looking at me as if I were mad."

"I keep an account at that coffeehouse. You needn't have paid. But do feel free to subtract it from your rent."

"You haven't yet told me what my rent is."

"Haven't I? How financially negligent I am. Then how much do you wish to pay? I will be content with whatever sum you like. But don't forget to add a few quid for late-night spying."

"An apology is obviously insufficient for you, after all. I told you, I had never had quite that much ale before. I was foxed."

"You were nonplussed." His gaze upon her was dark and complete. "By all that is holy, you are even prettier when you are furious. How is that?"

"Because you are a numbskull. I was not *spying*."

"My English is sometimes inadequate. Perhaps you prefer the word . . . what is it? Gawking."

"I don't. For heaven's sake, will you allow me to ask my question?"

Seating himself on the arm of the chair before the hearth, he gestured with his hand. "I am at your disposal."

"Last night in the pub my friends were discussing a matter that suggested to me acutely an area of study that, I fear, may cause me some if not considerable trouble in the future. Not only that, but being unable to share in even casual conversations about it is proving inconvenient."

He nodded encouragement for her to continue.

After last night, there was no other way to state this. She dove in.

"My knowledge of anatomy is lacking. Male anatomy, in particular," she clarified.

A single brow lifted. "Is it?"

"When the other students trade puerile banter, I am conspicuously silent. My studies on the subject are proving insufficient for the pretense of manhood I am living."

"I see." He glanced at her books stacked all over his parlor, about which he had said nothing for weeks. He was a generous host. She was depending on that now.

"Haven't you examined male cadavers?" he said.

"Those do not move, of course." She looked squarely into his eyes. In the candlelight they were the color of coal and, as always, very beautiful. "But you do."

"Ah," he said, smiling slightly. "I begin to see the direction of this conversation."

"Will you help me with this?"

"Your studies would continue to suffer." The knuckles wrapped around the end of his walking stick were stretched tight. "I, as you know, am not a whole man."

She stepped forward. It was unwise, especially now that she knew what she was capable of in his proximity. But she could allow nothing to hinder her project, not even memories of his spectacular musculature.

"If I am to succeed in this charade, I must know everything about being a man," she said. "And it is not male *legs* that interest me now."

His gaze snapped to hers, and in that moment it occurred to her that this man, who had agreed to her terms for living in his house, was neither celibate by nature nor inclined to remain so for much longer.

"No," he said, standing again and towering over her.

"Please don't misunderstand me," she said quickly. "I am not propositioning you. I would only like a brief demonstration, a purely clinical demonstra—"

"Absolutely not."

"Come now," she said, dragging courage into her lungs. "I know everything about both male and female human anatomy except how a live man functions in that manner. Textbooks are frustratingly foggy about the details, which is no doubt because only men write and are intended to read those books, and they all already know. The texts describe *lack* of function in more detail than healthy function, in fact. And now, of course, you and I have already conversed—and quarreled—about the most intimate subjects. I know it is an extraordinary request but you must agree that this is an extraordinary situation and I have no one else to ask. My success in this program may depend upon it."

"I am not a subject of laboratory study," he growled.

"Neither am I," she shot back. "Yet every Sunday I sit on a stool in your studio being precisely that. Why is it so shocking to you that I would wish to study one part of you when you have done exactly that to me? My nose. My ears. My fingers. What am I to you but a collection of parts to be described in pencil lead? How is what I am asking of you now any different than that?"

"If you do not know the difference, Miss Shaw, then on behalf of all your future patients not to mention your gentlemen admirers, I despair of you." He bowed. "Good night."

He left her staring at the open door.

Her words had come unbidden but she meant them. That she was to him a model only—a female face and figure to draw, and no more—hurt. She had never lived alone. Now she did, sharing a house with a man who despite all was as much a stranger to her as any of her fellow students.

She was a curiosity to her friends and father, an inconvenience, a burden, a responsibility that must be encouraged to pursue acceptable pursuits and think regular thoughts and kept safe, even from herself, and be *normal*. In her housemate's company, though, she never felt abnormal because he never expected her to be anything except her true self.

But that was false. To him she was nothing more than an oddity too, merely to be endured while he must.

As she stood in the flicker of the guttering candle, the loneliness crept up through the cold floor, into her legs, twined around her belly, and filled her chest.

Chapter 13

A Portrait

*E*ach time she sat for him she said nothing—not a word, neither in greeting nor in parting—no questions, no monologues, and no candid observations of the most inconsequential matter. She and the increasingly large piglet came and went like a Scottish mist, settling a layer of disquiet upon him that required hours to shake off. Days.

He missed her conversation. Her monologues. Her endless questions. Her outrageous requests.

It was better this way. The less he saw of her the more he could successfully pretend that he had no interest in more than the nose, ears, and fingers.

It was then a surprise when, at a supper party at the home of Lady Hart, one of his most avid patrons, Miss Elizabeth Shaw appeared before him and said, "I did not know that you had been invited to this party. I often overhear Mrs. Coutts telling Mr. Gibbs about the parties to which you are invited and complaining that you do not attend. But she never mentioned this one. You must have discovered the invitation to this party before she had an opportunity to look through the post."

He loved how her mind functioned: observing minute details, and then analyzing each of those details of every scenario to a logical conclusion. Her thoughts never rested. It made her recent silence with him especially troubling.

"I must have," he said, taking in the shape of her wrapped in white lace and cerulean silk that made her skin glow and left bare a moderate display of soft pink bosom. "You—"

"Don't," she said. "This is a silly frock and I only wore it to please Constance, who had it made up for me because the fabric matches the color of my eyes. If you compliment me now I might have to not speak to you for another month, and that would be inconvenient. And unpleasant."

"I see," he said. "I wasn't about to compliment you."

"You weren't?" In her hair was a comb studded with sparkling beads, the shorn length of her locks braided with satin ribbon and arranged like a coronet. Her lips had been gently rouged, obscuring their perfect hues. In the gully of her collarbone rested a cameo silhouette of ivory that hung from a gold filigree chain. He wanted to paint that neck and collarbone. He wanted to paint every inch of her.

"Then, what were you about to say?" she said.

"You are acquainted with Lord and Lady Hart, it seems?"

"Oh. Polite party conversation." A spark in the eyes dimmed. "No, I'm not. Constance and Saint are, and they brought me here. Papa made them promise to wrest me out of the house on occasion. I cannot turn down every invitation or they will begin to wonder where I have gone. But I am very glad you are here, because parties like this make me extraordinarily anxious and it is good to have a friend present."

A friend. That the word should induce an instant, quick thumping beneath his ribs was mere proof of his duplicity upon duplicity.

He wanted more than to paint her. He wanted to lay his lips upon that graceful collarbone and make her sigh.

"Now I will take you to task," she continued, "for Mrs. Coutts said that you were invited to dinner at the home of William Playfair. Playfair! The man who designed Surgeons' Hall! Yet you did not invite me to attend with you so that I could meet him and the plethora of influential surgeons in this city who will undoubtedly attend too. Why not?"

"It is not wise to be seen unnecessarily in society together."

Her brow crinkled. "Because to be always seen in the company of a youth of no impressive social connections would damage your reputation as a fashionable artistic genius?"

"Rather, to be always seen in the company of a youth with no apparent family or friends whatsoever, who is living in my house, would encourage gossip of the sort I do not wish for you. Malicious gossip that could harm you."

Watching the thoughts pass across her eyes was pure pleasure.

"Do you understand?" he said.

"I do. Thank you. But," she said, abruptly animated again, "I am dying to know what you have been drawing of me."

"Are you?"

"Yes. Of course."

"But you are making a point of silence when you sit."

"No. I am simply *being* silent. It is what you asked of

me. I am respecting that. And I am mad with curiosity. What are you drawing? My elbow? My left nostril? The tip of my shoe?" Her eyes rolled upward. "This exasperating curl that won't stay pinned or oiled down no matter how I try to tame it?"

"The whole of you."

She regarded him for a stretched moment.

"You are saying that now to make a point," she said. "You are endeavoring to prove that you can be a better man than I."

"I am not." He was beginning to see that he was in fact a much lesser man than she. Her candid honesty and sincere wish to always do good by others was showing him the hollow vessel that his life had become. "After you harangued me for drawing you in parts I began drawing the whole. I am not entirely unredeemable, Miss Shaw." Rather, a scoundrel of the worst sort. He was drawing the whole because the woman of curiosity, ambition, intelligence, and humor had departed his studio, leaving a shell. In drawing the whole of her, he was dangling before himself pleasure he knew he mustn't.

"I did not harangue you," she said. "Not any more than you harangued me, at least. But I should like to see the draw—*Oh*." Her startled gaze was on the doorway. Grasping his arm she shifted her body behind him. "There are Mr. and Miss Plath. I don't wish to see them. Hide me."

Across the room, a young man and woman greeted their hosts. Brother and sister by their appearance, they were fashionably dressed and obviously popular: as they entered, several people immediately approached them.

"Why don't you wish to see them?" he said over his shoulder, knowing he should tell her to release him but entirely unable to form the words. To have her hands on him was his daily fantasy. Rather, *hourly*.

"Because he is the assistant to my anatomy professor and has seen me any number of times as Joseph Smart yet does not recognize me. Not at all! Can you believe that? What a bounder."

"The youthful male company you are keeping is having an influence on your vocabulary, it seems."

"Also, they are awful. The Plaths, that is." Her grip was so tight around his elbow he could feel the impression of each of her fingertips. "When I tried to be friendly with Miss Plath, she and her friends snubbed me. Then he cornered me in an isolated place and stuck his tongue down my throat. He is a snake. It was disgust—"

Ziyaeddin pulled away from her.

"What are you—" She circled him and blocked his path. "What are you doing?" she whispered.

"Going to tell Mr. Plath that he must put his accounts in order because tomorrow at dawn a bullet will take up residence between his eyes."

"*What?*" She leaned close and grasped his forearm again, as though it were perfectly acceptable to do at a party, surrounded by other guests, several of whom were now watching them. "Are you *mad*? You will not call him out."

He extracted his arm. "Do move aside."

"*No.* What of your efforts not to draw attention to your acquaintance with me?"

"Not with you. With Joseph Smart. Now, Miss Shaw—"

She grabbed him again. "I will fight you to the ground to stop you from speaking to him," she whispered tightly. "I know you are taller and much more muscular than I am. Entirely. But I am stronger than I appear and you are at a disadvantage in terms of balance on that stupid peg. So if you wish for me to make a scene here with you now, go ahead and try to approach him."

The image of her wrestling him on the ground resembled

his greatest fantasy far too closely. He removed his arm from her grasp yet again.

"And don't even consider sending him a challenge either," she warned.

"I was not considering it." Rather, waiting until she departed to do so.

"Men are irrational. What if he chose swords rather than pistols?"

"Then I would tell him the space between his ribs will shortly be home to the tip of a blade." He had to smile.

She fell back onto her heels. "You weren't actually going to call him out, were you?"

He still was. "Wasn't I?"

"I don't know. But—actually—I have a question for you. An unrelated question I have been meaning to ask you."

"Another?"

"Yes. And, no, it is not at all similar to the last question I asked you. Request, that is. So perhaps you could stand down your artillery and turn your attention to more productive matters. Good heavens, men really are belligerent. That is a quality of masculinity that I will never adopt. A battle of wits, to be sure," she conceded with a shrug.

Across the room Mr. Plath was now watching them. His gaze slid downward, along the length of the cane, and his lip curled.

A rush of hot, sharp rage paralyzed Ziyaeddin.

Impotent.

He was impotent—not as Dallis had suggested weeks earlier, but in every manner that mattered, as he had been on ship deck years earlier, as he continued to be in the matter of his sister and people's well-being, and now even as a champion for this intelligent, strong woman who needed no champion but whose champion he wanted to be.

"What do you wish to ask me?" he said.

"What is it?" she said instead. "You look . . . not like . . . *you*."

He hardly knew who *he* was now. Not a prince. Not a complete man. A painter of elbows and nostrils and shoes.

"You are angry," she said. "You are truly angry, aren't you? At this minute. Not as you were angry with me on the street. Why are you—Because of what I said about your balance?"

"No. What is your question?"

"You are unwell now. That is, you are as handsome and elegant as ever. But I can see that something is wrong."

Plath had looked away from them, but Ziyaeddin could not unclench his teeth.

"I am well."

"You cannot lie to me. I am *trained* to notice when something is amiss with a person. We should go home now."

"I would be happy to convey you home. But we, Miss Shaw, are not here at this party together."

She blinked.

Then, as though she were bringing him into focus, from her eyes abruptly shone awareness that he felt in the pit of his belly and hard and deep in his chest.

He wanted to be at a party together with her—to be anywhere with her. He wanted Elizabeth Shaw on his arm. He wanted the world to know that this brilliant, ambitious, outrageously courageous woman belonged *to him*.

"How right you are," she said, a hitch in the words. "Now, master chemist, do tell me your thoughts on the following troubling conun—"

"Libby, how delightful to see you speaking with Mr. Kent." Lady Constance Sterling appeared on her husband's arm. "Good evening, sir."

"My lady." Ziyaeddin bowed.

The gold of her hair was like summer sunlight and her skin peach-touched cream. Her movements were graceful, her form voluptuous. She was a portrait of rounded glory, all of it ornamented in wealth and style. With this woman as her sole childhood companion, it was no wonder that Elizabeth Shaw could not see her own appeal.

He nodded to Constance's husband. Saint Sterling was neither aristocrat nor politician, rather a swordsman by trade. Over two years of lessons, Saint had taught Ziyaeddin how to use his loss to his advantage when fighting.

"I did not know the two of you were acquainted," Constance said.

"We met at Haiknayes once," she replied as blandly as though she were not living in his house now. When necessary, she was a fine actress.

"Of course," Constance said, her gaze shifting slowly between them. "I should have guessed that." Her perusal was too acute.

"If you will excuse me, ladies, Sterling," he said with the languid air of a bored poet he often adopted at parties, an attitude which suggested that although he enjoyed present company, inspiration called and he must heed it. "I must be going."

"You are leaving?" Elizabeth's gaze darted to Plath. "Now?"

"It has been a pleasure." He moved toward the door.

She followed him.

"You must not call him out," she said.

"I do not intend to." *Not tonight.*

"Then why are you hastening away, if not to sneak a challenge to him while I am talking with others?"

"One does not sneak a challenge."

"One might if one were trying to hide the challenge from a woman who does not approve of it."

"Do recall, Miss Shaw, how you told me that Lady Constance brings you to parties with the hopes of you discovering a man whose company you can endure."

"Oh. You and I were conversing for too many minutes just now, and I am following you to the door. You are correct, of course. Constance will begin to investigate."

"She has, it seems, the same inquisitive mind as her sister." It was perfectly foolish that he felt pride in saying this.

"Go, then. But I must have your promise that you will not call out Mr. Plath, tonight or ever."

"If you ask it, *güzel kız*, I will give you my promise."

"That was not a promise. It was a statement of your willingness to make a promise if I asked it, which I did not. I demanded it."

"You are too clever for my transparent wiles," he said.

"I am." Her lips were pinched. Still, they were a temptation. Every bit of her was a temptation.

"I give you my word, Saint George." He bowed.

"Saint George? Oh, of course. When you saw me beneath that statue of Saint George in the library at Haiknayes. But you said I looked like an angel at the feet of triumphant Lucifer."

"You remember."

"I have an extraordinarily good memory."

"Do you also remember that you corrected my catechism?"

"I reminded you that Lucifer in fact lost the battle. Yet you said he won a kingdom of his own in the end," she said thoughtfully now. "*Are* you Christian? Or are you a Muslim?"

"I am neither." No longer. Not since the sea had taken his faith. "Neither Christian nor Muslim, 'neither Jew nor Greek, neither slave nor freeman.'"

"Ha ha. That Bible verse continues 'neither male nor female.' How clever *you* are, sir." Her tone was dry. "And well versed in Christian Scripture."

"When in Rome . . ."

"One does as the Romans, as the saying goes, I suppose." She offered a small smile. She was pleased now and it was everything he wished to give her: pleasure, even such humble pleasure.

But he had not learned his Christian catechism in Rome. Rather, in Egypt.

During those years in exile he had never even remotely imagined this future—a future in which a young woman with lips that drove him mad would be gazing up at him with such delight and so many questions in the Mediterranean blue of her eyes.

"Have you another question for me, oh She Who Triumphs Over Dragons? Or may I finally leave?"

"It is an important question, in fact. But it must wait because now you are being ridiculous."

"What a man most wishes to hear." He could not resist the opportunity to touch her. He took her hand, bowed, and lifted it to his lips. "Good night, Miss Shaw."

She allowed her hand to rest in his.

"Good night, Mr. . . . whoever you are," she finished in an uncertain voice—a voice entirely unsuited to her character. Within the blue eyes was dawn, midday, and dusk at once, a fullness of emotion that made the irises glitter like stars.

Snatching her hand away, she pivoted and disappeared among the guests.

He went home.

And created a masterpiece.

"Did you rise before dawn for your duel?" she said, readjusting her position on the stool. With the crispness of the early December morning, the northern light made the studio seem especially clean and uncluttered. He too seemed particularly sober today, dressed in black trousers and a coat of such dark violet it was nearly ebony.

He did not reply.

"I suppose we will all read of it in the broadsheets tomorrow," she said. "'Mysterious Turk Slays Cad Over Insult to Lady Who Does Not Deserve Defending.'"

He continued working in silence.

"You refuse the bait," she said. "I intended you to reply with something to the effect of 'All ladies deserve defending, even those who dress in breeches.' Obviously you are not the sort of man to make pretty speeches but take no action. Rather you are profoundly gallant, a man who will actually call out another man for a small offense done to a woman, unless of course she makes him promise not to. My compliments."

Another minute passed in which the only sound was of a single bird chattering in the tree beyond the window, not even the usual scratch of his pencil upon paper. Today, for the first time since she had begun sitting for him, he was painting.

"Did you work all night? I saw the light beneath your door before I went up at two o'clock."

More silence.

"You are obviously weary," she said. "You should sit."

"Hush."

"I suspected that if I gave you a direct order you would complain."

"I did not complain," he said. "I instructed."

Earlier, when she entered, she had tried to glimpse the canvas on the easel, but he had not allowed it. He was painting with a rusty brown color.

"If I suddenly jump up and run around the side of the easel to see the painting now, will you stop me?"

"Does 'hush' have a second meaning in English, one which I have not learned, such as, 'continue speaking'?"

"Tired, yet cheerful. Interesting."

"Ask your question," he said, not quite smiling. "The question you warned me of last night."

"After the organ dissections in anatomy lecture, my friend Peter Pincher fell ill. So did several other students who worked on fresh organs, which had not been preserved in solution but had come directly from the hospital. They all suffered horrendous fevers."

"I am sorry that your friend was ill."

"Thank you. As you are a better chemist than I—"

"Not possible."

"Many surgeons are excellent apothecaries. Unfortunately I've never had the knack for pharmacy. In fact it is my least proficiency. Mr. Bridges always approves of the drugs I recommend for the patients at the infirmary, and I prepare excellent caustics. But pharmacy is a different talent altogether. I am still bowled over by the success of the adhesive you made for me. Last night I did not need to apply any powder to my face to cover blemishes or rash. None! That is how fine the adhesive is. I never would have thought of that combination of ingredients. Your natural talent as a chemist is far better than mine."

"Clean your hands."

"Now?" She inspected her hands. His hands were always beautifully manicured, like an aristocrat's. It had inspired her to keep her nails especially short, so that dirt could not hide beneath them, and to wash her hands every morning upon waking. "All right." She stepped down from the stool.

"Not now. After handling flesh. Scrub them thoroughly with soap, as though you seek to remove the skin. Your clothing and hair as well."

"Scrub my hands and hair? And clothing?"

"In the land in which I was born, men of medicine wash often. And they never wear the same tunics from day to day."

"Are they all vastly wealthy to have the laundresses to their houses daily?"

"They believe that illness is easily conveyed through touch."

Touch. The word had new meaning.

He had kissed her hand—his fingers around her palm—his lips on her knuckles—a simple series of touches that now made the word *touch* seem powerful. Magical.

Libby had never believed in magic. A natural philosopher could not; the world was a place of physical truths that were discoverable through investigation and experimentation. But she now understood people's susceptibility to notions of magic, the science of the unexplainable and marvelous.

His lips. Her hand.

Her belly was in knots of pleasure-confusion.

"Clean my hands," she said.

"Bid your friends do the same."

"You have never spoken of your homeland. I understand that you do not wish to tell me its name or location. I must accept that, of course."

"As you accept all else with alacrity," he drawled.

"Would you at least tell me *about* it?"

"It is verdant. There are green hills not unlike the Lothians and spectacular mountains. The sea as well. Great ships in the harbor. Magnificent mosques and churches, a synagogue—"

"Churches and synagogues?"

"Skies of sapphire and diamonds. Horses whose ancestors bore the great khans into battle. And a palace of such beauty and luxury, King George would blush with envy."

He was telling her something. She did not know what it was. Or perhaps she was imagining the hesitation in the strokes of his brush now.

"Tell me more," she said.

"In that land there are men of great learning and women of great beauty—"

A sigh of frustration came from her.

"—and power."

"Power?" she said. "The women are powerful?"

"Beautiful women are always powerful."

"But are there women of great learning there too?"

"Some," he said. "There, as here, they are rarely given their due."

On the other side of the house, the doorbell rang, immediately followed by pounding on the door. A voice came muffled from out on the street.

"Joe Smart!" It was Pincushion.

Here?

The bell rang again, then more pounding.

"Joe! Answer the door!"

Libby met her host's curious regard.

"You are expecting a guest?" he said. "A guest who, it seems, has been imbibing on Sunday morning? Fine men you consort with."

"He is twenty, hardly a man." She slid off the stool. "Since his illness and loss of weight, the spirits go to his head more quickly. You and I both know what havoc that can wreak, of course." She crossed the room. "I must quiet him or he will rouse the neighbors."

"Elizabeth," he said behind her, and her heart thudded against her ribs. He had never before said her given name.

She looked around at him.

"You cannot answer the door." His gaze slid down her skirts, slowly. He had been studying her for three quarters of an hour already. But this perusal was different. It was intimate.

"I will speak with him through the closed door." Her throat was a collection of pebbles. "You should tell me your real name."

He set down the paintbrush and went past her and out of the studio. Going after him, she ducked into the parlor. He opened the front door just as the bell sounded again.

"How do you do, sir? I'm Peter Pincher, a student with Joe." His usually nasal voice sounded oddly deep and formal. "Is he at home?"

"Not at present."

"Blast. That is, pardon me, sir! I've news from Bridges, and there's a ticking clock here."

"Perhaps you would care to write a message?"

"Yes, sir."

Libby ran to the drapery and tucked herself behind it.

"Mighty decent of you, sir. Thank you, sir," Pincushion said as he entered the room.

"There is pen and paper."

Libby heard the tip of the cane cross the floor toward where she hid. He must truly be tired to make such noise. Then, in an instant, she realized he intended the noise to warn her: there was no lamp lit in the room. She dove deeper behind the curtain a moment before he drew it aside to admit daylight.

"Any friend of Joseph's . . ." he said very close to her.

Pincushion wrote the note, said copious thanks, and finally Libby heard the front door close. She went into the foyer and found the missive.

"Thank you for that," she said to her host. "Oh! I should not have liked to miss this, indeed. Mr. Bridges invited a handful of students to attend a surgical dissection course in his private theater. Six of us only. He said it would begin as soon as anatomical subjects could be acquired, and now it shall, tonight."

"At nighttime?"

"I don't know why it should take place at night, but perhaps because Mr. Bridges is too busy during the days. By day there would be better light for our work. *Six* students only. It is thrilling! Each of us will have our hands in every part of the subject."

"Does it not concern you that this is taking place at a location other than Surgeons' Hall?"

"There are many private practical anatomy and surgical schools in Edinburgh. Most of the hosts are hacks, of course, selling dissections for students to supplement their income from pulling teeth and dispensing drugs. But Mr. Bridges is not one of those."

"You mustn't go."

"Of course I must. Mr. Bridges considers me one of the best among the new students. I cannot refuse this invitation. Now, shall I hurry and enter"—she gestured to the studio door—"ahead of you and steal a glimpse of your work in progress?"

He passed her by. "I will accompany you tonight."

"I have lived half my life in this city," she said, appreciating the beautiful breadth of his shoulders and the fall of his coat over his buttocks, and wishing she had had the presence of mind to study that when he had been shirtless. "I am not afraid to be out and about at nighttime, especially dressed as a man."

"Nevertheless, I will accompany you."

"I appreciate your concern, but—" Her words choked

up. In the bright morning light, she saw herself on the easel.

This. He had been working on *this* late into the night, after their conversation at the party.

She.

As Joseph Smart.

He had painted her as a man.

Hair swept back with oil, revealing her entire brow, the youth in the picture sported whiskers soft as feathers, a neck cloth tied neatly and tightly about his collar, a coat that flared at the hips where he perched on a stool, trousers tugging at his thighs, and shoes too big for his ankles. Beneath one arm he clutched a stack of books almost negligently, wearing them as easily as a woman wore a bracelet. A single crease dove from his brow down his nose like a trepanning perforator, and his eyes were brilliant. There was about him an air of both intensity and insouciance, as though even in his confidence he was unsatisfied.

"It is the under painting only," he said beside her. "Color will come when this has dried."

She opened her mouth, but words would not come.

"I will not be swayed," he said. "I will drive with you to the address and wait there with the carriage until you are finished."

"But I don't know for how many hours—"

"There is no use in arguing, Miss Shaw. While I would prefer that you not attend, I cannot make that so by locking you in your room, can I?"

She turned away from the portrait to him. "I would climb out the window and down the wall."

"I have no doubt."

"In pursuit of my desires, I have hidden beneath carriage seats, inside cabinets, and once in a museum after it was locked up for the night. I am tenacious."

"I have noticed that. Now, come. Seat yourself. For another quarter of an hour—"

"I am yours."

"No. You are your own. And I would have it no other way. Now, sit."

She went to the stool and said nothing else for the remainder of the hour.

Chapter 14

The Maiden

$\mathcal{A}$ rchie was waiting for her in the covered alleyway. "Got the fee?"

The five guineas snug in her pocket, Libby nodded and they entered the building.

Dozens of candles lit an octagonal room. Two tiers of benches rose from the floor, empty now. In the center, atop a table and covered with a crisp cloth, the subject waited.

To Mr. Bridges's left stood George, his complexion sickly already, and Pincushion. At the surgeon's right was Maxwell Chedham and two other students, all donning smocks over their coats. On another table surgical instruments gleamed invitingly: knives, lancets, saws, cauteries, trephines, perforators, elevators, probes, lenticulars, scrapers, forceps, catheters, cupping vessels, clamps, hooks, needles, and the like.

"Mr. Chedham," Mr. Bridges said. "Uncover the subject."

Chedham drew back the linen. The subject was of

middling age, his joints and skin revealing decades of labor and poverty. Libby had seen worse with her father. Yet she gaped.

"This man died only hours ago," she exclaimed. Even the cadavers of criminals who perished in prison came to students' dissecting tables older than this. Fresh cadavers were the sole privilege of master surgeons.

"That is for you gentlemen to determine," Mr. Bridges said. "Before sunrise you will entirely dissect the subject system by system, while preserving the organs for further study. Mr. Smart, your incisions are exceptional. You will begin tonight."

Chedham's stare was hard. George was pale and panting. Archie was grinning. Sweat dripped down the gully of Libby's tightly bound breasts.

Putting it all out of her mind she reached for a knife.

She stumbled as she climbed into the carriage. Ziyaeddin grabbed her arm and she collapsed onto the seat across from him, her eyes swimming.

"Did you—" She licked her lips. They were dry, her skin flushed despite the chill of dawn. "Did you wait here *all* night?"

"Yes." He rapped on the ceiling and the carriage jolted forward.

"That was . . . It was *amazing*. We dissected the subject from husk to marrow, the six of us, without any assistance. Mr. Bridges did nothing except instruct."

Reaching into his coat, he drew forth a flask and wrapped her hand around it. She drank deeply. Watching her exhausted eyes imbued with soft ecstasy, and the pink tongue licking wine from the glistening lips, he felt as though he were watching her pleasure herself. He could watch forever the simple act of this woman drinking.

Then she swiped her sleeve across her mouth and a great hiccough ushered forth.

"Thank you! That tasted spectacularly good. The surgical chamber was sweltering."

He folded his arms and tried to settle back against the squabs. "You smell wretched."

"No one asked you to smell me. But in fact I *feel* wretched. Wretched and magnificent. I understand so much more now." Her words slurred a bit. "To be able to study it all, at once, in such depth and detail, and so soon after death—it was revelatory. The subject perished only hours ago! That was the reason for Mr. Bridges's haste in alerting us today. He wished us to have the experience of working with a body that had not yet cooled entirely, which is nearest to working on a living patient. It was extraordinary."

The carriage halted. The street was empty and he descended and offered his hand, but she jumped down onto the pavement without aid.

He paid the drooping coachman and ascended the steps behind her. She was moving more slowly than he had imagined possible. But after two sleepless nights now he would barely be able to keep his eyes open if not for the pain.

"Mrs. Coutts will arrive short—" He turned from locking the door to find her slumped on the footman's chair. Eyes closed and lips lazy, she slept.

"Wake up, Joseph," he said, removing her cap from her damp curls and smoothing his hand around the side of her face. Her hair sliding through his fingers was silk and it filled him with the most insane sort of need. "Mr. Smart." Passing the pad of his thumb over her fuzzy cheek and the clean line of her jaw, he caressed her into waking. By Allah's grace, *she was so soft*. "Elizabeth."

Her eyes cracked open. "Did I fall asleep?"

"You did." He stroked the pale skin of her temple.

"I am extraordinarily tired," she said. "And you are touching me."

"Come now," he said, taking hold of her arm and assisting her to stand.

"I don't know that I can make it up two flights," she muttered, dragging her feet toward the stairway.

"I would carry you up, but we know that is not an option, alas."

"And you haven't slept either, I suspect. But you needn't have worried. It was all aboveboard," she said, climbing like oxen dragging a plow through mud. "Also, you should not carry me anywhere, even if you could, for we are not *that* sort of housemates, are we? I am Joseph Smart," she mumbled, "exceptional incisor and future surgeon." She disappeared into her bedchamber.

He went into the kitchen, put the largest pot on the stove, lit the fire, and began pumping water, never more seriously considering hiring round-the-clock servants than now, yet never more certain that he could not—not while Joseph Smart lived in his house.

When his housekeeper arrived he sent her up with the first buckets of hot water. Then he pumped two more pots full, put them to heat, and retired to his quarters. Not, however, to sleep.

He did not know Lewiston Bridges. If she would be spending entire nights in the surgeon's operating theater, he must assure himself of the man's character.

She did not want a champion, but he would serve her in that manner if necessary. Dipping quill into ink, he began writing letters.

LIBBY COULD HARDLY see around the beleaguered blood vessels in her eyes. Her neck and shoulders ached from bending over the dissecting table for hours. Her feet were swollen from standing through the night. And her coat smelled like a butcher's shop.

But she was happy.

Yet neither pleasure nor excitement could keep her eyes open. An hour of exhausted dozing while Mrs. Coutts was dumping pots of water over one's head did not equal a restful night's sleep. It occurred to her that Mr. Bridges had scheduled his nighttime dissection intentionally, to prove his students' abilities to withstand lack of sleep. She had been with her father in enough midnight sickrooms to know late nights were common for medical men.

At the infirmary, trailing Mr. Bridges beside Chedham— who looked horrible too—she wrote copious notes, said as little as possible, and marveled at her mentor's vigor. He had practiced surgery on battlefields in Spain and Belgium. Now in the big operating theater at the top of the Royal Infirmary he operated on patients and made them well again. Each time she sat on the riser watching him perform surgery, or stood beside him at the table, she felt even more certain that this was her destiny.

While she admired Charles Bell's scientific and surgical brilliance, she had no desire to lecture or write books in addition to caring for patients. She wanted only to practice as Mr. Bridges did. Mr. Bell had matched her to the ideal mentor, after knowing her only a few days.

Perhaps *he* had advised Mr. Bell: her housemate who seemed to understand her so well yet remained so adamantly distant—except when he had caressed her face, as though he had not even noticed he was doing so.

She wanted more of his hand on her face, more of his voice softly speaking her name.

By the time she emerged from the infirmary, she was ready to drop. Walking down the alley in which she usually sat on the wall and ate lunch, she saw Coira with two other women on the brothel's stoop.

"Good day," she said, giving Coira the pail. "I'm off to sleep till lecture, so you must eat the entire lunch today."

"Lad, you've a heart as big as the sky." Coira drew one of the others forward. "Joe, this be Bethany."

"I am pleased to meet you, Bethany."

"Sir," Bethany mumbled and looked at the ground, submissive like a pup.

Libby was becoming accustomed to this. As a man she was very young and small. Yet since she had been Joseph Smart, women who would have looked Elizabeth Shaw straight in the eye now deferred to her.

"This be Dallis," Coira said with a dismissive gesture.

Lounging against the railing, Dallis was slender like Coira, with eyes shaded by long lashes and the lushest lips Libby had ever seen. With a cat's smile on those lips, she winked.

"Bethany here's in the motherly way." Coira set her palm over her friend's flat abdomen. "For the sake o' the wee one she's gone off the bottle."

"An excellent decision, Bethany. I commend you."

"Now she's feelin' poorly," Coira said.

"How so, Bethany?"

"I've the shakes, sir," Bethany said like a mouse. "An' my belly's all twisted up."

"The headache too," Coira added.

"Your stomach upset could be a combination of the pregnancy itself with the sudden cessation of drink," Libby said. "The shaking and headache are probably signs of your body craving spirits."

"Aye, sir," Bethany mumbled. She looked *guilty*.

Suspicion tingled in Libby.

"Haven't you an older woman, a mother, or a procurer perhaps, who can give you counsel about this?"

"Aye, Joe," Coira said, her brow low.

"Oh. Then what you wish from me is not counsel but laudanum to calm the tremors and soothe the head. Am I correct?"

Bethany nodded.

"I am sorry, but I cannot provide you with laudanum."

"O' course you canna." Dallis's feline eyes narrowed.

At her father's side, Libby had seen people who had grown too accustomed to laudanum, and it was far from pretty. For this reason her father dispensed it rarely.

"For your stomach, Bethany, chew fresh ginger. I also recommend a tea made of *Hypericum perforatum*. Drink plenty of fresh water. Licorice root tea would be soothing too. I can supply you with those. You must also take sufficient sleep, especially when your meridian clock expects it."

"Her what?"

"The body's natural internal timetable. In ancient times—Oh, never mind. Just be certain to sleep through the night, Bethany."

Bethany dropped her gaze. Coira lifted her brows. Dallis chuckled with derision.

Heat rose into Libby's cheeks.

Forget that you are a maiden and instead be only a surgeon.

"Sleep at night as you are able," she amended. "I will bring the herbs tomorrow."

She did not now have time to rest but went straight to lecture. She gave only half an ear to Dr. Jones's discourse on malformations of the spine, which she could already recite from memory, and instead drafted a letter to the Duchess of Loch Irvine. Amarantha had once served at a hospital for paupers, and her teacher had been a woman. She would have ideas for natural remedies that were safe for Bethany and the baby, and which Libby would trust more than anything the apothecary in Leith could recommend.

She penned a note to Alice too. Given Alice's past, she must know of effective remedies for the discomforts of pregnancy that would be shared among sisters of the trade. Perhaps she even knew some local midwives with whom Libby could consult.

Her father had never asked her counsel on uniquely feminine matters, despite his many female patients. Nor to her knowledge had he ever consulted with a female midwife. Not once.

She folded the letters to Amarantha and Alice and tuned her ears again to Dr. Jones's lecture.

WHEN SHE ARRIVED in his studio on Sunday as the clock in the parlor chimed ten, he saw her for the first time since dawn the previous Monday. In the intervening days he had told himself it was for the best, but he suspected he had gone a little mad. The temptation of seeking her out had been such that he had taken on another commission, which would require him to spend every day for weeks at the client's home. The result was two portraits to be completed in insufficient time.

Now he turned her away.

This *was* for the best.

"But—"

"I've said I haven't the time," he repeated, and finally allowed himself to look to her. She wore the same plain gown she always wore for sittings. And whiskers.

Her eyes were full of mirth.

"Charming," he said.

She came toward him. "If you aim to depict me as Joseph Smart, then I aim to assist you in that. It is the least I can do to thank you for your care last Sunday night after surgical school."

He made himself return his attention to the canvas beneath his brush upon which, unfortunately, neither Joseph Smart nor Elizabeth Shaw sat.

"That is not necessary," he said, feeling her presence so close as one feels rain: on every surface of his skin and in every breath drawn into his lungs.

"I like that," she said.

"What do you like?"

"When you pretend not to smile."

"Away with you now," he said, "and think not to darken this door until next Sunday."

Without further comment, she went.

Hours later, the bell rang. He ignored it.

Shortly, his boarder appeared before him, this time without whiskers, sweeping into the peace of his studio with the force of a cyclone and coming directly to him, followed closely by the pig.

"This is not what I meant by not darkening the door," he said.

"Mr. Bridges has sent a message," she said, the missive still clasped in her hand. "He has secured another cadaver. There is to be a dissection tonight."

She had the most expressive hands, strong and lithe and capable. He could spend months painting even one and be content—if only he could do so without constantly imagining it on him. The place on his chest where she had touched him still felt hot.

"Why are you looking at the note when I have just told you what it says?"

He dragged his attention to her face, but it did not ease the thick pressure beneath his ribs or in his trousers. "At the same location?"

"Yes. Will you insist on going again?"

"Haven't you come to inform me in order so that I will?"

"I suppose I have." She turned her eyes to the canvas.

"That is Mr. Easterly. He is a friend of my father. I know his family well. His younger sons are beasts. They used to chase me around the drawing room and pull my hair. Ha ha! They would not be able to now. I should have cut my hair long ago. There are pencil marks there." She pointed. "How interesting. You have drawn on the canvas before painting it. Do you always do so?"

"I do." Then he added, unwisely, "Since the day I drew you at Haiknayes."

"You had never drawn on a canvas before that day?"

"I had never drawn a portrait before that day." He should not have said it.

Eyes rounding, she stared at him as no other woman ever did, as though she saw his bones and blood rather than all the outer aspects of him.

"What had you drawn before?" she said. "Or painted?"

"The human form."

Her brow wrinkled.

"The body," he said.

"The body? The body without the head?"

"Without clear facial features."

"I see."

"'I see,' only? I know not whether to be alarmed at this unusual brevity or intrigued."

"You needn't be either. Because I just lied. I don't actually see. Why did you begin including clear facial features after you drew me? Rather, perhaps it is more apt to ask why you did not include them before that?"

"I've no idea," he said, which was only a minor mistruth.

"It cannot be because you found me beautiful. For you met Amarantha at the same moment you met me and she is pretty while I am not." Abruptly her lips tightened together.

"What is it?"

"I should very much like to kiss you," she said.

The shock of heat that passed through him went directly to his groin. He returned his attention to the canvas and lifted the brush.

"Begone now," he said.

"You needn't be alarmed," she said. "I do not intend to throw myself at you. It is only that I have been wondering what it would be like."

She and he both. Although *wondering* did not suffice. *Fantasizing* suited.

"I thought perhaps you might be wondering it too. Given our proximity and that moment here the night I was intoxicated, it is reasonable for me to wonder. It might be for you too. Much more normal than anything else about this situation."

"There is nothing normal whatsoever about you. You are entirely unique."

"That has always been my problem, to be sure. But I—"

"No more confessions today," he said with credible calm, allowing himself to stare only down, at the hem of her gown, which was certainly a kind of pathetic desperation. "At what hour tonight shall I call for the coach?"

"Half past seven. You do not—"

"I do. I will. Now, go."

She went, pausing as she so often did in the doorway.

"It isn't that I go about telling all sorts of men that I wish to kiss them."

"For the sake of Joseph Smart's reputation, I am relieved to hear it. Now, if you do not leave me at this time, there will be consequences to pay."

She went, closing the door behind her, which was unusual for her.

Setting down the brush he ran his hands over his face.

This was a good thing, this abnormal situation. Good

for both of them. He had what he wished from it. And she did as well.

Soon it must be over anyway. The ambassador from Iran to Britain had shared a confidence with the foreign secretary in London, and Canning had written of it to Ziyaeddin: Iran would not long endure Russia's claim on its northern territories. War was coming. Whether the shah attacked northward first, or the tsar southward, either way Ziyaeddin could not remain impotently here while Tabir was caught in the middle of it.

Soon he would be gone from this place, and this temptation would be at an end.

Chapter 15

All the Secrets

The same six students were present in the private surgery, the candlelit room hot already. In preparation tonight Libby had not donned drawers. But she had not considered the discomfort of damp gabardine between her legs without the layer of linen between.

That the sensation of moisture on her inner thighs abruptly made her think of her host's hands on her face sent a little frisson of pleasure through her.

"Since Mr. Smart did such excellent work opening the chest cavity before," Mr. Bridges said, "he will begin again tonight. Mr. Armstrong, uncover the subject."

Archie grasped the linen and pulled it away.

"Initial observations, gentlemen?" the surgeon said.

"Female," Chedham said. "Seventeen or eighteen."

"No calluses on hands and feet," Archie said. "Skin intact, save mild scarring here and there from minor wounds."

"Still in rigor mortis," Pincushion said.

Libby's lungs had clogged. The subject on the table was Coira's friend Bethany.

"How—" She swallowed back nausea. "When did she die?"

"Mr. Chedham, you may assess the subject," the surgeon said.

Libby closed her eyes. She could not watch.

"I estimate three hours ago," Chedham said.

Opening her eyes Libby stared at Bethany's abdomen— at *the subject's* abdomen. Her head whirled.

"Mr. Smart?"

Her name came to her as though through a tunnel.

"Mr. Smart, are you with us?"

"Yes, Doctor," she forced through her lips.

"Make the incision."

She reached for the knife. But air would not fill her lungs and sweat trickled down the sides of her face.

"I believe I am ill, sir," she said.

"Taking a cue from Allan?" Chedham mumbled.

"That is enough, Mr. Chedham," Mr. Bridges said. "Mr. Smart, make the incision."

"I beg your pardon, sir." Her fingers were slippery about the knife handle. "I beg your pardon." She dropped the instrument. Pivoting, she pushed her way out of the room and ran to the door.

"Joe." Archie came behind her. "What in the—"

"I'll be all right. Go back in or Bridges will be displeased."

Libby fell out onto the street gasping and willing her thoughts to cease spinning. At the far end of the alleyway, the door to the carriage opened. She stumbled toward it.

He asked no questions, only instructed the coachman to go and closed the door.

The moon was dark and the night complete, lamps only illumining the carriage as it bumped along.

"I have never been so ashamed," she whispered.

"Were you ill?"

"No." This sickness was far deeper than nausea. She pressed her cold palms to her cheeks. Her face was clammy too.

When he removed his overcoat and offered it to her, she pulled it up to her chin.

"I knew her," she said. "The subject. I made her acquaintance only days ago. Her name was Bethany. She asked me for help. She was feeling unwell. She was . . . with child."

The rumbling of carriage wheels over cobbles filled the silence.

"It is common for poor folk to sell their deceased family members' bodies to surgical schools. But this has never happened to me before. I don't know what overcame me. Mr. Bridges will now think me a light-headed fool. An incompetent. He will eject me from his surgery. He might even refuse to keep me as his apprentice. Chedham has no trouble with this."

"Did Mr. Chedham know the woman too?"

"No. I don't know." She dropped her face into her palms. "What *happened* to me? I have seen the worst of illnesses at my father's side. I have treated patients with horrible diseases and injuries. I don't know what came over me. I failed. I am weak," she whispered.

"You are human."

"I cannot be human in that manner. If I cannot work on a subject I happen to have met before, how will I ever succeed at this?"

"You are not your father studying the dead to solve crimes. You are a healer of living people. That is your calling. That this happened tonight does not mean you are a failure. It means that you are a person of compassion."

"You don't know that about me! You hardly know me at all."

"I have known that since the day you offered a costly bottle of oil to an urchin, forgetting all in that moment except the need to heal."

The carriage halted. She went inside and directly to her bedchamber. Trailing her fingertips over the painting where the boys ran through the market, and feeling the immediate relief this ritual of touching the picture brought to her, she tore off her cap and cravat. Then she removed the whiskers and undressed. Staring at the discarded trappings of her masculinity, she felt trembling overtake her, and her thoughts spun.

She should return to the surgery and apologize to Mr. Bridges. She must wipe the smirk off Chedham's face. And what if they made mistakes tonight in her absence? What if they treated the body without care, without respect, coldly?

No. Mr. Bridges had taught them to always respect a subject. Still, she should have remained. She should have told him the truth. Now he would forever doubt her fortitude. And her notes would be incomplete.

She had failed Joseph Smart tonight.

But she had not failed Bethany. Not the living Bethany. Coira had said that since Bethany had begun drinking the mild tea and chewing ginger she seemed improved.

Tomorrow she would quiz Archie on the cause of Bethany's death. She would visit Coira. She would learn how a young woman in good health had suddenly perished. She would redeem herself for Bethany's sake and for her own.

"I WILL MAKE a prosthetic foot for you."

They were the first words she had spoken to him since

Sunday night in the carriage. Now as she entered the kitchen, the pig trailing after her, she seemed the same indomitable woman as ever.

She wore a plain blue gown that fit snugly to her arms, breasts, and waist, flaring out over her hips to create an exquisite silhouette.

"Why are you looking at my waist?" she said.

"That's new," was all he could manage.

"Oh. Another gown from Constance. Alice says Constance will notice if it hasn't been worn. But how unusual it is to live with a man who notices my gowns. Though naturally I understand the reason for that."

He doubted it.

"You must be working on glum Mr. Cook's portrait. You've black paint on your jaw."

"What do you want?" He returned his attention to the cup as he poured.

"Aren't we friendly today? Sleep poorly, did you? Actually, I know you did. I heard you wake up shouting in the wee hours. You frightened me to death."

"You seem alive enough now." He set down the teapot and took up saucer and cup.

"I have heard you shout in your sleep before, when I am studying late, which is why I know this is chronic pain and will now insist that you accept remedies for it, including a real prosthesis, one that includes hinges around the knee and ankle and other provisions which allow the substitute foot to mimic the movement of an actual foot."

"Leave me be." Setting his cane aside, he sat down at the table fashioned of a great slab of old gnarled wood. Assured of her absence, he had stayed home today to put the final glaze on a commission. She should not have returned for hours yet.

She grabbed a tin of biscuits and settled lightly on the chair across from him. Most often she barely sat, alighting even on the stool in his studio for an entire hour like a bird prepared to dart into flight again.

"I don't know if you have noticed," she said, "but your temper is poor today. Probably from lack of deep sleep. The body heals itself during sleep. I know that, by the way, from my father's wisdom and also from books."

"Aha." The teacup in his palm was warm. But not as warm as her skin had been when he had unwisely allowed himself to touch her. "Which books?"

"I have been reading about medicine of the East. And history. Turkish and Persian, especially."

"Have you?" he said blandly, because clearly she wanted him to show surprise.

"Yes. Did you know that Galen—he is the physician whose influence on Western medicine was greater than all other physicians combined for centuries—he was born in Pergamon. At the time it was part of Greece, but it had also been within the Persian Empire. It is now in Turkey. Although of course the Greek Paulus Aegineta was at least as celebrated as a surgeon, and hugely influential too. Anyway, I'm learning quite a lot. Paulus Aegineta, by the way, was eclipsed only by Albucacis. That is, his full name was Abū al-Qāsim Khalaf ibn al-'Abbās al-Zahrāwī. I don't know if I am pronouncing that correctly."

"Mostly."

"So you *do* know Arabic."

"I do."

"Interesting. Anyway, al-Zahrāwī is commonly known in European and British texts as Albucasis. He was a tenth-century Muslim physician from al-Andalus, the land that is now southern Spain. He is widely considered the father of modern surgery. Among his many advancements in medical science and treatment, he invented hundreds of surgical tools that we use now. He also emphasized the importance of a positive relationship between physician and patient. He wrote about all sorts of other matters too—compounding drugs, pills, ointments, plasters, and the like, and anatomy of course. My interest naturally tends toward his writings on surgery."

"You are peering at me meaningfully."

"I am."

"Yet the particular meaning of it escapes me."

"Ask me why I am Miss Shaw this afternoon when it is Wednesday and I should be at lecture," she said, taking a biscuit between two agile fingers and biting it as she did nearly everything, with energetic delight. And as with nearly everything she did, watching this got him hard.

"Why are you Miss Shaw today when it is Wednesday and you should be at lecture?" For pity's sake, he even sounded aroused.

"Dr. Jones has a wretched cold and has given us all a sudden holiday. I took the opportunity to call on a young surgeon who knows my father, James Syme. He is already famed on account of the hugely successful hip amputation he performed not three years ago. He is exceptionally clever with prostheses. Unfortunately I spoke with him at length about that mere months ago, when he and his wife invited Papa and me to dinner. I wish I could consult him as Joseph Smart, but I fear he will notice Joseph's particular interest in that same subject and recognize me. So I called on him today as Elizabeth Shaw and was again impressed with how seriously he considered my questions. I believe I could easily continue to consult with him and he would welcome it. I have decided to make it my candidacy project for the diploma, you see."

"What it?" he said warily. "Me?"

Her eyes glittered. "Of course not. Only the new addition

to you. I do not know why you content yourself with that wholly inadequate support when there are modern and wonderfully functional prostheses you could adopt instead. Whatever the reason for your stubbornness, however, I shan't let you continue in it."

"This is not amusing."

"I don't mean for it to be amusing. I mean to help you and also to send my teachers into raptures." She chewed on the biscuit, smiling a bit.

Apparently the experience of Sunday's dissection had not cowed her.

Of course it hadn't.

"You seem confident of success," he said.

"In creating for you the perfect prosthesis? Indeed I am. I am meticulous, which is ideal when working with mechanics."

"Success in your program of study," he clarified.

"If no one discovers that I am a woman," she said around a mouthful of biscuit. Abruptly she ceased chewing, the biscuit poised in midair between her fingertips. "Thank you for your words the other night. You were, of course, correct."

"Of course?" Leisurely, he crossed his arms. "This is a refreshing change."

She smiled and snapped the biscuit in half. "You will not quarrel with me about my project?"

"I will not quarrel. I will simply refuse."

"You mayn't refuse."

"Your humor today is especially high."

"There is reason for that." Dropping the pieces, she leaned forward onto her elbows. "I have news that is both a great relief and very curious."

Her posture leaning into the table pushed her breasts upward, making a cleft between them, and visible above the modest white tissue tucked into the gown there. She must think him a eunuch to display that so readily. He imagined freeing her breasts from the gown and caressing them—her—all of her, her beautiful breasts and her soft lips and *all of her*.

"Curious?" he managed, albeit huskily.

"I told Mr. Bridges that I had eaten bad oysters and he accepted that explanation."

Aha. The dissection. "That is good news."

"The news I've learned of Bethany is even better. She perished of heart failure. The arteries feeding the heart were normal. The bottom half of the left ventricle however was ballooned out and much larger than it should be. That could have caused cardiac arrest even in such a young woman. But there is some consolation, for she was *not* with child after all."

The soft smile that lit her eyes choked him momentarily. He untangled his tongue.

"You asked the other students?"

She waved her hand in that gesture that revealed every sinew and curve of her fingers and the taut strength of her palm, all of which he wanted on him.

"Archie and Pincushion are certain. I told neither of them that I recognized her, of course," she said. "No one knows. Except you. But you know all my secrets."

He wished he did not. He wished he could return to the day he had seen her at the public dissection, and instead have remained home that day. Then there would not be this desire for everything about her, breasts and lips and intelligent eyes and expressive hands and voice that tied him in knots inside.

"Do you believe she lied to you?" he said.

"No. I think she actually believed herself increasing. Her menses must have been delayed. That, added to chronic nausea from another cause, might make a young woman of her profession believe she was with child."

"Her profession?"

"Prostitution." She looked squarely at him. "Do you see the knot in this wood beneath my fingertip?"

He had been trying not to stare at that fingertip circling that knot—trying not to imagine it circling any and all parts of his skin. That, and the knot was not far from her breasts pressing against the table's edge.

"Yes." The syllable was hoarse.

"Do you see how it twists back on itself?"

"I do."

"That is what happens to your muscles each time you force the hip and back to do the work of the knee and foot. That is why you must allow me to build a prosthesis for you."

"For pity's sake—"

"All right! I shan't ask again. I will simply do it."

"You have no understanding of the word *no*, do you?"

"If I allowed *no* to halt me from doing what I know to be right, I would not be here now, would I?"

He caught his smile halfway.

"Do you wonder how I am acquainted with prostitutes?" she said.

"No. For I believe, Elizabeth Shaw, that your heart is sufficiently wide to fit within it all the people of the world."

Her cheeks flared with pink. It was beautiful. And disastrous. This show of mild embarrassment was tightening his cock unbearably. But he could breathe again. Honesty with her felt extraordinary.

"You should not compliment me," she said.

He allowed his smile now. "Why not?"

Abruptly she pushed back her chair and stood. "Because it makes me want to kiss you even more than I wanted it before. And do other things I have been thinking about too."

Other things?

"Allah, be merciful," he mumbled. "You have got to leave this kitchen. This moment."

"Of course I will." She sounded angry. "But I won't stop thinking about it."

"Yet you must." *Hypocrite.* He was a hypocrite through and through.

"I cannot," she declared. "I never stop thinking about *anything.* My mind does not *allow* it. When a thought occurs, an idea, my mind will not release it until it has come to a satisfying conclusion. But since you will not allow me to kiss you there can be no satisfying conclusion to my curiosity about it. So perhaps you could cease saying things that make those particular thoughts especially difficult to ignore, those comments about my appearance or character that no one else I have ever known has given me."

He couldn't believe it. "No one?"

"No. So you must cease saying compliments. And you must cease looking at me like that—like—" She shook her head. "Or you could simply let me kiss you and I could move past the preoccupation."

"Your remarkable mind notwithstanding," he said with as much control as he could muster, but her cheeks were full of color, her lips parted, and he wanted her in his hands, in his mouth, beneath him. "I cannot allow you to satisfy that curiosity, however much I would enjoy it."

Her lips fell open and her beautiful breasts rose on a tight inhalation. "*Enjoy* it?"

"I cannot. You cannot."

"Why not? It isn't as though I am a wilting maiden of the usual sort. I dress as a *man* every day and go about entirely with men."

"Because whether you wish to acknowledge it or not, at present you are dependent upon me, and a man who takes advantage of a woman in those circumstances is a knave. But far more importantly, you have a project to accomplish, a project that requires all of your attention. You haven't even a moment of time to devote to satisfying idle curiosities."

Astonishment shone in the Mediterranean blue.

"Do not think to argue with me," he said. "The moment you moved into this house you made yourself dependent upon me."

"I realize that."

"Yet my words surprise you."

"Not those words. What if the curiosities are not *idle*?"

He stood up. "Go. At once."

With a flip of her skirts she left. It was a small miracle, and a temporary reprieve only. She would return. He had no illusion that she would relent and no faith that he could resist her indefinitely.

Chapter 16

Desire

*L*ibby did not wish to hear again the heat of anger in his voice or feel the confusion that suffused her when he studied her with his inconveniently beautiful eyes. So on Friday morning when she discovered the little jar of adhesive empty, she waited to refill it from the large bottle in his workroom until he was not at home.

He had gone out each evening since she had confessed the truth about her thoughts, to avoid her no doubt.

Following her father from the homes of noble patient to noble patient, Libby had lived as an unwanted guest in enough aristocrats' houses—often hiding out in cabinets and stairwells—that she had glimpsed her share of gentlemen disporting themselves with servants. Her host's stance on the matter of female dependents living in his house made him either the most unusual man in Britain or the most honorable.

Perhaps from where he came, mores were stricter. Perhaps there, gentlemen did not prey upon women as they did in Britain.

Lamp in hand, she knocked on the door of his quarters. When no answer came, she entered.

The city at night shone through the studio windows: a light through parted draperies in the building across the mews, a lamppost, and a silvery moon embraced in stars.

She stared at his bedchamber door for the count of twenty before ducking beneath the bar and pushing the panel wide.

Adorned in subdued hues, the chamber boasted only a four-poster bed hung with midnight blue draperies, a clothespress, and an upright mirror. On the floor was a rug similar to others in the house, of Eastern design and rich, dark colors. The space suited his understated elegance, and it was redolent of his scent of cloves and paint and something else she could not define but was probably simply him—his unique essence.

Leaving the bedchamber, she crossed the studio to the easel upon which sat a portrait of a society hostess whom Libby had once met in Constance's company. Mrs. Lily Jackson was young and lushly gowned. The background by her head seemed unfinished: the brushstrokes rough and visible, so that the subject appeared to be dragging herself out of vexed shadow, leaning from the frame as though reaching out in supplication for help.

The artist had signed the piece; it was in fact finished.

Rumor had it that Lily Jackson's husband beat his servants with a carriage whip. And Libby had noticed that Mrs. Jackson wore thick powder, perhaps to cover abrasions. This portrait showed the truth of the woman. It was daring and extraordinary. Studying the colors and textures of the work, she felt the artist in it: his grace, his kindness and beauty, his darkness, and his acute understanding of human nature. Just as he understood her, he understood this woman and the others that he drew and painted, as though he could see into their souls.

Leaving the painting, she went into the workroom. Narrow and well lit by moonlight, it smelled of the oils used in painting and, faintly, of chemicals. On one side was a high table upon which sat bottles and jars filled with oils and colors, a terracotta jar bursting with paintbrushes, and another with the tools to make brushes: coarse hair, cotton string, wooden handles, metal ferrules, knives, and a tiny brass case. A burner and several glass flasks and pipettes populated the end of the table near the window.

Canvases stretched over wooden frames were stacked on the floor against the wall. All but one had been painted on. Setting down the lamp, Libby pulled the blank canvas away from the stack.

A nude woman gazed back at her.

Stretched out on a divan, the woman was gloriously relaxed, one arm draped on the back of the furniture and the fingertips of the other brushing the floor, her head lolling to the side and thighs resting gently together. There was no artifice to either pose or paint, only honesty and beauty. This picture was an adoration of the human body.

By the roundness of her limbs and the jewels on her fingers, Libby assumed the model was an aristocrat. That a woman of wealth would sit in the nude for a male painter was surely unusual. Libby knew that men of means often kept hired women for sex. Perhaps this model was his mistress. Perhaps in the evenings he went out to meet her.

How foolish he must think her naïve requests for kisses, he who had traveled across the world.

She drew another of the canvases forward and found another nude. This one was also bejeweled and softly round. But this time Libby recognized her. This woman was married.

She heard him enter the studio with enough time to glimpse another canvas, another nude, another married woman.

"Aha," he said, coming close enough to look over her shoulder. "Obviously I was wrong when I saw the light here and assumed the pig had learned to carry a lamp," he said dryly. "For Mrs. Coutts and Mr. Gibbs are not here, and I am quite certain I have forbidden you from entering my private quarters."

"I am smarter than a pig, and I have opposable thumbs, thus the ease with which I carry a lamp. I came for more adhesive. I know this woman, even though she is mostly looking away. I recognize those moles on her neck."

"Of course you do." On the cool air that yet clung to his coat lingered the scent of spirits.

"She is Lady Ainsley," she said. "Once at a ball at the Assembly Rooms I was so uncomfortable that I distracted myself by studying everybody's skin. Their gaits and postures too, of course." She gestured to the painting. "She looks as bored here as she did that night."

He chuckled.

But she had said it only to be contrary. The night of that ball Lady Ainsley had adopted an air of grand ennui. In this painting, instead, she glowed with sensuality.

"She sat for you in the nude? All three of these women did? Their husbands allowed it?"

"To my knowledge, their husbands did not know of it."

"Were they—*are* they your lovers?" She looked over her shoulder at him. "And don't you dare be angry with me for asking that. Not this time."

"They were not. They are not. They simply wished their portraits painted."

"Yet these paintings are here. I assume the women feared to claim them, but also did not wish them sold."

"Yes."

"Why did they come to you?"

"You must ask them that."

"I cannot, of course." She looked down again at the portrait. "It is unusual that they wished nude portraits, that they were not ashamed to be naked before you."

"Does a lady feel shame for undressing before her servant? Does an empress not step out of her bath before her slave?" His voice was without passion. There was no judgment in it, nor feeling of any sort. That flatness alarmed her.

"You are not a servant. You are a gentleman. No doubt they simply understood you as an artist, as eccentric and such."

"Perhaps."

"It angers you that they were willing to sit for you in this manner. Doesn't it?"

There was a moment's pause before he said, "Not any longer."

She allowed her fingertips to trace the edge of the painting.

"I will not ask you why you painted them anyway, despite anger. For it is evident in each brushstroke. It is the same reason that I study medicine. I am enamored of the human body. I am driven to repair it just as you are driven to depict it."

"You are not driven to repair. You are called to heal."

She felt him so intensely behind her. Her body stirred with heat. Yet there was something new too, which she had not felt with him before. He considered himself her protector. He wished to keep her safe, yet so differently from the manner in which her friends and father always had. They always wanted to protect her from the morass of her own thoughts and desires. He wished to protect her *for* herself, so that she could pursue her dreams.

He reached forward and laid his fingertips beside hers on the painting's frame.

"This is how I wished to paint you," he said.

She turned her head. Every shadow on his face, every gleam of light in his hair seemed precious now, too ephemeral, as though, were she to move, the night would steal him away.

Desperation surged up in her, a wild need for closeness—for *intimacy* with him.

He dropped his hand from the painting and met her gaze.

She could touch him. She could simply reach up and wrap her hands around his face and feel his heat and beauty and strength, and draw him to her and finally know the caress of his lips on hers. She could satisfy the hunger that only grew stronger the longer she denied it.

"Wished?" she said. "In the past tense?"

Those perfect lips made the slight smile on one side, the smile that carved such longing inside her.

"Wished," he said, "before I knew that you could not sit still long enough for it."

It was not the truth. She saw the truth in his gaze that now dipped to her lips.

She could lift her arms and wrap them around his shoulders and sink her hands into his hair and feel his body against hers. There was so little space between them already, she would hardly have to move to make it so.

Scooting around him, she went out into the studio and strode swiftly toward its exit.

"You have left your lamp," he said behind her.

"*Keep it.* Keep it, of course!" she shouted, and did not pause in her flight.

He wished to protect her. She could not deny him that satisfaction.

THE BELL RANG as his manservant was departing for the day.

"Package for you, sir."

"Thank you, Gibbs." Ziyaeddin accepted it.

"Sir . . . ? The young master . . ." The Scot's brow puckered up. "'Tis a mouse he's become, seems, sir."

Elizabeth Shaw was nothing like a mouse. Rather, a lion. "How do you mean?"

"He's got a corner o' the press stuffed full with torn stockin's. Least eight or ten o' them, all torn, as though he's makin' a wee nest in the drawer! Offered to darn 'em, I did. But he forbade me to touch 'em."

Perhaps she hid a gown or petticoats behind the ruined stockings.

"He'd hear none o' it! He tossed 'em in that travelin' trunk an' locked it up tight. Said I'd ne'er find the key. No' that I'd be lookin' for it, no' if the young master dinna like!"

"Of course you wouldn't," Ziyaeddin said reassuringly.

"For what he'd be wantin' torn old stockin's, sir, I canna be guessin'."

"No doubt he has a use for them." Mrs. Coutts had said that his houseguest had bought large shoes and stuffed them with wadding, to appear more manly.

"Aye, p'raps, sir. But I didna wish you to believe I've no' been doin' for the young master as I do for you."

"I trust you, Gibbs."

"Thank you, sir." The Scot nodded. "Good Sunday on the morrow to you."

"And to you." He closed the door on the chilly afternoon. *Good Sunday.*

Unlikely. Not while she lived in his house, confounding his manservant, winning over his housekeeper, and making him ache with even the quickest glance.

Hours spent away from this house were not proving sufficient to undo what happened to him each time she came close.

He should cancel the sittings. Better yet, he should send her back to her friend's house in Leith. Or he could write to Alice Campbell and entreat her to hire a house in Edinburgh and take on a young medical student as a boarder. Why hadn't the woman done that already?

Because she wasn't mad.

The package from the stationer's shop bore the name Joseph Smart. Gibbs could not read. But he cut hair extraordinarily well, shaved a man with a steady hand, and kept everybody's clothing free of paint stains on the one hand and blood on the other. And he was blessedly obtuse enough not to realize that the young master was a woman.

Ziyaeddin carried the package for her into the parlor. The stacks of books on tables had become towers and the writing desk entirely covered with piled papers. A page on top seemed to be a list of tasks to accomplish.

> ~~*Syme botany lecture notes*~~
> ~~*Fine grain files*~~
> ~~*Solution to Mrs. Bailey's scar tissue*~~
> ~~*Write out chemistry results*~~
> *Steel knee joint (Potts)*
> *Dorsiflexion and planter flexion*
> *Memorize Bell, Dissertation on Gunshot Wounds*
> *Monro secundus, Observations on the Structure*
>   *and Functions of the Nervous System*
> *Archie: how many sisters?*
> *Purchase 12 notebooks*

The list continued nearly to the bottom of the page, the penmanship neat, with close-set letters, the strikethrough lines equally tidy. Her mind was a cyclone of thoughts, ideas, questions, curiosities, and desires. Seeing this, her method for ordering that cyclone, brought heat into his throat. She was more extraordinary than any man would ever know. Any man but he.

Returning to the foyer he perused the post. It included an invitation from the Duchess of Loch Irvine to spend the Christian holidays at Haiknayes Castle. He would not accept. He would not leave Elizabeth. Wherever she was, he now understood, there he must be as well until his destiny took him away from her.

Another letter was addressed to him in a loose, confident hand. He read as he walked toward his studio.

Your Highness,

Intrigued by your wish for confidence, and conveniently on furlough (Titan is in dry dock receiving an iron hull), I have investigated thoroughly. I am delighted to assure you that Lewiston Bridges is above reproach. A man of no little skill, he is admired widely. His naval service of twenty years came to an end after an infection rendered him deaf in one ear and without perfect balance. Since then he has practiced surgery in Edinburgh, where he also teaches surgical students. While he is not known to be a scientific genius (as most regard your friend Charles Bell), Bridges's record is distinguished and his reputation unblemished by public quarrel.

I am curious as to your application to me for information when you live in a city well supplied with medical men. Yet I know that university towns can breed the worst petty gossip, and I would be a rogue not to comprehend your wish for discretion in this, as in all.

Respectfully,
Seamus Boyle, Surgeon, HMS Titan

The pain in Ziyaeddin's right ankle now was an illusion, for there was nothing there to feel pain. In repairing his leg seven years ago, Seamus Boyle had performed a miracle.

Crumpling the letter he walked into his studio.

"You should tell me your name."

She was perched on the stool, the winter light bringing to life her complexion that had lately turned toward pallor. She wore a skirt to her toes and a shawl thoroughly wrapped about her upper body, which she was holding tightly together beneath her chin.

"Obviously it was a mistake to allow you to know that Ibrahim Kent is not my name."

"If it were a mistake you would not have revealed it to me."

He leaned back against the doorjamb. "I have been known to do foolish things before."

"Such as?"

"Such as inviting a tenacious woman to live in my house while posing as a young male medical student. If I wished the world to know my name, I would use it."

"I am not the world."

She was. To him she was.

"There are sixteen hours yet until you are due on that stool," he drawled as though it mattered nothing to him that she was here, voluntarily, when she might be— *should be*—elsewhere. "Has the watch or perhaps your clever clock malfunctioned?"

Her hands loosened and the shawl fell to the floor.

"I decided to do this only this morning," she said. "But I discovered I was far too anxious to wait until tomorrow at ten o'clock. I heard Mr. Gibbs leave. So here I am."

Bare from the waist up, she was pale as the light that illumined her, save for the shadows beneath her breasts and arms and of her navel, and the aureoles that were the same hue as her lips: dark rosy pink. He saw her all at once, swiftly: the lowest ribs that protruded just a bit and gave way to a flat waist; the gooseflesh prickling the fine, silvery-gold hairs on her forearms; the squared bones of her shoulders that allowed young men to mistake her for one of them; the pulse that beat in her throat; and the blue eyes fixed on him.

Intelligent and determined, those eyes dared him to deny her.

"According to the terms of our agreement, which I only fully understood yesterday," she said, "I have come to sit for you."

Chapter 17

The Portrait

*H*e said nothing.

Libby's nipples tingled as they tightened, and heat filled her cheeks.

"Will you claim now that telling me your wish yesterday was also a mistake?" she said.

"I will make no such claim, for that wish remains."

He moved across the room and drew the draperies until they were almost closed. Then at the hearth he built up the fire. "That said," he added, rousing flames from the embers with the poker, "this is not the wisest idea you have had of late. And that is saying something."

"It was not my idea. It was yours."

He turned to her.

"Thank you for the fire," she said before he could reject her.

He bent his head and passed his hand over his face.

"Now that you see me," she said, "have you changed your mind?"

"On the contrary." His chest rose upon a hard breath. Then he walked to the easel.

"You have painted naked women before."

"As you have seen."

"With dispassion?"

"Yes," he replied, turning the page of the sketchbook on the easel and taking up a piece of black chalk.

"Not pencil?" she said.

"Not today." The muscles in his jaw looked like rock.

"What is the difference?"

"Do I ask you the difference between surgical instruments that I have no intention of ever using?" he said shortly.

"No. But this is of course different. I think you are uncomfortable."

"Do you?" Finally his gaze came to her, but not to her face, rather to her shoulder.

"I had hoped that, just as I as a woman of medicine would be able to work dispassionately on you if you allowed it, you as a man of art must be able to draw or paint me without distress."

"Hush now."

"Why are you always bidding me hush?"

His eyes moved over her body with the intensity of a scientist at his microscope, as his hand began to move on the page she could not see.

"Do you dislike my speech so much?" she said. "Is that the trouble? For you would not be the first. In fact you would be among the many."

"The trouble is not that I dislike your speech. The trouble is that I like it too much and would have you speak about whatever you wish, to the exclusion of all else, simply to hear the words and phrases and thoughts formed by your lips. In this manner I would gladly while away each day and subsequently accomplish nothing."

A surge of feeling fanned out beneath her breasts. Her tongue was abruptly useless.

"But," he continued, "I must paint in order to eat, and, not incidentally, to maintain this roof over not only my head but now yours as well, and to pay Mrs. Coutts and Mr. Gibbs for their services, and the butcher, and the candlestick maker. Et cetera. However unfortunate that all is, it is the tragic truth."

"You are not painting now. You are drawing," she said in a raspy whisper.

His gaze slid up to her face and his hand paused.

"I say again." His voice was also rough. "Hush."

She obeyed. But the throb of her pulse would not slow and her nipples were responding to his study without any subtlety or discretion whatsoever. She wondered if the women he had painted nude had felt this too, desire for this man who had made them so beautiful on canvas, Pygmalion and his creations.

"I dream of fire," he said.

"Fire?"

"Aboard ship," he said, his gaze shifting between the page and her body, back and forth again, smoothly, easily, the eyes of the artist at work. "It took the ship swiftly. When rescue arrived, I was barely conscious."

"Yet you remember it."

"I remember the flames as they overcame the deck. It is that of which I dream each night, and which causes me to disturb your sleep."

"You do not disturb my sleep," she said.

He glanced at her face and then again lower, then to the page, then to her body. He was either making a point of appearing unaffected by her nudity, or he truly was unaffected.

"No?" he said.

"I sleep little," she admitted. "I study until the candles and oil are gone."

"Hypocrite." He said it with a smile.

His confessions had burrowed into her belly and rested there now like a sunbeam hidden in a thick forest.

"I must succeed," she said. "I cannot have done all of this yet fail."

He said nothing more and for many minutes she watched him.

He set down the chalk and wiped his hands on a cloth. "Would you like to see it?"

She nodded and bent to take up her shawl from the floor, pulling it snugly across her breasts as he came toward her. She reached for the drawing.

In gray and ebony he had picked out her shape from the plane of ivory, raised it to valleys and peaks, and made it live. Her fingers curled around the page, her other fingertips skimming around the edges of the drawing. The lines of chalk were softer than the paper, like silk.

"Is it to your liking?" he said.

"You have made me appear . . ." Strong. Powerful. Even beautiful. But not in the manner of a man or even a pretty woman. "Elemental."

"I have done nothing but render on paper what I have seen with my eyes." There was color on his cheeks, his satiny hair was tousled over his brow, and he was watching her, it seemed.

She released the page. As it drifted to the floor, she shrugged her shoulder. The shawl slithered down her arm and slid across her breast and then away from it entirely.

"Touch me," she said.

Without hesitation he took a single step, and the toe of her shoe met his.

"You will?" she said, her heartbeats galloping in her ears.

With his knee he urged hers apart, and the shock of taking him between her thighs drew a gasp from her throat. Then he was between her legs, her thighs cradling his hips. She stared at the gold buttons on his coat.

"Do you know how medical texts describe female breasts?" tumbled from her lips. "'Two soft protuberances situated on the thorax in females.' It is accurate of course, but it does nothing to help a person understand the reason for their popularity with men. And it does not even begin to explain their extraordinary sensitivity or the sensations elicited when I think of you and—"

He touched her chin, gently tilting her face upward. His gaze traveled over her features, caressing her lips, cheeks, her chin and brow and eyes as though he would paint her now out of air and fire and heat.

"Will you call yourself a knave now?" she said, her body aching. *Hungry.*

"I will call myself Ziyaeddin Mirza," he said in a voice she did not recognize, rich with the cadence of another tongue and quietly confident. "But only with you, Saint George."

"Thank you," she whispered, "Ziyaeddin."

His throat constricted, the Adam's apple jerking upward. His fingers slipped from her chin to her jaw and then into her hair, so lightly, as though he barely needed to feel her to understand her. Then his palm curved around her face.

All her yearnings and loneliness and fear were now on the surface for his keen eyes to see. The pad of his thumb slid along her eyebrow, curving with the bone, then softly over her cheek and to her lips. Desire swamped her, throbbing between her legs and catching in her throat.

He was so close. Each black lash framing the dark irises seemed a miracle of shape and beauty.

"Elizabeth." Her name was a husky caress. "There can be nothing between us."

She waited for the retraction, the reversal that obviously must come, the *however*. For there already was something between them. He could not deny it.

"I ask you," he said, "do not offer me gifts that I cannot accept."

She nudged her face away from his hand. "Who *are* you?"

His brow knit.

"How can you not expect that question?" she demanded. Dragging the shawl to cover her chest, she swiveled off the stool and walked away from him, ordering her thoughts, so many thoughts.

"You know I am no featherbrain. Nor am I unobservant. You clearly hide here in Scotland. Or perhaps you are trapped here. Your closest friend is a duke, which is not in any way usual, you know. But perhaps you don't realize how unusual that is. Or how unusual it is to be fluent in no fewer than six languages. And you use a false name. So perhaps you are not simply a humble portrait artist who came to Britain to learn to paint in the European style and simply never got around to leaving. Perhaps you are not who you have convinced everybody you are."

"You have thought this through."

"Of course I have. I think *everything* through. And I am living in your house so I know you to be entirely unlike other men. I thought at first that was because you are a foreigner. But I don't believe that anymore. Even so, I cannot imagine any man who would reject what I have just offered you, other than perhaps an avowed celibate—a priest or holy man of some sort—or a man who prefers the intimate company of men. But I don't believe you are those, for the obvious reasons. I do not wish to bind you into any permanent arrangement. I intend to remain a man indefinitely. That of course makes impossible any intimate congress but of the most temporary sort. So I do not understand you."

She halted and faced him.

He said nothing.

"So be it." She squared her shoulders. "I won't bother you again."

"It isn't—" He seemed to struggle, and his knuckles were tight about the head of the cane. "You bring me such joy, Elizabeth Shaw."

The ache beneath her ribs was *unendurable*.

"I think from this moment forward you should only call me Joseph Smart. And I will only come near you as he. That will be wise. For I have a lot of natural confidence. But this is a new sort of rejection and I don't care for it."

His gaze went to where she was pressing her fist into her ribs. She tore her hand away from her chest and hid it in her skirts.

"I regret causing you pain," he said.

"Oh, sod off." She strode from the room.

Chapter 18

A Labor of Love

Archie invited her to spend the Christmas holidays at his family's farm. Libby declined. Packing her books and notes and necessary equipment into a traveling case, and making arrangements with a carter to transport the pig to Alice's house, she left a message for Mrs. Coutts and Mr. Gibbs on the foyer table with a pound note for each of them.

For her host she left nothing. He would know where she had gone, and if he so desired he could regret giving her pain from the distance of two miles.

Instructing the hackney to disgorge her at a busy posting house on the edge of Leith, she peeled the whiskers from her cheeks and changed into a gown, and hailed a different cab for the remainder of the trip. She had already done this thrice, once on the occasion that she encountered him at the party. That it made her stomach tight to remember that party, their conversation there, and the caress of his lips on her knuckles infuriated her now.

She could not be weak. Men were not weak in this manner.

"You are unhappy, Elizabeth," Alice said as by candlelight she poked a needle into an embroidery frame that read "Be sure to taste your words before you spit them out."

"You are mistaken. I am perfectly happy." Her fingers were tight around the metal file. After hours spent practicing the filing of joint hinges under the watchful eyes of Mr. Syme, she nearly had it.

Intrigued by her interest, Mr. Syme had asked her no questions when she applied to him for assistance. Young, and married to an intelligent woman, he already knew of Libby's fascination with medicine through his acquaintance with her father, and he applauded her wish to accomplish this. She worried now that if someday Joseph Smart came to be a well-known surgeon in Edinburgh, Mr. Syme would recognize her. But doing this project perfectly was worth that anxiety.

"You did not eat the pudding today," Alice said.

"I don't care for Christmas pudding."

"You did not eat the goose either. Or the haggis."

"I have been endeavoring to eat less meat of late. But I'm afraid I like bacon too much to entirely eschew meat. Don't worry, Pig," she said to the creature cuddled at the hearth beside Iris. "I shan't eat you."

"Of course not," Iris said. "For I intend to keep Pig when you return to Edinburgh." She stroked its back and it snorted and snuggled closer to her.

"You have grown unnaturally slender, Elizabeth," Alice said.

"I look more like a youth now."

"You are intentionally starving yourself? Elizabeth Shaw!"

"I'm not." She simply had no appetite of late. Eating had grown too complicated: the poultry must be eaten first and then the vegetables and only then the sweets. But Constance's cook had dressed the goose with berry jelly, which made all of it impossible.

She knew what was happening. It had happened in London years ago too.

She could control it.

"You are unwell," Alice said.

"And she has not laughed in days," Iris said.

"I am sitting right here, Iris."

"Your father would be unhappy to see you now," Alice said. "I am! Either your studies are distressing you or that man is."

"Alice, if you please. This is difficult work."

"What are you doing, Libby?" Iris asked.

"I am making a hinge for a prosthesis."

"A pro-what?" Alice said.

"A replacement limb."

"For a tree? Good gracious, what are they teaching you at that infirmary?"

"A limb for a human being, Alice. Now please do hush."

Hush.

She closed her eyes, willing steadiness into her fingers.

"For which human being?" Alice said into the silence of the crackling fire and sighing pig.

"For him, of course."

Alice's eyes went round. "Dear girl, you have succumbed."

"Succumbed to what?" Iris said.

"I have not succumbed to anything. This is my project for my diploma. If I succeed in this and pass the exams, I will be able to practice as an independent surgeon."

"And what of *him*?" Alice said. "Does he know it is a project for your diploma?"

"Yes. He does not approve. But when I return I will alter his opinion. It is for his own good." She turned up the wick on the lamp and took her tool in hand. "I have never been a ninny for a man, Alice. Trust that I will not begin now."

SHE RETURNED THE morning after Epiphany, before he could absent himself from the house. From his studio he heard the front door open, heard her call thanks to the hackney driver, and heard the light clomp of her boots across the foyer and into the corridor, then past the kitchen.

Not expecting her yet, he had unguardedly left the door to his studio open. Joseph Smart appeared in the aperture.

He had not seen her since the disastrous Saturday afternoon sitting, after which he had been sorely tempted to cut out his own tongue. To see her now was like coming upon a well in a desert.

"Felicitations on the new year to you, sir," she said coolly. "I trust you are well."

"Yes." *Now.*

"I am too. Iris developed an affection for Pig, so I left it at Alice's house. I didn't think you would mind it. Do you?"

"No."

"I must have your measurements. I can ask most of the necessary measurements of Gibbs, I suspect, whom I assume knows them on behalf of your tailor and shoemaker. But I must also study the particulars of your leg."

"There are a hundreds of veterans of war in this city," he said, returning his attention to the book open on his knee. "Use one of them for your experiment."

"You are being obstinate. That is a wretched trait in a man of power and authority."

Slowly he lifted his gaze.

She grunted, and her lips curved with a new sort of confidence.

"You know," she said, "I don't give a damn whether you want this prosthesis or not. This is not about you. This is about me and my project to impress my mentors, and you will do it or I will tell the world who you are."

"You don't know who I am."

"I have your name. And I have friends with connections to the government who can assist me in discovering to which foreign gentleman that name is attached."

"You wouldn't."

"You should have thought of that before you told me your name."

"You wouldn't. You actually would not divulge it. To anyone. Your conscience would not allow you to do such a thing. I know this about you."

She stared at him, her nostrils flaring above the downy moustache.

"Damn you, Ziyaeddin Mirza," finally burst forth. "Damn you, and damn every man who won't put a light in his window and stay up all night damning you."

He laughed.

The severity slipped away from her mouth. Then the lips he dreamed of both day and night smiled. The brittle light in her eyes became sparkles.

"Tears now?" he said. "Because I have complimented you on your conscience?"

"Of course not. I never weep. And do recall that you are not to compliment me on anything. Now, give me the measurements I require."

"I don't know them."

"No matter. I've a measuring tape." She reached into her pocket and started forward. "I will—"

"*Halt.*"

Frowning, she obeyed.

"Leave the tape," he said, "and a list of whatever you require, on the table in the foyer."

"Obstinate *and* vain."

"Not vain."

"Proud," she said. "Too proud to reveal any imperfection."

"Perhaps," he admitted.

"I am a person of medical science. Physical imperfections are the reason for everything I do," she said in clean syllables. There was no pity in her voice, and he thought he could love her for that alone.

"Yet I am merely a man," he said.

"You are a foolish man."

"And you are a woman with a brash tongue and a willful insolence toward a man who, though possibly foolish, should be accorded at the very least some respect."

Her lips twitched. "Fine. If you will not allow me to do the examination I will give you the direction of Mr. Syme, the surgeon I told you about that has had great success with amputations and prostheses. You must meet with him and he will gather from you the information I require to make the device. I have already told him your name. Your false name, that is. I told him that I am acquainted with you through the duke."

He nodded.

"This is ridiculous." She turned and he had the fleeting glimpse of a smile. "But men are weak creatures and must be treated accordingly, I suppose," she said breezily as she disappeared down the foyer.

WHEN SHE SAT for him fully clothed as Joseph Smart that Sunday, it occurred to Libby that it would be easier to take him between her thighs wearing trousers than wearing a skirt. With great ease she could also walk over to him and climb onto his lap and wrap her legs around him.

Thank heavens for *her* pride.

She had learned from Mr. Syme that Ziyaeddin had called on him. Neither of them mentioned it now. When the clock in the parlor rang the eleventh hour he said nothing, nor did she. She simply left.

Six days later he appeared in the parlor doorway.

"You have not slept," he said.

"Spying on me now, are you?" she said, not lifting her chin from her palm where it rested. "I thought you were out, by the way. Thus my feminine garb now."

"Mrs. Coutts is worried about your health."

"I am a medical student. If I were in poor health, doesn't she suppose I would know it? Don't you?" Finally she allowed herself to look at him.

The awl of pleasure-pain she always felt upon seeing him tunneled its way deeper into her belly.

"Have you come here only to berate me for my poor sleep habits?" she snapped, because it was that or begin speaking the thoughts that never let her be now—thoughts about trousers and laps and wrapping her legs around his waist.

"You are peevish," he said.

Dropping the pen, which splattered ink over her page, she sat back. "I sleep very little. Of course I am peevish."

He smiled.

Warmth fanned across her middle.

"Mr. Syme sent a message to me today," he said. "He said you have made progress."

"Yes. The plaster cast you allowed him to make has allowed me to fashion the socket. I have now done all that I can in preparing the device without having actually performed an examination of you myself."

"For what are you waiting?"

"To screw up the courage to approach you."

He lifted a skeptical brow.

"Yes!" she insisted. "You are a monster, a beast all burrowed away in his lair, striking out at any innocent maiden who crosses you. I am terrified."

"Every part of that statement was a fabrication."

"Except that part about being a maiden. Needn't I be terrified of you?"

"Perhaps of—" He halted his words and seemed to reconsider. "How may I assist you, Mr. Smart?"

His manner of address could mean only one thing.

She sat forward on the chair. "Now? You are offering to allow me to examine you finally, now? This minute?"

"Forgive me for my pride."

She stood up, her stomach a jumble of knots.

"Will you hate me for it?" she said. "Afterward? For wounding your pride? For if that is to be the price I must pay to have your cooperation in this, I will choose another project."

"Could you choose another project?"

"If I wished to lower myself to the level of a novice, as many of my classmates, yes. In that case, I could complete a suitable project in the time remaining."

"Shall I sit or would you prefer that I remain standing?"

Her heartbeats were thundering. "Can you promise not to hate me?"

"Yes."

"Should I believe you?"

"Yes," he said with the same maddening calm.

"Honestly?"

"Of course."

"And then there is the elephant in the middle of the room."

"I beg your pardon?"

"The elephant. The great big object that we are both not speaking of, but which is obviously there."

He said nothing.

"An *elephant*," she said. "One of those gigantic animals with—"

He laughed. "Yes. I know what an elephant is."

"Oh. Have you seen a real elephant?"

"No." Only his eyes were smiling now, the glimmer in them warm and wonderful. "Although I understand that my father once received a pair of elephants as a gift from the ambassador of some elephant-plentiful place."

Ambassador?

"Your father?" she said a bit weakly.

"He swiftly sent the animals away. He said they were so intelligent that his courtiers became jealous of them, and he feared for the creatures' lives if they remained."

"Courtiers?"

He tilted his head, his eyes questioning. He was asking her now that if he shared with her what he could, would she be content with partial knowledge? He knew her now. He understood that already she needed to know more.

For him she could do it. She must. This peculiar alliance they had forged was precious.

"The elephant in this room," she said, "is that the last time we were close enough to touch, matters did not proceed well. This situation, of course, is entirely different."

"Of course it is," he said.

"You do believe that, don't you?"

"Yes."

He often spoke like this, with such regal assurance, and now Libby had no trouble imagining him royalty—except that he lived as a common *mister* in Scotland, with only two servants, and he painted portraits to buy bread.

And she was a woman pretending to be a man and studying to become a surgeon.

"Shall we begin?" he said.

She went to the case in which she kept her tools.

"I have engaged a woodworker with considerable experience in fashioning false limbs. He has already consulted with your cobbler. And the coppersmith—" She turned and her footsteps faltered.

Cane propped against a chair, he was standing perfectly balanced on his foot and folding back the trousers fabric and unfastening the straps of the peg support from around his thigh.

He glanced up at her.

"Do not lose courage now, Mr. Smart," he said in an unremarkable tone.

"If you condescend to me," she said, swallowing her feelings and moving toward him, "I will tread very hard upon your toes with the heel of my shoe."

He chuckled.

She knelt before him and, as she reached for the trouser leg, their hands brushed. His hands jerked away.

"I am not boiling water," she said, folding back the fine fabric and pretending that delicious tendrils of pleasure were not now scurrying up her wrists. "I shan't scald you."

"I am not so certain about that," he murmured.

"Straighten your knee."

Three quarters of the calf remained, which she had guessed well enough already.

"But, this is better than I imagined!" Running her fingertips from the kneecap and around, over each tendon, she tested their elasticity. He was all hard muscle and healthy bone and tendons and fascia. "So much better." She reached into her pocket, withdrew a tiny hammer, and tapped it to the soft tissue beneath the patella. "Excellent reflex."

"Warn a man, will you?"

"Be quiet. I am working. *Oh*, how lovely for once to be the one to tell you to hush. The tibia, fibula, and the extensors are largely intact and the tendons are remarkably strong. The sawing and cauterization must have been done with great care. And flap-style rather than guillotine. Given that you were at sea this was an extraordinarily fine amputation."

"Felt dreadful," he mumbled.

"Even the scar tissue is minimal, and it has held up marvelously well despite that wretched peg. A surgeon must have skill to do an amputation of this quality. I assume he chose to amputate because the ankle shattered entirely." Her fingertips explored the thick, silky scar, then ran along the muscle again, and back up to the tendons and to the cuff of calluses above his knee created by the straps of the peg attachment. His skin was hot to the touch and dusted with masculine black hair.

"Who performed it?"

"Seamus Boyle of the Royal Navy."

She looked up. "The navy?"

"Captain Gabriel Hume's ship's surgeon."

"The Duke of Loch Irvine? That is how you came to know him? He rescued you from the burning ship?"

"Yes."

She should not notice the hard muscle of his thighs, nor marvel at his lean waist or the breadth of his shoulders or the taut beauty of his jaw, nor wonder why he had turned his head and was staring fixedly across the room. He was gripping the back of a chair, his fingers tight about the scrolled wood.

She sat back on her heels. "I wish to take complete measurements of your foot and ankle and calf."

With a single movement he twisted the chair around. He sat, removed his shoe, and then folded up the trouser leg and rolled off the stocking.

"It is instructive to see how a gentleman undresses," she said, a bit choked.

"Not much experience with that, hm?"

"No."

She was watching his hands as he laid them palms down on his thighs. Ziyaeddin willed the tightness in his cock to subside.

It did not.

"This man is now as undressed as he will be," he said, the syllables rocky. "Commence thine examination, Doctor."

Her gaze darted up.

On her knees. Before him. Eyes full of intention and curiosity. Brow creased with wisdom. Clever hands that could find bones and sinews beneath a man's skin. Ten agile fingers that could manipulate muscle like bread dough.

Yet he could think of *only one thing*.

He was a dog.

"Stand, please," she said.

He did so, and she touched first his instep and then the bones of his ankle and shin and generally spent too much time running her hands all over him until he was in agony. He was not a weak man. But there was only so much he could do to halt the inevitable. If she chose this moment to look up, she would get an eyeful.

He stared at the wall where hung a prayer rug upon which the tiny knots that fashioned the pattern spelled out a prayer in Arabic: *Allaahumma innee as-alukal-'aafiyah, wash-shukra 'alal-'aafiyah.* O Allah, I ask from You the well-being, and to be grateful for the well-being.

He was not a praying man. Nine years ago his faith had gone into the sea alongside his freedom. He did not keep the rug to remind him to pray. He kept it because, other than the watch, it was the only object from Tabir that he possessed. When shortly after his arrival in Scotland he had found the rug in a market in Leith, with the insignia of his family's dynasty woven into the pattern, he had thought it a blessing of sorts, a message that he had been meant to come to this land to heal. To live.

No longer.

Letters from London told him of unrest on Iran's northern border. It would soon be time to leave Britain. The brilliant woman on her knees before him would not know that he had accepted this gift not for her sake, but for his. He would not return to Tabir broken. She could make him whole.

She had set the measuring tape on the floor and was making marks in a notebook. It was a moment's reprieve from her touch, and he hated how much he wanted her hands on him again, even in this clinical manner.

"My father was correct," he said.

"That elephants are intelligent?"

"That his courtiers were fools. They perished in a single night, except those who betrayed him, of course."

Her eyes came to his. Her lips were a tight line.

"What caused those scars on your ankle and foot?" she said.

"A manacle and chain."

Her lashes made a single quick beat.

"I am finished here." Rising to her feet, she went to her writing table. "I will complete the prosthesis within the next several days. Now I must study. So you must go away and do whatever it is that portrait artists do when they are not telling gullible surgical students tall tales of the despicably tragic variety." Without looking at him she said, "What is the writing on the watch?"

"'Now do as princes do when prudent, pious, and beneficent—Serve God and him alone in good times and bad.'"

She waved her hand impatiently, shooing him away.

The impatience was like her. Avoiding his gaze was not. So he knew this was her way of telling him that she believed him.

Chapter 19

The Touch

"She isn't ill." Chedham stood beside her at the washing basin.

"Who?"

He glanced toward the cots in the ward. "Mrs. Small. She pretends pain so she can sleep in that bed and eat a hot meal each day."

"Mr. Bridges removed a tumor from her only six days ago, Chedham." Though if Mrs. Small were lingering in convalescence to ensure herself bed and food, Libby couldn't blame her. Ice clung to every rooftop in Edinburgh.

"She's taking advantage of charity," he said.

Wiping her hands dry, Libby reached for her lunch pail, carried it to Mrs. Small's bed, and opened it.

"I've extra cheese and bread today, Mrs. Small." She tucked it into the woman's hand.

"A heart o' gold you've got, dear lad."

Libby didn't bother looking at her fellow apprentice as she departed. She knew he would be sneering.

Later at the library Archie whispered, "Cheddar's up to something."

Libby dragged her attention from the chemistry text and blinked to bring him into focus. "Up to?"

"He's no' himself."

"It's the depth of winter and we all have piles of work to do. None of us are ourselves." Least of all her house-mate. The prosthesis suited him perfectly, so well that their conversation when she had given it to him had lasted only minutes. Now she was concerned. Mrs. Coutts had shared her worries too.

"He's in pain, lass. He'll no' tell a soul, bless him. The master's a proud man. But I've ne'er seen him like this."

Libby agreed. At her sittings she had noticed the whiteness about his knuckles and lips, the discomfort he seemed to have sitting and standing, his restlessness. Yet when she asked him about it, he said nothing.

The prosthesis was precisely designed. Mr. Syme agreed. She had done exceptional work. Her patient should now be walking more comfortably than he had since the amputation. He must have sciatica pain. Or . . . She didn't know. But he was avoiding her, and she was simply too busy to pursue it. Mr. Bell had sent letters of introduction for her to every medical man of influence in town, telling her that she must win the approval of these men too.

Someday, Mr. Smart, he had written to her, *you will be one of Britain's greatest surgeons.*

Now her studies consumed every moment. She hardly ever slept. Peevish with her friends, she often studied alone and spent lunchtime at the infirmary observing any physician or surgeon who would allow it.

"Archie, I don't have time to concern myself with Chedham's fits and starts."

"Last night he left the pub early, so I followed him. He went straight to Bridges's house."

"His house?" No student would ever call on a surgeon or physician at home late at night, unless invited.

"Aye." Archie nodded. "There's no good in that, lad."

"Perhaps he is having trouble with his project." As she was, *damn her subject's royal pride*.

"Then why didna he wait till tomorrow at the infirmary to ask Bridges?"

"We're always quite busy." But she and Chedham often quizzed Mr. Bridges on their studies as they moved between patients, competing over which of them could bring to their mentor the most knotty problem to solve together.

Knotty.

In her mind, a bolt slipped into place.

Shoving aside the chemistry text, she leaped up and went into the stacks. Running along the bindings printed in gold lettering, her fingers landed on the one she sought. Her eyes ran over the words as she turned pages. There were few diagrams; accurate engravings of human anatomy were too expensive for most printers to commission. But she remembered something she had read . . . *There*.

Snapping the volume shut, she threw notebooks into her satchel.

"Leaving already?" Archie said.

"I've got to."

Ziyaeddin was rarely at home—avoiding her, she assumed. Now on a Wednesday, when it was her habit after lecture to study at the library until she and her friends went to the pub for dinner, he would not expect her home. He might be there.

She understood what he was suffering. She would speak

with Mr. Syme about it, and write to Mr. Bell in London too. But she already knew. And she could fix it.

One last time she would disregard his wish for privacy, and make him listen to her.

STANDING BEFORE THE easel, Ziyaeddin shifted his weight from foot to false foot. The balance was sublime. But no position relieved the agony. Like knives buried deep in his flesh trying to cut their way toward his skin, the pain made every movement a curse.

She burst into his studio, flinging the door wide and striding in.

"You must allow me to—"

"No," he said.

She came directly to him, halting in a scented whorl of mint and lavender. Strong scent was unusual for her, unless it was of the surgery. It filled his head, clearing it abruptly of the muddle.

"Is there swelling?" she demanded. "Or streaks of red beneath your skin?"

"No."

"I know you are in pain."

"Leave here."

She glanced at the canvas, then at the deepening dusk without. "How can you paint when—"

A sound of warning came through his clenched teeth.

"Was that a *snarl*?" she said.

"Leave."

"I—"

"It is not Sunday at ten o'clock. You do not belong here."

"In fact I do."

The winter evening was rainy and his studio was dim. He had not lit lamps, for that would require moving about and bring the knives afresh. But he could see well enough her partial disarray. Her cheeks were hollow, and dark patches sunk the delicate skin beneath her eyes. She wore a shirt without neck cloth, trousers, and a dressing gown over them both, and boots.

"Remain to be drawn in that mélange of poor fashion, then," he said because he could not resist, "or begone until Sunday. But do not speak."

She grabbed him, the sleeves of the gown billowing momentarily, then her fingers clutching his back.

"Don't move," she commanded.

He swiveled to dislodge her, but she jammed her pelvis hard against his hip and her arms were clamps about him.

"Here," she said, and her strong fingertips dug into his hips.

Agony ripped through him.

"In the name of—"

"These muscles must be tended to," she said. "And these." Her fingertips gouged twin paths of torment down his thigh. "And these." She kneaded his buttocks and it was like shards of broken glass in his flesh. Stars exploded before his eyes.

He could hardly unclench his teeth to speak. "Take your hands off of me."

"If you do not allow me to relieve the tension in these fascia, it will only grow worse. Then the only solution will be cauterization of the femoral joint and I absolutely do not recommend that."

He wished he could enjoy the pleasure of her hips angled against his, her arms about him, and her hands precisely where he had fantasized them. The pain screamed. He struggled to breathe. And still her fingers did not cease the torture. Tears reared up in his eyes.

No.

No weakness. *Not with her.*

"I beg of you," he uttered.

She released him and took a step back.

"I am sorry for causing you pain," she said. "There, I can claim that too now, and I can even say it with sincerity. But you must allow me to help. For years those muscles have conditioned themselves to compensate for the missing limb. You must now recondition them. They require daily manipulation to release the knots in the fascia, and retraining. You must allow me to do this." Her brow compressed. "Unless, that is, you do not wish to be able to walk with ease and that is the reason you never before acquired a prosthesis. I don't understand how that could be, but I still possess all of my limbs and therefore cannot guess what it is to live without one. If it is obstinate pride that keeps you from comfort, I recommend discarding that at once and doing as I recommend."

"Recommend?"

"Insist."

"It is pride," he admitted. "And no true need for ease of movement before now."

"No need for ease of movement *before now*? You have not allowed this only for the sake of my project?" she said.

"No, *güzel kız*. I have not. I am to make a great journey. Soon. I wish only the physical strength and stability to do what I must do. You have made it possible."

The gold-tipped lashes fanned. "Then we must not delay."

She left the room.

Watching her walk away from him was pain he felt in every part of him now.

He was still staring at the empty doorway when she appeared again and proffered a scrap of paper.

"This is the direction of Mr. Murray. He practices the muscle manipulation you require. He learned it decades ago, in service for the East India Company. He is a little old Scot. I have seen him cure a lame horse and cause a chair-bound farmer to walk again, both without medications or surgery. Since you will not allow me to touch you, you must go see him immediately. And these," she said, handing him a second sheet of paper, "are descriptions of several repetitive movements you must do twice every day while the pain persists. Do them exactly as I have described there, without fail."

She reached into a voluminous pocket of the dressing gown and withdrew a bottle.

"Apply this twice daily to each place you feel pain. Work it into the skin until it is well saturated. It is a mixture of plant oils and will soothe and loosen the muscles without inflaming them. As you can smell, the scent is very strong and will overpower your usual scent, which is unfortunate, but must be endured temporarily."

She walked swiftly away from him again.

"It will be some time before you are free of all pain. But I think you will be happy with the outcome." In the doorway she turned. "The device itself is not causing you trouble, is it? Pain in the tendons or knee? Abrasions? Anything of that sort?"

"None," he said, wanting her body pressed against his again, her arms around him, more than he had ever wanted anything.

"Excellent." She began to turn away again but paused. "You know, I am incredibly busy. I have far too much to do each day. Yet I cannot cease thinking about you. It is exasperating. Is it the same for you?"

Every day. Every hour. Every minute.

He wanted to tell her that in seven years he had not allowed another human being to touch him as she had—to touch that which was both his greatest shame as a man and the greatest liability to his family and people. He wanted to tell her that until she had come into his life, into his house, he had been hiding, and that she had given him courage to hide no more.

But he said nothing, and she left him.

HE WENT AWAY. Having just completed and delivered three large commissions, Mrs. Coutts reported, the master had departed on holiday to Haiknayes Castle.

Obviously her confession had driven him away. Or perhaps her uninvited trespassing in his studio had—damn his stupid rules. Or both. Whatever the case, he left her no message and that was message enough.

The winter term brought an advanced practical anatomy course, with cadavers over which Dr. Jones gave her, Chedham, and Archie directorship, with teams assigned to them for the dissections, as well as considerably more surgical instruction in the infirmary's surgical theater. Her duties at the infirmary now occupied every day except Sundays.

When Mr. Bridges invited her to perform an actual surgery under his supervision, she could not believe his words at first. His assurance that the presidents of both the infirmary and the college had approved it hardly convinced her. It was unprecedented, a tremendous honor.

Preparing for the procedure, she was so anxious that she would be obliged to relieve herself during it, with others nearby, she consumed no food or beverage for twelve hours beforehand. The tactic succeeded and the surgery went splendidly. That such a young man could have such a steady hand, such natural instinct, such thorough command of both anatomy and procedure, and such speed and skill astonished everyone. Afterward, Mr. Bridges allowed her to regularly assist him in the surgery, encouraging her to take the lead again on several occasions.

She celebrated by commencing reading lessons for Coira.

"Why would I be needin' to read?" Coira said, munching on a crust of bread.

"Every woman should know how to read. The more a woman reads, the more in command of her own destiny she is."

"I'd as lief find a pot o' gold."

"That isn't likely to happen. Now, I've never taught another person to read. Usually I just recommend books. But we will begin with recognizing the letters in the alphabet, and hopefully that will go well."

Coira smiled. "I reckon you'll be as fine a teacher, lad, as you be a person."

Libby's own teachers made no secret of their delight with their youngest apprentice. Passing other students in the infirmary or on the street, she often heard whispers, yet fewer greetings than before. It was the same in her anatomy and clinical medicine courses.

She redoubled her studies. Always she had more questions needing answers, more notes needing organizing, more treatises to beg the librarian to unearth for her. If she made even the tiniest mistake with a patient, all of her work could come to naught.

Ziyaeddin sent no word. Tempted to write to Amarantha and ask after him, Libby did not. She could not. It would reveal her. It would reveal him.

Yet she could not cease worrying that if something had happened to him on the long road over snowy hills and icy waterways, if he had fallen afoul of weather or injury, no one would know to tell her.

The duke would surely send word to Mrs. Coutts—eventually. If anything at all happened to his friend, he would. He must. So Libby returned early to the house each afternoon, eschewing the library and the pub, to learn if Mrs. Coutts had heard from Haiknayes. But no message from Haiknayes came.

"MISSED YOU AT the pub again last night," Archie whispered to her over the library table strewn with books. "George was in his cups, railin' about Plath givin' him that bloody lung right there in front o' everybody. Pincushion laughed so hard he nearly split a seam."

Libby flipped through pages to find a detail about cartilage.

"Woulda done you some good, Joe," Archie said. "Laughin' a wee bit."

"I've a list of questions here that need answers, and only two hours to accomplish it." Archie did not understand. "Pass me that book."

He pushed it toward her and she found what she needed. As she struck the tip of her pencil across the question in her notebook, instant relief coursed through her like water down her throat on a hot day. Half of the questions were now struck through, another two dozen still to answer.

The words shifted, then swung left and looped back into place. She blinked, but now her vision was blurry too. She hardly knew what she should read next, Diderot's *Eléments de physiologie*, or perhaps Bichat's *Physiological Researches upon Life and Death*. Then there was Argellata's Latin translation of Al-Zahrawi's *Kitab al-Tasrif* to be read in full. Studying those illustrations alone would require days. There was so much to learn. If only she could sleep.

Exhaustion lapped at her.

She hadn't *time* to sleep. The months until her father's return were dwindling. If she maintained these successes, he would allow her to continue as Joseph.

She *must not fail.*

The next question on the list beckoned.

A quarter of an hour later she was packing her notebooks into her satchel.

"Where're you goin'?" Archie said.

"To the infirmary."

He tucked in his chin. "Is Bridges expectin' you back *now*?"

"No." She closed the overstuffed bag. "I've got to examine Mrs. Small's splint again."

"Small? I thought she'd gone weeks ago."

"She fell and broke her femur." The cancer had weakened her.

"Peter'll do it. He's on rotation tonight. We've got to get this report written."

"No. I must look in on her." First Mrs. Small's splint. Then Mr. Portman's sutures. Then the surgical instruments cabinet. The nurses and surgeons were forever storing the forceps beside the bone saws, and they often got stored soiled. If they were tonight, she would wash them. The cauteries would probably need to be put in order too. The surgical servants, who had very little knowledge, did not know how to arrange them sensibly from those used on the head to those used on the foot. "I'll write the report tonight and you can put your name to it."

"Now listen here, Smart, I'll no' be lettin' anybody do my work, especially no' if you'll be writin' it in that new chicken scratch o' yours. The letters were so pressed together in the last report I could hardly read it. An' they were all capitals. What's that about?"

"Our professor could read it. Listen, Archie—"

"All right!" Archie said, scraping his fingers through his gingery locks. "I'll do the diagram."

"Fine." She would draw the diagram anyway. It must be perfect.

Icy rain dribbled from the darkness above as she walked to the infirmary. Leaving her coat and bag with the porter, she went straight to the women's ward.

Mrs. Small's splint was perfect, just it had had been five hours earlier. After checking on Mr. Portman, Libby went to the surgical case and, finding the clamp on the left hook, she placed it back where it belonged on the right hook. She knew she should not. It was as well on the left hook as the right. No one would care.

But now it was fine. Better. Right.

Walking home, the bag full of books was lead on her shoulder. Archie had commented that she needn't carry her entire collection of Charles Bell's works with her every day. But he did not understand. She did not want to carry them everywhere. But she must.

Locking the front door, she hung up her overcoat and hat and removed her boots. Mrs. Coutts had left dinner for her on the dining table. Even the thought of eating nauseated her.

In the parlor she unloaded her bag and piled the contents carefully on the desk, keeping the stacks neat. It left no place to set the text she must read.

She could read it in her bedchamber. Later, perhaps she would write the report at the kitchen table.

Entering her bedchamber, she touched the feet of the boys in the marketplace painting, and then again, and got a moment's relief. The end of her bed was stacked three deep in books and papers. The dressing table too.

If she sat on the floor, she could use the dressing table chair as a desk.

She touched the edge of the painting again.

She was shaking. Her stockings were soaked through, her trousers were damp, and her coat too. Stripping them off, she made up the fire and hung them on a rack before the hearth, then stood before the dressing table mirror and peeled off the whiskers and placed them in the locked drawer. It was Saturday and Mr. Gibbs had long since come and gone. But she felt better with the whiskers locked in the drawer. Safer. Calmer.

But the ritual of folding the whiskers in oilcloth and packing them in their secret hiding place did not calm her *enough* tonight. Disquiet still prickled just beneath her skin and in her stomach. Excessive nerves. *Panic.*

She looked about at the books on her bed and dressing table and bed table. Standing in the middle of the room, every bit of her skin exposed to the cold, damp night air, she hugged her arms about her and felt the sour tightness of her throat, the salty, hot rise of desperation in her nose and behind her eyes, crackling, splitting open.

She had allowed this to happen. *This.* This mess. This insanity.

She knew better. *She knew better.*

She had known better since she was ten years old and her father had told her the stories of her real mother, stories that Libby swore she would never herself repeat, stories that she had worked so hard to hold at bay.

This could not be happening. The need to unlock the drawer, paste the whiskers back on her face, dress, and run to the infirmary tugged at her so hard. What if the nurse decided to move the surgical instruments? What if she rearranged the clamps? What if Mrs. Small's splint slipped and nobody noticed?

Libby's lungs would not fill.

The splint would be fine. She knew that.

She knew that.

It couldn't hurt to check *one* more time. Knowing Mrs. Small was sleeping comfortably with the splint in place would make her feel better—well enough, at least, to sleep tonight, perhaps.

Just once more.

She had unpacked her books already. If she went out, she would have to repack the books first. And don wet stockings, trousers, and coat. Rain was striking the window-panes of her bedchamber like tiny little fists.

Libby's limbs were heavy, cold. It was too much. *Too much.*

She could hardly lift her head. The bed was covered in books and papers. Only part of it near the headboard was even visible beneath the mess.

Her body was trembling. It needed food. When was the last time she had eaten?

She would go to the dining room and throw away the mutton, clean that bowl, and store it. Then she could eat the peas. Perhaps. *Perhaps.* If there were no droplets of jam on the counter or the kitchen table.

Insanity. *Insanity.*

Pressing her palms to her head, she heard a noise like the grinding of gears. It was coming from her chest, her throat, inside her head, consuming her.

Mrs. Small's splint required adjusting.

No. No no no.

She opened her eyes and the noise was still coming through her teeth, over her tongue, into the frigid chamber.

Breaking her hands away from her head, she ran to the clothespress, dragged a nightshirt over her head, then went to the fire and banked it. Through the darkness lit only by rain-speckled lamplight from the street with-out, she ran down the stairs, then along the corridor, her right shoulder brushing the wall to guide her. Twisting the handle of the door to his quarters, she opened it and tumbled inside.

The studio was in blackness. Without sight, she felt her way along the wall to the bedchamber door, and under the bar across the open doorway. The bed was three strides away—only three. She parted the heavy draperies, and climbed onto the cold mattress. The blanket was luxuriously soft and thick.

Without disturbing the blanket or linens, she burrowed into the bolster and pressed her cheek against it, willing the feathers in the cushion to reach out and warm her.

Chapter 20

Rescue

The list of items was the length of the page, the print entirely in Roman capitals and cramped, almost like the hand of another person.

TO COLLECT FOR PERSONAL APOTHECARY

~~TURPENTINE~~
~~THYME~~
~~NUTMEG~~
~~MINT~~
~~CARDAMOM~~
~~CINNAMON~~
~~GINGER~~
~~LICORICE~~
~~MORTAR~~
~~LAUDANUM~~

And the list continued. It was her writing, of course. Ziyaeddin knew it just as he knew that someone else had not entered his house and piled books the length of the left side of the foyer and on every surface in the parlor, littered the desk with papers, and left dishes of food on the dining room table around which a tiny mouse was nosing.

Her satchel occupied the floor beside the desk in the parlor. In the months since she had come to live in his house, he had never seen the satchel unless the woman was here too. Her overcoat, hat, and shoes by the front door were still wet.

The roads from London had been muddy everywhere and frozen in parts, and the journey northward slow. It was a remarkable thing to ride again, to put his legs around the girth of a fine horse and feel that power beneath him. A miracle she had made possible.

He intended finally to thank her, and to explain to her the real reason he had never had a suitable prosthesis made before. The truth. He did not know exactly how he would do that without coming within sight of her, and thereby putting himself in danger of grabbing and kissing her. But he would. It was far past time.

He had gone to London to speak with Britain's foreign secretary, Lord Canning. Sinking himself into diplomacy he had made modest progress in convincing Canning and the king that the war brewing between Russia and Iran—and smoldering on the borders of Tabir—would hinder the interests of Britain's East India Company in that region. It would also further weaken the Ottomans' eastern border.

The Duke of Loch Irvine had accompanied him on the journey. Disclosing nothing of Elizabeth's secret, Ziyaeddin had admitted to his preoccupation with her.

Gabriel had made his position on the matter clear: *If you break her heart, I will kill you.*

Ziyaeddin did not intend to die by the hand of his best friend. And away from Edinburgh he had gained a clarity of perspective on his houseguest that being always within grabbing-and-kissing distance of her did not allow.

Henceforth he was determined to maintain a wiser distance from her. It was entirely possible to reclaim the initial dispassion of their encounters by confining them to fully clothed one-hour drawing sessions only. Without conversation.

And there would be no more fantasizing. Or confessions. None.

He had this under control.

Leaving the traveling trunk in the cluttered foyer for Gibbs to tend to on Monday, he went to his quarters. The studio was frigid. He coaxed a flame forth in the hearth, then pulled the draperies wide to allow in the daylight.

Scotland in late winter: gray, rainy, cold. An ideal day to paint.

He had missed this studio, his easel, a paintbrush between his fingers.

Inside his bedchamber he set down his traveling case and only then noticed the lump on the bed. Parting the curtain entirely so that daylight from the studio illuminated the mattress, he took in the interloper: a slight, slender woman with short locks, curled up in a tight ball in the very center of the top of the bed.

Elizabeth Shaw. In his bed.

Every one of the well-intentioned lies he had told himself over the past weeks disintegrated.

Her cheeks and brow were ghostly, her hair slick against her scalp, and a voluminous white nightgown tucked around every inch of skin except her face. She barely stirred, her exhales so weak that the movement of her chest did not even touch her knees drawn up before her. Yet with each inhale her body shook.

He grabbed the blanket from the foot of the bed and draped it over her. She did not move.

Making up the fire here too, he then went to the kitchen, where he put a kettle on the stove and prepared tea. A simple task, it required stillness and patience. He needed that now.

When he had first come to Britain, broken and angry, he had railed against anything that moved more swiftly than he did—which everything had—yet also at every man who refused to move swiftly to help him unseat the usurper of his father's throne.

After months spent proving his identity to the prince regent and foreign minister, he had learned of how the general had captured his sister and forced her to wed him to legitimize his rule among the local tribes. With hardly the twitch of an eyelash the Russian ambassador to Britain had told Ziyaeddin that if he returned to Tabir, the general would kill Aairah, her children, and anyone loyal to her.

Reeling, he had begged his hosts for help. To no avail. Tabir was too small an ally to risk infuriating the Russians. And the general had the support of the local khans, who welcomed bribes of Russian gold and Russian weapons to wage petty wars among themselves.

Your Highness is welcome to remain the honored guest of Britain at your convenience.

At his convenience—as though remaining three thousand miles away from where he belonged was a matter of expedience.

Then, as he had climbed out of a carriage one gray London day, an assassin had plunged a knife into his side. Broken, hopeless, he had almost wanted death. That was when Gabriel invited him to Scotland. There, the duke said, he could continue to petition the ministers and regent and foreign ambassadors while healing.

In Scotland finally he had learned stillness. And patience.

Even when Elizabeth sat for him she was not entirely still. She asked questions, shifted position, told stories, looked about.

Now her utter stillness on his bed was worrisome. Given their last encounter, her *presence* on his bed was worrisome.

Climbing the stairs, he went into her bedchamber. Like the parlor, it was crammed with books and papers intermingled with cartons of plaster bones, broken pens, a box overflowing with empty chemists' beakers. It was chaos—a uniquely ordered chaos.

Searching for keys in the pocket of the damp coat hanging on the clotheshorse, he unlocked the traveling trunk and found what he sought: the torn stockings. *Nineteen* torn stockings, each rolled into a neat cylinder.

He scanned the chamber again, and prickling dread crept up his spine.

Descending to the parlor he made up the fire there and looked through a pile of scraps. Some were covered on both sides with lists: a list of book titles, another of cures for the symptoms of liver ailments, a third of cobblers in Edinburgh, and more, all struck through entirely. Another scrap bore hastily penned equations of letters and numbers and symbols he did not recognize, all of them struck through as well.

On a sheet of notebook paper in dark brown ink she had drawn a rudimentary torso, then several more garbed in coats, each with an increasing quantity of padding in the shoulders. Beside them, equations indicated the volume of padding required for each. Ziyaeddin recognized the coat; he had painted her wearing it.

He stared at the precise study of suitable shoulders

for a boy Joseph's age, and the back of his throat grew hot.

So much thought. So much labor. Nevertheless, she persisted.

Setting aside the page, he dropped the refuse into the flames.

"Don't do that."

She stood in the doorway. The nightgown fell to her feet, the thick fabric swallowing her shape but gaping open at her chest where she had not laced it. Nearly as white as the linen, her face seemed thinner, her cheeks and chin pronounced, her eyes pools of sharp blue surrounded by gray shadows.

"Good day to you as well, Sleeping Beauty," he said, taking up another pile of scraps, his heartbeats hard. "How was your repose? Fancy yourself the master of the house in my absence, did you?"

"What are you doing?" She lifted a hand to clutch the front of the shirt closed. Her fingers were bones covered in pale skin. "Don't. What are you doing in here? *Don't.*" She jerked forward, her eyes pinned to his hand outstretched before the flames.

"They are nothing." He gestured with the bits of paper. "Refuse. I am assisting you—and Mrs. Coutts—in decluttering this poor parlor. I hardly recognize it. Or you, for that matter. Have you dropped a stone?"

"No. My weight is none of your concern."

"I am a portraitist. Whether it is my concern, I will notice it." He would always notice every detail of her. "Are you ill?" he said, forcing calm into his tone.

"No." Her attention did not leave his hands. "This session is much more challenging than last. Put those down." One arm outstretched, she moved another step into the room. "Please."

"This," he said, lifting a scrap before him, "is a list of items to purchase at the chemist's shop. Every item has been crossed off the list. On the reverse is a crudely sketched diagram that has been scribbled over." He tossed it into the hearth.

"No! Stop! This moment, *stop*." She ran toward him and snatched away the remainder of the pile.

He took up another paper. "What of this list? A shopping list for the stationer's." Including sketching paper, chalk, and hog's hair bristles. Items for his work. None of them were struck through, however. His throat thickened.

"Stop!" She grabbed it with icy fingers. "These are not yours to discard."

"You are frozen. And barefoot, it seems. Go upstairs and dress. Then come have a cup of tea and something to eat."

"You will burn them if I go." The skin about her mouth and eyes was stretched tight.

"The rubbish, yes."

"*No.* You may not burn anything. Do you wish me to fail?"

"Fail?"

"You do. You wish me to fail."

"That is also rubbish, of course."

"I *need* these." Her eyes were fever bright in the pale oval of her face.

"You cannot need a ticket to the museum exhibit that happened months ago." To which she had invited him to accompany her, and he had declined.

"I do." She grabbed it.

He encircled her hand with his. "What is happening here?"

"Release me. Or have you decided it is acceptable for you to touch me when I don't wish it, even though you will not when I request it?"

"You are obviously unwell. What happened while I was away?"

"I said, *release me*." Slamming her palm into his chest, she grabbed the papers. They tore. She pried his hand open and took the scraps. Flying across the room, she tucked them beneath a pile on the desk.

"Tell me, Elizabeth," he said, controlling the panic rising in him. He had spent enough time among artists that he recognized madness. "Are you drinking spirits regularly? Or ingesting any medication, perhaps?"

"Of course not," she snapped. "Do not condescend to me."

"You are not eating. And this is not you." He gestured about them. "This chaos."

"You know nothing about me."

"In fact I know quite a lot about you. I know that your mind is capacious, your ambition high, and your determination boundless. I know that you are brilliant and talented and possess a streak of creative independence that, were you a man, would already have led to your fame as a surgeon, even at such a young age. And I know that this is not you." He reached for another pile of scraps.

"You don't—*Stop*! You mustn't." A sob escaped her. It sounded dry, empty. "How can you act with such disregard for me? How can you want me to fail?"

He placed the pile on the table and moved toward her. She backed to the doorway but did not cross the threshold, her eyes darting from him to the piles, back and forth.

"There is nothing I wish more than for you to succeed."

"You want to be rid of me, as everyone does after a time." Rounding him, she gathered up the piles of scraps and hurried out of the room.

He followed her up the stairs. She was closing the bedchamber door. He stopped the panel with his hand, pressing it open against her surprising strength. Retreating suddenly, she let the door swing open. Glass shattered.

"No!" Her scream echoed against the walls. She lunged toward the box of broken beakers as though to grab the jagged shards. He knocked the box away, smothering his shout as pain sliced across his palm. She fell forward. He grabbed her, pulling her up and away from the shards, dragging her back against his chest and wrapping his arms about her.

"*Stop*," she cried. "You do not understand." Her body convulsed and her sob rocked through him. Then another. He held her tight and pressed his cheek against her hair.

"No, I do not understand what is happening here," he said. "But I know this is not you."

"It *is* me," she choked out, straining against his grip. "I hate you. I do."

"I have lived in a palace pocked with assassins. I have fought as a captive in shackles. I have died on the deck of a ship aflame, cut into pieces beneath the burning sun. I can withstand your hatred for a time, *güzel kız*."

Limbs slackening, she groaned.

"They are legion," she whispered.

He bent his head aside hers, loosening his hold enough to test her reaction. She did not seek to break free.

"What are legion?" *Not voices. By the grace of Allah, do not say voices.*

"The rules. All of the rules telling me what to do, what not to do, how to do them. I cannot deny them. I cannot make them retreat this time. You must release me."

"If I release you, what will you do?"

"I will bring the remainder of the papers here." Misery suffused the words. She pressed against his arms. "*Release me.*"

He allowed her to slip from his grasp.

"Now, leave," she said.

"You said 'this time.' Has this happened before?"

"You disregard my demand, when you have expected me to give you privacy? That is rich. This is my bedchamber. Will you not allow me to be alone in it?" Color sat high on her cheeks and anger pulsed like waves from her.

Nothing could be done here now.

"We will speak of this later," he said, moving onto the landing.

"We will speak of it never," she said behind him.

He was not overly fond of spirits. His father had been a man of great faith, and Ziyaeddin had not learned an appreciation for the flavor as a boy, nor for the muddling effect it had on the mind. Now he went to the dining room and found the cognac. Blotting his bleeding hand with a kerchief, he drank down the glassful. Then he poured a dram for her.

Her footsteps clattered swiftly down the stairs. She passed the dining room and went out of the house. Through the window he saw Joseph Smart: quick stride, head down, no satchel.

He donned his coat and followed her out, but she had disappeared. It was Sunday; she could go to neither her favorite pub nor the library.

From the mews behind his house he commanded his horse. Daylight had gone and the rain had begun to fall in earnest. The streets, always quiet on Sundays, emptied.

He searched for an hour before finding her. She was not a fool, and she had walked to New Town where watchmen could be found even at this hour and in this weather. This alone gave him some hope; she was not so far removed from reason that she had lost her wisdom too.

"You have a horse," she said without looking at him, continuing along the footpath. She looked like a street waif, sodden and anemic. Her voice was weary but level now. "Did you purchase it at Haiknayes?"

"I borrowed it. Has this happened before?" he repeated.

"Yes."

"And you conquered it."

"Conquered?"

"Yes, Saint George. You conquered this dragon, I must assume."

"I believed I had."

"My hand is bleeding. Would you do me the favor of returning home and tending to the wound?"

She halted, and a great shudder seemed to pass through her. She nodded, turned about, and started walking again.

"Will you take this horse?" he said.

"I don't know how to ride astride. And you cannot walk the distance."

"Ride with me."

"I will walk. You may ride ahead. I will go directly home."

"Forgive me if I don't entirely believe you," he said.

"I cannot lie. I am not *allowed* to."

"What of Joseph Smart?" he said.

"Joseph is not a lie." Her lips were gray, her eyes hopeless. "He is the most honest part of me."

He rode to her side and reached down, and she allowed him to lift her onto the saddle before him.

She did not look at him. Settled snugly between his thighs, with her back against his chest and her body between his arms, she twisted her fingers into the horse's mane and allowed the rain to patter onto her face.

Silently he damned fate several times, and also that

madness in him that made him want her even while she was both ill and utterly unaware of him. Yet holding her, even in this manner, was a sublime pleasure he would not trade for all the world.

He thought she slept. But when they approached the house she swung her leg over the horse's neck and slid down to the ground in a single quick movement. She went directly inside, and Ziyaeddin deposited the horse in the mews.

After changing into dry clothing he went to the kitchen in search of tea.

"Forgive me," she said from the doorway behind him. She still wore the wet coat and trousers and whiskers. Her body quivered like the vibrating wings of a bee.

"You needn't ask my forgiveness," he said.

"You must forgive me," she said tightly. "Say the words."

"You are forgiven. Where—"

"Am I? In truth?"

"In truth. Where is your medical kit?"

From the pantry she drew forth a small leather case and unlatched it. It seemed to be a miniature version of her medical chest. The neat organization of the contents was a marked contrast to the disorder of her bedchamber, the foyer, and the parlor.

"Show me your hand," she said.

The wound was minor. But he had known she would put an injury before all else, and return here to tend it if he asked.

She barely touched him as she cleaned the incision, applied salve, and wrapped it with a thin piece of linen.

"I can control it," she said.

"Obviously not of late." He flexed his hand.

"It will be uncomfortable for you to hold a paintbrush for several days. You should not have used your dominant hand."

"I am, admittedly, unpracticed in the art of defending myself from broken bottles."

"When I was ten years old, I collected more than bottles and papers." Packing the bandages and salve away, she kept her head bent. "At that time it was much worse than now." She lifted her eyes. "You cannot help me."

"And yet."

"You are—"

"Dashingly heroic? Tenaciously protective? Impressively coolheaded?"

"Difficult to live with."

He suppressed his smile, for her lips remained taut, her entire face a study in tension.

"It seems you are moving with ease," she said. "Have you done as I prescribed?"

"I have."

"Is there pain?"

"Very little, thanks to you."

"How went your visit to Haiknayes?" She stood stiffly, so unlike her, as though chastened. Or defeated.

"I went to London," he said.

"Mrs. Coutts said you were at Haiknayes."

"That is what I told her."

"It hardly matters," she said dully. "Since your purpose in going was to be away from me, any destination served."

"My purpose in going was not to be away from you. I regret that you believed it was."

Disbelief colored her eyes, yet also a crackling defiance.

"What was your purpose?" she said.

He turned toward the kettle. "Change out of that wet clothing and then return here for a cup of tea." He looked over his shoulder. "Can you?"

"I can. You won't—"

"I will discard nothing. I will touch nothing. Tonight."

After a hesitation, she left.

When she appeared in the kitchen again she was wearing the blue gown, but it hung on her body as on a clothes stand. He placed the biscuit tin on the table.

"Eat ten of those," he said. "At once. Can you do that for me?"

She took up the teapot and poured. "Why London?"

"Not until I see you eat."

"That—"

"I have rules too, Miss Shaw, including refusing to converse with a woman who has not eaten a meal in a month."

"Not a month," she said, nibbling a biscuit. "I was not pining away after you, you know."

"I did not suppose that you were." He folded his arms and leaned back against the counter. "When was your last meal?"

"I eat at the pub. Mr. Dewey is accommodating to my needs."

"I won't be." He waited until she met his gaze. "Not in this. Elizabeth, tell me what I must know to help you."

"You cannot help with this," she said firmly. "It has nothing to do with you except that it is difficult for me to be alone. To live alone. When I must live among others, I am more able to quiet the rules. A bit." She turned her face away from him and seemed to stare at nothing. "No one else can help me. I learned that long ago."

"Then tell me what you must do to help yourself."

She consumed another biscuit.

"The rules you spoke of," he said, "they are voices telling you what to do?"

She shook her head, and relief wound its way through him.

"Not voices. My voice. My thoughts. My reasoning."

"There is nothing of reason in saving stacks of used paper."

"There is to me."

"What is it, then? Do you believe they are valuable in some manner?"

"No. Not valuable." She closed her eyes. "*Me*."

"You?"

"Each scrap . . ." Her hands fisted. "They are pieces of me. Don't you see? Can't you see how I cannot—"

He grasped her hand.

"This is a piece of you," he said, rubbing the pad of his thumb across her knuckles. "This clever piece. And this," he said, reaching up to brush the wild curl from her brow. "Not those old lists."

"I *know*. Rationally, I know."

"I am assuming that rationally you knew this a month ago too."

Drawing her hand away, she fisted it on her lap. "They are pieces of you too."

"Of me?"

"At first." She drew a shaking inhalation. "Notes I took while making the prosthesis. And . . . other things . . . about you."

A list of Edinburgh cobblers. A museum ticket.

"I don't understand."

She stood abruptly. "I was *frightened*." Her arms were rigid, her fists tight by her sides.

"I don't believe it," he said. "Not you. Not frightened. About anything."

"*Yes*. You left here barely able to move without pain and I imagined you on that road to Haiknayes and I was worried for your safety. I realize it was ridiculous. I know that you have traveled all over the world and survived much greater danger than a short journey into the countryside. But I could not cease worrying."

"So you saved scraps of used paper?"

She shook her head. Her lips parted, the pale pink revealing dry shadow within.

"Elizabeth, what do scraps of used paper have to do with your concern for my safety on the road?"

"If you had come to harm while away from here," she said, the cords of her neck straining. "It would have been because I discarded them."

"That is irrational."

"Of course it is!"

"Elizabeth Shaw, your mind is extraordinary. Agile. Brilliant. And chock-full of rationality."

Drawing her lips between her teeth, her throat working, she nodded.

"I am here," he said. "I am safe. Can you discard the papers now?"

"No," she said shakily.

"Why not?"

"It only *began* in that manner."

"Began?"

"At first I was not allowed to discard scraps associated with you. Then scraps associated with the house. Then . . ." Her throat constricted again.

"Any used paper?" The collections of oddities in cartons and boxes as well, no doubt.

She nodded. Her body wavered.

He pushed the teacup toward her. She sat again and wrapped both hands around the porcelain, but her eyes darted toward the doorway, as though she would spring away to the parlor in an instant.

He touched her jaw and guided her face back toward his.

"You overcame this before," he said. "How?"

"I am so ashamed. I hate myself for it. And you will hate me too, if you don't already."

"I do not," he said, sitting back and distancing himself

from her when all he wanted was to wrap his arms around her and assure her how thoroughly he could never hate her. "How have you bested this in the past?"

She was silent.

"When you do not obey the rules," he said, "what happens?"

"I . . ." She shook her head. "They tear at me. Obeying brings such"—her throat jerked—"such relief." Her eyes were pools of desperation, but thought too. "But when I *am* able to deny a desire, it weakens."

Would that his desire functioned similarly.

"That's good news," he said. "How do you deny it?"

"It is . . . difficult." Her fingers pressed into the tabletop. She glanced at the doorway again.

Standing abruptly, she grabbed the teapot and refilled both of their cups. Then she went to the stove and lit the fire beneath the kettle.

"I distract myself with other tasks," she said to the kettle. "That helps."

"I see."

She looked skeptically at him. "Do you?"

"I am trying to."

"Sometimes I only partially concede to the desire. That often lessens the heat too."

"The heat?"

"My father once said that the desires seemed to be like a fever in me that wished to consume everything rational." A smile flitted across her eyes. "He is a physician."

Even this hint of pleasure on her face loosened Ziyaeddin's chest.

"When you were a girl, the fever did not consume everything. For here you are."

"You mustn't look at me like that, as though I have already succeeded. You do not understand."

"Explain it to me. I am going nowhere. Not again," he added.

Her eyes were full of doubt. But also determination.

"It was not your departure that caused this. That is your arrogance interpreting it."

He bit back a smile. "Is it?"

"I did not know you when I was ten years old."

"No." When she was ten years old, he had been shackled to an oar in the belly of a ship. "Though I should have liked to know you then."

Her gaze shifted away.

"My father took us to London. I was accustomed to relocating. But that move was different. We had left all our furniture here. There was so much . . . newness." Her hand gripped the kettle's handle. "That was when the rules multiplied."

"What sort of rules?"

"All sorts." She stared at the wall. "There were a precise number of strides to be taken between the carriage and the front door, lampposts to be touched on each walk to the park, a special handwriting I could only use for certain tasks, pages of books that must be memorized before I could continue to the next, a rag dog to be arranged in bed exactly each night before I could fall asleep. One night I remember, I could not find the dog. I tore my bedchamber apart searching for it. The maid had washed it and it was hanging wet from a hook in the kitchen. I could not put it to bed properly, so I held it in my arms until morning and did not sleep. I took a horrible cold. That is the only time I can remember being ill in my entire life. Shortly after that, I began collecting useless items.

"I made life in London impossible for my father. We returned to Edinburgh prematurely." A smile came hesitantly into her eyes. "When I began studying medical texts, all the rules quieted. The worst of them faded entirely. You are thinking that I am studying medicine now," she said, the tip of her forefinger tracing the kettle handle, "yet this has happened. Again. That is what you are thinking, isn't it?"

He was thinking how he wanted that busy fingertip on him. All of her fingertips.

"Perhaps," he said.

"While you were away Mr. Bridges assigned me to my own operations."

"Congratulations." He could not make himself look away. Watching her move—any part of her—was pleasurable pain he should not have denied himself for even a day.

"There is quite a lot of responsibility in being the lead surgeon. And winter always brings many patients to the infirmary. Also, the new course in practical anatomy is much more challenging than last session. I've a lot of work. I have been skimping on sleep."

The image of her curled into a ball on top of his bed would never fade.

"When you are exhausted," he said, "the rules grow stronger. Don't they?"

"Yes."

"I beg your pardon for leaving."

"It isn't your responsibility. I should be able to command my own thoughts and actions. I am a grown woman."

An exceptional woman. Even light flesh and dull pallor could not hide that.

She lifted her lashes and he was caught inside the blue—his desires, his heartbeats, his every wish.

"Elizabeth."

"I must conquer this dragon myself, Ziyaeddin."

Hearing his name upon her lips again sent his foolish heart into wild somersaults.

Unnatural stillness shone on her bare features now.

"*Havā-tō dāram*," he heard himself whisper.

"What does that mean?"

"I am here, Elizabeth. Allow me to help."

Her shoulders dropped a bit. "Forgive me for sleeping in your bed."

"I am absolutely unable to accept an apology for that."

Flinty pleasure sparked in her eyes.

"In my bedchamber," she said, "there are too many tasks to be done perfectly each night. Saturday night I was beyond exhaustion. To avoid having to do all the tasks, I promised myself I would do them later."

"Later?"

"After I slept. Then I fled. The only place in the house where there was nothing to be done was in your bed."

"Not precisely what a man wants to hear."

"This is not amusing."

"No, that actually was amusing. Tragic. Nevertheless, amusing."

Slowly her eyes widened, and he dared hope she was thinking what he was: that she belonged in his bed.

"I forgot to do the tasks when I awoke yesterday, and when I left the house I did so without my satchel," she said. "I was so angry with you that I didn't even think about them."

He laughed.

"You mustn't laugh! Usually when I am angry the rules are even louder and impossible to resist, not quieter."

"Are you able to resist them often?"

Setting the kettle upon the iron pad on the table, she sat again.

"After London I taught myself to. Rather, I bribed

myself. I gave myself prizes for succeeding." Her brow furrowed. "I feel like a perfect fool telling you this."

"Prizes?"

"I made a list of the rules."

"Another list?"

"A good list. At the top were the rules I found easiest to refuse. At the bottom were the most difficult. I began at the top, refusing to obey the easiest first. When I succeeded every day for a sennight, I rewarded myself with a gift."

"Can you use that tactic now?"

She shook her head.

"Why not?" he said.

"I have everything I want."

He stood up and set cup and saucer in the washbasin. "There must be something that you want, however small, which you do not yet possess. An idea will come to you." He went out of the kitchen and she followed.

"You won't—"

"I told you I would touch nothing in the parlor. Not tonight."

"And tomorrow?" she said.

"Tomorrow you will begin."

Her hands twisted in her skirts. "I can. I shall. I do not wish to inconvenience you."

"Of course you do." He smiled. "But not in this manner. I understand."

"You will not throw me onto the street?"

He moved close to her and felt all the need that he had tried to deny grip him powerfully. "Do you truly believe that I could?"

"No. It will be dawn soon. Shall I come sit for you, since yesterday I did not?"

"At this time you will go upstairs and don your student's

garb. Then I will take Joseph Smart to breakfast to celebrate the successful completion of his first session of medical studies."

"That was weeks ago."

"I beg your pardon for missing it."

"You needn't. Before you left, that last time I saw you, you made it clear to me that you have not assisted me in my studies for my sake, but for your own."

He was a prize fool.

"I understand that," she continued, the earnest dart deep in the bridge of her nose. "I do not require you to celebrate my accomplishments."

"If I wish to?"

"Then I suppose you will." The lips hitched up on one side. "Princes typically do whatever they please, after all."

The ache inside him was too hard and deep. He could not escape it.

"I will not leave you again," he said.

For seconds that felt as though they were years, she said nothing. Then she picked up her skirts and hurried up the stairs.

Chapter 21

The Prize

S he chose her desired prize.

The proposal she made to him went thus: each Sunday she would choose a rule that she wished to bend—even break—and, at the end of a sennight of success, he must reward her with an illustration of an anatomically correct part of the human body. Drawn in ink, the illustrations would serve her studies. She explained to him that such drawings were dear and that students rarely possessed them.

Without fanfare, he agreed to it.

Beginning with the parlor clutter, she discarded first the used papers. On Monday she gathered up a pile of scraps and placed them before the fire, then left the room, her stomach in knots and throat sour with panic.

An hour later she returned, collected the pile, moved the screen from before the grate, and tossed them in. As the flames caught at the pages and consumed them, panic swelled in her throat. She stepped toward the fire.

"Have you dined?" he said from the parlor doorway.

She swiveled to face him. She had not known he was in the house.

"I want first a drawing of the shoulder," she said.

"You will have your drawing, madam, on Sunday morning. Now, however, you will take dinner. With me."

They dined and spoke of nothing and everything, of her studies and his commissions. When she went to bed she touched the picture of the boys in the marketplace only twice rather than the usual thrice.

By sennight's end the parlor was empty of scraps. Always besting any rule made it easier to best others, and on Saturday morning she threw all of the scraps in her bedchamber onto the grate as well.

After that she removed every book from the foyer and corridor, neatly shelving hers and her father's in the parlor and returning the others to their owners. She did the same with the piles of books in her bedchamber.

With lightness in her chest, she demanded of him her prize.

"The torso. Recto. Male, if you please."

He offered her a beautiful, simple smile and then shooed her away. She hardly ever saw him. He had taken on two new commissions at once, and hadn't even time for her sittings on Sunday mornings. But each Saturday when she requested another drawing to give her reason to resist the rules, he provided it.

"You've pink in your cheeks again, Joe," Coira said as they sat side by side on the wall in the alley, sharing Libby's lunch. "You're glowin'."

"It is because I am eating all of my sausages before you come outside and gobble them up," Libby said, and bit into a hunk of Mrs. Coutts's excellent oat bread. The sun was bright. Mr. Bridges had confided to her that Dr. Jones considered her the best among the first-year students and far beyond most of the advanced medical students as well. She had plenty of reasons to glow.

"No, lass," Coira said. "You're glowin' because you're in luve."

Libby choked on crumbs.

Coira proffered the flask. "Have a sip, lass. It'll soothe your agitation."

Libby stared at her companion.

"Who is he?" Coira said. "Or is he a lass?"

"He isn't a woman," Libby found her mouth saying.

"Have you told him he's won your heart? Or, if you do, is he more likely to run than drop his drawers?"

Libby's cheeks were hot. She jumped off the wall. Packing away the remnants of food, she muttered, "Share your lunch with a person, and get teasing instead of thanks."

Coira guffawed. Then she said seriously, "If he's no' a good man, he dinna deserve you."

"Coira, you mustn't—"

Coira made the motion of locking her lips closed with a key. "To my grave. Now go an' make fools o' all those men who canna see what's right under their noses."

That night, Libby carefully watched her friends at the pub. With each word Archie and the others spoke to her, each glance they turned her way, she wondered if they realized the truth too.

She had been too arrogant, too certain that her disguise and adopted mannerisms hid her femininity. But if Coira had realized it, who else might? Was Archie's admiration for her so strong that he could continue while knowing the truth? Could Chedham simply be awaiting the ideal moment to expose her?

No. Not Chedham. His jealousy of her was always so obvious. He would certainly reveal her if he knew.

Returning home, she went directly to Ziyaeddin's quarters.

Days earlier, when she had gone to demand the latest prize of him, she had found him standing at the easel, with the light of afternoon illumining his satiny hair and warm skin and white shirt, which he wore without collar or cravat. Her pulse had leaped. He always made her pulse quicken.

He had no idea. Each time the urge to confess it to him tightened her throat, she swallowed it, reminding herself that the relief of telling him would only last a moment before she must confess yet another private thought to him. The more she denied each urge, the weaker they all became.

Now she counted to ten in her head.

She had no drawing to demand of him, not for another three days. She needn't tell him about Coira either. Coira posed no threat. She had no real reason to speak to him now, only the desire to.

Returning to the parlor, she pulled out a book and got to work.

"I HAVE AN extraordinary request." She stood in the doorway of his studio, her hands tight around the jambs to either side. He had forbidden her to enter his quarters, even as Joseph Smart. He had also forbidden her to speak to him unless he had left his studio. Speaking with her— *being* with her—was unwise.

So he rarely left his studio.

Obviously she was not taking to heart at least one of his strictures.

"I would like drawings of the whole body, both verso and recto. The entire body. Male. All external parts."

That her words should produce an instant surge of heat

to his male external parts only proved his idiot susceptibility.

He returned his attention to the canvas.

"Thy will be done," he said, dipping his brush into fresh paint.

"You won't ask for what I am demanding this comprehensive illustration?"

"I trust you."

"You should. For this is different." As was her voice: subdued yet firm.

He paused midbrushstroke. "What is different?"

"The rule that I am determined to break."

He turned to her. "What is it?"

Her brows arced. "You wish to know?"

He had told her that she needn't inform him as to which rule she was conquering each sennight, only which prize she required of him to give her incentive to conquer it. In this way he had effectively removed one occasion for speaking with her each week.

He was a drowning man grasping at driftwood.

"If you wish to tell me," he said, "yes, I wish to know." He wished to know everything: her irrational rules, her studies, her worries, her triumphs, the scent of her neck, the flavor of her mouth, the texture of her body against his.

"Visiting the infirmary," she said. "Without Mr. Bridges, when I needn't. When I am not expected there. I go to check on the patients I have seen earlier in the day, to assure myself that their dressings haven't slipped or sutures burst, or that they are being given the correct medications. After Christmas I got into the habit of going several times a day—day and night, actually. Now I go only twice, once each afternoon and once every night on my route home from the pub."

"The infirmary is not en route from the pub to this house."

"That is true."

He bent his head and played the brush between his fingers. She was too somber and he was having the inconvenient need to go to her, take her in his arms, and make her forget about the damn rule and the infirmary—everything but him.

But that would not help her. That would help neither of them.

"Are there not competent nurses and physicians on call at night to see to that?" he said.

"It hasn't anything to do with them."

"I see."

"Do you? I know it is difficult to understand. My father never has entirely, nor Alice or Iris, or even Amarantha or Constance. None of them truly understand how I can be bound to irrational needs. I suppose that is a compliment of sorts." Her lips twisted a bit, as though she were trying to smile but couldn't. "I will not think less of you if you cannot understand."

"It is especially difficult to break this rule—visiting the infirmary multiple times—because it coincides with your actual concern for the patients."

A sound came from her abruptly. "You do understand."

"You call there twice every day, even when you have spent the entire morning at the infirmary and the afternoon in lecture?"

She nodded.

"Make it once each day for the duration of the sennight, and on Saturday I will give you what you wish."

Her features bloomed into a smile. "Thank you." Then she bowed. "Sir."

"Begone now, ruffian," he said.

Still smiling, she went, and he was again sunk in a peace that he no longer wanted or enjoyed.

"I DID IT," Libby said, entering the kitchen as spring sunshine broke from behind clouds and shone on the coffee and bread and butter on the table.

He looked from the newspaper in his hands to her. "Did what?"

"Don't play coy with me."

"I would never." His gaze was all over her, traveling across her face and down her neck and along her shoulders and arms and breasts. "You seem well."

"I am better. I have done it. You must pay up."

Folding the paper, he laid it on the table. "Before breakfast?"

"You've already had your breakfast." She gestured to the dishes.

"I meant your breakfast."

"I breakfasted before dawn. I could not sleep. I have been anticipating this for seven days. Unfortunately I have just received an urgent note from Alice that Constance intends to visit Leith this afternoon. I must be there. Apparently the last time Constance called, Alice had difficulty convincing her that I had not run away to join a troupe of traveling players. So I must be off to Leith now. But be assured, sir, I will collect on my prize the moment I return."

"As you wish, madam." He nodded.

"Are you truly royalty?"

He hesitated only a moment. "Yes."

"I wounded you. With that broken glass. Will you have me beheaded for it?"

"You have no respect for authority," he said, taking up his paper again. "I wounded myself with that glass."

"Not really."

"Yes, you will be punished for causing a scratch upon the anointed skin. Though not beheading. Barbaric practice, that."

"Indefinite imprisonment, perhaps?"

"Perhaps. I will see to it as soon as I can find the time. Until then, enjoy Leith."

WHEN SHE WAS gone from the house, finally he set down the newspaper he had stared at without reading, leaned his elbows on his knees, and put his face in his hands. With her will to succeed and her strength that teetered on the verge of splintery vulnerability and her intelligent sparkling eyes and her lips—by all that was holy, *her lips*—she would be the death of him.

The doorbell rang. No acquaintance of his would call this early of a Saturday morning. Taking up the paper again and determining to actually read it, he settled back in his chair.

Another ring sounded through the house. He folded the paper and went to the door.

A stranger stood on the stoop, a horse on the street below dark with sweat.

"Mr. Kent?" the man said.

"I am he."

He proffered a letter, then hurried down the steps and to his mount.

Ziyaeddin stared at the hand on the front of the letter. Ali had never before sent mail by a private messenger.

The grace of Allah be with you, Tabirshah!

I write with news from the princess: the general's health fails. He will not live through the summer.

His end is near, and with it the restoration of justice.

The princess sends to you now a trusted friend who will serve you upon your journey home.

Ali

Ziyaeddin reread the words until they ran into each other. His sister would be free, her captivity at an end, her children safe from threat. With the general's death, their family's allies would rise up in her defense. It was all he had wished.

Yet his breaths would not come.

Tabirshah.

King of Tabir.

WHEN LIBBY RETURNED home she did not find him in his studio or even in the kitchen. He often went out in the evening.

She went into the parlor to fetch a book.

He sat before the fireplace, a glass and bottle on the table beside him.

"You are here!" she said, then threw up her palm as he reached for his walking stick. "No, don't stand. It is only I."

He looked at her so singularly, as though she had spoken in a language he did not recognize. His eyes seemed full of darkness.

When he did not reply, she said, "Why are you here?"

"I live here," he said. "This is my house."

"You never sit in this parlor. In all the months I have lived here. Not once."

"Perhaps I do when you are not in."

She crossed the room and sat on the edge of the chair across from him.

"You so adamantly do not want to see me," she said,

"that even though you wish to be at home you remain away from it and never come into most of the house when I am here. Admit it."

"Yes," he said, leaning forward with his elbows on his knees and folding his hands. "I do everything in my power to avoid seeing you. How went your day in Leith with Lady Constance?"

"Awful. That is, she was not awful. It was wonderful to see her, and little Madeline, who is growing so swiftly. But Alice wanted cakes for Madeline, and Constance suggested we make a stroll of it, and somehow we ended up at the market. That went poorly."

"You have trapped your lips between your teeth," he said, looking at her mouth, but without pleasure it seemed.

She popped her lips free. "What of it?"

"You do so when you are especially distressed." He lifted his gaze to her eyes.

She stood. "Something is wrong. What is wrong? You were in excellent spirits this morning. What happened? Is it your leg? Are you in p—?"

"No. What went poorly at the market?"

She reached into her pocket and drew out several crumpled bits of paper. "There were so many people. And so much noise."

"There are noise and people on every Edinburgh street, yet you have traversed them successfully for a month. Have you not?"

"I don't know the reason that some places agitate me more than others. It never happens when I am tending the ill."

He glanced at the fire.

She tossed in the scraps. The relief of watching them burn was slow, a spring welling up to bubble over a dry rock.

"I am like an infant, learning how to walk and tumbling over again and again, a child who must sing the alphabet repeatedly to remember it. I suspect that is how you see me."

"I do not see you as a child, Elizabeth Shaw. Not in the least."

"Why are you drinking spirits? What has happened? I won't cease asking until you tell me, you know. My mind will not allow questions to go unanswered. You must tell me."

"Yet I will not, however many times you ask." Now the slightest crease appeared at one side of his mouth.

"I can break you," she said. "I broke my father. He grew so weary of it he fled to London for an entire year. I think he always hoped that I would outgrow my peculiarity. When I did not he needed a holiday from it finally. At times I have broken Alice and Constance too. I'm certain Alice allowed me to do this because even the idea of having me live in her house exhausted her. Dr. Jones is always exasperated by my questions. Archie laughs, but sometimes he looks at me as though I am mad or simply impetuous. I am not impetuous. It is only that my mind never rests."

"You will not break me."

"I might."

"If seventeen years of exile has had one benefit, it is that I have learned patience." His gaze traveled over her face and down her neck and shoulders. "Perhaps two benefits."

She could simply throw herself at him. *On* him.

"Seventeen?" she said, gripping the back of the chair to prevent herself from moving.

"Eight years in Alexandria. Two at sea. Seven here."

More bits and pieces of him. They did not satisfy her.

"Won't you tell me what has happened today?" she said.

He said nothing as firelight played in his eyes.

"Have you done my drawing yet?" she said.

"No. My apologies, madam. I shall at once." He rose.

"You needn't go. I have paper here, and as I would very much like to watch you draw, yet you have barred me from your studio, you must remain here and draw it."

"Must I, tyrant?"

"Oh, yes." She grabbed a sheet from the desk and pen and ink, but when she turned he was already at her shoulder and setting the lamp down on the desk.

"Here," he said, taking the items from her, and their hands brushed. Neither of them jerked away. "This table suits."

"I am glad you haven't done it yet," she said, pulling another chair to the desk. "I have decided I don't want the entire body. Only the hand and forearm. In detail."

He dipped the pen into ink. "Why the change?"

"Do you object?"

"To drawing a hand and forearm instead of an entire figure?" He looked aside at her, a single brow lifted.

"You needn't look at me as though I am insane."

"Forgive me. I am delighted to draw whatever you require. Left or right?"

"Please draw the left. Yours, specifically." A swirl of nerves went straight up her center.

He laid his left hand, palm down, on the desk. Pen met paper and a line of subtle grace appeared.

"You do not object to this either?" she said, her pulse quick.

"Why should I?"

"To me possessing a picture of you?"

"You already do." The pen moved swiftly across the paper, with utter confidence, the lines clean and sharp.

"I do not," she said.

"The picture of the marketplace in your bedchamber is of the market in the neighborhood in Alexandria in which I spent my youth."

"The black-haired boy?" The one she touched each day—the touch that had become a requirement from the first day she had come to this house. "It is *you*?"

"It is."

"Who is the other boy?"

"Joachim. He was my closest companion, nearly a brother to me, to the horror of my mother."

"What about him was horrifying?"

"Joachim's family was Christian. My father had always been a man of expansive mind and spirit, and welcomed all men of faith into his friendship. After we escaped we settled in a Christian quarter of the city in order to better hide. But my mother feared for her children."

"You had siblings?"

"Have. A sister." He set down the pen and pushed back the chair and stood.

"I beg your pardon," she said quickly. "Please don't leave. I won't pry any further."

"I am not leaving." He pulled off his coat and hung it on the back of the chair. "Unless you wish me to?" he said with a partial smile. He wore a waistcoat of midnight blue that fit snugly to his torso, and his shoulders stretched the fine linen shirt.

Libby shook her head.

He sat, folding the left sleeve to above the elbow. There was only dark skin and muscle and, on his forearm that was corded with strength, black hair. Again he took up the pen.

"Did your mother fear that you would be discovered by the courtiers who had betrayed your father?"

"No. At that time we were far from home and well hidden."

"Then what did she fear?"

"That we would be converted to the faith of our protectors. She needn't have had concern for my sister. Aairah's faith was immoveable as a mountain, even then."

"You draw so swiftly yet with such accuracy," she said almost levelly. "Your talent is astonishing."

"A gift from the creator of which this servant is not worthy."

"Obviously your mother needn't have worried about your faith either. Though I suppose Christians attribute such gifts to God too."

He smiled, but did not look away from his drawing.

"Who taught you how to draw and paint?"

"The uncle of Joachim. Joachim's father was a guardsman for a dignitary and had little time for us. But his uncle was a humble man. He owned a shop in the market where he sold icons for the pilgrims. From the roof of it Joachim and I would spy on the washerwomen at work."

"Why would you want to spy on washerwomen?"

"They rolled up their sleeves to work, *güzel kız*," he said, the movement of his pen precise. "When a boy is dying of thirst, he will revel in even a single drop of rain."

She stared at his forearm.

"His uncle's talent was prodigious," he continued. "It was wasted on those pilgrim icons."

"Not to the pilgrims, I suspect. Nor you."

Now he turned his smile upon her. "Indeed not."

"You are almost finished already," she said. "But I would like another."

"What other could you want? An icon, perhaps, of yourself slaying the dragon as you have so valiantly done these past weeks?" His gaze was moving over her face as it did sometimes, as though he saw not her features but the art he could make of them.

"Movement," she said. "I would like a series of pictures—"

"A series?" His quiet laughter spread warmth in her. "You are demanding."

"Four or five pictures."

"Ah, the tyrant seeks to take advantage of me now."

"Take advantage?" she said a little unsteadily.

"Mustn't you demolish another of your rules before receiving another prize?"

"Recall that originally you agreed to draw an entire figure."

"That I did, reckless fool that I was. So be it. What movement exactly do you wish to study?"

"This." With the tip of her forefinger she traced the ridge of muscle the length of his forearm.

He went entirely still.

"This muscle," she said, stroking slowly. The texture of his taut skin made wild pleasure inside her. "I wish to have a detailed study of its movement beginning with the fingers extended to the hand fisting."

After a moment he said quite low, "The hand."

"Your hand," she said. "Your hand that I felt pressed over my heart when I would have torn out every strand of my hair had you not been there, when I would have locked myself in my bedchamber and beaten at the walls until I collapsed from exhaustion, for the thoughts would not quiet no matter how I tried." Her fingers climbed past his wrist. "This hand that for days bore marks from the scratches I put there with my fingernails when you held me together, which you never spoke of," she said, running her fingertips over his smooth skin. "How sorry I am to have treated you so, and how grateful that you—"

"You mustn't be sorry." He spoke roughly. "And it is I who am grateful that you have trusted me to help you."

"I only wish—"

Lifting his head, he met her gaze and the restraint always present in the depths of his dark eyes was gone. Entirely gone. Only longing shone there, and desire.

"Ziyaeddin," she whispered.

Reaching to her face and curving his hand warm and strong around her cheek, he bent his head and kissed her.

Chapter 22

The Fire

It was as simple as that, as though their lips were meant to touch and their breaths, though trembling, mingle with intoxicating certainty.

His lips coaxed and it was so easy to respond, to do as he bid and let him taste her lips, her mouth, and take tastes of him in return. The scent of his skin and cologne and paint filled her senses now, his flavor of brandy and heat delicious, exhilarating. She met each caress of his lips with hers, flattening her palm to the table to push up toward him, to be closer. It was remarkable how she felt his kiss in her mouth and throat and chest and belly. *Everywhere.*

The tip of his tongue swept along her lips. Moaning, she opened willingly, hungrily, and reached for him with both hands.

Grasping her waist, he pulled her onto his lap.

She had no thoughts, only him—his satiny hair and

the evening's stubble on his jaw and his hard thigh and his hands spread on her back, holding her so tightly, and his mouth doing delectable things to hers. He was hot and hard, thoroughly alive and full of strength and *touching her.*

Need swelled in her, sweet and hot in her breasts and stomach. She needed to be even closer, pressed to him entirely.

His thumb stroked down her jaw, then over her chin, urging her lips apart. She complied, willingly, eagerly, and felt the caress of his tongue against hers. Lust jolted between her thighs. She tried the caress herself, and a sound of satisfaction rumbled in his throat. He delved into her.

It was an answer finally to all the frustrated confusion and yearning of months, he was kissing her and she never wanted it to end.

And she wanted *more*—more of his heat and strength and the glorious pleasure of touching him.

Sliding her hand down his neck and over his chest she felt the hard power of his body beneath linen and wool. Seeking his mouth even more closely, she slipped her palm over the fall of his trousers.

He caught her hand in his grip and with a groan tore it away from him.

"*No.*" His hand came around the back of her neck. "Elizabeth." Her name was a harsh whisper against her lips. And then the words came to banish any doubt of what he meant by *no* and *Elizabeth.* "You mustn't. We mustn't."

She broke away. Pushing off him, she stumbled to her feet.

Walking across the room on unsteady legs, she ran her fingers over her hot face and tender lips, and thoughts tumbled over each other, cluttered with lust and anger and guilt.

"Fine. Yes." She faced him and lifted her chin. "Fine," she repeated. There were too many other words wanting to be said, and she refused to give them rein. "Would you care for tea? I think tea would be a good idea at this moment. I will put the kettle on."

Biting down on confusion, in the darkness she went to the kitchen.

Her hands around the kettle and pump were steady, and they were steady as she lit the stove and a glow of light plumed in the room. She was a person of science with a life that no other woman in the world had. She was not a widgeon to melt at a man's touch as though she had no structure inside her to support her.

She went to the cabinet and reached for a cup and saucer.

He came to her, making no effort at silence, his footsteps like a hammer striking every one of her vertebrae. Grasping her waist, he turned her to him.

She lifted her face, and he captured her mouth beneath his.

It was right, perfect and delectable, and when she grabbed his shoulders he dragged her against him. Solid muscle met her—his thighs and hips and chest. Fingers threading through her hair, he kissed first her lips, then her throat and neck. The need rocking through her body was overwhelming, powerful, but honest and *good*.

Gripping his arms, she pressed herself to him, wanting to feel him everywhere on her, flesh to flesh, all of the skin and bones and sinews and muscle that made him beautiful on the outside.

"I did not understand it could be like this," she said.

His fevered gaze covered her features. "I knew it would be."

Stroking his thumb down her neck, he skimmed the edge of her bodice. She felt her body quivering, waiting for more, wanting more. His hand surrounded her breast.

"By all that is—" His voice caught. "Elizabeth," he whispered, and his thumb slipped across her arousal. She gasped and pressed into his hand. It was luscious. *Deliriously good.* Clinging to him she accepted his kiss and his touch and this new and perfect pleasure.

"Haw there!" The shout from the doorway echoed across the kitchen.

They broke apart.

Mrs. Coutts stood on the threshold, arms laden with parcels and mouth agape.

"Mrs. Coutts?" Libby exclaimed. "What are you doing here on a Saturday night?"

"Interruptin' a ravishment, by the looks o' it!"

"It was not ravishment," she said.

"An' no' a moment too soon." She cast him a dark glower.

"Why are you actually here, Mrs. Coutts?" he said.

"I've come to cook the lass dinner for the morrow. Now she's feedin' again I'll no' have her skippin' a meal an' wastin' away, no' under my watch! An' I'll no' have any man takin' advantage o' her, weak as she still be, no matter how fine a man," she said with a wag of her fingertip at the man who stood a head taller than her and paid her wages.

"He was not taking advantage of me," Libby said. "Rather the opposite."

"That statement is not accurate," he said, running his hand over the back of his neck and making Libby ache to touch him there too. She wanted to touch him everywhere.

"Oh ho! That's how it be? Each o' you takin' the blame for the other, now?" She shook her head, then pinned him with a hard stare. "Sir, you've a party to attend to-night."

"I do not."

"Aye, you do. Dr. Hope's supper party."

"Dr. *Hope*?" Libby said. "Dr. Thomas Charles Hope, vice president of the Royal Society of Edinburgh? The renowned physician and chemist! Yet you did not mean to attend?"

"I had another matter to attend to," he said in a tone that made heat ripple up through her.

"If he knows what's best, he'll go now," his housekeeper warned.

"Mr. Smart," he said, and bowed. "Good night, Mrs. Coutts."

Then he was gone from the kitchen, and Libby felt as though her internal organs were sucked out the door with him, which was ridiculous.

The discovery of so many new sensations was bewildering. Also instructive. She understood now why Constance, a noble heiress, had forced her father to allow her to wed a man who taught fencing for a living, and how Amarantha and the duke had sailed across oceans to find each other. And she finally understood why a woman and a man would find an empty room at a party and make love on an uncomfortable sofa. The need to follow Ziyaeddin now pressed outward beneath her skin like a fever. She felt at once excited and lost.

"Now, lass," Mrs. Coutts said. "We're to have a wee chat about the terms I put to the master for stayin' on in his employ when you came to live here."

"Oh. But you don't seem the overly pious sort. That is, you don't object to me *living* here."

"Aye, when I thought you'd nothin' in your head but those books." Her own head wagged from side to side.

"He's as fine a gentleman as I've e'er known. An' to be sure he's changed his habits since you've come to live here. But, lass, he's no saint."

Libby could not misunderstand Mrs. Coutts's meaning.

"Yet he lives so austerely," she said.

"Aye. But you've seen his paintings."

Full of depth and movement, they were all passion and beauty. And longing, she realized now.

"Dinna believe the man he shows the world to be the truth o' him." Moving forward, she took Libby's hands into both of her own big, callused hands, and clasped them warmly. "I know you've a good heart, lass. Only take care. He's no' a subject for you to study."

Disengaging, Libby backed up.

"Thank you for your words of wisdom, Mrs. Coutts. And I am very grateful for you coming here tonight to cook. I appreciate everything that both of you have done for me, more than I can express."

Snatching up a candle and leaving the room, she turned toward the door to his quarters. It was open and she went in.

He was gone, to the party or somewhere else. It hardly mattered. That he had kissed her, touched her, and then left her so easily only proved Mrs. Coutts's words. He had told her again and again to stay away from him, and she had pursued her desire anyway, because that was what she did when any desire pressed at her.

Now she could not return to the parlor where the drawing still lay on the desk. Running up to her bedchamber, she turned her eyes away from the painting of the marketplace, dragged her favorite medical tome to the window seat, lit a lamp, and settled in to read.

It was a futile effort. She thought of him caressing her and she ached for it.

Jumping up from the window seat, she went to the marketplace painting and touched her fingertips to the boys' running feet.

She returned to the window and curled up on the seat.

After a time she heard Mrs. Coutts bustle into the foyer and depart. Turning down the lamp's wick, Libby peeked through the drapery onto the street. The cobblestones glistened with moisture and a lamp at the corner showed the Scotswoman marching homeward. The clouds had parted to reveal a canopy of stars, and the moon cast soft gray stone in a silvery glimmer.

Of every place she had lived—all the grand estates to which her father had been invited over the years—she felt entirely at home here in this city of medicine. This fantastical life she was now actually living had been her dream forever. And she was succeeding, despite the charade she lived and the competition and the constant fear of discovery.

Yet she could not cease thinking about him and wanting him.

You haven't even a moment of time to devote to satisfying idle curiosities.

She stared into the sparkling night and thought that her wishes had conjured him from the darkness. But it was in fact him passing beneath the streetlamp with his silver-headed walking stick and handsome shoulders and uneven gait. Her body filled with yearning. *And happiness.* For the first time in months, beneath her breasts she ached with happiness.

As she watched he slowed at the edge of the streetlamp's aura, then halted.

A cloaked figure stepped away from the opposite building and then, pushing off the hood, moved toward him.

Coira?

It could not be a coincidence that Coira had come here to this street and was speaking with him now. Closing the curtain, Libby ran down the stairs.

"Sir?" A woman approached him.

Ziyaeddin did not pause. The swordstick in his cane was sufficient to deter a thief, but he had no will to harm a woman. Tonight, he had no will to harm anyone. With the texture of Elizabeth's body and the flavor of her mouth still crowding his senses, he had only one wish: to touch her again, and damn reason, destiny, and all wisdom.

He could not fulfill that wish—not even momentarily. With one taste his craving had become need. That need would lead only to a path neither of them could travel.

"You be the painter!" The woman sounded surprised. "The one that's painted Dallis, aye?"

"I am," he said.

Pulling back her hood she revealed a high brow thick with worry. "Have you seen her o' late?"

"I haven't. Not in several months."

"Then d'you happen to be acquainted with Mr. Joseph Smart? I'm near certain he lives on this street."

"In fact I am."

"Could you show me which door be his?"

"I cannot. But I will convey a message to him for you."

Three houses down the street, his front door opened and a fully cloaked figure stepped onto the dark stoop.

"*Coira*," she whispered in Joseph's voice, and gestured with her hand.

Coira dipped him a swift curtsy and hurried toward his doorstep.

He followed.

Inside, the women's conversation emanated from the parlor.

"Why, lass, you clean up pretty as a peach!"

"Never mind that. Are you unwell? How did you know where to find me?"

"I followed you to this block once, when Bethany and Dall—Sir! What're you doin' here?"

"This is my house," he said. "Although apparently that is not general knowledge these days." He went to the hearth and built the fire.

The woman was looking back and forth between them much like his housekeeper had earlier.

"He knows the truth o' you, lass?"

"I live here, so of course he must. Coira," she said with gentle impatience. "Now do tell me why you came looking for me. Are you ill?"

"'Tis Dallis. Nobody's seen her in days."

"Oh. Well, perhaps she has gone to visit family or friends elsewhere, in the countryside?"

"Dallis has no family," he said, setting the poker back in its stand.

Elizabeth's eyes were no longer hazy and full of pleasure, but crisply aware.

"How do you know that?" she said.

"She sat for me a number of times. In her boredom, she often spoke about herself."

"'Tis true she's got no kin," Coira said. "An' if she's e'er gone farther than the tollgate, I'll eat my hat."

"Where do you believe Dallis has gone?" he said.

"I fear the worst, sir." She clutched her arms tight about her.

"Do sit," he said, gesturing toward a chair. "Share what you are able with Mr. Smart." He went toward the door.

Libby's stomach was a storm of nerves, yet he was as self-possessed as always. It was as though nothing extraordinary had happened in this very room only two hours earlier, as though he had not pulled her onto him and made love to her with kisses, as though he'd no idea every cell in her body still wanted him.

"Where are you going?" she said.

"To prepare tea for our guest."

He left.

Coira was gaping.

"He's makin' *tea*? That fine gentleman, biddin' me, soaked hems an' all, sit in his parlor while he's off to make tea? For *me*?"

"We haven't a servant at nighttime. And he is generous."

"Generous'? Lass, he's a miracle! No wonder you're head o'er ears for him."

"Oh, do cease this. And tell me what you believe has happened to Dallis."

Ziyaeddin returned as Coira was describing the last few times she had seen her friend. Giving a teacup and saucer to her, he did not, however, sit.

"She's been feelin' poorly," Coira continued, "but I didna heed it. Truth be told, I thought she were play-actin'."

"Why would she playact illness?" Libby asked.

"To no' be obliged to—" Coira glanced up at him. "Help a lass here, sir?"

His gaze turned to Libby and her heartbeat performed the most astonishing somersault.

"She is a surgeon," he said, returning his attention to Coira. "You can speak candidly now. Indeed, you must if you wish her to aid you."

"Lass," Coira said. "I'd thought Dallis were pretendin' to be ill so she'd no' be obliged to take Reeve when he said so."

"Oh. Of course."

"James Reeve?" Ziyaeddin said.

"Aye." Coira's lips twisted. "Mongrel's got the leases. Bought 'em right out from under our noses an' now he thinks he can threaten we all with bein' cast onto the street any time he cares to. Dallis laughs at him so he's worst on her," she said with a scowl.

"Perhaps Dallis is with Mr. Reeve now," Libby said. "Do you know where he lives?"

Coira shook her head.

"I do." Ziyaeddin moved to the door.

Libby stood. "You know him too?"

"I will find him."

Motioning for Coira to remain, she followed him to the foyer. He was pulling on his greatcoat.

"You will go now? After midnight?"

"Men like Reeve are easiest to find at night. How does this woman know you are not a boy?"

"She guessed. I share my lunch with her and I am teaching her to read, and she is not afraid to sit close to a youth. Women are much cleverer than men, and far more observant."

"That has become entirely clear to me." He took his hat and walking stick in one hand. "Earlier, I should not have left you."

"Oh? Was the party that dull?"

A smile played upon his lips, but it was tempered with something else. Disquiet.

"What should you have done instead?" she said.

"I should have bid you return to the parlor," he said, donning his hat, "and drawn pictures for as many hours as you demanded it, simply for a thin excuse to remain in your presence."

"If you had done that I would have thrown myself at you again."

"You did not throw yourself at me. I kissed you."

"I remember it differently. I am now about to throw myself at you again."

"I will resist."

"Not successfully," she said.

Releasing the door handle, he came to her and bent his head to her. It was the merest touch of his lips to hers, but precious and perfect and sweetly lingering.

"That isn't enough," she whispered when he lifted his mouth from hers.

"It will never be enough," he said roughly, close above her lips.

She grasped his lapels with both hands and parted her lips beneath his.

He pulled her close. Then they were kissing again in earnest, her body filling up with heat and relief so profound it made her dizzy.

With a harsh sound in his chest, he broke away and returned to the door.

"Which part of 'I will resist' was that?" she said, tasting him on her lips and pressing her palms to the wall to steady herself.

"That," he said quite deeply, "was the last time."

"The last time you will pretend to resist?"

"The last time I will kiss you."

"You jest."

"Never again," he said.

Guilt poked at her. "Mrs. Coutts told me about her condition for remaining in your employ while I live here. Do you fear she will give notice?"

"This has nothing to do with her. It is about you. And me. Never again," he repeated as though forcing the words from his throat, as though by saying them he would make it so.

"That is ridiculous when we both want—"

"For your sake. For mine. For your future. For my sanity."

"For my future? Once before you claimed that you did not wish me to be distracted from my project."

"You remember that?"

"I remember everything. But I don't know if what you said is true, and I would rather have the truth than a lie or excuse."

He came to her, grasped her hand tightly, and lifted it to his lips.

"Believe that I wish only the best for you," he said. "And believe that if this mistake we have made today does not cease here, now, either you or I will have to leave this house at once. You must give me your promise."

His eyes looked into hers as though he sought to read upon her irises the promise he wanted from her.

"I do not understand why you would deny us this," she said, drawing her hand from his. "Unless . . . Are you truly royalty? The stories you have told me, are they not stories only, but actual history? Do you reject me because I am unworthy of you?"

"It is I who am unworthy of you, *güzel kız*—I who have hidden from my destiny while you have run toward yours."

"Establishing yourself in a foreign land is not running from destiny. It is surviving despite the evils destiny has thrown at you."

"Elizabeth, give me your promise now."

She nodded.

He left and she stood for a minute by the closed door, trying to make sense of how her happiness had abruptly turned upon end. Then she returned to Coira.

HE DID NOT come home until dawn. Slumped in the window seat of her bedchamber where she had dropped into fitful sleep, she awoke with a start to the sound of the front door closing.

She ran down the stairs.

"Did you find him? I am glad you have returned."

"Did you expect me not to return?" he said, pulling off his coat.

"You left in the middle of the night to search low places for a vile man, and you had only just said that one of us might have to move out of this house. So there were at least two reasons for you to never return."

His eyes were tired, but a smile shone in them. "Yet here I am."

"Did you find him?"

"No. But I now know where to find him."

"How did you even know where to search for him?"

"For a short time he was in my employ. After it became clear that he was inclined to violence, I broke off the connection. I haven't seen him in years." He moved away. "I will speak with him tonight."

"I will go with you."

"You will not. You will sleep tonight, and tomorrow return to the infirmary and lecture well rested and prepared to work."

"Don't patronize me." She followed him, watching the unnatural strain in his gait. "I will go with you. Two investigators are always to be preferred to one."

He halted. "No. You will not do this."

"I care about Coira and her friends. I wish to discover the truth of Dallis's disappearance as much as you do."

"Yet I wish you to remain safe." He continued toward his quarters. "Leave this to me."

"I cannot. Even were I not interested in it as Coira's friend I still would not be able to cease thinking about it and trying to solve it. And I certainly won't be able to sleep well while you are riding about Edinburgh's dark alleyways."

"You must make the effort, nevertheless."

"For months I have proven myself capable of going about this city as a man and suddenly you do not trust that I can do so?"

"I will not allow you to jeopardize your safety," he said sharply.

Metallic flavor came to her tongue. "You are *angry* with me?"

"I bid you do as I wish."

"There is the trouble," she said, "for I rarely do what others wish. Also, I can see you are in pain from this night you have spent in the saddle. I could relieve those muscles now if you would allow me."

"Thank you, no."

"Pride again?"

"Not this time. The spirit is entirely willing. The flesh is unfortunately weak." He turned to her and there was no weakness in his eyes or stance, only granite certainty. "I meant what I said earlier. This cannot be."

Sick heat filled her stomach.

He went into his studio and the door closed. For several minutes she stared at the panel, counting her quick heart-beats, but they would not slow.

Chapter 23

The Flood

"*E*ven my mother writes messages warmer than this," Iris said, swinging her heels against the wall as she passed the paper back to Libby.

"'Tis enough to freeze the tits off a lass," Coira agreed.

"I believe that was his intention. Metaphorically," Libby said, rereading the note he had left in the parlor for her in the middle of the night: *I have spoken with Reeve. He insists that he has not seen Dallis in some time. If you wish, I will pursue the matter.*

"I left him a message too."

"Poured your heart out, did you, poor thing?"

"No. I told him I was leaving. I paid the stable boy to collect my belongings from Mrs. Coutts and deliver them to my new residence today."

They were both staring at her.

"Don't look at me like that. It is the most sensible solution. I will not succumb to foolishness and he has made it clear that I am a nuisance." Rather, a mistake. He had called their beautiful kisses a *mistake*. "I will be fine in a new residence until my father returns."

"Are you coming to live with me and Mama?" Iris said. "My prayers have been answered!"

"Thank you, Iris. But I cannot be changing clothing and donning whiskers in hackneys every morning and night. Someone would discover me."

"I'd have you stay with me in a trice," Coira said, "if I could be sure you'd no' be topped by a lad lookin' for me."

"Topped?" Iris's brows were high.

"Penetrated in sexual congress," Libby said. "See, Coira? I understood that reference. But thank you, my friend. You are kind."

Coira clucked her tongue. "'Tis a fool man who doesna want you."

"You cannot live in Leith with Alice either," Iris said. "You must ask Tabitha and Thomas to take you in."

"No, I cannot ask them to lie." Yet she had asked it of him for months. And he had done so generously, requiring of her only two things in return: to sit for him and to otherwise leave him alone.

For months she had done neither. She owed him this.

"I will find lodging," she said.

"Aren't you anxious, Libby?" Iris said.

"No. I have learned that it is easier to do everything as a man." Except, it seemed, want one.

"You feelin' alright, Joe?" Archie peered at her across stacks of books. "You look peaked."

"Mm hm," Libby mumbled. Her head was heavy and thick. The letters on the page before her were crossing. She had spent the previous evening trudging from boardinghouses to landlords' homes, without success.

Finally Mr. Dewey had shown her the cot in the Bone's kitchen. Between the rats scratching around, the discomfort of the breast bindings, the anxiety of the whiskers falling off while she slept, and being woken before dawn, she'd barely gotten a wink.

"Looks like you slept in that coat."

"Sod off," she grumbled.

A pair of round thighs and a wide waist appeared beside the table.

"Well, that's that, lads!"

Libby looked up, squinting to bring George into focus.

"What's that?" Archie said.

"Plath's latest nastiness," George said, "making me measure every damn inch of that intestine . . . I've had enough, lads." He tucked his thumbs in his waistcoat. "I've just turned in my withdrawal. I'm done! No longer a medical student!"

"Congratulations, George," Libby said.

Archie extended his hand and shook George's. "Best wishes to you."

"I'm a new man, lads! It's law for me as soon as the new session begins."

"How'd the pater take the news?" Archie asked.

"Disowned me, the old bastard." George's grin broadened. "He's even already sent word to the pub to cut my tab and a letter to my landlord that he won't pay another night's rent."

"You're out on the street?" Archie gaped. With his large, affectionate family he never entirely understood George's acrimony toward his horrid father.

"Caroline's family's taken me in." His cheeks were rosy. "We're to wed next month."

"Congratulations again," Libby said, smiling finally.

"Aye, lad!" Archie said, slapping him on the back.

"Haven't felt finer in my life," George said cheerfully. "Who's for a pint?"

"George," Libby said. "Has your landlord leased your flat out yet?"

"No. Rang a peal over my head, in fact. Said it's impossible to find a tenant at this time of year, not till the new students come to town in the fall."

"I'll take that lease off your hands. Today, if that's all right with you. For the remainder of the session."

"Knew you slept in your coat!" Archie said, his eyes accusing.

"What are you, Joe, out of the mansion now?" George said.

"The mansion? Do you mean Mr. Kent's house?"

Archie nodded.

"It isn't a mansion. And how would you know? You've not been there."

"Pincushion told us all about it," George said. "He said it's the finest house he's ever been in."

"And he's been in my family's house, and George's too," Archie said with a nod. "What'd you do to get yourself booted out on the street, lad?"

"I did not get booted out. He would never do such a thing. He is a gentleman."

Archie held up both palms. "I meant no insult, lad."

"George, let's buy you that celebratory pint," she said, taking up her satchel that felt like a load of bricks. "Then we will go speak with your landlord."

ZIYAEDDIN CRUMPLED Alice Campbell's letter in his fist.

He had driven Elizabeth away. He had not intended it. But after Mrs. Coutts's tale of his houseguest's swift departure, and his initial shock, he had made himself believe it was for the best.

Fool that he was, he had not worried for her safety.

"A load o' courage, that lass has got," Mrs. Coutts said, nodding sagely as she stirred a pot. "Poor dear doesna even realize her heart's no' made o' steel."

She was brilliant and capable and strong, and he assumed she had returned to her friend's house in Leith. But he had missed her, and finally he had given in to that weakness and sent a message to Leith.

"She is not at Miss Campbell's house." His throat was nearly too tight to speak. "You would tell me if she were staying with you now, and Mr. Coutts. Wouldn't you?"

The Scotswoman glowered. "'Tis your worry speakin' nonsense now, sir."

Then where in the hell was she?

Tearing off his paint-stained shirt as he went to his quarters and dressing quickly, he was certain of one thing: she would never abandon her studies.

She would be angry with him for seeking her out. She had left—decidedly, permanently, without word. She no longer wished to see him. But a twisting fear had invaded his gut as he thought of the people Joseph Smart had befriended and to whom he might have gone for aid: young university men, and women who sold sex for shillings.

From the outside, the Dug's Bone seemed an unprepossessing place, the marquee a crudely painted image of a dog skeleton chewing on the foot of a human skeleton. Inside it was a tidy, warm warren of nooks and tables upon which books were strewn and the heads of the handful of patrons all bent to their studies. Ziyaeddin went to the bar.

"Have business with young Mr. Smart, do you, sir?" the pub master said, eyeing him curiously. "He cured my missus o' the rheumatism, after twenty years o' it! Lad's a wonder."

"Do you know where I can find him?"

"Havena seen him since he slept on the cot in my kitchen."

Allah, have mercy.

He should have anticipated this.

"He an' his mates come in here most Thursdays. They should be here in a bit. A pint while you wait, sir?"

He wanted only her.

When Peter Pincher entered he came with two others: a stocky ginger-haired youth with an open, intelligent face liberally dusted with freckles, and a stout, pale young man whose stodgy dress and features shouted his provincial English origins. From her stories Ziyaeddin guessed them to be Archibald Armstrong and George Allan.

Armstrong slapped coins onto the bar and commanded ale. The barkeep gestured to Ziyaeddin. Armstrong's head swiveled around, his brow darkening.

"Sir," Armstrong said, the pleats across his brow comical, but his stare severe. "I understand you've been waitin' here for Joe Smart."

"I have. You are Mr. Armstrong, I believe."

"Aye." The Scot's eyes narrowed. "Joe's mentioned me, has he?"

"He has told me about all of you. I am pleased to make your acquaintance." He extended his hand.

Armstrong paused, then shook it firmly.

"I'll no' beat about the bush, sir," he said, the frown deep again. "I didna take kindly to you tossin' Joe out on his arse. For all he's cleverer than me an' the lads combined, he's still a green'un to the ways o' the world. Though I'll admit if it werena for that stubborn streak o' his, I mightna be so vexed with you, sir. For I'd have him to the house an' Mum'd be pourin' soup an' tea into him now."

"Mr. Armstrong, do you know where he is?"

"If he's no' told you himself, I'm no' inclined to either."

"I did not toss him out. Nor do I hold any malice toward him."

"Aye, 'tis what he said, an' I've ne'er caught him in a lie. An' now that he's refusin' to see us, somebody's got to talk sense into him."

"Refusing to see you? Why?"

"Peaked with a fever for days now. Then he didna show at the infirmary yesterday or this mornin'. Skipped lecture yesterday too! Pincher an' I went o'er earlier today."

"Over where?"

"To a flat he's taken. He's locked himself in. Sick as a dug, but he willna let any o' us inside to tend him."

"And you *accepted* that?"

Armstrong started back. "Said if I entered he'd remove my spleen. He could do it!"

Of course she would not allow them to tend her. She would die of fever before risking exposure and ruining her dream. "Take me there. At once."

Armstrong obliged.

The rooming house was exceedingly modest, but inside it was clean-swept and dry. Ziyaeddin knocked, then tried the door handle.

"Where is the landlord of this blasted place?"

"I'll find him!" Armstrong scampered down the stairs again.

Ziyaeddin pressed his knuckles to the wood and, for the first time in a decade, prayed.

A quarter of an hour later, Armstrong appeared with the landlord.

Slowly the man looked Ziyaeddin up and down.

"What exactly you be wantin' with the lad . . . *sir*?"

"He is my ward."

The landlord's eyes narrowed. "A wee bit young to have a ward, ain't you?"

Ziyaeddin had long anticipated this. In public he had stayed far from Joseph Smart because of it. Until now, he had been very careful.

"The boy is gravely ill," he said, shaping his vowels and consonants carefully, as though born to speak the king's English. "If you've a wish to explain to the police that you allowed a gentleman's son to die for lack of care, then by all means do not provide me with the key. If not, give me your price and I will pay it."

Shortly Ziyaeddin was unlocking the door and instructing Armstrong to wait without.

The flat was minuscule and cluttered with her books and boxes. He opened the door to the bedchamber, crossed it in a stride, and went to the narrow cot. Buried in sodden blankets, she was shaking.

Rounding her flushed brow with his hand and taking her wrist between his fingers, he felt the burning in her flesh and found her thin pulse.

"Elizabeth," he whispered, stroking his fingers around her cheek from where the whiskers had peeled away. "Open your eyes. Show me through those beautiful eyes the spirit that cannot be cowed by a mere fever."

The lashes twitched.

"That's it," he said. "Look at me."

Irises the color of the sea were coated in glassy stupor. Her lashes drooped again.

Lifting the coverlets away from her, he took in the sweat-soaked shirt, breast wrappings, and man's drawers that clung to her body.

Bending his head, he searched for the core of his strength. Then, tucking the blankets snugly around her, he gathered her in his arms.

Chapter 24

Deltangam

"*There* you be!"

The sound came to Libby through the thick clog of sleep.

"'Twas a nasty fright you gave us, lass." Mrs. Coutts put an arm behind her and leaned her forward. The room spun. Then the lip of a cup was between her lips and water was dribbling down her chin and, wonderfully, over her tongue. It hit a wall of dry throat.

"Now dinna be tossin' it all back at me, daftie."

Mrs. Coutts was chuckling, her arm firm and solid behind Libby's head.

"Wh—"

"There now, lass. You needna talk just yet."

Her limbs clung to the mattress like the limbs of a rag dog had once long ago clung to her. Above, the parted draperies of a silk canopy allowed morning light to filter in and shine on a small painting of a marketplace.

Her bedchamber. In his house.

"Why am I here?" she rasped.

"The master brought you home in his own arms. Ne'er thought I'd see sich a thing! But he'd no' allow anybody else to carry you. The poor lad didna sleep a minute after that either, sittin' outside this room night an' day, then just there so I could catch a wink myself, no' till the fever broke."

Libby's thoughts would not right themselves. She was so tired.

"An' he'd no' allow one other person in this house," Mrs. Coutts continued, "only me and he. He even hired my niece to keep *my* house these past three days an' cook for Mr. Coutts. 'Tis a considerate man, in spite o' frightenin' you off."

"I wasn't frightened." Weariness pressed down on her eyelids. "I . . ."

"Rest now, dearie."

The next time Libby awoke she was able to sit up and drink a cup of tea and a bowl of broth.

The next time she roused, she was ravenous.

"I have a strong constitution," she said around a mouthful of bread and butter. "Usually."

"A sore heart'll bring a body down swift as rain."

"There is no such thing as a sore heart unless it is caused by an infection of the pericardium, Mrs. Coutts. And one does not take a fever simply because one is sad."

"Aye, there's a wee bit o' wisdom you've still to learn, lass."

Libby snuggled back in the soft blankets. "What day is today?" she mumbled, her eyelids heavy.

"Saturday, lass."

"Must . . . get . . . my . . . books . . ."

She woke by the bell at Greyfriar's ringing the Sunday

service. Staring at the canopy above, with metallic detachment she watched her thoughts accelerate as one might watch a carriage gaining speed.

She had made a hash of it. Trying to save him trouble she had caused him more. And Mrs. Coutts. And Archie. Where were her notebooks? Had the awful landlord thrown them out? She must apologize to Dr. Jones for falling asleep during his lecture. And to Mr. Bridges for disappearing. Had she paid her bill at the pub? Her stomach burned. Where were her clothes, and her whiskers? She could not waste another moment here. There were so many mistakes to repair.

No.

No.

Lifting her weak arms, she pressed her palms into her eyes.

It had happened this way: she had read his curt message about Reeve, and the desperate urgency to immediately right all that was wrong between them had propelled her into action—anything to quiet the thoughts, the regrets, the guilt.

You conquered this dragon.

Turning onto her side, she stared out the window at the early gray spring morning.

With a deep inhalation, one by one as the worries scrolled she set each on the windowsill and then tipped them off onto the street below. By the time Mrs. Coutts came with stew and bread, Libby was almost smiling.

Mrs. Coutts helped her wash and change into a fresh nightgown. Worn out by the activity, Libby fell again into bed.

When she awoke it was to abrupt wakefulness and a bedchamber lit from the hearth and a lamp. Swinging her feet free of the covers, she tested her strength. It did not impress her, nor did the achy tenderness of her chest. But the rug was warm to her bare feet.

Taking up the lamp, she went onto the landing. The house was silent.

Holding on to the railing, she descended to the ground floor and her toes sank into the soft rug running the length of the corridor. She studied the sumptuous, intricate pattern beneath her white feet.

A mansion, her friends had said. Months ago, when she first came, she had noticed its simple elegance. But it had seemed such a natural extension of its master, she had catalogued the details of its beauty in her mind, then had given them little thought.

Little thought. A miracle, to be sure.

Now she allowed her fingertips to run along the smooth wooden wainscoting to the parlor doorway, then around the bright brass handle that was cool to the touch. Just as in her bedchamber where the canopy was in perfect proportions, gorgeously designed to be at once restful and beautiful, the entire house was gracious in every detail: carefully carved wall paneling, painted plaster moldings in the ceiling, the exquisitely designed furniture and finely woven draperies, the porcelain that she used every day. All of it was enhanced subtly with bits of luxury: lapis stones set into drawer handles, garnets dangling from sconces, a paper-thin line of gilding the length of the stairwell railing, which at its base curved in upon itself like the petals of a glorious flower, a perfect spiral of satiny wood for the pleasure of the human hand.

Without ostentation, this house reveled in beauty. It was the home of an artist. And a prince.

Yet he had welcomed her here. And he had treated her as his equal.

In the parlor her notebooks were stacked on the writing

table. Her boxes of bones and plaster models, her case of surgical instruments, and her medicine chest were set carefully on the floor. A sharpened pen, pencils, page cutter, and a half-empty bottle of ink remained exactly where she had left them weeks earlier.

She recrossed the room and went out, and there he was. In shirtsleeves and waistcoat marked here and there with brilliant streaks of paint, he was standing perfectly still near the base of the stairs.

"I thought I heard something." His eyes were lustrous. "Rather, someone."

She went to him, and without pausing wound her arms about his waist and pressed her face against his chest.

He wrapped her in his arms.

"Forgive me," he whispered roughly beside her ear, and his hands spread on her, holding her. "Forgive me."

She wanted to burrow into him, to remain in his embrace and to be held in his strength and peace and stillness forever.

She drew away and stepped back.

He seemed to release a slow breath, his gaze never leaving her eyes. Libby had seen this many times before at the hospital. This was not the usual studying regard of the artist, but the watchfulness of a man who believed the one he watched might at any moment expire.

"You needn't worry now," she said. "You rescued me. And how like a fairy-tale hero you accomplished it, besting my landlord, then carrying me away to safety."

"This would presuppose you are a damsel in distress, which is balderdash."

"Mrs. Coutts said Archie took you to the flat and that you carried me out. But she is inclined to exaggeration and more importantly, I don't think the latter would have been possible."

"You underestimate your skill."

"Not once in my life have I underestimated my skill. The prosthesis allowed you to carry me? Truly?"

"You are light. And I was well motivated."

"Archie could have carried me. Or the hackney driver."

"Not while I live."

"You are . . ." Her throat was closing.

He tilted his head in question.

"You are very strong," she said. "With strength of both body and character."

"I weary of hearing your praise of me. I do not deserve it."

"As usual we see matters entirely differently. I wish to stay. Here. In this house. May I stay?"

"This is your home."

Fierce prickling erupted behind her eyes. "I may stay until my father's return to Edinburgh?"

"For however long you wish."

"What if I wish it to be forever?"

"Then forever it shall be."

Heart tight, she turned to the stairs and went up as swiftly as her bandy legs would carry her. When she paused on the landing and looked down, he stood there still, watching her.

"My father and I have always lived wherever his patients wished. I have rarely stayed in one house for long. I have never had a home that could be mine forever."

"Now you have."

"Until my father's return."

He nodded, and it was so regal that she wondered she had ever thought him anything but a prince.

"I won't bother you," she said.

"I have very little confidence in the predictive value of that statement."

Air shot out from between her lips.

"Was that noise an agreement?" he said, a beautiful smile shaping his mouth.

She laughed again, and pain shot through her lungs.

"I missed that sound," he said. "Your laughter."

She clutched the linen over her chest. "It hurts."

"Yes," he said. She didn't mean the laughter hurt, but she thought perhaps he understood that.

"I will try not to disturb you," she said.

"Don't," he said. "Disturb me. Every day. Every hour. Every minute if you wish."

"You were wise. Before. When you said that I mustn't—that *we* mustn't . . ."

"I was," he said. "But it is too late to undo now, isn't it?"

Salty heat swamped the back of her throat, and her hands were tight about the bannister.

"Sleep," he said. "Recover."

Going to her bedchamber and crawling beneath the soft blankets, she slept deeply through the night.

LIBBY RETURNED TO the infirmary early the following morning.

"I had gotten so accustomed to your absence, I entirely forgot you," Chedham drawled. "Pincher said you were at death's door."

"Apparently death shoved me back out onto the street."

"Pity. I suggested to Plath we purchase your corpse for our final dissection in Jones's course."

She went past him to Mr. Bridges, who was entering through the gates. The pleasure on her mentor's face was genuine.

Archie and Pincushion had taken up her duties during her illness. Visiting her patients, however, she learned that her nemesis had helped.

"I'm obliged to you for seeing to my patients, Chedham," she said as they followed Mr. Bridges between wards.

"I didn't do it for you."

They stopped before the first bed in the women's ward. It was empty and Libby peered down the row of cots.

"Has Mrs. Small been discharged?"

"Unfortunately she succumbed to the cancer," Mr. Bridges said. "Mr. Chedham removed the tumors. We will study them tomorrow." He proceeded to the next bed, but Libby could not tear her eyes from the clean white linen stretched across the cot.

Chedham bent to speak over her shoulder. "Perhaps we'll use her corpse for our next dissection, since we can't use yours."

"You are an unconscionable prick, Maxwell."

"Say that a bit louder. I don't think Bridges heard you." With a tight smile he followed the surgeon.

The remainder of the morning was a whirlwind of tasks that kept her late, past the time she usually met Coira for lunch.

"I'm glad to see you, lad! Gave me a fright, what with you vowin' to search for Dallis, then disappearin' as you did."

"Has she returned?"

Coira shook her head. "P'raps she's gone down to Newcastle. They say the sailors pay more there."

"I will ask Mr. Kent if he discovered anything from Mr. Reeve."

Coira's eyes twinkled. "Taken him back, have you?"

She had not taken him back. He had taken her back. That she now wanted to spend every moment with him only proved that he had been wiser than she all along.

Dr. Jones had learned of her illness from Archie, and instructed her to complete the missed work and be well prepared for the final dissection of the term.

"A public dissection, Joe!" Archie said as they took their seats in the lecture hall. "Folks'll pay to watch us perform it."

"Why would anybody pay to watch students do a dissection?"

"While you were down, the college published the names o' the top apprentices this year. You're famous, lad!"

If that were indeed true, when her father returned how could he deny her?

On Saturday, after both Mrs. Coutts and Mr. Gibbs departed, Libby changed her clothes and knocked on the door to Ziyaeddin's quarters and heard him say "Enter" from within.

She found him in the workroom. He did not remove his attention from his task, and she watched as he deftly worked the painter's knife into a dollop of gray paint that became greener with each pass of the tool.

"For what are you mixing that color?"

"Mrs. Planchett-Spinner's eyes," he said, the knife gliding and pressing and scraping the paint with mesmerizing rhythm.

"I have met Mrs. Planchett-Spinner. She is an awful gossip. Her eyes are not that green."

"Indeed."

"You do not paint what you see. That is why you so often break the rules of portraiture."

"Do I?"

"I saw your picture of Lily Jackson, in which the background seems unfinished. It was intentional. You wished to show the truth of her. You do not paint by the rules because you are not content with depicting what everyone sees on the surface."

There was tension in his jaw muscles. "Perhaps."

"How do you do that? How do you see what is beneath the skin?"

"You do as well."

"I see bones and muscles. You see the soul."

He did not reply.

"Mrs. Coutts says that you are busy with commissions."

"She has not misspoken. You are wearing Joseph Smart's dressing gown and your legs are bared," he said, his head still bent to his work. "Why is that, I wonder?"

"I want you to paint me. All of me."

Finally he looked at her.

She swallowed over the thickness in her throat.

"Art," she said. "I would like you to use me as you initially intended when we made our agreement, to paint what you long to paint. A nude. Or perhaps a mythological subject. Or a historical piece. As you wish. There is the oddest light in your eyes suddenly. I think you are about to reject my offer. But you cannot. I wish to thank you for everything you have done to help me, but I have nothing else to offer."

"There is no need. You have already made me whole."

He did not gesture to the prosthesis or otherwise elaborate on this astonishing statement.

"Like your paintings," she whispered, "will we always now be saying more than our words suggest on the surface?"

He turned his attention again to the palette. "I require no thanks."

"Yet my conscience must be satisfied that I have paid my fair share in our agreement. It won't rest until you allow it."

His fingers tightened about the knife. "All right."

Nerves spun through her belly. "I am ready to sit for you now. Can Mrs. Planchett-Spinner's eyes wait?"

He set down the knife and turned to her. "Everything can wait."

She pivoted and went into the studio, dropped the dressing gown, and perched on the stool.

"I am somewhat spare of flesh because of my illness. But you can embellish, of course. How would you like me to pose?"

He still stood in the doorway to the workroom.

"As you are," he said quite low.

"If you choose to do a classical piece, I would prefer not to be one of Zeus's unwilling conquests. No swan arranged between my thighs or bull looming over me, if you please."

"Have mercy." He gripped the back of his neck.

A flush of heat was spreading across her chest and cheeks.

"You once told me to set aside the maiden and be only the surgeon. Now you must set aside the man and be only the artist."

"There is no artist without the man. Not today."

"I shall not speak now," she said. "And you shan't either. Then neither of us will say anything unwise, subtly or not."

He took up a canvas stretched over a frame and set it on the easel.

"Don't you wish to sketch on paper first?"

"I needn't."

"Had you already prepared that canvas for a commission?"

"For this."

"For this? But I never said—"

He came toward her. Libby's skin tingled all over with feeling. The eyes of the artist were assessing her, slowly, carefully, lingering here and there.

"Like a journey one longs to take," he said, "and thinks

of to the exclusion of all else, I have been planning this piece for months." He touched her knee. "Lower this."

She obeyed, sliding her foot along the floor to stretch her leg, her calf brushing his trousers. Spirals of pleasure raced through her.

His hand came around hers and she allowed him to set it atop her thigh. She shivered.

"I am not cold," she said. "Only nervous. I have never before sat around in the nude, of course."

"What happened to neither of us speaking?"

"A chimera, obviously."

His fingertips strafed her elbow and her eyelids fluttered. Moving her arm, she followed his gentle pressure until she was reaching toward the ceiling. Then he cupped her chin in his palm and tilted it upward.

"Perfect," he said quietly, huskily. His thumb caressed her lips and his eyes upon her were positively luminous.

"You mustn't make love to me now," she said shakily. "Priorities, sir."

"Making love to you is my priority."

"Since when? Since you told me this cannot be?"

"Since the moment I first saw your face, heard you speak, watched you move. I have been entirely dishonest with you, and with myself even more so."

"Not dishonest," she whispered. "Wise, to be sure. Shall I now recite a list of the various complaints of the stomach? Or perhaps the diseases of the skin? Either can effectively dampen ardor."

"Unless you can recite them in someone else's voice, it will not suffice." His fingertips carved a line of decadent pleasure along her throat, like a sculptor smoothing a curve. "For the sound of your voice is to me at once golden sky and cerulean sea, storm and sunlight."

"Poetry," she whispered.

"You," he said huskily.

"Dyspepsia," she said in Joseph's register, "is a complaint of the central digestive organs which causes the patient to experience—"

His hand fell away from her.

"Rest when you wish," he said, returning to the easel. He took up a pencil, but then only looked into her eyes.

"Why are you not drawing?" she said.

"Elizabeth, I am—"

"*Draw.* You must now draw. And then paint. And this time I truly won't say another word and you mustn't either."

They said nothing else. He became to all outwardly appearances the expert draughtsman, his gaze shifting rapidly between her and the canvas. When he completed the sketch he collected palette and brushes from the workroom for the under painting. But the tension had not gone from his jaw and there was none of his usual restful peace or even insouciance in his stance. The tendons on his hands and neck were taut.

Occasionally she rested her arm and stretched her neck and felt the heat of his gaze upon her, and she imagined all of the ways he might touch her if she invited it now. Every atom of her skin was ready for that, every part of her body primed—for him.

When the daylight waned he lit lamps.

Finally he set down the paintbrush. Walking to the workroom, he said, "That will be all."

"All?"

"The under painting must dry. Return when you are able. I will be here. Always for you."

She drew her dressing gown over her shoulders, pulled the sash tight around her waist, and walked across the studio. Inside the workroom, he stood with his back to the doorway, one hand covering his eyes.

Laying her palms on his scapulars, she smoothed them across his back. The muscles flinched. Slowly she swept her hands down along either side of the rigid line of his spine that had long borne the torment of his lack.

"Why did you not use a real prosthesis for so many years?" she said. "Why did you allow yourself to be hobbled?"

"So that I needn't leave here."

Her hands halted.

"You do not wish to leave Edinburgh?"

"When I leave, Elizabeth, it will be to war."

"War?" Her throat was hot. "In your home?"

"That is my birthright. My blood. My responsibility." He lowered his arm to his side. "This is my home."

Leaning forward, she pressed her body against him, the pleasure of it dislodging the bristling fear inside her. She ran her hands around to his chest.

"It is a miracle," she said, "this body, such unyielding strength, yet encasing a heart of such gentleness."

His lungs expanded against her palms. "There is nothing gentle in this heart at present."

Laying her cheek on his back, she stroked the contours of muscle to his waist, feeling the tension in him and the shudder of his flesh where her hands passed.

"Since that night I have thought of little but this," she said. "I knew it would be pleasurable. But I did not know how it would be consuming. I did not know that once we kissed, once we touched, I would want only this."

"This is not the half of it." He did not move. "Not the quarter."

"I should have known. It is the way of my madness. The more I feed it, the more it craves. My body is positively humming. No distraction serves to lessen the hunger. I want so much to satisfy it finally."

"Go," he said. "Upstairs. Anywhere else. Away."

But her hands would not release him. Her body would not peel itself away from the heat of his. Here, touching him, she felt safe, both at peace and utterly alive.

The bang of the front door knocker echoed through the silent house.

"Jooooooooooe!" From the stoop Archie sang in a full-throated warble. "Joe Smaaaaaart! Be you home, Joe?"

The bell rang.

"We're celebrating!" George shouted.

"Georgie's gone and tied the knot!" Pincushion cried.

Their voices burbled together, and then copious laughter.

"Joe!" Archie called again. "Where you be, young Joe?"

Ziyaeddin broke from her hold, moved around her and swiftly crossed the studio. She followed. When he reached to open the door, she slid behind the panel.

"There you be, J—*Sir!*"

She heard scuffling footsteps, then more laughter. Rain fell without, pattering steadily on the stoop and cobbles.

"Can young Joey come out to play?" Pincushion said in a nasal twang, then he and George fell into laughter.

"Good evening, sir," Archie said. "George here's gone an' wed his lass today o'er the anvil. We're celebratin'."

Ziyaeddin's profile illumined by their lamp was the most beautiful thing she had ever seen. He was hardly older than her friends—four or five years at most—yet he had crossed the world, endured shackles, and made a life for himself in a foreign land, and still he would go into danger because he must. No wonder she thought only of him.

"Congratulations, Mr. Allan," he said.

"Thank you, sir!"

"Is young Joe in?" Archie said.

"He is. I will tell him you've come."

"Much obliged!" George said.

"Seein' as we're soaked, sir, we'll wait out here."

They were singing as Ziyaeddin closed the door.

"They are not entirely drunk, but certainly on their way," he said, then started toward the back of the house.

"This is unsustainable—what we are doing now."

He paused and turned partially toward her. "Go. Celebrate your friend's happiness—your friend who ought to be with his bride tonight," he added in a lower register, "but some men are idiots."

"I am tired of you being honorable!"

"This is not honorable. This is self-preservation and a healthy dose of fear. Now, go."

"Fear?"

He came to her, grasped her waist, and took her mouth beneath his. She wound her arms about his neck and accepted his hands sliding upward to part the dressing gown and cup her breasts.

It was a wild kiss, urgent, deep, hot. His skin against hers was scalding, his thumbs stroking over her nipples making pleasure she had never imagined. She pressed her naked belly to his waistcoat and shifted, parting her knees to feel this thigh harder against her need. He groaned and his hand swept around her hip, surrounding her buttock. Bending to her, he pulled her thigh up alongside his.

Pleasure spiraled in her, thick, perfect, his body between her legs hard, his arousal massaging her where she most wanted it—most wanted *him*. He kissed her throat, her neck, rocking her against him with his fingers splayed on her behind, and she could only make sounds without words, the pleasure spinning higher, quicker.

"This is all I want," he said, his mouth on her skin, his hands holding her tightly to him. "In every moment, to touch you, to feel you in my hands, to taste your lips and hear your voice."

"Yes," she said, aching unbearably, on the cusp and needing his mouth on hers—*everywhere* on her. "*Yes.*"

"Joooooeeeey!" The singsong call came from the street.

Ziyaeddin lifted his head. His eyes were aflame.

"This hunger will never be satisfied," he whispered harshly. "If that does not suffice to give you fear, then you are a far braver man than I, Joseph Smart."

He released her and she slid back against the wall as the rhythm of his footsteps receded into his quarters and her friends called her name from the street.

Chapter 25

Rules, Disregarded

$\mathcal{S}$he saw nothing of him. She spent her days at the infirmary, the lecture hall, and the library or pub, and her nights in the parlor with her head bent to her books. But always her body was strung with the memory of desire and restless anticipation.

"Sunday night, gentlemen, will be our final meeting in my surgery," Mr. Bridges said, scrubbing his hands at the washbasin. On her insistence, they had taken to washing between each examination on the ward. Respecting Ziyaeddin's wish to remain as inconspicuous in Joseph Smart's life as possible, she had searched every medical text about disease she could find for justification of hand washing. Finally she had found it in a treatise on maternal health by an English physician.

Drying his hands, Chedham cast her a swift glance. "Yes, sir."

The surgeon departed.

Chedham turned to her. "You think they'll name you top apprentice this year, don't you?"

She grabbed her satchel and started out.

"I will win," he said behind her. "Whatever I must do, Smart. I will win."

Hurrying out into the courtyard flooded with sunshine, she gulped in air.

Whatever I must do.

She had said that to Ziyaeddin months ago.

Alice had accused her of succumbing, and perhaps she had. Certainly she had. She thought of little but him—his touch, his hands on her, the scent of his skin. But neither she nor he was free to follow that desire. She understood that now, but understanding brought no peace, no relief, no satisfaction, only a hunger so deep it made her dazed.

"Cheddar's up to something," Archie said later, eyes narrow. "I dinna trust him."

"He only wants to succeed," she mumbled, turning a page in her book. "Just as we all do."

"Aye, to be sure. My future's set on it. But you want it more. I've ne'er seen the like, lad. You want it like a man wants opium."

"What?" she said. "What do you mean?"

"It's unnatural, Joe," Pincushion mumbled against the edge of his glass.

Unnatural.

George entered, and the conversation turned. But Libby could not retrieve her concentration.

She packed away her books, bid her friends good-bye, and left the pub. She was walking through the gateposts of the infirmary courtyard before she realized her feet had carried her here.

She wanted to believe she had come out of habit. But she had not. Need had guided her here. At the bedsides of her patients and in the preparation chamber where clean instruments hung in neat rows, relief beckoned.

Drawing the cool, damp air into her lungs, she pivoted about. With each step away from the infirmary, the desperation receded.

Her friends thought her unnatural. And she was. But not as they believed. Only Ziyaeddin understood. Yet he had never judged her for it. Not once.

A half block from the house Mrs. Coutts came walking toward her.

"Dinner's on the table," she said. "Mr. Coutts an' I be off to our son's farm tomorrow, so I'll no' be seein' you till Monday. I've made up plenty o' food. You'll no' need to be spendin' every night out, as the master."

"I thought you liked him to attend parties."

"No' when he's attendin' simply to be outta the house," she said with a shake of her head.

"Is he at the house now?"

"He's gone to church."

"*Church?*"

Her merry eyes winked. "Aye, driven him to religion you have."

"I very much doubt that."

"See for yourself." She gestured to the steeple nearby, then bustled off.

Libby walked around to the church's entrance and into the sanctuary. It was empty—no sacristan tending to candles, no worshippers—only him, sitting in the last pew, head bowed and hands clasped between his knees.

She dropped her heavy satchel on the ground and sat beside him.

"Do not tell me you are praying. Not in a church."

"A man must find succor somewhere, mustn't he?" He lifted his head and met her gaze and it was as though the wind whipped about beneath her ribs. He looked at her like no one else ever had, as though he knew all the thoughts in her head and found each of them beautiful.

"I don't believe you," she said.

"Give me your hand."

She did, and he lifted it to his lips.

"You are trembling," he said, pressing his lips to her palm.

"I am overwhelmed. I had no idea this was what lovers do."

"It isn't. Lovers actually make love."

"Why are you really in this church?"

He laced their fingers together.

"A man is coming to Edinburgh to speak with me. I will not allow him to call at the house. I await the vicar now. I will ask him the favor of meeting with my visitor in the privacy of the rectory."

"From where does this visitor come that you choose to meet him in secret rather than at the Gilded Quill?"

"My homeland." His thumb stroked over her knuckles. "He is coming to bid me return."

Withdrawing her hand, she said, "I will leave you to the vicar."

She went home. With no appetite for the dinner Mrs. Coutts had prepared, she put it away and climbed the stairs. Passing the mirror in her bedchamber she saw Joseph Smart.

In the church when he took her hand she had forgotten she was a man. She had forgotten she was a *woman*. She had only attention for him, for his touch, and for the news he had shared with her as though it meant so little, as though it had not torn the earth out from beneath her.

Changing her clothes with shaking hands, and scrubbing her face free of adhesive, she resisted the heat gathering at the back of her throat and eyes. Descending to the parlor, she opened her books. But her thoughts spun and the sentences folded back on themselves.

She should eat.

Leaving the parlor she went instead into his studio. The painting—her painting—sat on the easel. Finished.

He had not painted her as a damsel of ancient mythology, nor as a religious figure or even a simple nude.

Partially draped with a tissue-thin cloth from one shoulder to one thigh, she grasped in her right hand a surgeon's instruments as though she had just plucked them from the heavens. Beneath her right foot was a toppled barber's pole. She looked upward with the same crystal gaze of intelligence, curiosity, and confidence of his painting of Joseph Smart, but this time with a hint of vulnerability that looked like nothing less than humility.

Tears surged into her eyes.

"Do you like it?" he said behind her.

She whirled around.

"Why must you be so dreadfully good?" she exclaimed.

"I don't know. For it has not been convenient."

"I didn't mean good as an artist."

"I didn't either."

"If you were cruel or selfish or violent or even inconsiderate I could dislike you easily. I have no tolerance for those qualities."

He folded his arms and leaned a shoulder into the doorjamb.

"You are angry with me because I did not paint you as a bored aristocrat draped in jewels?" he drawled.

"I am not *angry*. I think I am in love with you."

His lips parted. His arms fell to his sides.

She dashed tears from her cheeks. "I tried to convince myself that it was only lust. But that was a lie. I am aching for you, as though I am ill with a disease that I haven't any idea how to cure. It is both horrible and wonderful and I am furious about it, for *this* isn't at all convenient."

He came toward her, slid his hands beneath her dressing gown, and took her waist in his strong grasp. Gently he drew her to him.

"I am a disease?"

"I did not say you are a disease. Only the feelings. Though I try I cannot rid myself of them. I have never failed at anything so thoroughly before in my life."

"Don't try," he said. "Kiss me."

"I pursued you when you warned me not to. I am so sorry."

"You should be. It is a terrible mistake. Now kiss me." He lowered his lips to hers and she met him, felt him, opened to him, and drank him in. Wrapping her arms around his neck she pressed her body to his and he kissed her fully, deeply.

"Say you will make love to me," she said, welcoming his mouth on her throat and running her fingers through his hair and needing to feel every part of him. "Now. Do not make me wait another minute."

His hands spread down her back and around her hips.

"Another minute?" His whisper against her skin sounded like laughter. "I have been waiting three years."

Breaking free of him, she shed her dressing gown on the studio floor, and ducked beneath the doorway bar. Beside the bed she awaited him, but he paused on the threshold.

"Why are you waiting?" she said. "It cannot be from nerves, at least not as wildly agitated as mine. You are not a virgin too, are you?"

"Elizabeth, are you certain?"

"Entirely."

But he did not come forward. So she went to him, spread her palms on his chest, and willed her hands to express her certainty. The quick, hard beating of his heart buoyed her courage.

"I am not a typical woman."

"I have noticed that." His smile was marvelously unstable.

"I haven't the modesty, nor fear of the sexual act. And when you put your hands on me, when you kiss me, I want to feel you inside me so much that I am mad with wanting it. And I wish to finally see"—she slid her hand downward and felt the hard proof of his desire—"*exactly* how this functions."

His hand covered hers, the other sweeping around the back of her neck and drawing her to him to kiss.

She had already been naked while sitting for him, yet removing her gown now was a new adventure, for as he assisted he touched her. Standing behind her he unfastened the stays, removed her shift, and his hands circled her waist, spread over her belly, then swept up to cup her breasts. He kissed her neck, and his fingers trailed about her tight nipples tantalizingly, then across them.

"What are you doing?" she said upon a shiver of pleasure.

"Making love to you, as you have requested and as I have wanted to do to the exclusion of all else."

"I didn't know this was part of it."

"Anything you wish is part of it."

She swiveled in his arms. He kissed her beautifully. Then, with exquisite care, he taught her what she wished to learn about the male body. His body.

As he undressed she took her turn assisting.

"I never imagined that the experience gained in my imposture could be put to such compelling use," she said as she released the fasteners on his trousers.

"I did," he said.

She looked up into his eyes that in the firelight were full of desire. Full of *her*.

"You did?" she said.

"Every day."

Her mouth opened, and closed, then opened anew. "I did not know. You are excellent at dissembling."

"Touch me, *joonam*. Learn what you wish, and bring my endless craving for your hands on me to satisfaction finally."

She already knew he was beautifully formed. Now she found that he was so in every part.

His skin, taut and smooth over hard muscle, revealed past abrasions: some scars small, but others evidence of grievous wounds.

"What will happen if I do this?" she said, doing to him what she had wished to do for months. Against her palm came the pulse of his body's reaction and a rumbling groan sounded deep in his chest.

"That," he said rather deeply.

Awe and a sensation of feral power coursed through her.

She continued the experiment. It was thoroughly intoxicating: his grasp tightening on her, his rapid breaths against her brow that told her she was dismantling his perfect composure, and the increased throbbing of her own arousal. He was satin and heat and hard desire, and she wanted to feel all of him, to taste him and make him hers. She opened her lips against his neck and slid her hand downward.

Five strong fingers clamped around hers.

"If you do *that*," he said with glorious roughness, "this demonstration will come to a rapid end."

"But it can be repeated."

Upon laughter he pulled her against him and kissed her quite thoroughly.

She had believed him a man of restraint in all things. Now she discovered that in this, with her, he absolutely was not.

As she laughed in happiness, he touched her everywhere—lips, throat, breasts again and again, caressing until she was gasping and sighing more often than forming actual words. His hands on her body were nothing like hers when she had touched herself, for they were large and not at all callused.

"Your touch," she said, clinging to his shoulders. "It is so gentle. It makes me feel desperate inside."

His hands rounded her hips, fingertips strafing the undersides of her buttocks, and he kissed her throat, her neck, her shoulder. "It is to your liking?"

"It is perfect yet I want more. *Much* more. I beg of y—"

He stroked along her arousal. Like liquid fire, pleasure licked up through her. Light and soft, his touch was maddening, gorgeous, *drugging*. Legs weak, arms banded about his neck, she parted her thighs and her hips moved as though bidden to do so by his hand. "*Ohh*. This is—" She was wild with need, undulating to his caress. "Please. Now. Give me more. Give me *you*."

So he did. Upon the soft bed linens he gave himself to her. First his hands that were both gentle and full of power spread her knees. Then he lowered his body to hers and she took him into her.

For many moments, perhaps minutes, they were still except for the deep, awed breaths that neither of them could fully draw moving her breasts against his chest. Cupping her face in his hand, he stroked her cheek and her lips with the pad of his thumb.

"This feels good." Her words would not rise above a whisper.

"That it does," he murmured, and kissed her softly, then again.

"It feels . . . proper," she said between his kisses.

"Proper? You?"

"Us, proper. That is, *right*."

"Yes." Fever was in his eyes as his hand traveled along her throat and neck, and curved around her breast. As he caressed her peaked nipple he moved inside her.

"*Oh*. That was *perfect*. Do it again."

He did it again, and again, and again. Faster, harder, they came together more urgently with each thrust, and shortly she understood on a purely animal level how it was that people so frequently wished to do this.

His hands on her were no longer gentle, but greedy like her hands were on him, as she gripped his waist and heard herself whispering his name, then crying it aloud. Everything was wet and hot: her lips, his skin, their bodies locked together.

Yet still he played her body with his clever caresses precisely where they made her wild and his sex deep inside her, until the spiral of tight ecstasy exploded. It rolled through her, deep and hard and complete. The sounds she made were barely human.

She did not have to ask him to identify the moment he found the peak of his pleasure; she saw it in the straining of the sinews in his neck and the flexing of the muscles in his chest and arms, and felt it within her own body.

Still in his embrace, when she was again able to fill her lungs entirely, and he was setting beautifully tender kisses on her cheek and jaw, she did ask him how it had felt to him and also whether it was always both this satisfying and this wet.

In response he wrapped his arms around her, kissed her hair, then her brow, then her lips. She loved his mouth, the sweet heat of his tongue, the little bites upon her lips that made languorous rapture skitter about in her sex anew and her nipples tighten.

Her heart was still beating far too swiftly. She was full—
so full.

Drawing away from her, he reached for a pitcher of
water and a garment that had previously been discarded
in favor of mutual nudity—her shift or his shirt, perhaps.
Beginning with the sweat in her hair he began bathing
her. He accompanied this with kisses.

She allowed it. As always she had many questions, but
she had no words sufficient to express her feelings now.
When eventually he reached her hips and gently applied
the linen between her legs, she forced words over the lump
clogging her throat.

"I have no particular awe for royalty."

"I have in fact noticed that." Smoothing his palm over
her damp belly, he smiled a bit.

"Still, I don't think you should be bathing me as a
nurse bathes a child or a servant bathes a great lady. That
is, not precisely like those, for a nurse or servant would
presumably be dressed."

"Presumably."

"You shouldn't."

"Yet you must allow it this once."

She needed to know whether by *this once* he intended
for them never to do this again, or if she must only allow
it this first time although there would be many more occasions when he might bathe her but would not.

"Ask what you wish, Elizabeth," he said, somehow
knowing that questions now teetered upon her tongue.

She swallowed them.

"Thank you," she whispered instead, surrounding his
face with her hands, and drew his mouth to hers.

Soon he slept but she could not, instead hovering in a
semiconscious haze of aching satisfaction and another kind
of sensation that was not satisfying, rather uncomfortably

desperate and lodged beneath her sternum. It made her watch him in sleep, the slow, shallow rise and fall of his chest, the handsome face without any care now, his features at peace.

Eventually he stirred, turned his head, opened his eyes, and met her gaze.

"I expected you to shout," she said.

"When?" he mumbled, still partially asleep.

"In your sleep," she said. "From the nightmare."

He turned onto his shoulder and faced her, the flexing of firelit muscles magnificent.

"The nightmares have gone," he said.

"Gone? How wonderful! When?"

He rose above her and kissed her on her mouth and on the tip of her nose and on her brow. Her palms reveled in each ripple of his spine. His lips were in her hair.

"Before you," he said, "there was only fire."

"Am I the rain?"

"You are the flood."

Her hands clenched on him.

"I do not wish to be the magical cause of your nightmares ceasing," she barely whispered.

"There is nothing magical about it." He kissed her jaw and she lifted her chin so that he could set kisses on her neck just beneath her ear where his lips truly did magic. "Why are your fingertips drilling holes in my arms?" he said against her skin.

"Because I want to swallow you with my hands. I want to touch you everywhere. And I want you to tell me that the nightmares will not recommence as soon as I leave this house."

"To the last I can give you no promise. To the first two, you have my eager consent."

"And to my statement that I will leave this house?"

"I know that you will leave it." He looked into her eyes. "I am not your destiny, *güzel kız*. And you are not mine."

A sound escaped her throat: a sob of some sort, coming from her lungs and belly and heart all at once. It was impossible—this pain in the midst of such pleasure. Irrational. *Unbearable*.

He took her face between his hands and kissed her mouth. Caressing her lips, he parted them. Their heat became one.

He kissed her throat and neck, working his pleasure-magic along her collarbone and between her breasts, stirring her skin to a hot flush, and making her whole body wake again with hunger. Teasing the soft flesh of her breast with light kisses, he stroked the nipple and it hardened. When his lips closed over it she groaned, arched up from the mattress, and welcomed his teeth on her, and his tongue.

His fingertips stroking the length of her side to her hip tickled and tormented at once. He followed them with his mouth, soft and beautiful on her ribs and then her belly and then the skin stretched over her pelvic bone. She felt positively worshipped. It was the most ridiculous notion, yet his touch, his caresses, the beauty of pleasure twirling through her body echoed the glorious majesty of the goddess he had painted.

When his hands urged her thighs apart she did not resist, but spread them, eager for the hard thrust, the deep penetration, the wild pleasure.

Instead, he licked her. She choked upon a gasp. Their gazes met. His tongue stroked her flesh slowly, decadently. A sound rumbled in his throat and he closed his eyes, as though tasting her gave him pleasure. A wash of fragile elation cascaded through her.

"Touch your breasts."

She surrounded them with her hands, stroking her fingertips over the taut tips, and watched as he kissed her sex again, and again.

Bringing her to climax required very little of this. She groaned as he licked her, repeated the soft caress, then penetrated her. Holding her thighs apart he took her entirely with his mouth. She panted, finally thrusting, telling him with words and her body that she needed him inside her.

He obliged, sliding up into her, their bellies brushing as he stretched her with slow, wet, gloriously confident ease that only drove the torment higher, tighter, then drawing out until she was gasping. Desperate to reclaim the pleasure she gripped his hips and tried to force him in.

Finally he thrust hard. She shouted an assent.

"This pleases you?" he said.

"Yes. *Yes.* Again."

He did as she wished. As his hands wrapped around her hips and he pushed deeper and deeper into her, touching a place so magical that words tumbled from her lips without shape, she had never more appreciated his great strength. Her cries and moans entwined with his.

When all had subsided to a gratifying languor and he was lying beside her, kissing her shoulder and arm, sending tingles of delight all over her body, she said, "I finished bleeding two days ago."

The kisses ceased.

He rose onto his elbow to look down at her. "What are you saying?"

"That I shan't get with child from this."

Bewilderment glistened in his eyes. Turning onto his back, he laid a forearm across his face and his chest moved with deep, uneven breaths.

She shifted onto her side and took in the beauty of him, all taut, bronzed contours in the candlelight.

"Women do not typically speak of such matters to men, of course," she said, "unless the man is a physician, and even then infrequently. But I should think this a very useful thing for lovers to discuss."

His arm slid away from his face and he stared up at the canopy, his lips that had given her such pleasure closed, but his breathing still fraught.

"Are you familiar with how a woman's menses function," she said, "that there are certain days in each monthly cycle in which she is unlikely to conceive?"

"Yes."

"I did not imagine this of you," she said. "That you would be reticent to speak of it."

"I am not reticent to speak of it."

"Then what now is causing you discomfort?"

"Not discomfort." He met her gaze. "I am thinking how much I want you to bear my child."

Now she could not breathe properly either.

She climbed onto him and saw him watching her as she trapped him between her thighs and he wrapped his hands around her hips—saw the questions and confusion in his eyes.

"Do not speak," she said, placing two fingertips over his lips, then replacing them with her own lips. "Do not say another word."

He met her kisses, wrapped his arms around her, and pulled her against him.

SHE AWOKE TO thin silvery light peeking through the draperies and the scent of toasted bread. She was alone in the middle of his bed, the linens tucked up around her shoulders.

A dressing gown of sapphire blue satin lay at the foot of the bed. She donned it and went to the kitchen. A fire in the hearth warmed the room. Standing at the stove, he wore only breeches.

"You are unusually domestic," she said, clutching the doorjamb. His bared shoulders and arms and back were all power and fluid beauty. "Shockingly so. I know no other man who can so easily prepare a pot of tea."

"A boy far from the comforts of home swiftly learns what he must to survive. And a man with secrets to hide does for himself as often as possible." Finally he looked over his shoulder. "That color suits you."

The shadow of morning stubble darkened his jaw and around his mouth. As she remembered the things that mouth had done to her, her limbs grew liquid.

"As a boy living in a foreign land," he said, returning his attention to the kettle, "I learned that taking tea together, dining together—they are rituals of friendship."

Her satchel was on the floor nearby. On the table was breakfast: toasted bread, jam, cheese, eggs, and a beautifully painted dish of chickpeas from which arose the woody aroma of cumin.

"Tell me your story," she said, sitting down.

"My story can wait. First you must eat. Then you must study. I will not allow this to distract you from your purpose."

"A few hours"—she had to clear her throat—"away from studying will harm nothing."

He leaned back against the counter.

"Breakfast." He gestured.

"You have seen the worst of me," she said. "The ugly and the irrational, the desperate and arrogant and selfish. All the worst."

"If this has been the worst of you, *güzel kız*, then your god has truly favored you."

"Why don't you want to tell me your story? I will share it with no one."

"I trust that."

"Then why?"

"Thousands of miles away. Years ago. It is a story that can hold no interest for a woman so thoroughly in this place and this moment." But shadows again were in his eyes and she knew that his words were only a partial truth.

Reaching for a piece of toasted bread, she played it between her fingers.

"It is a story about you," she said.

After a moment, he spoke.

"Tabir is a small kingdom, under the watchful eyes of nearby powers, yet independent. My father was an educated man, well traveled in his youth, and a friend to all. His first general had been his closest companion since childhood. But the general wanted more. When in secret he offered our Russian neighbors a monopoly on trade from our port, they assisted his coup. My father was killed. My mother, my sister, and I escaped with three servants. We traveled far in haste. We settled in Alexandria in Egypt under the protection of the patriarch of the Orthodox Coptic Church."

"A *bishop*?"

"Thus my excellent catechism." He almost smiled.

"But why not—?"

"The shah in Tehran? The emperor of the Ottomans in Istanbul?" He shook his head. "Both Iran and the Turks have tried to swallow Tabir into their borders many times. Fearing the very Russians who gave support to the general, the shah had only just made a treaty with France. As for my mother's family in Istanbul, they had never much liked my father, and would have encouraged her to ally with the general, if only to give them an excuse to go to war with the Russians. It was best to allow them to believe us dead."

"But why did you hide among Christians?"

"Egypt's pasha then, and now, is a brilliant but belligerent man. My mother believed he might use us in his battle with the Ottomans. She knew not whom to trust. Napoleon had abducted the Catholic pope and was holding him captive, and he had long had designs on Egypt. Perhaps the patriarch had reason to fear as well. Alliances were often unlikely in those years, as now." His gaze slipped down her dressing gown. "Necessity makes strange bedfellows."

"I am not strange."

"You are beautiful." His voice was husky.

Beneath his hungry gaze, her skin flushed with warmth. "You repeat yourself."

"I shall do so as often as I please."

"You said you lived eight years in Alexandria."

"The patriarch resides in Cairo usually, but he believed that until I was older we would be best concealed in Alexandria. It is a vast port. All the world passes through it. No one would take notice of a few more strangers."

"It was there that you learned to paint from Joachim's uncle."

"I was a boy when we arrived, and knew only that I was free at last from responsibilities. No more weapons training. No more endless hours memorizing treatises on tactics or law. No more dour holy men forever chastising me for my every misstep."

"Your father had men like *that* in his court?"

"He believed all men worthy of respect."

"In Alexandria you were free of responsibilities."

"I ran through the streets of that city as any boy

might. I grieved my father and his friends who had fallen to the sword that night. But I did not feel trapped in my anonymity." The memories of happiness were bright in his eyes.

She understood the freedom anonymity offered. Entirely.

"You loved it there," she said. "Didn't you?"

"I did. From my father's betrayers I had learned that one cannot always trust one's friends. In Alexandria I learned to trust strangers. And I learned that a man needn't look or sound or eat or pray like another to become his brother."

"Did your mother and sister feel as you did?"

"Aairah was always impatient that I should return and fight for our father's throne. I used to tell her she would have been a much finer ruler than I. Eventually I could resist her pleas no longer. It was decided I would travel to Istanbul and seek the aid of the emperor of the Ottomans. Leaving my mother and sister in the patriarch's protection, on my sixteenth birthday I set sail with my tutor. Only a day out of port, brigands boarded us. My tutor, an old man, told the pirates that I would bring them gold in ransom. They laughed as they killed him."

Libby gasped. "You *saw* them kill him? Why didn't they believe him?"

"We had fled Tabir with nothing. I had with me only two items to prove my claim to the throne: a letter from the patriarch and—"

"The watch?"

He nodded. "The captain recognized its obvious value and kept it for his own. It looks better on you, by the way."

She could not smile. "He did not believe it was a king's, did he?"

"None aboard could read the inscription, and the letter from the patriarch meant nothing to them. Many such letters are forged. Upon the sea, among thieves gold is the only language of worth."

"What did the pirates do with you?"

"I was young and strong. At first they put me in the galley to row."

Thickly embedded in his ankle and foot, the scars had been months in the making. "At first?"

He did not reply and the darkness now in his eyes spun fear up her spine.

"What about after that?" she said.

After a moment's pause, he said, "They made use of me."

There was no anger in his voice. There was nothing. No emotion. No life.

She stared at his handsome face, at his beautiful mouth, his graceful artist's hands, his lean body, and anguish crawled through her insides.

"I have learned, Elizabeth, that there are men of God on this Earth," he said softly. "Men of honor and men of great faith, sons of Allah and Yahweh, brothers of Jesus, all of them striving for goodness—for truth. I have been blessed to know many such men."

Throat closed, she waited.

"My captors," he said, "were not among those men."

Fists tight in her lap, she forced her voice to evenness. "What of the patriarch's sailors?"

"Some survived the battle and were taken aboard too. I did finally convince the captain to seek ransom for me. I promised it would make him a wealthy man. The general's mercenaries eventually came, but they were interested only in wealth that could be gotten immediately. They cut down the brigands. Shackled to the mast, I watched, assuming my death would follow."

So much violence and death. No wonder he cherished

the homey task of making tea. No wonder he loved painting the nude female body, which was full of strength and generative life.

"Was that when the ship caught fire?"

"Yes. The mercenaries fled to their vessel. As they did, a boy tried to free me. He had no key or axe and he wept. I told him to shoot the chain. The bullet chose bone instead of iron."

"*You* told him?"

"The men and boys with whom I had been bound to oars—some of them had become friends, such as we were. Chained in the hold, they would perish because of my arrogance. I had to try to free them."

Even in chains he had been a hero.

"Did any of them survive?" she said.

"Some."

"How did the British navy find you?"

"The crown prince of Iran as a boy had met my father and admired him greatly. One of the mercenaries, it seemed, had sold the information to him that I still lived, and he requested Britain's aid in finding me. The navy sent Captain Gabriel Hume's ship. He sailed along the coast for months searching for me. It was pure luck that his lookout sighted the smoke."

His nightmares had been of that which had saved him.

"Gabriel took me to London where I asked your prince for assistance. He declined. Russian power is growing along the Ottoman and Iranian borders. Britain plays them all carefully for whatever advantage it will give its own East India Company's ships and caravans. My father's realm, although a gem, is caught at the crossroads of empires."

"What of your sister and mother?"

"I was in England only months before I received word

that my mother and her servants had been struck down, and my sister taken to Tabir to be married to the general against her will to legitimize his rule. By the time I heard the news, she was to bear to him a second child."

"She was a *captive* wife?"

"I was told that if I ever returned to Tabir, she and her children and all who supported us would be killed. That threat remains." He folded his arms. "You know the rest of the story."

"Why do you use a false name? Why do you not live in London or Paris, anywhere you wish, and be feted according to your blood, and where you might petition government for aid?"

"I do petition the British government. And Iran. The emperor as well. Regularly."

"But you might live as befits royalty."

"Spending hours each day with my tailor and valet? Drinking up gossip at parties to spit out again at the next entertainment? Sleeping all morning so that late into every night I can be a marvelous curiosity for the fashionable elite to fawn over? And all the while ceaselessly currying the favor of allies whose armies are larger than the entire population of Tabir?"

He fell silent.

"I beg your pardon," she said.

"After all that I have seen, Elizabeth, all that I have done and been, how could I live that life?"

"But you are still waiting to return. For your sister's sake."

"No longer waiting. War is coming. When the shah's army rides to retake lands that Russia now holds, that army will pass within miles of Tabir."

Chill skittered across her skin. "Will you go *now*? To war?"

"My sister is safe at present. She has allies in the palace and among the neighboring local lords. The general still has the promise of Russian protection. Iran remains quiet as yet. There is time." He bent his head. "And I am needed here."

Standing, she took up a slice of bread and went around the table to him. Breaking the piece into two portions, she gave him half and bit into the other.

He smiled. "What are you doing?"

"Eating as you bid me do, and feeding you too, so that we will both have sufficient energy for how I wish to spend the day."

Dropping the bread on the table, he circled his arms around her and drew her snugly hip to hip with him.

"And how do you wish to spend the day?" he said, kissing her cheek, then the other cheek.

"In your bed," she said, resting her palms on his chest, then sliding them up and over his shoulders. He was warm and beautiful. "Or wherever else in this house you wish to give me pleasure and receive it in return."

He answered by giving it to her right there, great pleasure that left her clinging to him and suffused with satisfaction and thoroughly alive.

The day passed in that manner. He had, she discovered, extraordinary reserves of virility. When she asked if this was common, he peered at her like she was daft and said he hadn't any way of knowing, and what sort of a gentleman did she think he was anyway? She dissolved into laughter, which gave him opportunity to show her precisely how virile her laughter always made him.

When the clock in the parlor chimed six and Libby left his bed to dress for the final meeting of her mentor's private surgical course, she kissed the sleeping prince on his lips, but was not surprised when he did not wake.

Chapter 26

Tabirshah

"Seems you're feelin' fine, Joe," Archie said, casting her a quick glance as they entered the alleyway.

"I do feel well." Spectacular, except for the soreness in parts she had never before used as she had used them over the past twenty-four hours. She wondered if healthy young men got sore from extensive lovemaking. She would ask Ziyaeddin. Then she would make him make love to her again.

"You truly all right, lad?"

"Yes, Archie. Why do you ask?"

"Your cheeks an' chin are all reddened, like you've sprouted a rash . . . or such."

The powder she had donned to cover the burn from his whisker stubble had disintegrated beneath the adhesive. She had hoped her whiskers would hide it. Apparently not.

"I'm well." She halted before the door and reached for the bell.

"You're thinkin' I'm an old hen for worryin' o'er you," Archie said, frowning. "But somebody's got to."

The door opened and she was saved further probing stares as they went into the surgery hall.

When they were all present and smocked, Mr. Bridges said, "Mr. Smart, make the initial incision."

Libby drew back the linen.

Dallis.

"I know this woman. She has been missing—my friend—*her* friend has been searching for her." She looked back down at the pretty face. It was pale now, the lush lips dulled. "I know her."

"The woman you knew is no longer present," Mr. Bridges said. "Now, do make the incision or Mr. Chedham will."

The long eyelashes lay peacefully on the beauty's cheeks, as though she had only fallen asleep. Libby's hand around the knife was damp and cold.

There was nothing she could do for Dallis now. She could only discover for Coira the cause of her friend's death.

She got to work.

SEVENTEEN: THE AGE of Elizabeth Shaw when she had intruded upon him in the library of Haiknayes Castle and altered the course of his life. But there the similarities between her and the girl who sat before him now ended.

"Dear me," Miss Hatch said, batting her eyelashes, "I believe I've a tear in my flounce." Bending over to examine the imaginary tear, and affording him an ample view of the bosom spilling from her bodice, she lifted to him eyes filled with limpid helplessness.

It was the fourth such excuse she had invented to lean over. She had fabricated three excuses to lift her skirts to her knees too.

He'd had enough.

Wiping his brushes clean and taking up his walking stick, Ziyaeddin left the room.

"Mr. Kent!" Mr. Hatch rushed into the foyer. "Are you leaving? Already? We thought you would remain all day. My wife is laying a splendid lunch for you. Perhaps you have forgotten a brush or another item at home? Allow me to send a footman for it."

"I have forgotten nothing. Your daughter, however, seems to have forgotten common civility."

Hatch's head jerked back so that his chin became the multiple chins of a tortoise.

"I beg your pardon, sir?"

"Rather, she ought to be begging mine. You and your wife, as well, for raising her with truly poor manners yet giving me no warning."

"Oh, dear." His cheeks grew ruddy. "I am exceedingly embarrassed. That is, I—" His eyes were the eyes of a father who knew exactly of what his daughter was capable. "I beg you to tell me your recommendation for going forward."

Ziyaeddin leaned in as though to speak confidentially. "Find her a husband. Swiftly."

Spring sunshine flooded the cobblestones as he rode toward Old Town. Elizabeth would not return home for many hours yet, but he had plenty of work to occupy him until then.

Climbing the steps to his door he felt watched. Across the street a man wearing a cloak of russet that concealed his head stood too immobile.

Ziyaeddin descended the steps, and the man drew back the hood. His hair shone with gold and his eyes were as familiar as the gray Scottish sky.

"*Joachim?*"

"Your Highness," the Egyptian said, "I come according to my vow made to you ten years ago, and at your sister's bidding."

Taller and broader than when last they had run together through the streets of Alexandria, Joachim's skin was light, his beard thick, and his eyes an age older than Ziyaeddin remembered. Now he wore on his hip a blade and on his chest the insignia of the patriarch his father had once served.

"My friend." Ziyaeddin extended his hand. "My brother."

Bowing his head, Joachim clasped his arm, as they had practiced when they spied on the patriarch's soldiers and spoke of how someday they would be men too. But now Joachim was not speaking his native tongue, rather in Persian, the language of Tabir.

"I had forgotten," Ziyaeddin said.

"Forgotten me?"

"Never." On the dock before the ship's departure, Ziyaeddin had finally told his friend the truth about his family. Joachim had gone to his knee and promised life-long fealty. "I had forgotten your vow to me."

"Yet I never have."

"Come. You have traveled a great distance. Allow me to offer you hospitality."

Inside the house the Egyptian remained stiff, his eyes assessing.

"Sit and take refreshment," Ziyaeddin said when Mrs. Coutts had left a tray of coffee.

"Your Highness, bid me kneel or stand, but not sit."

"Call me Ibrahim, or Ziyaeddin if you prefer, or speak to me not at all. And sit."

The soldier sat with obvious discomfort.

"This house . . ." he said, looking around the parlor. "What is it?"

"My home."

Joachim frowned.

"Now, old friend," Ziyaeddin said, "tell me how it is that my sister sent you here and that you speak now in the tongue of my homeland rather than yours."

"His Holiness sent me to Tabir."

"To *Tabir*? When?"

"The year after you sailed, when I went into service for His Holiness, I thought it right to tell him of my vow to you."

"Of course you did." Ziyaeddin smiled.

Joachim titled his head. "The memories are not entirely lost to you, then?"

"Not entirely. Why did you so easily accept as truth what I told you about my family that day on the dock before my departure?"

"My father had always known. When you arrived in Alexandria, the patriarch had given him the responsibility of protecting your family. Then after you set sail, when your sister was taken and your mother slain by those dogs . . ." He shook his head. "My father has never forgiven himself or his failure to protect them. Neither has His Holiness. When word came that you had been lost at sea, His Holiness sent me to Tabir to ensure the princess's safety. In the guise of a merchant I have kept watch on your palace ever since. Eventually I was able to communicate with her."

"But . . . This is *incredible*."

"No more so than a prince hiding among soldiers' families a thousand miles away from his realm."

"How can my sister have communicated with anyone outside the palace? Is she no longer the general's prisoner?"

"Ziyaeddin, the general is dead."

"*Dead?*" He stood, sweeping a hand over his face. He had waited so long for this, it seemed unreal. His sister was free of her captor. Finally. "Ali wrote to me of the general's illness, but not of—Are you the messenger he wrote of, the servant that my sister would send to me?"

"I am."

"Is she well? And her sons?"

Joachim nodded. "She was well prepared. She holds the loyalty of Tabir and negotiates already with the general's remaining allies among the khans. But war has come. The very day of the general's death, Russian soldiers appeared on the mountain and news came from Tabriz that the shah's army had begun its march north. With His Holiness's help, the princess is now securing Istanbul's promise to aid you."

Istanbul. As though the years had simply vanished, his sister was seeking aid from the Ottomans—from their mother's people.

Thousands of miles away. Years ago. Yet all of it was now again his reality.

"Ziyaeddin Mirza, Prince of Tabir," Joachim said, descending to one knee, "your throne is at long last yours to claim. Your exile is at end."

Chapter 27

The Accusation

*H*e was not at home when she returned. Libby changed from her clothing that smelled of the surgical hall, washed thoroughly, and paced the parlor until she heard the front door open.

She went to him. "I have—"

Cane clattering into the stand where he tossed it, he took her face between his hands and captured her mouth beneath his. She gripped his waist and allowed him to bear her up against the wall, and she filled her hands with him. There was no hesitancy or gentleness in him now, only urgency she tasted in his mouth and his body pressing into hers.

When he drew away it was only to consume her face with his gaze and then kiss her again.

"Is this what will always happen when one of us enters the house?" she said.

"If your god favors us, *delbaram*." He stroked her

forehead where the errant curl refused to be tamed. "What is amiss?"

"Was that Turkish?"

"Persian."

"Why have you ceased calling me *güzel kız*?"

"You are not a girl. You were not, had I but known it."

"How do you know that something is amiss with me?"

"Your brow is taut even as you kiss me. This face, every feature, every shade, every texture is a masterpiece I have long since memorized. Tell me."

"You must speak again with Mr. Reeve." Her fingertips dug into him. "I found Dallis tonight on the table in Mr. Bridges's operating theater. There was laudanum in her stomach, but she died by suffocation."

His face paled. "*Dallis*."

"Yes, I am so sorry. You knew her well."

"Not well. Then it was no accident."

"Bethany's appearance in that same operating theater is too great a coincidence for it to be otherwise. I must go tell Coira, so that she will be cautious. I waited only until you returned to ask for your aid."

"Elizabeth, with great respect for your intelligence and abilities, I ask you to allow me to speak with Reeve alone. Will you agree to this?" He spoke gravely.

She twisted her fingers around the lapels of his coat. "I cannot remain idly here, of course."

"You will not be idle. Write to Bridges and request a private audience with him. Do not disclose your reason for the audience. When he agrees to it, I will accompany you."

"You believe Mr. Bridges is hiring resurrectionists, don't you? For I do. Although I haven't an idea of how resurrectionists are still operating in Edinburgh. There are guards posted at nearly every cemetery in the city."

"I will speak with Reeve." He released her. "Your promise now?"

She nodded. "I have no wish to end up beneath Maxwell Chedham's scalpel."

Lightness came into his eyes. "Of course you haven't."

She took up his cane.

"I liked that," she said, offering it to him, "being kissed immediately and so thoroughly at the door here."

"That does not make it particularly easy to walk out this door now. Say nothing more, temptress."

She cracked a laugh.

He reached for her and, wrapping one hand behind her neck, bent his head, but he did not kiss her.

"There is nothing in the world I want more—nothing," he said, "than to kiss you thoroughly not only here and now, but everywhere and in every moment."

"That would be impractical."

"Practicalities be damned." There was a rough defiance in the words that made the hairs on her arms stand.

He released her and departed, and she went to write her letter.

YEARS EARLIER, WHEN Ziyaeddin had used the Duke of Loch Irvine's house in Edinburgh as a studio, he had first encountered James Reeve there. Reared on the streets of Edinburgh, Reeve had a desperate, childlike fondness for art. Delivering firewood to Gabriel's house one day he had glimpsed several of Ziyaeddin's paintings. Thereafter he had become a devotee, and proved useful for certain tasks. Ziyaeddin had even painted for him a small still life of the farm Reeve dreamed of someday purchasing for his ailing mother.

When Reeve accidentally set the fire that burned Gabriel's house down, fearing for his life he had returned to the alleys of Old Town to hide.

Now Ziyaeddin found his quarry in a tavern.

"Sir! You've no need to be comin' down here to find

Jimmy Reeve! Only send a note an' I'll be at your door-step in a cat's whisker!"

"Take a seat, James."

A nervous scowl twisted Reeve's lips, but he obeyed.

"Are you robbing graves?"

Reeve gaped.

"There is no need to lie in this, James, and every reason to tell me the truth. At least two women of your close acquaintance are dead. If you did not murder them, you will not hang. But I must know the truth if I am to help you."

Reeve nodded. "Aye, I've dug up a few graves. But only them that's properly buried an' prayed o'er. I'd no' nab a stiff whose ghost's still close by."

"To whom do you sell the bodies?"

Reeve's lips tightened.

"You have an appreciation for beautiful things, don't you?" Ziyaeddin said.

"Aye," he said tentatively.

"That is a fine gold ring you wear on your left hand. No doubt a token of gratitude from the man for whom you rob graves of their occupants?"

"For a job well done." Reeve grinned. "I'll be givin' it to my mum when she's out o' jail."

"The band is so carefully wrought. And the name inscribed on it delicate. All contrived with grace. The name? Of course. You cannot read. So you cannot have realized that inscribed on that ring is a proper name, no doubt the name of the woman from whose lifeless finger he took it. With that name it will be easy to find her family. I am certain they will be happy to have that ring again."

Reeve's nostrils flared.

"Now, James," Ziyaeddin said, "to whom do you sell the bodies?"

"He hasna told me his name," he spit out. "Said I didna need to know it to find them."

"Them?"

"The lasses."

Ziyaeddin pulled air into his lungs. This was no time to imagine Elizabeth in that alleyway with Coira, in danger. Perhaps he should not have persuaded Joachim to leave for London immediately, giving him a letter to carry to the foreign secretary and instructing him to begin making arrangements for their journey. Perhaps instead he should have asked his old friend to remain in Edinburgh, where the guardsman's strength and skill could be of use in protecting a woman who wanted no protecting.

But yesterday Ziyaeddin had not been ready to trade his present for his past. Not yet.

"Which lasses, James?"

"Them's as s'eptible to a fine toff. Bonnie ones lookin' for work. He dinna care for the dugs."

"Are you telling me that you act as procurer for a gentleman who murders prostitutes and then sells their bodies to surgical schools?"

Reeve screwed up his brow. "Well there, Master," he said, scraping his fingers across his scraggly beard. "I'm no' certain how he's handlin' 'em after they go with him."

"You make the introductions only, and this man pays you well for it?"

"Aye."

"Do you understand that in giving you that ring he placed proof on you which the police will seize upon when they discover these crimes?"

Reeve frowned. Then, as though the ring were aflame, he pulled it off and slapped it onto the table.

"Have you any further assignations planned with this man?"

Reeve shook his head hard.

"Have you an address for him?"

His head wagged back and forth again. "Always sends word for me here."

"Are you telling me the truth?"

"Aye, sir! You know I'd ne're lie to you."

"If he should send word to you again, I wish to hear of it. You may find me here." He slid his calling card across the surface of the table. Pocketing the ring, he left and made his way swiftly home.

She was not there. The pot of adhesive sat open on the dressing table in her bedchamber, as though she had donned her whiskers hastily. In the parlor he found a message: *Called to emergency at infirmary. Will speak with Bridges while there.*

The swell of emotion in his chest came suddenly and violently.

Frustration—with her.

Fear—for her.

Pride—in her determination, her intelligence, her independence, her confidence.

Yet all he could think of was getting her back in his bed. He was an utterly lost man.

The clock in the parlor chimed twice. Standing at the base of the stairs in the darkness, silently he cursed her, then himself, and then her again. Then he went to bed. Alone.

LIBBY WATCHED HER patient sleeping now, and her last remaining mote of energy slipped down into the soles of her feet.

"Excellent work, Mr. Smart." In the gray light of early morning, Mr. Bridges stood in the doorway. "The nurse has told me what you did, hastening here when the surgeons on rotation were already engaged in surgery."

"Only three bones needed setting, sir," she said, following him out of the ward.

"You have saved the young man the use of his hand. Well done."

"Thank you, sir."

"I received your message last night. Mr. Chedham has not yet arrived. What is it you wish to speak with me about in private?"

"I believe that the cadavers used in your surgical dissection course are obtained through foul means."

He was silent a moment. "You imagine it to be the work of grave robbers?"

"No, sir. Actually, I believe it could be murder."

His brows snapped together. "That is a serious accusation. Have you any evidence?"

"Insufficient as yet. But I hope today to have more information. Sir, would you tell me from whom you purchase the cadavers?"

A frown pulled his face into vertical lines. "You are an exemplary apprentice and student, Mr. Smart. I advise you not to endanger your future with baseless accusations."

Chedham was entering the hall.

"Yes, sir," she said quickly. "I will speak with you about it only when I have strong evidence."

With another frown, the surgeon led the way to the ward.

Hours later Libby's toes were dragging and she could hardly keep her shoulders square.

"Smart," Chedham said, easily catching up with her as she crossed the courtyard. "What did you do to offend Bridges?"

"It's none of your business." But she feared it was.

Archie's observation that Chedham had gone to Bridges's house late at night would not leave her mind, nor the surgeon's quick dismissal of her suspicion.

"It didn't seem so to me," Chedham said. "But don't worry. When you fall, I'll be right here to pick up the pieces. And toss them in the rubbish bin with the rest of the offal."

As he sauntered off, exhaustion coated her.

Shucking off the feelings, she walked to the alleyway. Coira came from her house.

"Tell me you've that kidney pie today, lad, an' I'll kiss you," she said with a cheery smile.

"Coira, I've news about Dallis. And I need information. I need you to tell me how Bethany came to believe she was pregnant. Exactly how. By whom and when. And then I need you to go to my house and repeat it all to Mr. Kent."

"To the pub, lads?" Archie said, as the lecture hall emptied.

"Mr. Smart is required elsewhere," Dr. Jones said as he ascended the steps toward them.

"Sir?" she said.

"Come with me at once," he said, and passed them by.

Archie and Pincushion's eyes were round.

Libby gathered up her books and followed. "Doctor, have I—"

"Silence will do you well for once, Mr. Smart," he said grimly.

He led her across the courtyard and into a chamber furnished with a long table and sober portraits of men on each wall. Late afternoon sunlight illumined similar men seated about the table, including the Lord Provost himself.

Mr. Bridges stood just inside the doorway.

"Mr. Smart," the Lord Provost said. "I understand

from Dr. Jones that you suspect the cadavers that Mr. Bridges uses in his private surgical school to be acquired illegally."

"Yes. But, whether it is true or not, I don't understand what business of the university it is. Mr. Bridges's school is independent. If what I suspect is true, it is a matter for the magistrates and the police."

"You have an insolent tongue, young man."

"An honest tongue, actually. It is one of my greatest faults."

"You will answer only the questions I ask you."

"Mr. Smart," Mr. Bridges said. "Tell them everything you know."

She told them. But she knew it would not matter. If her guess were correct that Chedham had illegally procured the cadavers for their mentor's surgery, they would all protect him before believing her. She had been here before, after all. Chedham was from a wealthy family, the sort where sons molested servants in stairwells and no one listened when a little girl reported it. She was no one, despite her accomplishments, still the odd one out, still the one who said the wrong things—always the wrong things.

Of course this was happening now. Of course.

"I discovered today, before Dr. Jones's lecture, that the first woman I recognized, Bethany, had recently taken up with a gentleman of means," she finished.

"Taken up with?"

"She had become his mistress. My friend, the one who knew both Bethany and Dallis, said that the man had just let a house for Bethany nearby. Unfortunately my friend does not know his name."

"Are we to trust the word of a female of the trade, now, gentlemen?" one of the old men said.

"You should if it exposes a criminal," Libby said.

"Then that will be all," the Lord Provost said. "Dr. Jones will inform you of our decision."

"What decision?"

"You have gravely insulted the honor and integrity of the Royal Infirmary, the college, and this university, which have all long considered Mr. Bridges an esteemed colleague."

"But I haven't accused *him* of doing wrong, or even of knowing about it."

"A surgeon," Mr. Bridges said soberly, "should know from where his subjects come, Mr. Smart."

"Mr. Bridges and Dr. Jones have requested that we not bar you from further study at this university or the Royal Infirmary. But you may not return this session, and you will not be permitted to apprentice at the infirmary until further notice."

She choked. "But—"

"You are dismissed."

Dismissed.

She was ruined. Above reproach for his entire career, her father would never allow her to continue her ruse after this.

Numbly she followed Dr. Jones from the room. Archie, Pincushion, and George stood in the corridor, hair askew and faces flushed.

"Gentlemen," Dr. Jones said, "if you have come intending to plead a case for your friend, Mr. Bridges has already done so, without success."

"We've come just in time!" Pincushion exclaimed.

"We've brought this, Doctor." Upon Archie's palm was a small gold ring. "'Twas a gift from a gentleman, Mr. John Sheets, to a lass named Bethany."

"A real looker she was, sir," Pincushion interjected.

"She'd a fondness for laudanum, so she gave the ring as payment to the bloke who got the laudanum for her. That bloke gave it to a fellow called Reeve, in payment for havin' made him known to the lass."

"I am not following this narrative, Mr. Armstrong. Make yourself clear at once."

"'Tis Plath, sir!"

"*Plath?*" Libby exclaimed.

"Mr. Robert Plath," George said in clean, crisp, lawyerly syllables. "Plath hires a low fellow Reeve to introduce him to girls of the trade who've already got a liking for poppy seed syrup. Then Plath befriends the girls, sells laudanum to them on the cheap till he needs a cadaver, then while they're in a stupor does away with them."

"Robert Plath?" The physician said in an astonished hush. "My assistant?"

"Aye, sir," Archie said grimly. "Murders them, then sells them to surgical schools."

"And not only Mr. Bridges's," Pincushion inserted.

"Plath is making a fortune," George said.

Dr. Jones's face was pale as a cadaver. "What proof beyond that ring do you have?"

"Peter here spoke with the lad who carts the cadavers to the schools," Archie said.

"Wait here, all of you." Dr. Jones went inside the room.

"How do you know this?" Libby whispered, wrapping her arms around herself to hold in the shaking that was rising from her feet into her stomach.

"Kent found us at the pub," Archie said. "He was lookin' for you, but when we told him Jones marched you away, he told us how he'd tracked down the goldsmith who made the ring, then Sheets himself. Pincushion ran off to find the cadaver carrier. Then we threaded it all together till we'd a whole cloth. Here's the ring Kent took from Reeve," he said, putting it in Libby's hand. "'Tis a shame about your friend, lad."

"What're you thinking to make friends with girls like that, Joe?" George said.

"She was ill," Libby said. "She asked for my help."

The door opened and both Dr. Jones and Mr. Bridges came into the corridor.

"Gentlemen," Dr. Jones said, "do you know where to find Mr. Reeve and Mr. Sheets?"

"We will, sir," Libby said. "Immediately."

"No. Mr. Smart, you will remain here. Before lecture I told Mr. Plath of your accusation, which Mr. Bridges had shared with me in a message. I could not fathom that you would speak rashly and I admit that I was in need of re-assurance. I realize now that was unwise. If what you and your friends believe is true, you could now be in danger from Plath. The Lord Provost is writing letters to both Mr. Sheets and Mr. Reeve, requesting an immediate inter-view. When the police arrive you gentlemen"—he looked at her friends—"must assist them in finding both men."

"Aye, sir," Archie said. "Lads?"

Pincushion and George nodded.

Libby wanted to throw her arms about them all. In-stead, when Mr. Bridges motioned her back into the room with the men who held her fate in their hands, she followed.

Chapter 28

The Ravishment

She burst onto the darkening street. For hours Ziyaeddin had watched for her. Praying. Now he crossed to her.

"You saved me again," she said below the sounds of a passing carriage. There was deep color in her cheeks beneath the whiskers, and her eyes were thick with exhaustion. "You and my friends." A smile flitted over her lips.

"What happened?"

"Did Mr. Sheets tell you that he is married?" she continued quickly as she started off along the footpath. "With three children. The bounder. He did not wish anyone to discover his attachment to Bethany. Speaking to the Lord Provost just now, though, he seemed truly devastated over her death. How clever you were to have found him and Mr. Reeve and wrested the truth from them. But of course you are excellent at seeing into people's souls."

"I would have preferred you to not have met either of them."

"I am exonerated." She was staring at the dark opening of an alley ahead. "The police went to Plath's home and found him packing for a journey. Dr. Jones and Mr. Bridges asked me to wait with them until we got word that they had taken him to jail. I think they were the longest hours of my life."

His, as well.

Abruptly grabbing his coat sleeve, she pulled him around a corner and then several yards along a dark alleyway.

"What are you—"

She grasped his waistcoat. "Kiss me. Kiss me without delay."

Wrapping his hands around her shoulders, he took her mouth beneath his. She met him with her lips parted and her hands twisted in his shirt.

He laughed.

"*Kiss me.*" Her eyes opened wide. "Why do you laugh?"

"I have never before kissed a person with whiskers." He stroked a finger along her throat. "It is a new experience for me."

"It repels you. Does it repel you?"

"Nothing about you could ever repel me."

She planted her lips on his, the whiskers tickled his skin, and he kissed her. Her lips trembled and he curved his hands around her back, and beneath the texture of a man's coat he found her entire body shaking.

She broke away. "We must go home." She slipped out from between him and the wall and ran out of the alley.

By the time he reached the street, the darkness and traffic had swallowed her.

He found his front door unlocked. Setting down his hat and walking stick, he listened for her.

Nothing. No sound. But she was in the house. He knew

it as well as he knew the bows of her upper lip and the arc of the lower.

Not in the parlor. Nor the kitchen. Nor his studio. Nor—wishful fool that he was—in his bed.

He climbed the stairs and found her draped across the bottom of her bed, dropped off in the process of removing her stockings, and the whiskers so hastily removed that a patch still clung to her chin.

Setting down the lamp, he pulled off his coat and found the vial of oil on her dressing table. Then, sitting beside her on the bed, he unstuck the final hairs from her chin. She did not wake.

There was plenty to be done and he proceeded slowly so as not to disturb her sleep. He untied the crushed cravat and discarded it, then unfastened the single button at her throat and parted the shirt. Scissors did swift work of the binding about her breasts. Still she did not rouse. Peeling the stockings from her feet and tossing them away, he followed them with the trousers.

He left the drawers and the shirt.

Lifting her legs onto the bed, he noticed a lopsided lump in her undergarment. Quite swiftly he convinced himself that an artist must always satisfy a burning curiosity. Untying the drawers, he discovered yet another ribbon attached to the waist. He tugged, and out popped a cluster of three small pillows.

Setting them on the bedside table, he swallowed over the rise of feeling in his throat and leaned his head back against the bedpost.

"Why do you weep?" From half-lidded eyes she was watching him.

"I am not weeping, of course," he said, bending to fold up his trouser leg and unfasten the straps from around his knee.

"There is a tear on your cheek."

"You are dreaming." He set the false limb aside and stretched out on the mattress beside her.

Her eyelids drifted shut again. "I don't . . . know why you should weep. We . . . won."

He stoked the hair back from her brow, loosening the oiled locks and using the ruined cravat to wipe away the remnants of her uniform. When he was certain she slept again, he closed his eyes too.

IN DARKNESS SHE roused him. When she climbed atop him and he lifted his hands to her, he found only her skin, warm in the spring night, her sweet body: bony hips, soft thighs, curving waist that gave way to the ripple of ribs and then her breasts.

Tugging at the tail of his shirt, she worked the linen free and he pulled it over his head. Then her fingers were opening the fasteners of his trousers and she was pulling the garments down and away.

She slid atop him, bringing her body along his, stroking his skin with her hands and breasts and supple arms and stretching herself out on him. Her mouth came over his, open and hungry, seeking, her tongue a live, wonderful thing, sweeping over his lips and touching his tongue, his teeth. Her fingers speared between his and her palms pressed hard atop his, holding his arms to either side as she undulated against him, kissing him as though she wanted to consume him—his mouth, his throat and neck and chest.

When her lips closed around his nipple he groaned, feeling her hunger in his hardening cock. He shifted to free his hands. But she held him even tighter to the bed, and he allowed it and drew in the scent of her: salty sweat and earthy oil and her skin, damp now and emanating her fragrance of sexual heat. Teeth grazing him, she pressed her nose to the meeting of his ribs and moaned.

Releasing his hands abruptly, she swept hers down his sides, wrapped them both around the base of his cock, and took the full length of him into her mouth.

As in all things, she was astonishingly clever. It was over far too quickly.

She kissed a path back up his abdomen and chest and finally put her mouth on his and he tasted his own seed on her tongue. She laughed, a chesty, broken cascade of sheer delight and, stroking him with one hand from lips to bollocks, made him constrict and groan anew. Then she climbed onto him once more, spread her thighs, and pleasured herself on him.

When she collapsed onto his chest, her face buried in the crook of his neck, he wrapped his arms around her and held her as close as her jagged breathing would allow.

"The next time, Prince Virility," she whispered in his ear, and the feathers of the words made him catch his breath, "I want you inside me. Can we do that?"

"I am," he said, stroking his fingers up her willowy back, "as always, at your command."

The laughter came again—laughter of pleasure and relief and simple happiness.

They slept. The next time he awoke, a candle burned on the bedside table and he found her sitting beside him with a book open on the blanket that covered her lap but not her breasts and delicate squared shoulders. The wavering candlelight made her eyes glittering mysteries.

"You discovered Joseph's genitals," she said, gesturing to the three little pillows. She closed the volume. "What do you think?"

"That you sew remarkably well."

"Mrs. Coutts sewed them. And of course I sew well. I am a sur—" Her eyes flared. "You said that to tease."

"Possibly."

Her mouth broke into a toothy smile. Tossing the book aside, she leaned down to him and, still smiling, kissed him on the lips. Then again. Then she was wrapping her arms around him and he was pulling her tightly against him and running his hands over her arms and sides and hips and the sweet plane of her back.

"There is an hour yet until dawn," she said, sliding her leg around his hip and pressing to him. "Two until I must be at hospital."

"What do you wish to do with those hours, I wonder," he said, taking her earlobe between his teeth and loving how her body shuddered in response.

"I wish to use my lover shamelessly," she whispered against his throat. "Then go off to my studies and leave him in this bed thinking of me and longing for my return." She brought her lips to his. "How does that suit you, Your Highness?"

He found that he could not speak. So he kissed her. And she did precisely what she wished.

HE DID NOT allow her to leave him in her bed. While she dressed, he went to the kitchen and made coffee and breakfast. Flavored with sugar, the coffee was strong and delicious.

"Like my prince," she said, and he leaned forward and kissed her, which she had intended. She scraped her fingertips over the night's whisker growth across his jaw. "These abrade my skin."

"I will instruct Gibbs to shave me more closely."

"How do my whiskers feel?"

"Soft. Silky." He leaned back and crossed his arms

over his chest. "Like your hair, which in fact they are, transferred artificially to your face."

"You are reminding me of this unnecessarily, I think, to emphasize that you would not kiss just anybody with whiskers."

"I have no desire to kiss anyone else, whiskers or not. And I am simply answering your question."

"So he says." She stood and threw her satchel over her shoulder. "What will you paint today?"

He shrugged. "I am at my leisure."

"How magnificent you are," she murmured. "Perhaps you should go back up into my bed and long for me all day, after all."

"Perhaps I shall."

Walking to the infirmary as the city awoke to the day around her, it seemed her feet hardly touched the cobblestones.

As they did their rounds of the wards, Chedham was as stony as usual, Mr. Bridges was his regular measured self, and their patients offered their typical litanies of complaints and gratitude. It was as though nothing horrible had happened the previous day. Even the memory of Dallis's and Bethany's pale, still faces could not dull Libby's contentment.

The newspapers would undoubtedly drag Mr. Bridges, the college, and the university through the mud for being unaware of the viper in their midst. But Mr. Bridges's excellent reputation would allow him to weather the scandal. Perhaps it would even inspire the college to finally regulate the acquisition of cadavers for use in its fellows' surgeries.

At lunchtime she called on Coira and delivered the news. Her friend accepted it with the practical fatalism of a Scotswoman and the thoughtfulness of one who had known the weaknesses of her friends and loved them anyway. Libby promised she would report on Mr. Plath's fate, although it would certainly be in the broadsheets. A scandal of this sort could not remain hidden within the medical community.

Finishing her lunch with Coira, she went to the library where Archie and Pincushion already occupied their usual table. She greeted them in a whisper. Pincushion didn't even look up. Archie glanced down the length of the reading room, then back at her. Libby unloaded her texts.

A while later, Pincushion returned from a trip to the water closet with his cheeks red as beets and his neck cloth askew.

"Time to go, lads," he said tightly.

Archie frowned. Then he gathered up his books, and gestured for her to follow.

Moving out onto the street and turning in the direction of the pub, Pincushion flexed his shoulder and winced.

"What is it, Peter?" she said. "Are you having trouble with your shoulder again? I can help with that."

Without looking at her he said, "I know you can, Smart. Clever as a cat with joints." He pushed open the door of the pub with his other hand and headed straight for the bar.

"Is it dislocated again?" Libby said to Archie.

"Aye." Archie's gaze slewed about the pub. It was early still, and the place was only half filled.

Pincushion carried over two pints and set them on the table, but his face was strained.

"You must allow me to treat it," she said. "I have been practicing external rota—"

"It's fine, thanks," he said, shifting in obvious discomfort.

"How did it happen? Did you fall?"

He glanced at Archie, then shook his head.

Libby looked back and forth between them. "What is amiss? Has Plath broken free of jail or the Lord Provost changed his mind? For after our triumph yesterday I cannot imagine why you've both got such grim faces."

Archie said, "You dinna know, then, lad?"

"Know what?"

From across the pub, several students burst into laughter. Their eyes were all on her.

Libby's heartbeats tripped.

"This mornin' at dawn," Archie said quietly, "somebody found a paper placard affixed with tar to the door o' Surgeons' Hall."

"With tar? How disrespectful. A placard about what?"

"About you, Joe."

"*Me?*"

They knew.

"I didna see it," Archie said. "Nor Peter. Whoever found it tore it down. But everybody's talkin' about it."

"What did it *say*, Archie?"

"There was a crude picture." He muttered. "An' a caption."

"What was the caption?"

Archie's eyes were on the floor, Pincushion's on the other side of the pub. Neither of them spoke.

"You must tell me," she said.

"It said . . ." Archie frowned. "'In a fine dark alley, the Turk buggers a Smart young surgical apprentice.'"

She hardly knew how she lowered herself to a chair.

"It doesna matter a thing to us, Joe," Archie said quickly, taking the seat beside her. "Peter an' George an' I, we'll shoulder forward with you."

Pincushion's head bobbed up, his skin a bit green. He pivoted on his heels and marched back to the bar.

"That is," Archie said, "no' literally, o' course. No' Peter's shoulder, at least. What I mean to say is, we'll stand by you, lad."

Everybody in the pub was staring at her now, whispers and snickers from young men who for months had treated her with respect, even deference.

"How did his shoulder dislocate this time?" Her eyes were so dry. She couldn't manage to blink.

"Bounders roughed him up at the water closet," Archie scowled. "They said—well, you can guess."

"Because of me. Because of his friendship with me."

This could not be happening.

Someone must have seen them in the alley the night before. Someone had seen him kiss her. The words on the placard had exaggerated it, but someone had clearly seen them. And now her friends were suffering for her carelessness.

And . . . *he.*

Sodomy was a hanging offense.

"Kent's a fine bloke," Archie mumbled. "What, after you were ill, an' yesterday, an' the lot o' it. Still, I'd like to break his neck for puttin' you in danger."

"It is not his fault," she said. "You believe the accusation?"

Archie's brow dipped. "Few nights ago," he whispered, "you were actin' mighty queer after lecture. I was worried about you, lad. Wanted to be sure you'd get home all right, so I followed you." He paused a moment. "I saw you in the church. With him."

Nausea crawled through her.

"I'll ne'er tell a soul, lad."

She tried to fill her lungs.

Pincushion returned to the table and sat down, but he wouldn't look at her.

"It is unwise of you to be near me. Both of you. And George too." She felt hollow inside. "You should distance yourselves from me."

"Bugger that," Archie spat out. "Er, uh, beggin' your pardon, Joe. But we'll no' abandon you. An' these piss-ants can go suck rotten eggs," he said, glaring at the snickerers at the other table. "Hypocrites, at least two o' them, an' probably others."

"You must protect yourselves," she said.

Pincushion pushed a glass toward her, then finally looked into her eyes.

"Bugger them all, right?" he said and lifted his pint in salute. "To Joe Smart, the cleverest lad in Edinburgh."

"It'll blow o'er, Joe," Archie said, and tossed a thick text onto the table. "Now to the books."

An hour later George arrived. Face grave, he settled in the chair beside Libby and looked about at them pointedly.

"Aye, lad," Archie said. "We've heard."

"I heard it from my father," George said. "First time he's called on me since he threw me onto the street. He remembered we're friends, Joe."

"Your *father*? How does he know of it?"

"Everybody in Edinburgh knows, lad," he said soberly. "Gossip's spreading like fire."

She must go home, tell him, warn him.

"'Tis a grim business," Archie said, sipping ale. "But we'll stick by you, Joe."

Pincushion nodded.

"No need, most likely," George said. "Jones and Bridges have already spoken up for young Joe here."

Libby froze in stuffing her books into her satchel. "Already? But Archie said the placard was only found *this morning*. How can this be?"

"Kent's a celebrity, Joe. He's got the respect of half the men of power in town, and the dislike of the other half. Some will believe any nasty story about a foreign chap they hear, and they're pouncing on this quick. Father says Jones and Bridges made the case that you'd never have agreed to it." His lips were tight but he spoke dispassionately, professionally. "They're saying it must have been force."

Worse and worse. *A nightmare.*

"Father says you're likely to be exonerated."

"But what of him?"

"Indictment, most likely. Police haven't any evidence to bring before the magistrates, only hearsay."

"Plenty o' lads o' low character envy young Joe." Archie shook his head. "Evidence'll surface, even if it's false."

"That was my thought." George looked her in the eye. "Joe, whatever I can do, I'll do. Damn, but I wish I'd stood up to my father years ago so I'd be able to legally represent you now."

"Thank you." She could not tell them that she had friends far more powerful than even George's father, more powerful than all of them combined. She could not tell them that her heart was breaking. "I will write to my father."

She must now. The scandal with Plath paled in comparison to this horror.

A footfall sounded beside the table. She looked up into Maxwell Chedham's eyes.

"Pity to hear you're in trouble, Smart," he said. "I am all broken up over it. Truly. But don't worry. I'll care for your patients after you're gone." He sauntered off.

Archie's gaze followed him. "I wonder who posted that placard," he muttered.

But watching Chedham greet his friend Pulley and his other toadies with a smile, Libby already knew.

MRS. COUTTS BUSTLED from the kitchen. "He's had callers, lass," she said. "Police investigators! Stayed a full hour, drank two pots o' tea, an' gobbled up all the biscuits too. I listened through the door, o' course. 'Tis wicked slander! They can clap me in shackles an' lead me to the noose, an' I'll defend the both o' you till my last hour."

"Thank you, Mrs. Coutts. Where is he?"

"Where else? I'm off to cook for Mr. Coutts. But if you need me, lass, send a lad an' I'll return straightaway." Mrs. Coutts chucked her under the chin as though she were a child—the child that the scandalized population of Edinburgh believed her to be—and departed.

In his studio he sat on the stool before the easel, the portrait on it only partially colored over the underpainting. It was a pair of boys standing proudly in red coats and black breeches and surrounded by a pack of hunting dogs.

He would never have another commission like this.

Setting down his brush, he came to her. He stroked the hair back from her brow, kissed her there, then kissed her lips.

"We must talk," she said between kisses.

"Later." He peeled the coat from her shoulders and unbound her cravat.

"Not later. Now."

"If I am to be publicly accused of ravishing you," he said, pulling the shirt out of her trousers, "then I should be permitted to actually do so in private."

"You did not ravish me," she said as he released her and went into the workroom. "You ravished Joseph Smart."

He returned with oil and a cloth.

"Although I am becoming accustomed to the tickle of these whiskers," he said, dabbing the oil onto her skin and peeling away the down, "I prefer kissing you without."

"You will not acknowledge what I have said?"

"In point of fact I ravished neither you nor Joseph Smart. Both of you grabbed me and kissed me. As ravishments go, the public will be disappointed. I found it very enjoyable, of course."

"You must be serious. Someone wishes to hurt me, or perhaps both of us, yet because of Joseph's youth you are to bear the whole burden of it."

He unfastened her trousers. "I have never believed my time on this earth would be lengthy, *joonam*. Indeed for two decades now I have expected death to come at any moment."

"It will not happen," she said, laying her hands on his shoulders as he bent to push the trousers down. "You must write to the duke. We will ask for his assistance."

His hands stroked along her bared thighs. "These legs. I want them wrapped around me. Now." He looked up into her eyes and she was shocked by the fevered haze of lust in his.

"Will you do nothing to save yourself?"

He took her hand in his and kissed her knuckles like a knight kneeling before his lady.

"Whatever you wish, I shall do, *jan-e delam*." He stood and started across the room toward his bedchamber. "Now, come. There is ravishing to be done and I don't particularly care who does it, only that it is accomplished without further delay."

She went, and shortly there was not ravishment but passion, and when he brought her to crying pleasure she hid her tears of desperation against his skin and held him tight.

Chapter 29

The Sacrifice

The following morning Libby went to the infirmary for her usual rounds. Mr. Bridges said nothing regarding the accusation, but his face was drawn.

"It's in all the papers," Chedham muttered to her as they stood side by side at the chemistry table. Mr. Bridges had gone to the men's ward alone, he said because there was an unknown illness there. But Libby feared it was for her sake, an attempt to protect her.

"Plath's indictment is front page," Chedham said, mixing a vulnerary salve in a brass bowl. "But your depraved little imbroglio is on page two."

She added a pinch of turmeric taken from Mrs. Coutts's kitchen to her own decoction. "You did it. Didn't you?"

"Skulking around in dark alleys hardly suits a man of my character. Anyway, I had theater tickets that night. Opening night. It was excellent entertainment."

At lunchtime she walked directly to the theater nearest

the alley in which she had grabbed her lover and kissed him.

"Aye, lad," the box office clerk said. "Two nichts aby. *As You Like It*. Openin' nicht always sees a mighty crush."

Chedham wanted her to know that he had posted the placard—that he had won. She could only pray that he alone had seen that kiss. Then the judge might consider it biased evidence.

But the evening's gossip broadsheet dashed her hopes. According to reports, recently Mr. Kent had rudely rejected the delicate advances of a maiden of great beauty and charm whose father had commissioned a portrait of her. Given that young men threw posies at this maiden's feet, her father suggested that the artist's indifference must surely be due to his "unnatural" proclivities.

"It is all lies!" Tearing up the broadsheet, Libby threw it onto the grate. No fire burned there. So she grabbed a candle and tossed it onto the newspaper and watched it all crackle into ash. "She hated you for rejecting her, didn't she? And her father did too. They are jumping onto Chedham's accusation out of spite."

"Seems so." He reclined in a comfortable chair.

"How can you sit there and do *nothing*?"

"I am not doing nothing. I am watching you wear a trough in my favorite rug."

Going to him, she climbed onto his lap and banded her arms about his neck and pressed her face into his shoulder. His hands came around her waist and he kissed her hair.

"They will come to take you away."

"They will not," he said.

"They will."

"They have no proof beyond Mr. Chedham's word. And as you have noted, his reason to see you fail is well known."

"Everybody in town with any minuscule complaint with you will add their disgruntlements to the fray until the magistrates can no longer brush it off as one student's vendetta against another." She leaned back and stroked her fingers along his jaw. "Chedham's family is wealthy and influential. But so is Constance's."

"You must not tell her. You must tell no one."

"I wrote to Amarantha."

His hands loosened and he tilted his head back and looked up at the ceiling.

Her fingers twisted in his waistcoat. "The duke can help."

"Only three years ago the Duke of Loch Irvine barely weathered a scandal far worse than this. Edinburgh has not yet forgotten the devil it loved to hate. I will not repay my friend for his generosity by embroiling him in yet another scandal."

"You needn't. I already have."

"Elizabeth—"

She leaped off his lap, her fists tight at her sides.

"It was *my* need that put you in danger, my need for reassurance, for forgiveness and all the foolishness that I can be. I am at fault. *Me*. You have done nothing of blame and I cannot bear that you will be hurt."

"Before your father returns you must complete this extraordinary year's accomplishment," he said with infuriating calm. "Until then, put this from your thoughts."

"How can you be so indifferent to your fate? My father will hear of this. My future is already determined. Yours is not."

"Your father need not know Joseph Smart is his daughter."

"I have already told him."

His features fell into disbelief.

"I had to allow him time to accept the truth before he returns. I did not tell him about you. But now he will know. He will hear of this scandal into which Joseph has fallen." She turned away from him. "How wretchedly I have served every person I love. I wanted this so desperately that I cared nothing for the pain or danger it would bring anyone, only for the satisfaction it would bring me."

"Happiness."

She swung around. "What?"

"It has not only brought you satisfaction," he said. "It has brought you happiness. And me as well. Happiness I thought never to enjoy."

She stared at him.

"You must leave here at once," she said. "Go anywhere. To London. Alexandria. Istanbul. Leave here and save yourself."

"I will. When your project here is finished."

A great, hard scream pushed its way up into her throat. She choked it back and strode out of the parlor.

HE FOUND HER in his bed. Taking her into his arms, he held her until her rigid acceptance of his embrace became acquiescence, and in the stillness he counted each of her quick breaths and equally swift heartbeats.

When finally she turned to him and wrapped her arms around him and lifted her lips to be kissed, he gave her what she desired.

THE DUKE AND Duchess of Loch Irvine arrived before breakfast.

"Tuppin' lads now, Your Highness?" the duke said.

"Ladies present, Your Grace," Ziyaeddin murmured to his friend.

"Only one lady, properly," Elizabeth said. Moving forward, she grasped the duchess's hand. "Thank you for coming."

She did not curtsy to Gabriel, or even nod, and Ziyaeddin felt that powerful pride thickly in his chest. Elizabeth Shaw would bend to no man's superiority. She was perfect. Perfect.

"Of course we came," the duchess said. She was a beauty in the English mode, with pale skin and freckles scattered over her nose and cheeks and fiery tresses.

"How are the little ones?" Elizabeth asked.

"My son is a bundle o' drooling good nature," the duke said.

"Like his father," Ziyaeddin said.

"Aye." He was a giant of a man, with shoulders like a stevedore's and features weathered by a decade at sea. "My daughter's a holy terror, o' course, just as I like a female." His brow grew thoughtful. "Speakin' o' holy terrors . . ."

"There is nothing holy about what I have done." Elizabeth stood alone now near the desk upon which were arranged her books—too neatly. A new pile had gathered on the floor, atop it a small stack of scraps of used paper.

Brilliant, ambitious, bighearted, and determined to succeed.

These setbacks coming one upon another had ignited the demon that within her always awaited a moment of weakness, of fear. He must wrest her free of this. Swiftly.

"Gabriel," he said, "can you open your house here?"

"Aye."

"Of course," Amarantha said. "Libby, you must come live with us. If Joseph continues to be seen entering and leaving this house, it will only stoke the flames of gossip. If he is no longer seen here, people will swiftly forget.

Such is the nature of scandal. When do you expect your father here?"

"Soon." Her hands were clasped tightly together.

"He will be our guest as well, and it will appear a regular merry party of friends."

"But what if he is arrested?" Her blue eyes swung to Ziyaeddin. "And don't say it will not matter because you have experienced worse."

"I was not intending to say that."

"You were thinking it. I can see it in the very set of your mouth, you know."

He strove not to smile. She was too sober, her brow too taut.

"We'll cross that bridge when we come to it, lass," the duke said.

"Your Graces!" Mrs. Coutts stood in the doorway, parcels in her thick arms.

"Good morning, Mrs. Coutts," Amarantha said. "I am afraid we have descended upon you even before breakfast. Libby, perhaps we could assist Mrs. Coutts in preparing a repast." She nodded toward the door.

"As you wish, Amarantha." Elizabeth followed, and as she passed into the corridor Ziyaeddin heard her say, "But he is the one who always makes breakfast."

"Son o' a bitch," Gabriel grumbled.

"Insult my deceased mother, Scot, and I will show you that your paltry three inches of additional height have nothing on my strength and general creativity."

"I wasna referring to you." The duke threw himself down into the chair opposite. "Who's this Chedham? A spoiled lad?"

"His parents have wealth."

Distant clinking of china came from the kitchen into the silence of the parlor.

"You've no choice," Gabriel said. "You've got to let it be known who you are."

"I cannot. Not now." Not with this accusation attached to him. In Tabir as in Britain, the law had no mercy for men who did with men. He could not bring that to his sister or people, not as war seethed on their borders.

Gabriel nodded solemnly. "What'll you do?"

Ziyaeddin stared at the open doorway through which she had gone. "Whatever I must."

Mrs. Coutts and Amarantha helped her pack and it was swiftly accomplished. Before leaving the house, Libby sent notes to Iris and Alice. Then she dressed as Joseph and went to the infirmary where she was expected as always.

Chedham said nothing out of the ordinary, nor did Mr. Bridges. She prayed that this meant the police had decided the accusation had no merit.

After lecture she told Archie and Pincushion that she had moved to another residence and that it would take her some time to walk there before dark, so she could not join them at the pub.

At the appointed location at the edge of New Town, a plain carriage collected Joseph Smart. A quarter of an hour later, Elizabeth Shaw descended from it before the door of the elegant home of the Duke and Duchess of Loch Irvine far out past the toll gate.

Libby thanked her hosts for their welcome, but declined dinner; she had no appetite. In her luxurious bedroom, she unpacked her books and turned again to studying.

The following morning, the footman opened the door of the little parlor Libby had taken over for her studies and said, "Miss, you have a caller."

Iris bounded through the door.

"You are here!" She threw her arms about Libby. "It is positively refreshing to see you wearing a gown, Libby. How pretty you are with your short hair and sad eyes. Will you give up Joseph Smart forever now?"

"Iris, I have missed you too. Thank you for being such an excellent friend. I dearly hope this scandal does not reach you."

"Alice and I think it's an adventure and are determined to defend you!"

A knock sounded at the door. This time her father stood there.

"Papa!" She sprang up and flew into his embrace. After a moment, he put her gently to arm's length.

"My daughter," he only said, his kind eyes smiling. "Good day, Miss Tate."

"Welcome home, Doctor. I'll go find the children." Iris departed.

"Papa, how good it is to see your face. I have missed you dreadfully."

"Yet you have been occupied." Glancing at her books spread out he added, "Joseph."

"You received my letter."

"I left London that very day." He shook his head. "Elizabeth."

"Do not be angry with me, Papa. Few people know who I am, and none of them will tell a soul. You needn't be ashamed."

"I am not ashamed. I am astonished. Never could I have guessed that leaving you would inspire you to this. But I should have. I have known for two decades what an extraordinary person you are."

"Thank you." She grabbed his hands and squeezed them. They were warm and dry and softer than she remembered.

"Daughter, has Kent used you poorly?"

She released him. "No. He has been generous, kind, and patient. All that is good."

"Is this accusation—this unseemly rumor—does it have truth?"

"None that merits concern."

"That is a relief. I could not forgive myself for having left you if it were otherwise."

"Papa, it was my choice. My doing."

"And Alice Campbell's," he said grimly. "I should have arranged for you to live with Constance, or at Haiknayes."

"You asked Alice because you believed that I would be happiest in her home." He had not wanted to disturb her, to throw her into the social whirlwind of Constance's life in Edinburgh or the duke and duchess's busy estate. He had wanted her to remain calm, quiet, *unchallenged*. "You must not blame yourself or even Alice. She only did what I begged her to do, and you know how impossible I am to refuse."

He took her hands again. "I also have news to share, Elizabeth. The college has invited me to remain in London through the year. And I have an additional reason to remain there now."

"Madame Roche? Alice guessed."

"Yes. I wish to ask Clarice for her hand. But I shan't make my feelings plain to her if the idea is abhorrent to you. Twenty years ago when I accepted you as my own, I made a vow to your mother and no less to myself that I would care for you. I will allow nothing to come in the way of that."

Libby now saw his fatherhood like a heavy yoke upon him. He had never denied her, never demanded of her, never forbidden her anything. He was first and always a physician. He had given her unquestioned love and affection, an extraordinary education, and his respect. But he had never asked of her anything it was uncomfortable for her to give.

Ziyaeddin had. He had demanded she heal herself. And now he was demanding that she finish what she had begun. He expected it of her.

"Papa, I like Madame Roche very much. Nothing will make me happier than your happiness."

"This gives me great relief," he said, mirroring her smile in his measured way.

"Will you—both you and she—allow me to continue as Joseph Smart?"

"Daughter, the question must rightly be upon you. Can remaining as Joseph Smart bring you happiness?"

Two DAYS LATER the indictment came. Libby stood stunned on the street corner as traffic clattered by and pedestrians jostled her, making the broadsheet print before her eyes wiggle. But the text was clear: Mr. Ibrahim Kent, portraitist, had been arrested for the crime of "unnatural acts."

In a daze she walked toward the pub.

"This way, Joe," Archie said, grabbing her arm and dragging her out onto the street again.

"Archie. Where are you—"

"To Miss Coira's house. Your cousin's got somethin' to tell you."

"Iris? How do—"

"She's insistin' on seein' you. She didna know where you'd be so she found Coira at the bawdy house. Your cousin's an audacious lass, Joe. I think I'm in love."

They rounded the corner and Iris and Coira both leaped off the wall at once and came forward.

"I brought him!" Archie's chest puffed out.

Iris ignored him. "Joseph, I must speak with you in private. Immediately."

Libby nodded to Coira and Archie, and they moved away.

"Amarantha hadn't any idea where to find you," Iris said, "so I told her I would. I didn't want to reveal that you have lunch every other day with a prostitute, of course. She's a duchess and—"

"Iris, please. What have you come to tell me?"

"Mr. Kent is to be indicted."

"I know. I've just read about it. I was going to the pub to write a statement for the police, denying it all."

"It won't matter, Libby. Mr. Kent is repudiating you."

"Repudiating? I don't understand. In what manner?"

"In the most fabulously heroic fashion! He has admitted to the crime, but claimed that the witness only assumed it was you because you live in his house, but that it was not in fact you."

Libby's stomach rose in her throat.

"He has *admitted* to it?" Panic swirled in her. She knew why he had done this: to ensure that she would not be physically examined—that *Joseph* would not be physically examined for proof of the deed. He was doing it to save her future. "*No*. No, he cannot."

"What's more, the accuser has been revealed. It is Mr. Maxwell Chedham. Do you know him?"

The crushing weight of every decision she had made pressed down upon her.

"He cannot. He *must* not," she heard herself saying as though through a tunnel.

"He already has! Though not publicly, it's true. The duke said only the Lord Advocate knows as yet. I wasn't supposed to know, actually, but I happened to be in the playroom with the children when he was telling Amarantha in the next room. I pretended I hadn't heard. But it seems they all agree that the accusations will not be withdrawn and that it is the only way to save y—Libby? Where are you going?"

"Archie, please see Iris home."

"Aye, lad."

"Thank you, Coira. Thank you, all of you."

At the corner she hailed a hackney. Asking the driver to deposit her at the rear of the ducal mansion, she entered through the servants' entrance so that none of her friends would see her. It did not distress her. She had used servants' entrances throughout her life. As a bastard child, she had long since grown accustomed to her place.

Now she would be the cause of a prince's destruction.

In her room she removed all traces of Joseph, donned the most elegant frock Constance had bought for her, pinned ear bobs in her lobes, and tied a pretty bonnet, to which Iris had attached a length of her cut hair, atop it all and then called for the gig.

She drove herself to New Town.

The square she sought was no more than thirty years old, the houses austere and imposing. She refused to be intimidated. Joseph would not be. Neither would Elizabeth.

A servant bid her wait in a drawing room. When her nemesis finally entered it was immediately clear that he did not recognize her.

"How do you do, ma'am?" He bowed. He was dressed expensively and soberly in a coat of dark blue with a stiff white stock and cravat pinned with gold.

"Good day, Mr. Chedham."

"You have me at an advantage," he said with a natural smile she had never seen before: open and appreciative. "Miss . . . ?"

"Elizabeth Shaw."

"To what fortune do I owe this call, Miss Shaw? Or"—the pleasure in his eyes dimmed—"has Sawyer perhaps mistaken it and you have come to see my father?"

"No. I wished to see you. You don't recognize me."

"I do beg your pardon. But I am certain I would recall such an attractive lady had we met before."

"All the plain women be damned, is that it? I'm not surprised. You truly don't recognize me. It is extraordinary."

"Miss Shaw," he said coolly now, "I fear I am at a loss."

"Oh. There is the Cheddar I know well."

Something flickered in his eyes. Then his shoulders fell back and his lips parted.

"Yes," she said in Joseph's voice. "It is I."

He stepped backward a full pace. His nostrils flared.

"You are . . . Smart's sister?"

"His twin, perhaps?" she said in her natural voice. "No, Chedham. It is truly I, the young man beside whom you have worked for months, whom you have tried to best yet never have, and whom you have recently accused of a crime that could have me and a man who is worth one hundred of you hanged by the neck."

"What—what sort of a man are you?"

"I am not a man. I am a woman, as you can plainly see."

"You *cannot* be."

"Must I undress before you for you to believe it?"

"No woman—"

"Could have bested you? Could have bested everyone? Could have pretended to be a man for so many months without detection? Yes, a woman could have. For I did."

He shook his head.

"Shall I recite to you every misstep you have made at the infirmary these many months?" she said. "Shall I tell you about the time you dosed Mr. Finch with too much camphor and had I not noticed and opened his air passages he would have died? Shall I describe to you the details of Mrs. Small's fatal tumors at which you scoffed? Shall I tell you how you jested about using my cadaver for dissection? Of course it is I. That you worked beside me for so many months yet never once suspected I was a woman, and that you stand here now agape, only proves that you are as stupid about actual human beings as I have always thought."

Finally his gaze narrowed. "You unnatural creature."

"I am not unnatural. I am, like you, called to be a surgeon. Can you not understand that? Can you not pity the woman whose talents and skills are suited to a calling she is not permitted to pursue? Can you not try to understand why I have done what I have done? You know now that what you saw in that alley was not what you believed it to be," she said. "You know now that he has committed no crime."

"Do I?" The arrogance was back.

"Tell them that you mistook it. Retract the accusation. Don't do it for my sake. For they will not come for me, you know. They believe Joseph Smart is too young to have done it voluntarily. They are accusing him of force. Retract the accusation. You must."

"I do not care to."

"You would send an innocent man to the gallows?"

"If it will ensure that Joseph Smart's reputation will be smeared, I will. Gladly."

"What do you want, then?" she said. "What must I do so that you will retract it?"

"You—Joseph—must admit to cheating. Throughout the year. Then you must quit."

She was numb.

"You don't want anyone to know a woman has bested you," she said.

"It is not my fondest wish," he said tightly.

"I will do it. I will quit and disappear. I will leave you to your Pyrrhic victory. But I will not admit to cheating. I accomplished this year what no other woman and few men have accomplished. I will not lie about that."

"It seems it's to be the noose for the Turk and ignominy for his poor young victim, after all."

"You *must not*. I beg of you." She gripped her hands together. "See me now, begging? You have me at your mercy. Tell me what you want of me and I will do it. *Anything*."

His eyes gleamed. "You care for him."

Her throat was full of tears she refused to reveal. She nodded.

"Admit to cheating on every assignment, and I will withdraw the accusation." He went to the door. "You can see yourself out."

Chapter 30

The Truth

The papers eagerly awaited the Turk's fate while chewing on every detail of the medical community's other scandal. Plath had begun his grisly commerce by befriending the sick and homeless in Edinburgh's back alleyways, helping them along prematurely to the afterlife, then selling their fresh corpses at exorbitant prices to private surgical schools. Promising to supply cadavers to too many surgeons at once, he had turned to murdering those he believed were friendless and transporting them to the surgery along the city's ancient underground passageways.

As one, Edinburghians looked forward to Plath's hanging, yet squabbled in disagreement about the other possible hanging.

Some broadsheets insisted that the portraitist was an innocent victim of jealousy and slander while others claimed that foreigners could never be trusted. Most agreed that, given the suspect quality of the accusation, since he might not be condemned to hang he should at least be sentenced to the public pillory. There the crowds would see to his punishment.

Constance reported that it was all anybody wanted to gossip about. People who had once clamored for his presence in their drawing rooms and for his paintings on their walls now excoriated him publicly.

"How easily they turn against a man whom they have adored," Constance mused.

"The moment he steps out of the role they have assigned to him," Alice added. "Ignorant fools."

He had understood this long ago, Libby realized, and had chosen in his quiet way to resist that.

"I am less interested in gossips than in the young men who have served our dear Elizabeth poorly," Alice added. "But young men are wretched as a species. Elizabeth, I hereby offer to snip off the jewels of each of them that has caused you pain."

"Thank you. But I don't think that would be wise." Anyway, Joseph had no such jewels, and it was he who was causing everybody the most pain. "Papa and Amarantha and the duke believe that behaving normally will be the surest path toward exoneration."

"What does Mr. Kent have to say about that?"

Nothing. Ziyaeddin had not written to her, nor sent any message via the duke.

The following morning, dressed as Joseph, she went to the infirmary as usual. Mr. Bridges met her with his customary sobriety. A surgery was scheduled, and as she stood across the operating table from Chedham, assisting their mentor, her fellow apprentice offered her a hard glare, then looked away. Obviously he would not reveal her. His pride would not allow the world to know that a woman had gotten the best of him.

Later, in the lecture hall, she settled into her

regular seat beside Archie and pulled out her pencil and notebook.

"Dinna fret, lad," Archie whispered. "We'll find a solution. It'll be all right in the end."

"Yes. It will."

Dr. Jones lectured on the male reproductive organs. Watching Chedham's cheeks grow red, and knowing that her presence in the hall caused it, Libby nearly smiled.

Two hours later the physician dismissed them.

Libby stood up and removed her coat. With steady hands she unbuttoned her waistcoat, pulled her arms from it, and unknotted her neck cloth.

"Joe? What're you doin', lad?" Archie chuckled uncomfortably. She could feel the attention of others around her as she tugged the long tail of shirt linen from her trousers, dragged the garment over her head, and dropped it onto her chair.

With only the binding around her breasts and the eyes of everyone in the hall on her, using an oiled cloth, she peeled the whiskers from her face and wiped the cosmetics from her brows, and shoved the hair back from her brow.

Then she unbound her breasts.

"As you see, gentlemen," she said in Elizabeth Shaw's voice—*her* voice—the voice that Ziyaeddin had said he could listen to forever. "I am a woman."

Below, Dr. Jones was staring at her with eyes full of shock.

The hall had gone silent.

"Won't anybody say anything?" She swept the hall with her gaze. "Or would you like me to drop my drawers too, so that you haven't any doubt of it?"

Archie leaped up and threw a coat over her chest.

"O' course we dinna doubt it, lad—*lass*." He was

holding the garment around her and grinning like a fool. "Lord almighty, I shoulda known it. Joe—*Joséphine*—whoever you are—Well done, lass!" He made a whooping sound. "Lads," he shouted across the theater that was finally erupting in chatter. "I'll have you recall that she chose *me* for her mate! That is, no' her *mate*. That is to say—her—" He choked on laughter.

Pincushion pounded him on the back, his grin shining. "Wait till George learns of this. He'll split his breeches." Shaking his head, he thrust out a hand to her.

Libby shook it, then the hands of half a dozen other students. Most of her classmates cast her glares.

"Mr. Smart," Dr. Jones's voice cut through the chaos. "At once." He strode from the chamber.

She clutched the coat to her, accepted her belongings that Archie had gathered up, and followed her professor from the hall.

SHE COULD HARDLY sit still.

Arrayed across the table from her were the Lord Provost, the president of the college, the president of the infirmary, several members of the University Senate, Dr. Jones, and Mr. Bridges.

"The ignominy you have cast on this university, the Royal Infirmary, and the college is unforgivable," the Lord Provost continued his speech that had already gone on for a quarter of an hour. "Never before has this ancient, august city harbored such a brash, willful, disrespectful mockery of morality."

Given Robert Plath, this was patently untrue.

"How do you know that?" she said.

Dr. Jones's lips flattened.

Mr. Bridges's cheek twitched.

"I beg your pardon?" the Lord Provost snapped.

"How do you know that no other woman has done this before? You didn't know I was a woman, and I only revealed it to exonerate an innocent man. How do you know there haven't been other women that have fooled you too, only never revealed themselves?"

"Elizabeth," her father said beside her.

She swallowed her next words. Within minutes of this harangue it had become clear that these inestimably moral scions of this community were far more upset that a woman had succeeded in studying medicine at the highest levels than the fact that a gently reared maiden had been living with a bachelor for months. They were positively hypocritical. But she did not wish to shame her father any further.

"Be grateful, Miss Shaw," the Lord Provost said, "that none of us are taking more severe measures against you for perpetrating this heinous farce. Transportation has been suggested."

Her father jerked forward. "My lord—"

"Your influential noble connections have, however, pleaded in your defense," the Lord Provost said tightly. "Your indenture fee is forfeit, but this council will not remit you to the magistrates. You are a fortunate young woman to have such friends."

"Mr. Bridges has requested that you call at the infirmary to bid your patients good-bye," the president of the infirmary said. "I however am concerned that, given the circumstances of the baths in which you have treated patients, if the male patients discover the truth of this"— he gestured in the general direction of her torso—"it will distress them. I give you permission to complete your responsibilities at the infirmary today as you are."

"Thank you, sir."

"Dr. Shaw," the Lord Provost said gravely, "you have

long been an esteemed colleague and friend to this university. Yet you, sir, have contributed to this travesty. I trust that you will impress upon your daughter the gravity of her insupportable charade, and keep her well in hand forthwith."

"My father is generous and wise, and does not deserve your censure." She reached over and grasped his hand. "Thank you for never clipping my wings, Papa." Releasing him, she stood up.

"Be seated, young woman," the Lord Provost said. "We are not finished with you."

"But I am finished with you. Unfortunately. For I would have liked to complete my studies and become a fellow of the college and a practicing surgeon. But you will not allow it despite my accomplishments, and for that I have little respect for you." She looked at her teachers. "Dr. Jones, Mr. Bridges, I am deeply grateful for the superlative education you have given me, and I am sincerely regretful to have caused you embarrassment. But I hope that my successes have planted a seed of doubt in your excellent minds about the exclusion of women from the highest ranks of the medical profession. If I have done that, at least in a very small manner I have succeeded. Good day, gentlemen."

Her father followed her out. When the door closed she took both of his hands.

"Thank you for standing with me, Papa. You will be ostracized here now."

"By none that deserve my respect."

Leaving him, she went out of the building. She had spent hours awaiting the gathering of her chastisers and then being chastised—hours during which she had heard the news that the charges against Ziyaeddin had been withdrawn. Now late afternoon had settled over the streets in the busy press of traffic. Taking extra-long strides as she walked with graceless speed to the infirmary, she reveled in these final moments of freedom from the constraints of skirts and stays, her heart at once aching and magnificently light.

At the hospital, only one of her patients mentioned her scraggly whiskers—the remnants of her attempt at removing them in the lecture hall. The nurses watched her carefully and she suspected they had already heard the rumors. News traveled swiftly in the medical community, and in less than a sennight Joseph Smart had been at the center of two scandals.

As she was setting her examining tools back in their rightful place in the preparation chamber, one of the nurses passed by.

"I knew it all along," the woman whispered. "The Lord bless you, lass, an' bless your sainted father an' that fine Mr. Kent." Then she was gone and Libby was staring at the empty doorway.

How many people had known? How many *women*? How many had suspected it but never said a word? How many had simply reveled in knowing that one of their own was secretly accomplishing what none of them were permitted to even attempt?

Awe and gratitude filled her as she walked across the infirmary courtyard and toward home.

For the first time since she had moved into his house, as she lifted her hand to the bell ringer, anxious tingles beset her belly.

Mr. Gibbs answered the door.

"Evenin', miss," he said, beckoning her inside. "Heard you'd been found out."

"Mr. Gibbs, have you always known I was a woman?"

"Naw, miss! Anly heard it from the master an hour aby.

Will you be wantin' a fresh neck cloth? That one you've got on there's in a fine tangle."

"No, thank you." She swallowed back her laughter. "Is he in?"

He shook his grizzled head. "Went out like cannon shot after the police left, must've been twenty minutes aby or so. Said he'd to see a dug about a bone."

The Dug's Bone.

"The prodigal daughter!" Mrs. Coutts exclaimed, bustling forward. "Mr. Gibbs, we've a celebrity in the house."

"Actually, leaving it," Libby said, the nerves dancing in her stomach like little mice around a block of cheese.

"No' with that tangle o' fuzz on those pretty cheeks! Mr. Gibbs, fetch the oil."

Minutes later, free of whiskers, Libby pushed open the pub's door.

"She's here!" Pincushion was shouting as the door flew wide.

And there Ziyaeddin was, meeting her gaze, and all of the wicked nerves in her belly melted into brilliant happiness.

She flew at him, wrapped her arms around his neck, and kissed him. She thought she heard cheering, but his mouth and the strength of his hands holding her were all she cared about.

"You should not have done it," he said to her as the whoops and whistles and applause continued. She heard Archie call for ale for everybody, and the place erupted in yet more cheering.

"The Lord Advocate agreed to delay matters until I am gone," Ziyaeddin said beneath the cheering. He took both of her hands and spoke close to her. "Elizabeth, I am leaving. Very soon."

"I suspected that," she said, gripping his hands too

tightly. "You told me as much. I wanted you to be able to leave without fear of this rumor chasing you, and to return without fear of the noose—if you should ever find occasion to return."

His eyes smiled.

"Come," she said, circling her fingers about his arm. "I wish to have my likeness drawn at once, and I am willing to pay a fairly respectable price for it."

"Fairly respectable?"

"That will depend on the quality of the likeness, of course."

HE NEVER FINISHED the picture. Every few minutes her curiosity impelled her to leap up from the chair and inspect his progress. Each time she had to touch him and sometimes kiss him.

On the tenth such interruption he pulled her onto his lap and made love to her there, she tearing off his coat and shirt even as she rode him, laughing and crying and generally making such a ruckus that it was a very good thing he did not hire round-the-clock servants.

Later, twisted in the bedclothes, their limbs thoroughly entangled, as she drifted off to sleep she heard him whisper, "Thank you." But she had not done it for his thanks. She had done it because she was finished with living a lie and finished with bending to irrational rules. She snuggled closer into his heat and slept soundly.

In darkness permeated by the first suggestion of dawn she sensed when he rose. Drowsily she felt his fingertips stroke along her jaw and then over her lips, slowly, tenderly, as though he sought to memorize the texture and shape of them. Then his lips pressed against her brow.

She heard the echo of his wooden footstep across the studio floor, and she smiled with closed eyes. Turkish coffee or English tea: either would do for breakfast. She drifted back into slumber.

When she awoke bright sunlight glimmered through the crack in the draperies. Rising, she wrapped his dressing gown around her and went to the kitchen. On the table beside a pot of tea that had long since gone cold were a large folio and a thick packet of papers.

The folio was the drawing of her from the night before, now finished, a young woman wearing only an oversized satin dressing gown, her face radiant. As she read the words he had written beneath it, her lungs would not fill.

Be well, extraordinary one. I will not forget you.
—Z.

The packet contained the deed to the house, written over into her name, and signed and stamped by a notary. There was another document too, that indicated all moveable property within the house likewise now belonged to Elizabeth Shaw, daughter of Dr. John Shaw of Edinburgh. The contents of his bank account were now hers as well.

She wandered the house. Her bedchamber was as she had left it. The parlor too. In the studio he had left everything: brushes, oils, pigments, and finished paintings. She did not find the portraits of her.

Returning to the master bedchamber she cocooned her body in blankets and allowed herself finally to weep.

Chapter 31

The Champion

When the afternoon was advancing Libby arose, cleaned her face, dressed in one of Mrs. Coutts's gowns, and hailed a hackney coach to the Duke and Duchess of Loch Irvine's house.

After speaking with her father, Alice, and the duke and duchess, and informing them that she intended to remove to her own residence immediately, she was standing in the bedchamber she had used for the past sennight and staring blankly at the array of hair ribbons Iris had given her to console her for having to become a woman again.

Beside them on the dressing table was his watch that she had worn for months.

Caliphs and kings.

He was a world away.

The morning broadsheets had printed the shocking news that Mr. Kent had done all in order to protect Miss Elizabeth Shaw's reputation. He was exonerated for the hangable crime but castigated for dishonesty and his immoral influence on an innocent maiden.

All foolishness.

"Miss," a maidservant said from the doorway, "there be a Mr. Chedham here to see you."

Dropping the ribbons, she descended the grand staircase to the drawing room. Chedham stood rigidly by a bookcase.

"What do you want now?" she said.

"I suppose I should not have expected any other greeting from you."

"Of course you shouldn't have. And I should not have agreed to speak with you, but here you are and I have a curious nature. So? What do you want?"

"To apologize."

She folded her arms. "This is unexpected. And far too late."

"I was wrong not to retract my accusation after you called on me," he said as though it required every muscle in his body to force the words over his tongue. "It was the worst sort of ungentlemanly behavior."

"You could pass a bladder stone now with the pressure you are putting on your diaphragm."

"Pulley told me that he saw you and Kent enter the alleyway. That is all he saw. In order to ruin you, I embellished it."

"You are an arrogant prick and if it weren't for your extraordinary skills in medicine I would wish you banished from this earth. But I cannot wish that, Maxwell, for you have a gift for healing that has already helped many people. I have witnessed that. I only wish that the gift had been granted to you with a human heart as well. Even a fraction of Archie's heart would do."

"Did he tell you that he challenged me?"

"Challenged you? To a duel? *Archie?* Oh, no! Do not say that you—"

"Not Armstrong," he said. "Kent. He won, of course. We met this morning at Arthur's Seat, at dawn. I haven't any skill with either pistol or sword, so I chose pistols since I suspected it would be easier. I think he knew I was unprepared. He did nothing while I fumbled, didn't even raise his weapon. I shot and missed him. Only then did he fire into the air. He told me it was for your sake that he had not killed me."

"You are *sworn* to heal others," she said. "Yet you *intended* to shoot him?"

His gaze shifted away uncomfortably, then he seemed to notice the room they were in, the subdued ducal elegance. "You are not the person I thought you were."

"People rarely are what others think of them."

"His Grace seconded Kent." His lips tightened. "Pulley was so impressed to meet a duke, he nearly soiled himself."

"Your friends are idiots. You needn't surround yourself with fools, Maxwell. You are brilliant. You must fulfill your potential. You owe me at least that."

"I should take my leave now," he said stiffly.

She walked to him and extended her hand. After a moment's hesitation, he shook it.

He left, and Libby returned to packing her belongings, the pain in her heart no lighter but for the first time in months her head entirely clear.

The Royal Academy
London, England

ZIYAEDDIN WATCHED AS, in the crowded exhibition hall, a couple with a girl approached the painting.

"Fine-looking lady," the man said, trying not to peer too closely. Like his womenfolk he was dressed simply, his hands red and chapped from labor.

"Look how she grasps the tools, Louisa," the woman said to the girl. "Like she'd do battle rather than give them up."

"She is beautiful, Mama." The girl stared without shame.

"Yes," her mother said. "Her eyes are full of fire and wisdom."

"She's got the brawn of a lad," the man said, frowning.

"She is strong," the mother said.

"Is she a doctor?" the girl said, her eyes on the surgical instruments.

"Must be one of those old-time goddesses," the man said, "or she'd be wearing a proper dress."

"No, Mr. Dunnell," his wife said. "She is merely a woman who has seized a gift from God."

The family wandered away.

"The form of a woman and the mind of a man." Charles Bell stood beside Ziyaeddin, studying the painting. "Yet still my foolish colleagues reject her."

Ziyaeddin nodded. But she did not have the mind of a man, rather of a woman. And the courage of a hero. None would know that she had accomplished far more than success in her medical studies. None would know that she had slain a dragon. None but he.

"Thank you, sir," he said.

"Oh, you needn't thank me. The directors were thrilled I was able to convince you to allow them to hang your work in this year's exhibition."

"I thank you for your forgiveness for my lie, and for your promise."

"I would continue to support her even did you not request

it. But I am honored that you have asked it, Mr. Kent. I only hope she does not weary of the fight."

She wouldn't—not this warrior.

Ziyaeddin bid the surgeon good-bye and went out from the exhibition hall onto the street. Joachim waited by the carriage, a conspicuous foreigner in even this cosmopolitan city.

"You tarried too long," Joachim said.

"The foreign minister will wait."

"But a naval ship will not," Joachim said as a footman opened the carriage door. "We must be aboard it in mere hours." He climbed in behind Ziyaeddin and the carriage started forward. "Yet you would rather remain here in this building full of pictures and commoners. You have become attached to this land. Haven't you?"

Around them, London in all its ambitious complexity bustled. But his heart was not in this city.

He missed Edinburgh. He missed the Old Town's narrow alleys, the coffeehouse in which he drank wine with artists and poets, the bustle of students, the bookshops, and the brilliant blue skies cluttered with clouds and emerald hills, and the roll of Scots in his ears.

He missed his house, his studio, his paints. Only a fortnight away from them, yet his fingers were hungry for a brush. He missed the scents of walnut oil and linseed.

He missed her. He missed her so much that sometimes he forgot to breathe.

"Edinburgh," he said.

"Cold stone and constant rain?" Joachim screwed up his brow. "The house in which you lived was smaller than the servants' quarters in your palace."

Ziyaeddin smiled. "It is a fine house, actually." Hers now. He imagined her in the parlor, books strewn about, a cup of tea abandoned by her elbow.

"Do you remember, Ziyaeddin, how the brilliant summer sunlight bathes the courtyard of your palace in warmth?"

"In truth, I remember little of it."

"Your sister will help you remember it all."

Ziyaeddin glanced at his friend, who now stared out the window. In the days he had spent with Joachim, he had seen this often: the gray eyes turn sightless when he mentioned Aairah. Now he could not help but wonder how Joachim seemed to know so well the courtyard's summer warmth. The general had died during the chill Caspian winter, and Aairah had taken control of the palace only then. Ziyaeddin wondered if his old friend's vow of fealty had brought him here, or another bond—a bond with a captive princess—forged in secret in a courtyard bathed in summer sunshine.

Surrounding a busy port, for centuries Tabir had been a land of many faiths and many peoples. The people of his realm had long since learned to negotiate their differences, to learn from and live in peace with each other. Still, to a Muslim royal princess the love of a Christian soldier was forbidden—as was the love of a royal prince for a bastard orphan girl, a commoner who was anything but common.

But he was no longer that prince. In exile from her now, he knew that the moment he had met Elizabeth Shaw he had been nothing more or less than hers.

Rapping on the carriage ceiling, he reached for the door handle.

"We have not yet arrived at Westminster," Joachim said as the carriage halted.

"There is a stationer's shop just there." He gestured with his stick, then climbed out. "Go on. I will walk the remainder of the way."

"But, Your Highness—"

"Have no fear. I will come."

Frowning, Joachim pulled the door shut and the carriage moved away.

Gripping the walking stick, Ziyaeddin started toward the shop. He would purchase a sketchpad with thick linen sheets that took both chalk and lead well.

The day was warm and the street was peopled with all the world, the highborn and the lowly, fashionable men in black coats and tall crowned hats and stylish women in muslin and silk of green and burgundy and blue, the dusky and the pale from all across Britain's vast empire, starchy tradesmen and humble beggars and nurses marching behind prams.

As he went, to give himself pleasure he looked for a riot of guinea curls and bright sea-blue eyes and lips that drove a man mad, and pretended that someday he might accidentally see her pass by and again, for a precious moment, be home.

Chapter 32

A New Agreement

May 1828
Edinburgh, Scotland

"There. No, there. *There.* Good heavens, Archie, can't you see?"

"Aye, I can see, Miss Perfection," he said, lifting his attention from the half-stitched wound to glare at her. "I'm doin' it my way, thank you verra much."

The patient, a weathered old fisherman, looked warily from one to the other.

"It's all right," Libby said to him gently. "Mr. Armstrong stitches a superlatively good suture." She folded her arms. "It would just be a lot quicker if he allowed me to do it."

"Aye," Archie said. "But then both o' us would be barred from this place for a fortnight. *Again.* I'll no' be riskin' that so close to sittin' for exams."

"You'll do fine."

"Chedham's ahead o' me."

"He has always been ahead of you."

"Done!" He straightened up and nodded at the fisherman. "How does it feel?"

The fisherman bent his arm. "I woulda rather the lass done it."

"Ha!"

Archie rolled his eyes. Snatching up his suture kit, he moved toward the washbasin.

"Why has nobody taken my recommendation to run a pipe from the pump into this basin?" she said. "Running water is far better for cleaning instruments than still water. It would save lives."

Archie dried his hands. "You'd be president o' this place someday if—"

"If the college would allow me to become a fellow. I don't know how much longer I will have the patience for this, Archie," she said as they left the building. "My tutors are all wonderful, especially Mr. Bridges and Mr. Syme."

"Bridges was braggin' about you again the other day. Canna help himself."

"But to be forbidden to work at the infirmary after all I have proven again and again, and forbidden from the other teaching hospitals as well . . ." This morning she had received yet another joint warning from the town council and the Church of Scotland that if she attempted to perform surgery at any established medical institution she would face the full displeasure of the law. "Even the apothecaries guild has closed its ranks against me. There is no place in Edinburgh for a woman surgeon."

"What'll you do, Lib?"

"Continue to assist at the paupers' hospice in Leith, and to study." And wait. She could not say it aloud, but the truth was that for two years she had been waiting. Waiting for a miracle.

She pasted on a grin, much as she had once pasted on whiskers.

"And I will continue to pester you and Pincushion to let me work on your patients here when no one is watching."

"Someday we'll open our own private surgery, the three o' us. George'll be our solicitor an' we'll be the most popular sawbones in Scotland."

She smiled genuinely now.

They had come to the corner of her block.

"You've time for a pint?" Archie said.

"Not today. I've got to finish writing up notes on the strangulated hernia I repaired yesterday."

"Tomorrow, then."

"Tomorrow perhaps." She watched him lope away.

She would not join her friends at the pub tomorrow, nor the next day, nor the next. She adored them. They had remained loyal companions even as her private studies took her abilities and knowledge far beyond theirs. But they were so young. Like Iris, they were playing at life without fully understanding themselves yet, while she was a grown woman who knew her heart and mind, but was still waiting for a day that would never come.

It was time to leave Edinburgh. The community of medical men was too strongly set against her. According to some in Edinburgh she was still an unnatural female and a fallen woman, disguising herself as a man only to be seduced by the Turk, then abandoned, and now scandalously living alone. That she was accused of both, side-by-side, was a pile of irrationality. The worst, however, was the ignominy she brought upon her mentors and friends for merely associating with them.

She needed to go elsewhere, perhaps to a remote village

so desperately in need of a healer no one would chastise her for it. She would miss Alice, Iris, Coira, and Mrs. Coutts dreadfully. But she could no longer endure this partial life.

And she needed to go away from the places in which she could not help but think of *him*.

The grief of rising every day without him in the house would not entirely fade. Memories kept it fresh. She had not even changed his studio. He was ruling a kingdom thousands of miles away, yet she could not make herself discard a single paintbrush.

Leaving Edinburgh was the wisest solution.

She could live with her father and Clarice in London. Mr. Bell had promised to take her on as a private assistant. But the hospitals and the College of Surgeons there would not accept her either, and anyway she didn't care for London. She did not want to leave her friends here, and the coffeehouse on the corner, and the little church where she liked to sit in the last pew, and her perfect house.

She did not want to leave behind the memories of her portrait artist. Her prince.

The *Times* from London had announced the end of the war between Iran and Russia, and praised the fair-minded ruler of Tabir for helping to negotiate the treaty.

War was brewing anew between Russia and the Ottomans. But for now, a world away, he was well. She wanted only that.

Two years of waiting was long enough. Life must be lived.

Swiping at a ticklish spot on her cheek, she climbed the steps to her front door and reached into her pocket for the key.

"Are you prepared for this?" came a voice behind her— the most perfect voice in all the world.

She pivoted and there he stood on the footpath below,

a tall, lean, dark figure of exceptional elegance with a walking stick tipped in gold, completely still and watching her.

The most extraordinary sensations broke from her tight heart and spilled through every part of her. Astonishment. Desire. *Joy.*

"Prepared to live entirely among men?" she said, not particularly stably. "To learn their ways and pretend to be what I am not so that they will not know me for what I truly am? To be always alone?"

He offered that beautiful tilt of his head she had always thought so princely even when she had not known he was a prince.

"No," she said. "For now I know who I am, and I wish only to be me."

He ascended the steps and she remained immobile while all inside her was a tumult. So close now it was impossible not to see the changes two years had wrought in him: his hair was longer, and short whiskers framed his mouth and jaw. His coat was very fine, the style regal, his waistcoat threaded with gold. He looked like a ruler of a foreign realm. Like a stranger.

He was looking at her as though she were a stranger too, his dark eyes questioning. Hesitant uncertainty hovered in the air between them.

"You've plaster stuck to your cheek," he said into the awkward silence, his voice a little rocky too. He reached up and picked it off her skin, and his fingertips lingered for an instant—for only an instant—*for long enough.*

The uncertainty wavered, then vanished.

"I forgot to look in a mirror before leaving the infirmary," she said, drawing the scent of him into her and getting dizzy. "Archie's patient was howling so I mixed the plaster even though I have been prohibited from assisting him. It was hours ago. But I was distracted. Actually, I was distracted all day."

He bent his head and she saw the shifting of muscles in his jaw. "Tell me it is because today is the anniversary of the day I left."

"It is because today is the anniversary of the day you left." With shaky fingers she tucked a loose curl behind her ear and hope pounded in her. "It is not possible that you arrived today by coincidence."

"In fact it required a fairly significant effort on my part to arrive by today. Winds do not always blow in the direction one wishes."

Tingles of happiness were spreading inside her. "Metaphors again?"

"Actual winds too, as it happened. My ship was delayed arriving in port. I was obliged to ride from Newcastle to arrive here today."

"You haven't yet even changed your clothing. You smell of horse."

"And you smell of camphor." His eyes smiled.

Joy went wild in her breast.

"I have been following news of the war." *Following.* Gobbling up. Twisted with anxiety that one day she would read that Tabir had fallen, that he was gone forever. "I—I was happy to read of the treaty—that your kingdom is well, and your—your people."

"Stuttering?" He lifted a brow. "When did this begin?"

"This moment. This is extraordinary. I did not actually think to ever—to ever see you again."

"Of course you did."

"I didn't. I wanted to. I imagined it. Of course. I thought every day of how this conversation might go were you to ever return: what you would say, what I would say, where it would take place, all the particulars.

Sometimes I thought of it every hour. Eventually it became so distressing that I was obliged to give myself rewards for not allowing my mind to spin around this potential conversation."

"You bested it."

"I did, first by allowing myself to spend a quarter of an hour each day writing out what I imagined we would say to each other. The following fortnight I allowed myself only to *think* about it for a quarter hour each day. But the latter proved impossible, for you were always in my mind anyway. Finally I allowed myself to think of anything about you except this conversation."

"Is this conversation resembling what you imagined?"

"Bits and pieces of it. The part where you said you made a significant effort to return, yes. Not the part about plaster."

His mouth was resisting a smile. "How I have missed you," he said very beautifully and reached up to tuck the errant curl behind her ear. This time his fingertips lingered for more than a moment, caressing the slope of her jaw and sending sparks of pleasure through her.

She laid her palm flat upon his chest, and the solid reality of him filled her as his lungs filled deeply beneath her hand.

"You are here," she whispered.

"I am here," he replied softly.

"This is a gorgeous coat, never mind that you smell of horse. You are dressed magnificently. Royally. That walking stick is the most beautiful piece of carving I have ever seen."

"I wanted to impress you."

"*Me?*"

"When we first met, I drew your face to impress you. Afterward I could not make myself forget any detail of these features. Yes, I have always wanted to impress you, *jan-e delam*."

She curled her fingers around the lapel of his coat, knowing she should not do so here on the stoop, but unable to release him, and anyway she had made a life out of doing what she should not.

"I asked for news of you," he said.

"Did you? From the duke?"

"Every fortnight."

"Every *fortnight*? What did he report?"

"That you remain undaunted. That you have continued your studies. That you are brilliant."

"You knew the last already."

"And that you have not married."

"Why should I?"

The reluctant smile she loved so much creased his cheek. "Why should you, indeed." It wasn't really a question.

"Are your sister and her children well?"

"Very well." His gaze was traveling over her face slowly. "After the treaty, once I was assured that all was stable, I abdicated."

Her arm dropped. She gaped. "You—you—"

"We must do something about this stuttering. It doesn't suit you."

"You *abdicated*? But—can you do that?"

"I did. So, yes, I can. That is, first I formed a parliament. That took some time, of course," he said as calmly as though he were reciting errands. "When that was settled I wrote a petition to parliament that my sister should serve as regent for her sons until they come of age, and in its first official act the members ratified it. It all went quite smoothly, actually. This is the modern era, you know. Constitutional monarchies are all the rage."

"You mustn't jest about this."

"I am not jesting."

"You *abdicated*."

"How can you doubt it?" he said, now soberly.

"One does not simply abdicate!"

"One does when the woman one wants is on the other side of the world." He lifted her hand to his lips and kissed it tenderly—so tenderly. "I am not the first monarch to abdicate for love."

For love.

This could not be *real*.

"When you left here," she said, "I believed that you would never return."

"When I left here I knew within a mile that I am no one without you." He bent his head so that their brows were nearly touching. "Elizabeth Shaw, you fill my heart. You fill my head. I have thought only of you, wanted only you. Away from you I have been like a man sleeping while awake, always in a terrible dream from which I could not wake. Without you I am half a soul. With you I am whole." He looked into her eyes. "I am home."

She could not breathe. "But you cannot have given up your crown."

"I would give up more than a crown. For you I would give up the world."

With a cry of joy, she threw her arms about him.

He kissed her brow, her cheek. "I am not too late?"

"You would never have been too late."

"Will you accept me?" he said with gorgeous fierceness. "Will you allow me to care for you and make love to you and watch you be extraordinary in the world, this time for a lifetime?"

"Yes, yes, I will, of course, now kiss me. For this was the part I imagined every time."

He smiled, and kissed her smiling, and stroked the pad of his thumb over her lower lip.

"Then we are agreed?" he said.

"We are agreed." She pulled the key from her pocket and pressed it into his palm. "Welcome home." She smoothed her hands down his chest and felt all the glorious strength of him. "Where is the portrait of me that you took with you?"

He kissed her again, savoring her lips. His hands wrapped around her waist and he pulled her snugly to him.

"Hanging in a gallery in Paris," he said between kisses. "Why do you ask?"

She clung to his shoulders and accepted his mouth on her throat. "Lately I have been wanting a likeness done of me."

"Have you?"

"Yes. Only of my chin, though."

He kissed her chin. "This beautiful chin."

"Also my earlobe."

"Exquisite earlobe," he murmured, trailing his tongue along the sensitive appendage.

"And perhaps my left ankle."

"And these lips," he said, kissing them anew. "These perfect lips."

"Lips too," she said upon a sigh because those lips were in heaven beneath his.

"I happen to know an artist who can do those likenesses." His timbre was rich and husky and just as she loved it.

"I hoped so."

"He is available now."

"Splendid," she said. "Let's see to it immediately."

"Absolutely. No time to waste."

They went inside.

They did not reach the studio. Not directly, at least. Somehow they got caught in each other's arms and the parlor was close by and their eagerness to confirm their new agreement went well beyond the need for a gentlemanly handshake.

Afterward, there was tea to be enjoyed, and then a great quantity of kissing in the kitchen too, since it proved difficult to cease touching even to drink a cup. In all of this they relearned each other, imprinting on their senses again the cadence of laughter, the texture of skin, the beauty of sighs, the glimmer of affection in blue eyes and brown, and the radiance of love.

Eventually they did reach the studio. She had installed a well-cushioned couch in the room, and explained it was because she liked to rest there in the afternoons, sometimes to read, and sometimes to mentally catalogue the branches of the trees in the garden and pretend she was not thinking of him.

They made love again on that couch. Kissing her he murmured the words *atashe delam*. When she asked him the meaning of that he said she was the fire of his heart, and then he showed her.

Later, when she was flushed and hot and damp and entirely satisfied, he went to the workroom, brought forth canvas and pencil, and began a new portrait.

The following days went much like that, including an efficient visit to a parson amidst the sittings and lovemaking.

When the portrait was completed, Ziyaeddin hung it on the wall in the master bedchamber. Libby said it was silly to have a big nude picture of herself in their bedchamber, what's more a picture in which she was quite obviously in the throes of sexual gratification. He replied that it must remain, for whenever she happened to be away from home late at night at a patient's bedside, it would provide him company and afford him enormous pleasure.

She teased him for it, and he caught her up in his arms and told her that he loved her, was mad for her, and that he commanded her to obey him in this because he was, after all, of royal blood. She said she would never agree to *obey* him in anything, but that she would make love to him at once, and then perhaps they could have some tea and biscuits and sit on the couch and read to each other, and then probably make love again, and wouldn't that be much more fun anyway?

To that her prince responded as she desired.

Epilogue

Ever After

May 1868
Scotland

The world was changing.

The postal clerk looked out onto the tracks of hard wood and black iron. The navvies were all gone away now, taking their brickmaking machines, their ramshackle huts, and their strange foreign tongues, leaving only the tracks behind. No engine or cars had passed through yet. The timetable said the first would arrive Tuesday, and with them the quickest mail delivery to ever arrive in the village.

Aye, change would come whether a man liked it or not.

Some things remained the same, though. The bells in Saint Margaret's still announced the Sunday service. The little river that wended its way alongside the village still teemed with trout. The old mill's wheel still turned with a creaking groan. And the doc and Mr. Kent still walked the riverbank path each evening after dinner—rain, snow, or sunshine—as they were doing now.

The clerk rocked back in his chair, watching the pair stroll alongside the sparkling water. Days past, there'd be three little ones running alongside, skimming stones on the water and tumbling in the moss. Those young ones, each of them brighter than the next, had long since grown up and moved on—one to the Royal College of Physicians in London, another to Paris to sculpt fancy statues, and the last to some far-off Eastern land. An ambassador, that one. Aye, this village had been too small to satisfy those three.

Only the doc and Mr. Kent remained.

The postmaster still remembered when the pair had first come. He'd been a boy, and till then he'd only ever seen Turks in the pages of books, with their turbans and ballooning pantaloons and great curving swords. If he hadn't heard the alderman insisting on it, he wouldn't have believed Mr. Kent was one of those. Dressed like an Englishman, and better spoken than even the reverend, he'd fascinated everybody in the village. Rumor had even gone about that he was some sort of royalty. A bigger tara-diddle the clerk had never heard. What prince would live in a village in the middle of nowhere?

Whoever he was, folks had taken to him quick. The drawings he'd done for the village's wee ones had won him the mothers' favor. But when he painted the laird's favorite hound so it looked like the bitch was leaping right out at a body, the whole parish had welcomed him.

Not her. Not at first. Lady Surgeon, they'd called her, and not kindly.

Eventually she'd won over everybody, of course. When

wee Willie Pudding fell from the old ash and broke the bone clean through the skin, she'd known what to do—then, and any number of times after that.

She still kept up a busy practice in her office in the village, sometimes stepping out to assist with a troublesome birth in the tenant farms, at other times aiding the gentry in the sorts of woes only the wealthy and comfortable seemed to have: megrims and sleepless nights and gout. Mostly she helped those who couldn't pay.

Together the pair had always lived quietly in their cottage at the end of the village. Everybody liked and respected them.

The postal clerk glanced again at the tracks and the sparkling new platform. It was a shame the doc didn't travel as much as she once did. On the railway she'd arrive in Edinburgh or even London speedily—much quicker than in those fine carriages her patients sent for her. Once, he'd heard, Her Majesty herself had required the doc to call at Buckingham Palace.

Strangers still visited them at the cottage regularly, some grand, others modest folk, sometimes for weeks on end. The clerk himself occasionally saw to the shipping of Mr. Kent's paintings. Only the wee pictures, though. The doc had once told him that Mr. Kent's patrons preferred to retrieve the bigger paintings in person.

"Each is worth a veritable fortune in gold, of course," she'd said to him as though she'd no care for a fortune or gold or any of it.

The postal clerk didn't know a thing about art. But he knew the Kents paid their servants twice what every other household in the parish did. And according to the butcher and grocer they'd never been late paying bills. So the clerk supposed the doc hadn't exaggerated about the worth of those pictures.

He watched them now as they strolled along the river-bank in the pinkish glow of the fading day. As always they walked hand in hand, slowly, her strides short, his bumpy, as though in the busy bustle of modern life they'd nowhere to be but side by side, enjoying the peace and quiet of a spring evening together.

Stepping onto the footbridge, she took his arm. They halted at its center, and turned their faces toward the sun setting over the water.

That sunset surely was one of the prettiest sights in Scotland.

Then the doc turned her face up to her husband and spoke, too far away to be heard, but her lips moved quickly—a mile a minute that woman could talk. Mr. Kent replied, and she smiled. Then he lifted his hand to her cheek and bent his head.

The postal clerk looked away. It wasn't right to stare, even if the couple did this every evening, exactly in that spot, rain, snow, or sunshine.

Some folks, he supposed, never forgot what it was to fall in love.

Of Marvelous Matters Historical, & Fulsome Thanks

All men and women are to each other
the limbs of a single body, each of us
created from the life God gave to Adam.
When time's passage withers you to nothing,
I will grieve as if I'd lost a leg;
but you, who will not feel another's pain,
you've lost the right to call yourself human.
—SAADI, *Gulistan* (13th century, Persia)

*M*y Dear Readers,
    Thank you for joining me on this adventure. I hope very much that you enjoyed Libby and Ziyaeddin's love story.

When characters request that I write their story, I always

say yes, whatever that entails, even if it seems incredible. For, happily, it turns out that actual history is more astonishing and historical people much more extraordinary than we often expect. And sometimes the stars align. On a single glorious day in Edinburgh I discovered Surgeons' Hall, Sir Charles Bell, and Dr. James Barry. In Charles Bell, a brilliant surgeon and a painter of no little talent, I saw immediately how I could bring together my hopeful surgeon heroine and my portraitist hero. Filled with excitement from this, I was poking around in Surgeons' Hall's delightful little gift shop and found the biography of Dr. James Barry by Michael du Preez and Jeremy Dronfield. And *The Prince* was born.

Libby's disguise is based on James Barry. Eager to become a physician, a young Irishwoman Margaret Buckley befriended a pair of liberal-thinking and influential patrons and in 1809, dressed as a man, began studying medicine in Edinburgh, soon becoming Dr. James Barry. Entering the army's colonial service and spending decades in posts abroad, Barry lived the remainder of his life as a man.

I drew from Barry's story not only the idea for Libby's disguise, but many details, including a foreign patron embedded in British society who had plans to return to his home country and rule it; Barry's self-imposed isolation until he became close friends with another intelligent student; the carefully crafted little pillows he used to fill out his trousers; his brilliance and successes; the anonymously posted placard accusing Dr. Barry of being "buggered" by his friend and patron; and the severe illness he suffered during which—in Barry's case—his secret was discovered when his fellow medical men sought to care for him. On each of the few occasions when it appears that others did in fact discover Barry's female sex, it was always hushed up, probably due to influential allies, but possibly also because of the respect many held for Barry's abilities.

In the nineteenth century in Britain most men believed women lacked the physical and moral nature to be physicians or surgeons. In the scene in which Libby first tells Ziyaeddin she wishes to be a surgeon, I gave her the words of Elizabeth Davies, LL.D., in her 1861 piece "Female Physicians" in the *Englishwoman's Journal*: women's medical accomplishments to date were themselves evidence of women's intellectual and physical power—and all accomplished despite being denied formal education.

My inspiration for Ziyaeddin initially came from a number of historical people. Mirza Abul Hassan, the Iranian ambassador in London in 1809–10 and 1819, wrote a memoir of his time among high society, and English people wrote about him as well, including newspapers. He was a very popular guest: handsome, charming, and beloved by fashionable hostesses, the prince regent, and many others.

Perhaps more importantly for Ziyaeddin's rather less exalted lifestyle in Britain, I drew from the experiences of six Iranian students who sojourned in England between 1815 and 1818 to study literature, history, engineering, medicine, and weapons manufacturing. One of them, Mirza Salih (who again visited England in 1823 on a diplomatic mission), kept a journal of his travels and wrote many letters. As with the ambassador, others wrote about these young men, including friends they made in England and eager journalists. Nile Green's wonderful history of these students suggested to me—among other details—Ziyaeddin's appreciation for tea and dining as rituals of friendship.

Portrait painting was hugely popular in Persian culture at this time, and, although the style of portraiture

Ziyaeddin adopted was European, it was easy to root his interest and aptitude in portraiture in his childhood. The English artistic prodigy Thomas Lawrence, his natural abilities and mentors as well as his style and desires, provided me particular inspiration too.

The early nineteenth century was a global era, with regular warfare between the armies of titans whose expanding mercantile empires were ever hungry. Inventing Tabir—and making its ruling family descended from Persian royalty—I placed it at the nexus of Russia, Iran, and the Ottoman Empire, and near the trade routes of Britain's East India Company and the lands of Napoleon's imperial ambitions. Here the mingling of peoples of many origins, languages, and faiths was not uncommon, and especially so in port cities.

For centuries Europeans referred to the ruler of the Ottoman Empire as "the Turk." But by the early nineteenth century in Britain and America, "Turk" was often used indiscriminately to describe any Muslim. In Western news and entertainment Muslims were regularly depicted wildly inaccurately. The "caricatures" drawn in Lord Byron's bestselling, Orientalizing poems and the diplomat James Morier's popular novels, which Libby refers to, included gross misrepresentations of Muslims, Islam, and Eastern cultures intended to sell copies to a public thirsting for titillating entertainment. The opera offered further clichéd portraits. Literary correctives to these did exist, but they were never as popular.

To my knowledge, Charles Bell did not travel to Scotland in the fall of 1825. My timeline for this story was constrained by the actual Russo-Persian war of 1826–28, however, so I sent him briefly to Edinburgh to serve Libby's purpose. Also, at this time in Britain there was an actual renowned physician named John Shaw. I discovered him, however, after my fictional character of the same name appeared in print in my novels *The Rogue* and *The Duke*. Libby's father is not intended to be the real historical Dr. John Shaw.

The nineteenth century saw extraordinary advances in medical science in Britain, especially in surgery, with Edinburgh at the apex of these scientific developments. "Resurrectionists" made good money by robbing graves of their inhabitants and selling the cadavers to Britain's expanding network of private anatomy and surgery schools. The grisly story of stealing corpses turning to *creating* corpses comes from Edinburgh too: in 1827 two unscrupulous yet enterprising grave robbers promised a surgeon more cadavers than they could find, and turned to murdering poor people who, they believed, would not be missed. One of their victims, however, was in fact missed, and the villains were convicted and hanged.

While researching I discovered lots of other fascinating stories too. For instance, young Charles Darwin studied medicine in Edinburgh at the same time as Libby. Bored and put off by his anatomy and surgery courses, he busied his brilliant mind learning the art of taxidermy from John Edmonstone, a formerly enslaved man from British Guiana who was living and working in Edinburgh. It's hard to imagine that this work with rebuilding the bodies of animals didn't have a profound effect on Darwin's later theories. And then there are tiny bits of magically delicious information I learned that do not appear directly in this novel, like the fact that the word *caliber* has Arabic roots—via Italian, then via French, and finally into English—and refers to excellent shoemaking.

Many people helped me with this book, for all of whom I send up copious cheers and offer oblations.

Thank you to my editor Lucia Macro, who is good and wise, and to Carolyn Coons and Eleanor Mikucki and all the patient, talented folks in Managing Editorial; Jeanne Reina, Patricia Barrow, Anna Kmet, and Adrian Jiminez for this beautiful cover; my publisher Liate Stehlik; and Caroline Perny, Pam Jaffee, Angela Craft, Kayleigh Webb, and everybody at Avon who contributes to making my books so beautiful and helping readers find them.

Thank you to my superlatively wonderful agent Kimberly Whalen of The Whalen Agency.

For the generous people who read this manuscript and offered sage counsel, and for the amazing novelists, historians, medical experts, and artists without whose research, writing, and consultation I could not have written this book, I am profoundly grateful. These angels are Marcia Abercrombie, Sophie Barnes, Dan Bensimhon, Georgie C. Brophy, Georgann T. Brophy, Noah Redstone Brophy, Helen Dingwall, Hussein Fancy, Donna Finlay, Nile Green, Mona Hassan, Jean Hebrard, Paty Jager, Deborah Jenson, Arash Khazeni, Adriane Lentz-Smith, Mary Brophy Marcus, Vanessa Murray, Cat Sebastian, SrA Misty R. Sow, USAF, Ret., Martha P. Trachtenberg, Amanda Weaver, Barbara Claypole White, the Royal College of Surgeons of Edinburgh, the librarians at Perkins Library and the Rubenstein Rare Books and Manuscripts Library, and the writers and teachers at the Persian language and culture blog Chai and Conversation.

To the Lady Authors, Caroline Linden and Maya Rodale, whose laughter and encouragement I cherish, and to the beloved memory of Miranda Neville, whose own book research and wit lent Libby words that will forever make me smile: all my heart.

To my readers who make this adventure so much fun,

and especially to The Princesses, I adore you and am grateful for you.

Thank you from the depths of my heart to my beloved husband, son, and Idaho, whose support and love sustain me and who inspire every one of my books.

For new readers who found me with this novel, welcome! Libby and Ziyaeddin's romance is the fourth novel in my Devil's Duke series. For more about the series, including bonus scenes and even more history, I hope you will visit my Web site at www.KatharineAshe.com. There you can also find my schedule of appearances and lots of other nifty extras too.

Next month, don't miss these exciting new love stories only from Avon Books

Cajun Persuasion by Sandra Hill
Alaskan pilot Aaron LeDeux came to Louisiana with his brother to discover his Cajun roots. But any hopes he had of returning home are extinguished when he agrees to help a crew of street monks and nuns rescue sex-trafficked girls. Plus, he's in love with a gorgeous almost-nun named Fleur . . .

Moonlight Seduction by Jennifer L. Armentrout
Nicolette Besson never thought she'd return to the de Vincents' bayou compound. It's where her parents work, where she grew up . . . and where she got her heart broken by Gabriel de Vincent himself. Avoiding Gabe should be easy, but escaping memories of him, much less his smoking-hot presence, is harder than expected—especially since Gabe seems determined to be in Nikki's space as much as possible.

Dark Challenge by Christine Feehan
Julian Savage was golden. Powerful. But tormented. For the brooding hunter walked alone. Always alone, far from his Carpathian kind, alien to even his twin. Like his name, his existence was savage. Until he met the woman he was sworn to protect. When Julian heard Desari sing, emotions bombarded his hardened heart. And a dark hunger to possess her overwhelmed him . . . blinding him to the danger stalking him.

Discover great authors, exclusive offers, and more at hc.com.

REL 0618

THE SMYTHE-SMITH QUARTET BY
#1 *NEW YORK TIMES*
BESTSELLING AUTHOR

JULIA QUINN

JUST LIKE HEAVEN
978-0-06-149190-0

Honoria Smythe-Smith is to play the violin (badly) in the annual musicale performed by the Smythe-Smith quartet. But first she's determined to marry by the end of the season. When her advances are spurned, can Marcus Holroyd, her brother Daniel's best friend, swoop in and steal her heart in time for the musicale?

A NIGHT LIKE THIS
978-0-06-207290-0

Anne Wynter is not who she says she is, but she's managing quite well as a governess to three highborn young ladies. Daniel Smythe-Smith might be in mortal danger, but that's not going to stop the young earl from falling in love. And when he spies a mysterious woman at his family's annual musicale, he vows to pursue her.

THE SUM OF ALL KISSES
978-0-06-207292-4

Hugh Prentice has never had patience for dramatic females, and Lady Sarah Pleinsworth has never been acquainted with the words *shy* or *retiring*. Besides, a reckless duel has left Hugh with a ruined leg, and now he could never court a woman like Sarah, much less dream of marrying her.

THE SECRETS OF SIR RICHARD KENWORTHY
978-0-06-207294-8

Sir Richard Kenworthy has less than a month to find a bride, and when he sees Iris Smythe-Smith hiding behind her cello at her family's infamous musicale, he thinks he might have struck gold. Iris is used to blending into the background, so when Richard courts her, she can't quite believe it's true.

**Discover great authors, exclusive offers,
and more at hc.com**

JQ4 0916

At Avon Books, we know your passion for romance—once you finish one of our novels, you find yourself wanting more.

May we tempt you with . . .

- **Excerpts** from our upcoming releases.

- Entertaining **extras**, including authors' personal photo albums and book lists.

- Behind-the-scenes **scoop** on your favorite characters and series.

- **Sweepstakes** for the chance to win free books, romantic getaways, and other fun prizes.

- Writing **tips** from our authors and editors.

- **Blog** with our authors and find out why they love to write romance.

- **Exclusive content** that's not contained within the pages of our novels.

Join us at
www.avonbooks.com

An Imprint of HarperCollins*Publishers*
www.avonromance.com

Available wherever books are sold or please call 1-800-331-3761 to order.

*G*ive in to your Impulses!

These unforgettable stories only take a second to buy and give you hours of reading pleasure!

Go to *www.AvonImpulse.com* and see what we have to offer.

Available wherever e-books are sold.

AVONIMPULSE

IMP 0811